Bronwyn Parry's first novel, *As Darkness Falls*, won a prestigious Romance Writers of America Golden Heart Award for best romantic suspense manuscript in 2007. Her second novel, *Dark Country*, was named the Favourite Romantic Suspense Novel of 2009 by the Australian Romance Readers Association (ARRA) and in 2010 was a finalist in the Romance Writers of America RITA Awards – the Oscars of romance writing. *Dead Heat* was named the Favourite Romantic Suspense Novel of 2012 by the ARRA and is a finalist in the 2013 RITA Awards. Bronwyn's active interest in fiction and its readership is reflected in her PhD research and she is passionate about the richness, diversity and value of popular fiction. Bronwyn lives in the New England tablelands.

ww.bronwynparry.com

Praise for Bronwyn Parry's novels

'An impressive debut.'
The Australian Women's Weekly

'A great thriller . . . gripping.'
Herald Sun

'This is a fine debut novel from go to whoa, a desperate thriller that also works as a moving love story.'
Crime Down Under

Also by Bronwyn Parry
As Darkness Falls
Dark Country
Darkening Skies

Dead Heat

BRONWYN PARRY

hachette
AUSTRALIA

hachette
AUSTRALIA

First published in Australia and New Zealand in 2012
by Hachette Australia
(an imprint of Hachette Australia Pty Limited)
Level 17, 207 Kent Street, Sydney NSW 2000
www.hachette.com.au

This edition published in 2013

National Library of Australia
Cataloguing-in-Publication data:

Parry, Bronwyn.
Dead heat / Bronwyn Parry.

978 0 7336 3013 2 (pbk.)

Murder investigation – Fiction.
Suspense fiction, Australian.

A823.4

Cover design by Josh Durham, Design by Committee
Cover photographs courtesy of Getty Images and Bigstock
Text design by Bookhouse, Sydney
Printed in Australia by McPherson's Printing Group

ONE

Vermin.

They had to be the worst thing about her job. The feral dogs, pigs, cats, goats and horses did enough damage, but the vermin Jo really disliked – the ones responsible for the vandalised camping ground in front of her – were the two-legged, hoon variety.

Five days since the State Minister and her entourage of hangers-on and media had, at this very spot, declared the new National Park open, and already the vermin had left their mark. Not only had they hauled down the information board – the one she'd dug the post-holes for herself because they couldn't get the mechanical digger repaired in time for the Minister's media event – they'd cut the posts into pieces with a chainsaw.

The door to the loo hung crookedly on a single hinge, the watertank beside the covered cooking area was riddled with bullet holes, and, judging by the copious amounts of broken glass around the campfire remains, they'd also smashed – or perhaps shot – a fair number of beer bottles. Presumably after drinking the contents.

They sure hadn't come out here to appreciate the natural environment.

But they weren't here now. She could see the whole camping area – no cars, no tents, no people.

She reached into the cab of the vehicle for the radio mike and rattled off her boss's call sign. 'Are you there, Mal?'

'Yeah, Jo.'

'Can you give the police a call? A mob of *Homo idiota* has been rampaging. The tank's full of bullet holes, the loo door is cactus and the info board's down – they took to it with a chainsaw.'

'Damn it. Are you all right? How many of them are there?'

'I'm fine, Mal. They're gone.'

'Are you sure?'

'Yes. Brazen louts aren't likely to be skulking in the bush, afraid of a lone woman.' Being out in the wilderness by herself was a normal part of her job, and if she spooked easily she wouldn't have lasted a week, let alone ten years.

'Okay. Can you wait until either the cops or I get there? I might be an hour. And even if there are police available, they'll probably be at least that long.'

Jo stifled a sigh. She would just have to hang around and wait for the police to take whatever evidence they needed before she would be able to start clearing up the mess.

'No worries. I'll photograph and document the wreckage.'

Photograph and document – a standard procedure she'd completed too many times, although she'd hoped such deliberate vandalism would be less frequent out here in the north-west of New South Wales than in the parks she'd worked in further east, closer to cities and city hoons.

It would take all of thirty minutes, if that. Then maybe she could map the track to the lookout while she waited, so the morning wouldn't be a total waste. Checking and updating the maps they'd inherited from State Forests was only one task on the long list of jobs to be done now that the area had officially become a National Park.

The sun's heat already warm on her back, she retrieved her camera from her day pack in the rear of the vehicle. Taking a moment to scan the large camping area, she watched, listened, alert for anything that didn't belong. The typical morning birdlife filled the air with sound. A flock of corellas, white on the dark branches of a eucalypt near the river, squabbled among themselves. A young magpie, fatter than its parents, squawked on the grass, demanding more food, and a treecreeper hopped up the bark of an iron gum, foraging for insects. At one end of the car park some of the local mob of kangaroos sprawled lazily in the shade, their morning grazing completed.

Nothing out of the ordinary, nothing disturbing the peace. Other than the wildlife, she was alone out here. Exactly the way she liked it: peaceful, without distractions, just her and the natural beauty of the wilderness. A different beauty from the parks she'd worked in for most of her career, on the eastern fall of the Great Dividing Range, but this dry, scrubby landscape of the western slopes and plains brought her almost full circle, back to the kind of landscape where she'd grown up.

She drew in a deep breath of warm, dust-dry air. A good decision, moving here, away from the constant reminders of loss and grief, as well as an enjoyable professional challenge, establishing the new park. Definitely plenty to keep her busy.

This vandalism added a few more tasks to her list for the day. Nate Harrison, the lone constable based in Goodabri, might come the twenty or more kilometres out if he was in the area, but the chance of any other police driving the fifty-plus kilometres from Strathnairn, let alone bringing a crime-scene officer, was close to zilch. Yet, just in case, she took care to disturb as little as possible as she photographed the destruction and recorded the details in a notebook.

On the edge of the camping ground, among the undergrowth, a family of fairy wrens flittered in the bushes. Two young males, just coming into their adult plumage, chased each other, the half-grown tufts of blue feathers on their heads punk-like.

'At least *you* don't go around wrecking camp sites, boys,' she murmured, zooming the camera on them.

From this distance her voice didn't disturb them, but as she snapped a few shots they flew off, startled. She turned the camera to the dingo emerging from the low bushes, breakfast in its mouth. She caught its face close-up in the frame, the eyes watching her warily, ears upright, jaws clenched tightly around . . .

The image in the viewfinder began to shake violently but she snapped the photo, and another. Five fingers. A tattoo winding past the knuckles, up to the stump of the wrist, blood dark against the pale skin.

The dingo turned away and she yelled at it, desperate for it to drop its find, but it disappeared back into the undergrowth.

'Shit, shit, shit, shit.' Indecision held her motionless while she ran through her options, her heart racing as quickly as her thoughts. Follow it and see what she could find, or radio Mal to report it? She flicked the camera back to the two images she'd taken. No, it wasn't a joke artificial limb left over from a Halloween prank. Real flesh, mostly whole, so it had not been lying on the ground for days. Whatever had happened, it had to be recent. Not a minor injury. So where, and in what condition, was the person the hand belonged to?

She jogged back to her vehicle. With insufficient mobile phone reception for a call, she radioed her boss again. First things first: find out if there was still reason to worry. 'Mal, have you heard anything about someone being injured out here? Calling an ambulance, yesterday or overnight?'

'Nothing I know of, Jo. Why?'

She hesitated. No, not information she wanted to broadcast on an open radio channel, with farmers, truckies and others potentially listening in. 'There's some signs of a major injury,' she explained briefly. 'I haven't heard anything about an ambulance call-out last night, but maybe they left here by car. If you hear anything, let me know.'

Still on edge, she surveyed the camping area and surrounds, the key questions ringing in her mind: How the hell had someone lost a hand out here? Where were they now, and in what state?

The hoons had felled the posts with a chainsaw, but it would be pretty damned hard to accidentally cut off your own hand with one. Likewise with an axe or a hunting knife. Fingers, easily enough, or a chunk out of a leg or foot, but not your own hand.

That meant a much higher probability of foul play than of accident.

If the injured man was out here, the sooner she found him, the better. Aware of the isolation, kilometres from anywhere and anyone, while she checked her backpack for first-aid kit, satellite phone and portable radio she listened again for any indication of company.

Nothing but bird calls, insects and the breeze stirring the leaves.

Not far from where the dingo had trotted back into the scrub, she found drag marks, half a metre or so wide, and a few ants still gathered, here and there, around dark smears in the gravel. Pairs of footprints flanked the drag marks.

Boot prints, not wild pig or dog tracks.

She stared at them, the skin on her arms prickling despite the heat of the sun. No, there couldn't be any sort of innocent explanation for this.

Wary, making herself breathe slowly and evenly, she followed the drag marks and tracks over the rough, rocky ground among the trees.

Less than forty metres in, she found a pile of broken branches under a tree, glimpses of denim visible through the thin, dry foliage.

She'd done her share of search and rescue over the years, and dealt with more than her share of injury and death. And she could do it again.

She steeled herself and pulled aside one of the branches to check what lay beneath . . . and then jerked away, gagging, her mind reeling in horror. Not an accident. No way an accident. The man whose body lay semi-hidden had been coldly, brutally, tortured and murdered.

ॐ

The cow stood in the middle of the narrow dirt road and stared at him. Nick stared back and inched the car forward. The cow didn't budge.

A second blast from the horn finally had it ambling to the verge, and he pressed down on the accelerator as soon as he was past.

'Turn left in one hundred metres,' the female voice of the sat nav intoned.

Down a rough track with a locked gate across it, and an 'Authorised Vehicles Only' sign?

'That'd be another "no", honey,' he muttered and turned off the useless system.

An hour since the call had come in and he still had to travel at least ten kilometres to get there. Assuming his constable's directions for the 'shortcut' route between Strathnairn and the National Park were correct. Assuming he hadn't taken the wrong road. Both the map and the sat nav had proved useless – the scale of the map not large enough to show the minor roads, the sat nav thinking every farm track and fire trail was a public road.

He mentally added *decent maps* to the list of resources he would request. Only three days into the job and his list was already long. His predecessor in the senior detective position at Strathnairn might have been content to work without adequate resources, but Nick wasn't. Although, given the large number of open cases Nick had inherited, he wondered if the word *work* had been in the man's vocabulary. That made his own posting to the almost-outback command not just a banishment but a poisoned chalice as well. Detective Garry Coulter, killed in a car accident over a month ago, had apparently been held in high regard by the locals, so raising questions about the man's competence or integrity would not make Nick popular with his new colleagues.

He would worry about that later. Right now, he had a murder to investigate – once he reached the crime scene. At least the body that had been reported wouldn't get any deader. Just – he flicked the airconditioning up a notch – just riper, in this heat.

The road joined another at a T-junction, and a National Parks sign helpfully pointed to Ghost Gums Camping Ground. After another ten minutes of winding road through dry, rocky bush he descended to the camping ground on the river flats, the parking area already busy with three police cars, an ambulance and two National Parks utilities.

The two paramedics stood beside their ambulance, idly talking, but as Nick got out of his unmarked car, one strolled across.

'Are you the new detective?'

'Yes. Nick Matheson.' He shook hands, unblinkingly meeting the man's frankly curious and not entirely trusting gaze. So, the gossip had gone beyond his new colleagues in the Local Area Command to other emergency services. So be it. He had a job to do, and he'd do it.

'Where's the victim?'

The paramedic nodded towards the police cars at the other end of the camping ground. 'In the bush over there. He definitely doesn't need us.'

'But you're hanging around anyway?'

The guy shrugged. 'It's pretty gruesome. Someone might faint or suffer from shock.'

'Who found him?'

'Jo did.' He waved a hand towards two people in khaki shirts and trousers, leaning against the bonnet of a National Parks vehicle. 'Jo Lockwood. She's a bit shook up but she doesn't need us, either. Jo's tougher than she looks.'

Jo would be the slim one with the light brown hair held back in a ponytail. Nick couldn't see the woman's face, but from her hands-in-pockets, straight-backed stance, Jo Lockwood clearly wasn't falling apart in hysterics. That would make his job of interviewing her a hell of a lot easier.

'Thanks. I'll talk to her after I've seen what she found.'

What she'd found, he discovered when he followed the local constable through the scrub to the scene, was enough to give most people nightmares for months.

The smells of death – piss, shit and blood – turned Nick's stomach, but he quelled the response automatically. *Never show weakness.* That had been life's first lesson growing up on the docks of Newcastle, and kids who didn't learn it early suffered constant beatings and degradation.

The constable stayed to one side, staring intently at the body. 'Must be a sick bloody psycho, to have done that,' he said.

Nick crouched and, without touching a thing, surveyed the body. Facts. Evidence. That's what he needed to focus on. A rope tied tightly as a ligature above the amputated hand; another above a mangled and bloody foot. A major wound to the other knee, covered in blood, dirt and grit. The gunshot to the head probably the final of many other cuts and injuries.

The sustained violence and torture of this death – the patterns of blood flow suggested that the injuries were ante-mortem – were among the worst of the innumerable violent crimes he'd seen.

'No,' he mused, as much to himself as to the constable. 'Not *a* psycho. This guy's big, and he fought. It would have taken more than one man to restrain him.'

'From the looks of the camping-ground damage there were a few crims here last night,' the constable said. 'And he's got some unusual tattoos. Haven't seen anything like them before. Must be some sort of gang thing. You'd know about that, wouldn't you, Sarge?'

Another one who'd heard the rumours. The question might have been asked out of curiosity, but the sly grin suggested insolence.

Nick kept his expression carefully neutral and muttered a noncommittal 'Hmm.' Yes, he knew about gangs. Street gangs, bikie gangs, criminal mobs. The possibility of a gang connection in this youth's death was on his rapidly growing list but, far more than most cops, he knew there was no such simplistic crime as a 'gang thing'. He knew the complexities, the constantly shifting dynamics of power and personalities, of opportunity and risk, of adrenaline and testosterone and fear.

No, tattoos on the man's arms – which weren't any gang tattoos he was familiar with – didn't amount to evidence of an organised gang. If there were even any such thing out here in the north-west of New South Wales.

He stood and glanced at the constable's name tag. Harrison. A senior constable. Young, confident to the point of cocksure; the know-it-all type who probably didn't like taking orders. Too bad, because Nick would be giving plenty of them.

'This area needs to be taped off, Harrison. From the grassed area to past here. I called Forensic Services when you first reported in and the Crime Scene Officers are on their way from Inverell. They're contacting the forensic pathologist.'

'Don't expect one to come in person, Sarge. We're too far from Newcastle.'

Eight or more hours' drive, Nick knew. Too far from city resources . . . but not far enough from his memories. Not that Newcastle had a monopoly on bad memories. He'd collected more than enough of them from all over the map during his career. The poor dead bastard in front of him was just another drop in the ocean. Just one more crime that might, or might not, be solved.

'Have you got an ID on him? Or found his car?' he asked Harrison.

'No. None of us know him. He's not local. CSOs will search his pockets for ID.'

Nick nodded but he doubted they'd find anything useful. And judging by the burns on the remaining hand, identifiable fingerprints might be almost impossible to obtain.

He also doubted they'd find a car. If the guy had driven his own car, the assailants had probably taken it, could be a few hundred kilometres away by now.

He couldn't learn much more from the victim until after the crime-scene officers arrived, so he would have to start with the nearest thing he had to a witness.

'The National Parks officer who found him – do you know her?' he asked.

'Jo? She's a newcomer to Goodabri. Setting up things for the new park. She's the quiet type, doesn't socialise much. Seems to work hard enough though.'

Nick had taken a detour through Goodabri on his way to Strathnairn on Sunday, scoping a fraction of the large region covered by the police command. The town was thirty kilometres off the main road and consisted of fifty or so scattered houses, a police cottage, a small primary school, a row of empty shop buildings in the main street and a run-down pub. Not a thriving community, and presumably reliant on the larger Strathnairn, seventy kilometres away.

A woman who kept to herself in a small community . . . He mentally filed that piece of information. Jo Lockwood turned as he walked towards her across the grass, assessing him in the same kind of way he instinctively assessed her during those few moments.

She's the quiet type . . . Her emotions tightly leashed behind her pale face and closed expression, she shook his hand with a firm grasp when he introduced himself, and the constable's description underwent a swift revision in Nick's mind. Quiet perhaps, but from reserve, not shyness.

The calloused hand briefly in his, her lean, fit frame and her lightly tanned skin confirmed the 'seems to work hard' part of Harrison's description.

Despite her control, the haunting determination in her hazel eyes held his attention. Shock, yes – she still fought to keep it from overwhelming her. But she knew she could. He'd seen that same determination in the eyes of too many colleagues over the years – people who'd seen incomprehensible death, and survived it.

He guessed she'd be in her early thirties, but those eyes were older. No makeup, no artifice, nothing *pretty* in her face, only a stunning, stark beauty he found compelling.

Her colleague stepped forward and extended his hand. 'I'm Malcolm Stewart, senior ranger for the Strathnairn National Parks division. Do you really need to interview Jo now? She's had a tough morning.'

Before Nick could answer, Jo threw her boss a glance that mixed affection with slight exasperation. 'I don't need mollycoddling, Mal. The sooner we get this done, the sooner we can all get on with our jobs. I presume you'll want this part of the park closed, at least for today, Detective?'

'Yes. Perhaps you could liaise with the uniformed police, Mr Stewart, while I ask Ms Lockwood a few questions?'

'It's Doctor Lockwood,' Stewart corrected him. 'Doctor Joanna Lockwood. She has a PhD.'

With a gentle hand on Stewart's arm, Jo said, 'It's just a piece of paper, Mal. The title is irrelevant.'

Irrelevant? Not in Nick's estimation. He added intelligence and perseverance to his impressions of capability and control.

For all the cool calmness of her manner, the late morning was already hot, and she'd been standing around waiting for a couple of hours. Nick dragged his gaze away from a trickle of sweat running down her neck and disappearing below her open collar.

'Can we find somewhere in the shade to talk?' he asked her.

She nodded. 'There's a table down by the river. I don't think we'd be disturbing any evidence there.'

She slung a small backpack over her shoulder and led the way, skirting around the edge of the camping ground, along a thick line of trees and rough undergrowth that obscured the river from view. He could hear it – water running over rocks – but only caught glimpses now and then. So he looked, instead, at the open area of the camping ground. He would go over it closely later, but for now he concentrated on getting the general layout, the context in which the crimes had occurred. Even from this distance, the damage was obvious.

'They sure made a mess. I don't suppose you collect names, addresses or car registrations from visitors?'

'Names and postcodes sometimes – when they fill in a form. But that's hit and miss.' She turned on to a path through a break in the trees, into a clearing beside the water's edge. 'However, I can tell you that there were at least two vehicles here. And two dogs.'

Hope sparked in him. 'You saw them?'

'No. I was only here yesterday morning, and it was after that. The tyre tracks are there, though, and dog tracks and faeces beside where they were parked.' She rested her backpack on the wooden picnic table and drew out a camera. 'I have photos. I was compiling evidence for a long list of offences – criminal damage, bringing dogs and chainsaws into a National Park, lighting a campfire during a total fire ban – but I guess . . .'

She sat down abruptly on the bench seat, her bitter, somewhat shaky laugh a small crack in her control. 'Murder pretty much trumps all of those.'

'It would. *If* the people who did the vandalism committed the murder.' Avoiding a lump of bird shit on the seat, he sat opposite her, taking the camera she offered and flicking through the images while keeping half his attention on her. It was incongruous, sitting in such a cool, restful spot under the trees, the river winding its way over rocks less than ten metres away, when thirty metres behind him havoc had reigned in the night.

She stared at the table, circling a knot in the timber with her fingertip. Short, unpainted fingernails, he noticed. And tanned wrists and hands that, although small, were corded with lean muscle.

After a few moments of silence, she looked up at him and said, 'If it wasn't them, then the timing would have had to be close.'

'Why do you say that?'

'When I arrived this morning, the dog faeces were still moist. Only a few hours old. And the . . .' she steadied her voice and continued, 'the victim – there was no sign of rigor. And few insects.'

She had all his attention now. He considered her argument, and explored possible holes in it. 'The dogs might belong to the murderer.'

'The vehicle the dogs were tied up beside is the same one that rammed down the information board. There's a distinctive tyre track.'

'You're very observant.'

'I'm a scientist.'

She said it simply, as though it explained everything. Which, he supposed, it did. Scientists relied on logical processes and evidence – just as he did.

But he also relied on gut, on the sense of what fitted and what didn't fit, on his experience of patterns of behaviours that might not seem rational but could all too easily be the caustic results of mixing personalities, power and passions.

With the niggling certainty that the elements of this crime scene didn't fit neatly together, he flicked through the images on the camera one more time. She had taken some broader context shots as well as detailed close-ups, and despite the small screen, from her photos and the general view of the destruction he'd seen he could construct a fair picture of some of the night's events.

He handed the camera back to her. 'Can I get copies of those images, today?'

'Of course.' She opened the side of the camera, slid out the memory card and passed it to him. 'Take the card. I've got spares.'

'Thank you.' He waved a hand at the camping ground behind them. 'This kind of vandalism – does it happen often?'

'It happens sometimes. A mob of louts, full of beer and testosterone, with no respect for others' property, having what they'd call "fun". There's something about the isolation and the wilderness that can bring out the Neanderthal. But—'

She stopped and, curious about her thought processes, he prompted her, 'But?'

'It's just . . . Look, I'm no detective or psychologist, but I've been going over it these past couple of hours and it seems to me that the murder doesn't fit the same behavioural pattern. The vandalism is . . . well, if we were talking about animal behaviour,

I'd call it marking a territory. I suppose it's the hoon version of it – refuting authority and order and claiming the space.'

'But you think the murder is different.'

'Yes. Possibly. It's intense, over a period of time. Focused on a person, not property. And I know that cruelty can be about power – it usually is – and vandalism also is, but vandalism is general, and cruelty . . . well, this seems more personal, more emotional. Anger or hatred or punishment.'

He stared out over the water, flowing along the path it had carved out over millennia, and considered her thoughts. She'd put her finger on what was unsettling him: the two crimes didn't naturally evolve from one into the other. If they had been perpetrated by the same people, then something must have happened to shift the mood. Something or someone.

His instinct guessed *someone*. Someone who'd manipulated the restless mob's energy and adrenaline, turned it, focused it on a target and let it loose.

He'd seen it happen before, countless times. And he knew exactly how it was done, because he'd been that kind of ruthless, manipulative bastard himself, more than once.

TWO

Jo took a gulp from her water bottle, despite her still-queasy stomach. The heat and her fatigue from a late night and early morning had dampened her appetite even before she'd made her gruesome discovery, but in this weather dehydration was too real a risk to ignore.

She studied the detective as she made herself drink another couple of mouthfuls. The new detective, mentioned in last week's Strathnairn newspaper. Much easier to consider him than to let her mind recall the sight of the victim.

Nick, she remembered from his brisk introduction. Detective Senior Sergeant Nick . . . Morrison? Matheson? Something with an M. All business, focus. Nothing boyish or soft in his face. Attractive, in a hard-edged way. Compelling, with dark eyes and equally dark hair.

When he turned his attention to her and their eyes met, she caught a glimpse of power before the mask of cool detachment

18

slid into place. The kind of power that marked him as predator, not prey.

Her instincts told her his steadiness, his self-possessed strength, would make him a formidable opponent. Just as well they were both on the same side of the law.

'You may be right about the murder,' he commented evenly, 'but it's too early in the investigation to rule anything in or out.'

'Of course.' The victim's image appeared again in her mind, and she fought to diminish its effect, black humour the only weapon her brain could find. 'Except, I presume, natural causes.'

His sharp glance seemed to assess her mood before he let a thin, wry grin crack the inscrutable demeanour for just a moment. 'A machete-wielding dingo is low on my list of possible causes, I admit,' he said dryly, as if he knew that belittling a horror with absurdity could almost, for a short while, make it manageable.

He was a cop, a detective – he'd probably seen far more than she'd ever have to deal with. She didn't envy him.

'You said you were here yesterday morning. Was there anyone else here then?' he asked.

Good, something easy to answer, to focus her thoughts on. 'Yes. A retired couple in their van – grey nomads. They were here for a few days and were just packing up to leave. As I was talking with them, there was a guy on a motorbike on his way in. He told me he wasn't staying, just visiting the lookout.'

'Did any of the other staff come by later in the day?'

'No. We're a small division, based in Strathnairn, and we're responsible for four parks and three conservation areas. Yesterday afternoon there was a grass fire at Campbell Creek, so we were all out there.' Would he understand the size and range of the areas they managed? Perhaps. The Strathnairn Police district covered much of the same area, and presumably he'd done some research on his new posting. 'I'm currently living in the old Riverbank homestead on the edge of this park, which we use as a depot and staff quarters, so I usually do the camp fee collection, toilet paper and loo-cleaning rounds here. Officially this park is new, but we took over management from State Forests a few months ago.'

'You mentioned camping fees. What happens when you're not here when people arrive?'

'There's a lock box on the info board. People are supposed to fill out an envelope and put the money in it, in the box. The box is still there, among the debris. I didn't touch it, just in case they left fingerprints, or their names. I assumed your people would check it.'

'I doubt vandals are the kind to do paperwork and pay fees, but yes, we'll check it. The average crim can be pretty stupid.'

She could agree on that. Trashing a public campground was hardly an intellectual exercise.

'Are there other camping grounds nearby?' he asked. 'Other people who might have heard or seen something last night?'

'There's a picnic area at Casuarina Falls, a few kilometres up the river. I've already been there this morning, and there was no sign of anyone having spent the night. We should probably check the path up to the lookout.' She nodded across at the hill behind the camping area. 'People aren't supposed to camp there, but sometimes they do. There's no unattended cars parked nearby today, though.'

'Any farmhouses or other residences in the area?'

There had been gunshots and a chainsaw . . . perhaps somebody had heard. But, thinking about the land around, she shook her head. 'Riverbank, where I live, is probably the nearest residence, but that's a good ten kilometres as the crow flies, and well off the main road. I didn't hear anything last night. McCulloch Downs is the next property to the west, about ten kilometres from Riverbank, but Jack McCulloch moved into town last year and there's no-one living there now.'

He fell silent again, a frown narrowing his eyes. She hadn't been able to give him much to go on.

She couldn't keep her mind from straying back to the victim, and she gave up trying. Far better to think about the practicalities, the process from here, than to succumb to emotion and become useless. Not here. She would not be a burden to anyone.

'What happens now?' she asked, straightening her spine. 'Will you be able to take him away soon?'

'The deputy coroner and crime-scene officers are on their way. It may be a couple of hours before they've finished.'

Unsure she wanted to hear the answer, she asked, 'Do you need me to stay?'

Candid dark eyes studied her for a long moment, making her even more determined not to fall apart. He must have seen that in her face because he answered, 'If you can stay, and are willing to, the CSOs will probably want to talk with you, and I'd like you to show them the tracks you noticed.'

'Of course. I'll do whatever I can to help, but I'd rather keep busy instead of just hanging around. I was going to walk up to the lookout, map the track with the GPS. Would that be okay? It won't take long – it's less than a kilometre.'

'You said that the guy on the motorbike yesterday was going up there?'

'So he said. Most people who come here do. It was in the morning, though, so I doubt he stayed overnight.'

The detective's face remained impassive while he considered. 'Okay. But give me five minutes to make a couple of phone calls first. I'm coming with you.'

Delivered politely enough but a statement of fact, not a request. She didn't argue. His crime scene, his decisions.

'You'll be lucky to get much phone reception out here. A text might get through.'

They returned to the car park and as soon as he'd left her by her vehicle he had his phone out, texting as he walked across the grass to where Mal was deep in conversation with Nate Harrison and another police officer, presumably trying to agree on which park roads to close and where.

She refilled her water bottle from the cooler she kept in the back of the ute and filled a second one, tucking them into the pockets of her backpack; anything to keep busy. Taking a map from the front seat, she walked across to join the men.

'I was just telling your colleagues that there's a group of fifteen year-eleven students and a couple of teachers camping in the park,' Mal was explaining to Nick, 'I'm wondering if we should evacuate them. Do you know exactly where they are, Jo?'

Jo unfolded the map on the bonnet of one of the police cars and the men gathered around.

Beside her, the detective reached out to catch a corner of the sheet and hold it down, restraining it from flapping in the breeze. Momentarily so close to her that she caught the faint tang of aftershave and the undeniable awareness of powerful *male.*

Pheromones. Just damn pheromones, and of no relevance to her responsibilities here – the park, the students and any other visitors. No relevance to her at all.

'I've already radioed to check on that group,' she assured Mal and the others. 'They're fine, and they've seen no-one else around. They're over here on the north-west side of the park.' She saw Nick glance from the place she pointed at on the map, to the scale. 'It's about fifty kilometres from here as the crow flies, but there aren't many access roads into the park and no roads directly through it. It'd be about a hundred-and-twenty-kilometre loop around to get to where they are.'

'This lot had vehicles and resources,' Nick said decisively. 'There's no reason I can see for them to stay within the confines of the park. Assuming they left a few hours ago, they could be hundreds of kilometres away by now.

'We need to isolate this area around the crime scene until forensics have examined it thoroughly,' he continued. 'But there's no need to restrict access to the whole park. If the access road is closed there, at the intersection, are we shutting off any sites other than this one?'

'No, it's fine,' Jo answered. 'Visitors can still reach the waterfall viewing area by that other road, and it has toilets and barbecue facilities. There's basically nothing down this road except for what you can see here.'

'Good,' he said, turning to his uniformed colleagues. 'Harrison, get a team to put a road block in place there. I don't want anyone else down here except police and the deputy coroner. We'll also need an operations base closer to here than Strathnairn, for at least a few days. Does your station at Goodabri have suitable space?'

'No,' replied Nate. 'It's just a century-old police cottage, designed for one or two officers. Three people in the station makes it feel crowded.'

Having been to a couple of meetings with Nate and others, Jo could agree with that. 'We're leasing a double-front shop building and only using half,' she offered. 'There shouldn't be any problems with you guys using the other half, should there, Mal?'

'No worries at all,' Mal agreed. 'We've used the second shop space to coordinate joint emergency exercises a few times. There's power, water and basic furniture. Your people could set it up with mobile comms and such in no time.'

They could, and they would. With the old Mechanics' Institute hall closed for repairs, there was no other suitable empty space in town. So, for the next few days at least, the peace of her office environment was going to be disturbed.

⁂

Nick checked finding an ops base off his mental list. While not police, Jo and Malcolm must know the kind of requirements for a critical incident operation centre, so he would trust their judgement. On to dealing with the other practicalities. 'Is there suitable accommodation in Goodabri? A couple of specialist homicide detectives are on their way from Sydney.'

'The hotel is okay,' Jo assured him. 'I stayed there when I first arrived. It's clean and the rooms are a good size. The food's standard pub food, but quite reasonable.'

Luxury, compared to some of the places he had stayed over the years. 'Good. Sounds like that's the best plan. Assuming we can get the arrangements made quickly.'

Malcolm already had his satellite phone out. 'I'll contact the Strathnairn commander and make the offer, and get over to Goodabri to liaise with your people. And I'll take Jo back home on the way, if you don't need us any more.'

'I'm not going yet, Mal.'

Definitely a woman accustomed to speaking for herself. Nick nodded at both of them. 'I'll leave you to discuss it.'

As he walked away towards his car he heard Malcolm say, 'Jo, you know we have to follow all the incident procedures. I should be making sure you see a counsellor or a doctor.'

'I don't need a counsellor, Mal,' she retorted. 'I'm perfectly capable of over-analysing my own emotions.'

Nick almost grinned. Along with her independence, the scientific Dr Lockwood had a wry sense of humour.

His phone vibrated in his pocket and any trace of amusement evaporated when he read the text message from Aaron Georgiou, his detective constable: *Dalton & Brock ETA Goodabri noon.*

Dalton? It was standard procedure for the Homicide unit in Sydney to be involved in murder cases, but why the hell were they pulling Hugh Dalton off Strike Force Dragon and sending him up here? Unless Hugh knew something he didn't, at this stage Nick could see nothing to suggest a connection between the murders of a prominent Chinese–Australian couple in Sydney, and a dead, non-Chinese man in the scrub nine hundred kilometres away.

He would ask Hugh soon enough.

He disregarded the twinge of tension in his neck. He *could* work beside Hugh, despite the competitiveness that characterised their personal history, from long before they'd joined the police force. They had done it before. Hugh would strive hard for success, strive to show himself as good as, or better than Nick, so the case could only benefit. Not the most comfortable of working relationships, but then when, in the past ten years, had he ever been *comfortable* in his work?

Nick didn't know Brock – quite likely a detective constable like his own offsider, Aaron Georgiou. Nick had already arranged for Aaron to collect the Homicide detectives from Goodabri's landing strip and bring them out to the park.

He'd have to wait for the CSOs, for Hugh, for the deputy coroner, liaise with the forensic pathologist, and make sure the area was searched thoroughly before he'd be finished here. It was shaping up to be one hell of a long day.

He keyed a message back to Aaron: *Bring lunch.*

He tossed his phone and keys on the roof of his car and pulled out the bag from the back containing his search-and-rescue uniform. Far more practical for the tasks ahead than the business shirt and trousers he wore.

Jo Lockwood was the only woman around, and he doubted that she'd be offended by the sight of a man's skin, so for the sake of expediency he changed beside the car. The sun's heat prickled on the scar on his side as he swapped shirt for police T-shirt, but his bad leg held his weight without harsh pain while he changed into the dark blue overalls and heavier boots.

Never show weakness. He'd had plenty of practice at that through weeks in hospital and recovery. The bullets had narrowly missed arteries and vital organs, but the nerve and muscle damage would take months to properly heal, particularly in his leg. Determined *not* to spend months on restricted duties or sick leave, and accustomed to full body-contact street-fighting and martial arts, concealing pain from the doctor who'd assessed his fitness for duty had been no challenge.

He transferred his Glock from the light holster he'd worn with his street clothes to the one on the full equipment belt, and was buckling that around his waist when a shadow fell on the ground nearby.

'Now you look like a copper.'

Jo. The broad brim of her hat shaded her face, and he couldn't tell from her dry tone if she thought it was a good or a bad thing.

The ambiguity of her comment heightened the mixed emotions of pulling on even this informal uniform. After so long in plain clothes and undercover, the sense of pride and rightness in wearing a police uniform was dulled by the knowledge that a good many of his colleagues believed he no longer belonged to the tight-knit police community, and should be in prison overalls instead.

∞

Jo silently willed the heat rising to her cheeks to pass as an overdose of sunshine. Definitely not the most intelligent comment she'd ever made. Probably the damn pheromones again, taking advantage of her emotional shakiness, making sure she didn't miss, after several years of celibacy, the prime example of male before her.

She'd classed him in animal terms earlier as predator rather than prey, but in human terms he fitted the warrior archetype.

His close-fitting T-shirt emphasised muscular strength that his shirt had camouflaged, and the darker colour and military lines of the uniform gave his appearance a harder, rougher edge.

But so what if she found him sexually attractive? He was an unknown quantity, and she was much more than the sum of social conditioning and biochemistry.

He was a police officer doing his job, she was doing hers, the day was getting hotter the higher the sun rose, and professional friendliness was all that was called for.

She took the spare water bottle out of her pack and held it out to him.

'Have you got room on that serious-looking belt for this? It's going to be a scorcher, and there's not much shade on the way up to the lookout. You might need it.'

His hesitation in taking the bottle was so slight she might have imagined it. But years of working in a predominantly masculine environment had ingrained the habit of humouring her way around macho behaviour. 'Don't worry. There shouldn't be any girl germs. I washed that bottle this morning.'

'Oh, I think I've developed a pretty good immunity to girl germs. They won't kill me.' His grin softened the hard lines of his face, and the playboy look might have been convincing if it had made it as far as his eyes.

He'd probably returned her light teasing to put her at ease, a courtesy to a possibly traumatised witness. But she recognised a performance when she saw one; despite his undoubted physical attractiveness, those eyes belonged not to a playboy, but to a man who hunted murderers.

His focus on that task had him noticing, before she did, the tyre marks around the bollards at the start of the walking track to the lookout.

Another motorcyclist who couldn't understand the plain-English sign, 'Pedestrian Access Only'.

'Did you happen to notice what kind of tyres the motorbike you saw yesterday had?' he asked her.

'No. It was a BMW bike, though. I figured him for a corporate-type, out for a road trip. We see a few of them.' She cast a sideways glance at him. 'It seems to be a fashionable male ritual.'

This time, his grin seemed to come naturally. 'A man, a bike and a long, straight road? I can see the appeal.'

She understood the appeal. Not so much the powerful, status-symbol bike, but the escape, the freedom to choose what she did next and when, being alone and unfettered. She'd done it herself, many times. On horseback, as a kid, exploring beyond the large family grazing property. Later, in a ute or a car, taking to the roads during uni vacations.

A comfortable silence between them, they walked side-by-side up the track. Jo scanned the way ahead continually, keeping an eye out for snakes, and noting out of habit the animal tracks crisscrossing the dusty path. Wallabies, lizards, a dog – perhaps the dingo she'd seen, perhaps a feral dog – and here and there a few shoe prints, all interspersed with traces left by the motorbike.

In a sandy area, sheltered from the winds by a large boulder, she paused to take a better look. 'The bike tracks may have been the man I saw,' she said. 'Looks like they're from yesterday.'

He stopped beside her. 'How can you tell?'

With years of experience educating park visitors with limited knowledge of non-suburban environments, she explained simply, outlining the facts. 'The tracks are blurred in many places, blown by the wind, and quite a few animals have crossed the tyre marks.'

He knelt down, studying the ground with interest, and she crouched beside him. 'Those marks are a wallaby or a young kangaroo – you can see the imprint of the long hind legs and the tail.' She picked up a twig to indicate a much smaller line of indentations in the sand. 'That's a lizard – see the drag line of the tail and the footprints either side? And that one there – see those brush lines? That's a snake.'

'Impressive. I guess most people – including me – never think to look properly. And don't have the knowledge or skills to know what we see.'

She rose to her feet again and shrugged. 'It's no special skill. I'm familiar enough with some of the wildlife to recognise a few animal tracks. The rest is just logic.'

He studied the dust in front of him for a few more moments, as if committing the marks to memory. 'Logic requires knowledge to interpret the evidence. You're a useful person to have around, Doctor Lockwood.'

The compliment sounded genuine, a statement of fact rather than an attempt at flattery.

'Drop the "Doctor" stuff,' she said. 'I'd rather be called Jo.'

'Then call me Nick. I didn't have to work as hard for the detective title as you did for your doctorate.'

She wasn't so sure about that. A person didn't get to the rank of detective senior sergeant without considerable experience, and she'd far rather tackle a mountain of research papers and analyse gigabytes of data than face the kinds of things he must deal with on a regular basis. Like a murdered man, and the twisted humans capable of such a brutal killing. And whereas she could walk away once she'd given her statement and answered any questions, he'd be living with the investigation and whatever it turned up for days, weeks, maybe longer.

No wonder his smile rarely touched his eyes.

༄

If the hoons who'd vandalised the camping ground had come up to the lookout, Nick saw no evidence of it. The granite boulders on the summit held only pockets of sand and their surface retained few identifiable tracks, human or animal, to indicate who'd been there before them. He'd wondered, the whole way up, what they'd find, but the wooden benches, viewing platforms and information boards were all undamaged, and the wind, though hot and dry, carried no trace of the death stench.

They hadn't climbed a great distance, but the lookout was the highest point in the area and had a good view over the river gorge and across the undulating hills to the south and west.

They stood on the first platform, overlooking the camping ground and the gorge. The cleared camping area was dwarfed by the bush as far as the eye could see; dry scrub, eucalypts, cypress pines and plenty of trees and bushes he didn't know, thick on the river flats, a little sparser on the rocky slopes of the lines of hills beyond.

'There's a hell of a lot of bushland out there to dump a body in,' he mused aloud. 'So, why so close to the camping ground?'

Jo leaned on the wooden rail beside him. 'Most people don't venture very far away from the roads and walking tracks. And carrying a body across rough ground, through scrubby undergrowth, is hard work. I've done a few rescues. Even with a stretcher, in that kind of ground, fifty metres might as well be a mile. If I hadn't seen the dingo this morning, chances are no-one would have discovered the body for weeks or months. It happens, often enough. Usually suicides, or accidents.'

Yes, he'd worked a case like that – where the victim had lain, undiscovered for a couple of weeks, in a reserve backing onto suburban housing.

He had to hope that if the killers had assumed their victim wouldn't be quickly found, they might have been careless and left evidence.

Jo crossed to the other viewing platform, GPS in hand, comparing the reading to the landscape around.

Doctor Lockwood. It hadn't surprised him. The way she'd defined herself as a scientist, the seriousness and focus beneath the easy manner and humour, all added up to an intelligent professional. A stark contrast to many of the women he'd been surrounded by in the past few years: drug addicts, prostitutes, gang girlfriends and victims . . . women trapped in poverty, violence, addiction, and crime.

He dealt with female police officers often enough, and lawyers, but rarely professional women outside law enforcement. Twice this morning he'd caught himself wondering how to play his role with her, only to remember as soon as the thought occurred that he no longer had to perform, or be anyone else but himself. A detective senior sergeant with a cooperative and observant witness, and no reason for the uneasiness working its way through his muscles, at least as far as she was concerned.

She tucked the GPS into her backpack as he joined her.

'I just saw a couple of cars on the road in,' she said. 'So we'd better go back.'

'They can wait a few minutes, if you need to finish anything.'

'No, I'm all done. Except I just want to duck down to that tree stump. Someone's stuffed some plastic in it.'

In the direction she pointed, sunlight glinted on the plastic in the hollow of a small stump, poking up among the rocks in the rough ground, twenty metres beyond the platform.

'You'd think it would have been easier to take their rubbish home,' he commented.

'You'd be surprised how many people have an aversion to carrying rubbish in their cars.' With the agility of a gymnast, she climbed easily over the railing and readied herself for the drop to the smooth boulder below. 'You head back. I'll catch up with you in a minute.'

He took a few mouthfuls of water from the bottle she'd given him and waited while she strode through the low-growing scrub among the rocks. Perfectly at home and capable in this environment, she didn't need protecting, but he waited nonetheless.

She reached the tree stump, picked up the plastic – and then stopped, her hand holding it mid-air. A spider on it, maybe? Or some other bug? From this distance, in the sun's glare, it didn't seem large enough to hold anything grim.

She turned and called out to him, 'You'd better come here. This isn't rubbish.'

Plastic bag, not rubbish . . . not good, whatever it was. Normally he'd have followed her over the railing, but with his leg less reliable than usual, and no urgency requiring the risk, he took the conventional route around the side of the platform.

In the sand around the cement supporting one of the platform's legs, he saw the bike track again. Not far away, in the shade of a small tree, the smudged marks and a single indentation suggested the bike had been parked there. A boot print pointed towards Jo.

Nick swore under his breath. His suspicions hardened when he reached her and saw the bag she held by its corner. A ziplock bag the size of his hand, containing a dozen smaller plastic bags, each half-filled with white powder.

He pulled an evidence bag from his belt and held it open as she dropped it in.

'Is it what I think it is?' she asked.

'If you're thinking cocaine, then yes, probably.' He'd look at it more closely when they were back in the camping ground. 'There's bike tracks just up there, so it's possible the man you saw yesterday might be involved.' His voice sounded harsher than he intended, his thoughts racing, too crowded with possibilities and implications for courtesies. Because if they were connected – a biker, a violent death and a stash of cocaine – it signalled a dangerous combination.

THREE

Questions, questions, and more questions . . . By the time they'd reached the camping ground again after a grim, silent descent, the crime-scene officers were waiting for her with their questions: where she'd walked that morning, what she'd seen, what she'd touched or moved. She went over the scene with them, patiently answering each of the queries.

As she finished, a car arrived with Aaron Georgiou and the two detectives from the Homicide unit in Sydney: a man, probably in his thirties, tall, blond and well-muscled under the suit; and a slim woman in her twenties, short blonde hair sharply bobbed, neat in navy trousers and a fitted white shirt.

Drinking some more water, Jo watched Nick meet them, and her idle observation sharpened to curiosity as his subtle body language contrasted with the male detective's lively greeting – a vigorous handshake and the slap on the back of an old mate. Nick returned the handshake with equal strength and direct eye contact, not giving an inch of ground. Not rejection, not unfriendliness, but although he smiled and exchanged a quip with the man, Jo saw a practised and finely enforced dominance.

They knew each other, these two, and despite the ease of familiarity and friendship between them, she didn't read a relaxed affection.

Not that it was any of her business how two men chose to relate to each other. It was only the lack of anything else to do that had prompted her observations.

Okay, that and the fact that Nick had caught her intellectual interest. Cool and calm on the surface, like the waterhole beyond the trees he probably needed a sign warning of hazards and dangers in the depths. Not a man who could be neatly categorised.

After a brief conversation, the four detectives crossed the ground towards the place she had found the victim, and disappeared from sight into the bush.

With her head starting to throb from the heat and tension, and probably from lack of food, she returned to her utility and sat on the tailgate in the shade to eat some dried apples from the cooler.

The fruit giving her system a little sustenance, she washed down a couple of headache tablets with another swig of water and struggled not to retch them back up as the last of the adrenaline faded and a wave of reaction hit her.

She closed her eyes, shutting out the sight of the vandalised camping ground, trying to still the jumble of ugliness in her head. Drugs and murder in the area she'd worked hard to make safe and welcoming. A camping ground that should have families and kids and grey nomads enjoying the environment, instead of police cars and crime-scene officers and a mortuary van making its way down the road to collect a young man's remains.

⊗

'You said the ranger discovered him?' Hugh asked, kneeling near the victim. 'Did she disturb anything?'

Nowhere near as much as a parade of police and crime-scene officers had. Nick surveyed the trampled ground, the pile of branches moved away from the victim.

'She knows to preserve a crime scene, Hugh. CSOs have been over it all with her. She pulled aside a branch to see him, that's all.'

The sun beat down on Nick's head, heightening the ever-present, low-level irritation of dealing with Hugh. He had long acknowledged the truth to himself; he was never entirely easy with Hugh because Hugh was here and Patrick wasn't, and his brother's ghost hovered silently between them.

Hugh beckoned his constable, waiting nearby with Aaron. 'Shelley, come and look over this unlucky bastard, take some notes on what you see. Another fine example for you of humanity's barbarism.'

Typical of Hugh, that cynicism, but darker, more biting these past few years, the lighter humour he'd used as armour during his youth left far behind. Not unusual for cops. Given they'd both started their careers with more experience of violence and crime than most cadets, and their respective paths had taken them deep into criminal underworlds, Hugh's black cynicism came as no surprise to Nick.

From the struggle for composure evident in both Aaron's and Shelley's ashen expressions, they hadn't – yet – witnessed as much violent death as he and Hugh.

They'd have to get used to it, learn to channel revulsion and anger into analytical investigation that could ultimately bring killers to justice.

Nick indicated the victim's wrist, drawing their attention to observable facts. 'The tourniquet stopped him bleeding out. But you can see that blood flowed from the other wounds there . . . and there . . . and there. The autopsy will confirm that the injuries were inflicted when he was still alive.'

'Yep,' Hugh added dryly. 'Not much point going to all that effort if he was dead.'

'Bastards,' Aaron said, through clenched teeth.

Shelley gasped in a breath, trying to swallow a sob, and she turned away, fumbling for a handkerchief. Not hardened to it yet, for all she worked in Homicide.

Nick saw Hugh watch her for a moment, his face wooden, before he turned in the other direction, abruptly leaving the scene and heading back through the scrub.

'Aaron,' Nick instructed in a low tone. 'Bring Brock when she's ready. And tell the CSOs we've finished here, so they can bag him whenever they're ready.'

'The ranger – did you say her name's Lockwood?' Hugh asked when Nick caught up. 'Was she around Gloucester, Barrington Tops, five years or so back?'

Was she one of Hugh's many former girlfriends? Not a comfortable thought, but he refused to let it linger. He held aside a low branch for Hugh and answered impersonally, 'She's been in the district a few months. There was no reason to ask from where. Why?'

'Just curious. Might have come across her on a case. Anyway, I'd like to ask her a few questions.'

Nick briefly considered objecting, but held his tongue. Technically, in murder cases such as this, Homicide had charge, although collaboration was the norm, and he and Hugh held the same rank. Nick had no intention of giving over control, but nor would he push Hugh into claiming it. And in Hugh's shoes, he'd want to speak to the key witness himself.

As they emerged from the scrub, he scanned the area, looking for Jo. She rested on the tailgate of her ute, head against the canopy frame, not stirring while they crossed the camping ground towards her, opening her eyes only as they came close. Nick saw no recognition of Hugh register, but he could see shadows of a headache or tension in her eyes, and her skin had paled despite the heat.

'Jo, this is Detective Senior Sergeant Hugh Dalton, a specialist from the Homicide unit in Sydney. It can be useful to have several perspectives in an investigation, so he'd like to ask you a few more questions, if you're okay for that.'

She nodded, despite her evident strain. 'I'm fine. What do you need to know, Detective Dalton?'

If Hugh recognised her, he gave no sign nor made mention of it, but Nick caught the quick, challenging grin he tossed at him before addressing Jo with cool, distant professionalism.

Nick would have stayed, ensured Hugh kept the conversation brief, but Harrison had more questions about the search area.

As he walked across the dry grass, away from Jo and Hugh, he resisted the urge to look back. A respected senior detective and a competent professional ranger – neither needed him to monitor their discussion.

❧

The high-spirited friendliness Hugh Dalton had shown in greeting Nick was nowhere in evidence in his manner towards her.

After ten minutes of detailed questions, Jo reminded him, 'I've already told Nick all of this. And your forensic people.'

'I know. Sorry. But I have to note it all down for the case records.'

And in case you're lying. The man didn't say the words but the suspicion was there, in his coolness and the insincere apology.

She'd met the type before, run the gauntlet of the questions and insinuations and suspicions even while she grieved. She mentally braced herself for the ordeal.

'Can you tell me where you were last night, Doctor Lockwood?'

Yep, here we go again. With nothing to hide, she gave the honest answer. 'We were fighting a grass fire sixty k's west of here well into the evening. I must have left there about eight-thirty and drove home. I'm staying in the old Riverbank homestead that's now part of the National Park. It's about ten kilometres this side of Goodabri.'

'Do you have a partner or housemate who can verify the time you came home?'

'No. We use the homestead as staff quarters, so there's sometimes others there when we have major projects on, but I'm currently there alone.'

40

That would be another black mark against her in his notebook – no alibi at all.

'So, let me get this right, Doctor Lockwood: you saw no-one between around eight-thirty last night until the police arrived here this morning?'

'That's correct.' She looked him straight in the eye, determined not to be cowed or to lose her temper in frustration. Keep cool, keep calm, keep repeating the truth until he believed it. 'And I was nowhere near here between ten a.m. yesterday and eight this morning. Now, as I have told you and your colleagues everything I know – multiple times – I am going to get back to my job.'

'I'd prefer you to remain here a little longer, Doctor Lockwood. We may have some more questions for you.'

Not just routine enquiries, then. He seriously thought her a suspect. Either that or he was being annoyingly methodical and painstaking in his investigation and suspected everyone unless they could prove otherwise.

'I didn't murder the man, Detective Dalton. It would be very stupid to commit a murder and then draw attention to the body, instead of leaving it hidden.'

He smiled, as if he was enjoying this. 'Oh, you'd be surprised how often killers who think they're being smart try that tactic. Don't go too far away, Doctor Lockwood.'

The spring in his step as he returned to the others was almost joyous, and he clapped Nick heartily on the back as he joined them. Nick looked around, as if to check on her, and he made some brief comment to Dalton – chilling, if she read the expression on his face correctly – before he turned back to speaking to Nate Harrison.

She waited in the back seat of the ute, the doors open to catch the breeze. She'd been just as innocent last time as now, but there'd been more justification for the questions in that case. She'd coped by reminding herself that an investigation should be a logical process, devoid of emotion, open to all possibilities until excluded by rational evidence. She could, at one level at least, understand that approach, even if being in the spotlight made her uncomfortable.

She'd give them ten more minutes. After that, unless they arrested her, she'd go into the office and try to get some work done. And maybe try to shake off some of the horror of the day.

But sitting in silence with her eyes closed only allowed the gruesome images she'd seen to resurface in her mind. The old grief of Leon's death, mixed with the irritation of the detective's inquisition put her in a poor frame of mind to still her thoughts and memories.

The crunching of footsteps on the gravel made her open her eyes. She braced to confront Dalton again but it was Nick Matheson standing before her, with more concern in his expression than suspicion. Still the reserve, though. Tight. In control.

'How are you holding up, Jo?'

She stepped out of the ute. 'Other than tiredness, caffeine withdrawal and fatigue from not eating much today, I'm fine.'

He nodded slowly. 'I'm sorry we've kept you so long. I really appreciate your help. But I have one more favour to ask you.'

A favour, not an order. Obviously she wasn't on top of *his* list of suspects. Or else they were playing bad cop, good cop with her. If they were, then Nick, despite all the potential power she'd glimpsed beyond his cool, courteous exterior, was doing a damned good impersonation of a good cop.

'The deputy coroner has given permission for the victim to be transported. Jo, I need to know if he is the motorcyclist you saw yesterday morning. You can say no to this if you wish – I know it's not an easy thing I'm asking. But if you could look at his face, and tell me if it's the same man, it would be a huge help.'

'The motorcyclist? But why do you think—' The answer hit before she finished the question: because some bike gangs dealt drugs.

'With the bike tracks near where you found the drugs, we have to consider him possibly involved,' Nick explained. 'He may simply have been admiring the view or taking a leak, but the coincidence raises questions.'

She recalled her encounter the previous day, tried to remember any detail about the man that might be relevant. 'He looked more like a tourist than a gang member. Neat haircut, no tattoos or insignia that I saw. And it would have been a good ten hours before dark that he was here.'

'You saw his haircut? He had his helmet off?'

'Yes. Not while we spoke – he was on the bike then, just slid the visor up – but he parked a short distance away while I was talking to the caravan couple, and he took off his helmet then.'

Could he be the victim? She hadn't clearly seen the victim's face under the branches he'd been covered with. The prospect of seeing the dead man's face shouldn't have unsettled her, but it did. He was dead, there was nothing left but a physical shell and the need for justice. Justice she might be able to help to find.

She thrust her hands into her pockets and squared her shoulders. 'I'll do it. I doubt it's the same man, but you're right – we need to be sure.'

He stayed close beside her as they walked across the grass to the mortuary van, and he remained beside her in silent support when the attendant unzipped the body bag on the trolley just far enough to expose a face.

A young face, round and soft with easy living, framed with tousled dark hair, the skin marked by blotches where blood had settled after death. Green eyes stared blankly; lifeless, bloodshot, empty of emotion.

Tears stung her own eyes and she turned away.

'It's not him. Not the motorcyclist. He's too young. He's . . .' Her voice clogged in her throat, and she hugged her arms around herself, as if that could stop the cracks in her control from becoming crevices.

'Take your time, Jo.' She was grateful he didn't touch her, but the unspoken understanding in his voice steadied her.

'Sorry. It's stupid. I should be able . . . I don't even know him.'

'It's never easy, whether you know them or not. It's a natural reaction, Jo. Sit down over here for a minute, if you want to.'

The crime-scene officers had finished at the nearby sheltered picnic table, and she sat on the bench, facing the river. Behind her, the trolley rattled, sliding into the van, and someone closed the door on it as the engine started.

Whoever the young man was, they were taking him away.

Jo dug in her pocket for a handkerchief, blew her nose to clear the remnants of her tears, and kept her reddened eyes averted from the man who sat beside her. She had to pull herself together, to focus on facts and do what she could to help, instead of recalling the way the body bag had framed the young man's face, and the painful memory of Leon's face, framed in similar plastic.

Focus, describe and let the police do the analysis. Nick sat beside her, silent, undemanding; leaning forward comfortably, forearms on his knees, hands loosely clasped, as though he had all day to admire the view. She turned her head towards him, and immediately he shifted his gaze to meet hers, as if he'd been aware of her every movement while he waited.

'The man yesterday seemed older than the victim,' she began. 'Maybe in his thirties. His hair was just as dark, but more closely cut. What I saw of his face was thinner. Higher cheekbones, and his skin . . . well, not quite an olive complexion, but he wasn't fair. His eyes were darker. They were—' She stopped, catching the thought before she vocalised it.

'They were what?' he prompted.

She shook her head. 'It was just an impression I remembered, not a fact.'

'Impressions can be useful.'

'They can also be biased,' she argued, her own experiences after Leon's death clear in her mind. 'They can be based on nothing but the observer's assumptions, beliefs and culture.'

'Or,' he countered evenly, 'they can be the result of the subconscious mind instinctively recognising and interpreting small signals from body language and voice tone. You're observant, Jo, which is why I'm interested in your impressions.'

He had a point, yet still she hesitated, seeking among her memories of the short encounter for evidence she could trust.

'We only talked for a couple of minutes. I said hello, asked a few polite questions. On the surface he seemed relaxed, but he was . . . watchful, I guess would be the right term. He made plenty of eye contact, but he didn't smile and he didn't volunteer much or ask any questions himself. Some people are very open and friendly, and are ready for a long yarn as soon as you say hello. Others are curious, they want to know about the park, where to go, what to see. He wasn't like that. But maybe . . .' She had to be fair to him, non-judgemental. 'Look, maybe that was just a cultural thing. His English was fluent, but he had a slight accent. I'm not sure what it was. Some American pronunciations, perhaps, but I don't think he was American.'

'You said he was watchful.'

'Yes. But then, so are you.'

He threw her a rueful smile. 'It's a habit that comes with the badge.'

'No. It's more than that.' She rose to her feet and strolled a couple of metres away, stretching her arms back to loosen the tension in her shoulders. While she worked her muscles, her mind avoided emotions by tackling the intellectual challenge he'd handed her. 'Your colleague, Detective Dalton, was watching me only to find what he wanted – evidence of my guilt. He was pleased that I have no alibi for the time that the man was killed.'

She thought she saw his eyes narrow slightly, and an almost imperceptible firming along his jaw line. But the instant passed and she could no longer discern any change. She took the risk of prodding that control.

'In contrast, while you may be playing the good cop right now, you're constantly observing. Not so much looking for threats, not looking for guilt, but a continual scanning, gathering data, analysing it. The motorcyclist was like that, too, but he gave no indication of warmth or emotion. Just that detached study. Like a predator.' She tilted her head to one side and watched for his response. 'Like you.'

She'd surprised him, and he allowed himself to show it, raising an eyebrow as wry amusement curved his mouth. 'I'm a predator?'

She shrugged. 'Classifying things is a habit that comes with my type of work. I don't mean it with the nasty human connotations. In animal terms, a predator has strength, skills and intelligence to hunt prey when it needs to eat. On the basis of our few hours' acquaintance, I think you're a person who knows your own power and exactly how and when to wield it. On the basis of only a few minutes with the motorcyclist, I'd lean towards a similar category for him.'

Rather than arguing, taking offence or making light of her comments, he leaned back against the table, considering them.

'Do you think you could describe him to a police artist?' he asked eventually.

'I could try.'

'Good.' He stood and reached for his phone, and as simply as that their discussion was done, bar the practical arrangements from here. 'I'd like to get your fingerprints, too,' he said, 'so we can exclude them from the drug package and the fee box.'

'One of the crime-scene officers has already taken them. Do you want me to see the police artist this afternoon?'

'No. I have to go back to Strathnairn now, then down to Newcastle for the autopsy, so I won't be able to arrange it today. And you've done more than enough for one day. Perhaps you should head home, take the rest of the day off. I'll be in touch tomorrow sometime, but here's my card, in case you think of anything or see anything that might be relevant.'

His phone beeped, and with a faint smile of apology he checked it, walking away from her as he read, keying a response with nimble thumbs, all focus and work.

A small group of police officers emerged from the bush, their search completed, and milled around one of their vehicles. The forensic team packed the last of their equipment into their car.

She stood alone by the picnic table, where the activities should have been light and happy instead of shadowed by violent death.

Home. She'd planned to go into the office, but she needed the peace and silence of her own space more than she needed to keep busy, and Mal wouldn't object if she took the last few hours of the day off, in the circumstances.

She slid Nick's card into her pocket. She'd done all she could, and they no longer needed her here.

And she hoped she'd never have another day like this one.

&

During the trip back to the temporary operations centre in Goodabri, Jo's assessment of him echoed again and again in Nick's mind.

I think you're a person who knows your own power and exactly how and when to wield it.

Yes, she'd pinned him, probably more accurately than she realised. That was who he was, who he'd been, what he did. And that's what he'd taught Hugh. Survival in the world they'd grown up in, and then worked in, required more than martial arts skills and fighting strength. Power mattered. Personal power, intellectual power, psychological power. Power and control.

As for the predator definition, if one counted criminal dealers, killers, traffickers and extortionists as prey, then yes, in a way that fitted him too. A predator of predators. But while Hugh's temperament matched that of a jaguar or a tiger, Nick couldn't see himself in that light. More of a hunter, camouflaged in the same criminal stench, behaving in the same criminal ways – to all observation, exactly like his targets – until he'd found enough evidence to draw the web tightly around them.

Dangerous tactics for dangerous work. Three days into his return to normal duties after ten years, and he doubted he'd adjust to 'normal' again. Not that a brutal murder of this kind equated to normal, even for Homicide.

He made it to Goodabri five minutes before the first scheduled briefing, to find the old shop building buzzing with activity, the basics already in place. As well as a mobile ops van, a van with the logo of the regional television station was parked out the front, beside a car from the three-times-a-week Strathnairn newspaper. Avoiding them, he parked around the back of the building and entered through the rear door, passing an office, storerooms and a small kitchen to reach the main room, already looking like an incident room. Blinds on the front windows kept curious eyes from peering in, several tables already had computers set up, and screens divided the room into sections. In the larger space, photos of the victim and the scene were up on a board; the second board, headed 'suspects', was empty.

At the urn set up in a corner, Hugh was helping himself to coffee.

He'd known Hugh long enough to dispense with courtesies and get straight to the point. 'What's happened with Phoenix that they sent you up here?'

'A dead end. All the signs point to a hit from China – some old family feud – but the Chinese government isn't much interested. This came up, I'd heard you were here, so I volunteered. Change of scene, catch up with an old mate, catch a villain or two.'

Catch up with an old mate . . . Nick poured himself a glass of water. An easy term for a complex relationship. Perhaps the complexities were as much in himself as in their relationship. Whatever the case, he didn't feel entirely *matey* towards Hugh just now.

'Why did you press Jo Lockwood for an alibi?'

Hugh casually stirred sugar into his mug, seemingly unperturbed. 'She knows this area, she had the opportunity, she's got no alibi, and she very conveniently discovered the body without any witnesses.'

Classic Hugh thinking: regard everyone with suspicion, consider everyone capable of murder. Everyone *was* capable of murder, Nick knew, but not everyone was capable of every murder. 'So what about the minor details of means and motive?' he challenged, low and direct. 'I grant you she's a fit and strong woman, but even you or I would have had difficulty committing that murder alone.'

Hugh tried to cover his hesitation by taking a sip of coffee, but couldn't disguise the way he watched Nick for a reaction, despite the pretence of nonchalance. 'She could have had help. Look, mate, fact is, I've come across her before. It's not the first time she's been involved in a death. She obviously doesn't remember me – I didn't interview her then – but I recognised her name from that case in the Barrington Tops four, maybe five years back.'

Five years ago Nick had been working an undercover drug case in Queensland, out of touch with his colleagues. Few family connections or close friends were among the prerequisites for the specialist work he'd spent the past decade doing.

'What case?' he asked.

'Her fiancé – he was a park ranger too – fell off a cliff in the Barrington Tops during a search-and-rescue one night. She was the only one with him. Turns out he was about to head off for a job overseas without her, but he carked it and she inherited a tidy sum. Coroner ended up ruling it an accident, but there were a few of us not sure about that.'

Others were coming into the room now, gathering for the briefing, so Nick dropped his voice. 'You seriously think she pushed her fiancé off a cliff?'

Hugh shrugged, gathering up a file in one hand while balancing his mug in the other. 'Means, motive and opportunity, mate. She certainly had all three. And experienced abseilers don't usually walk off cliffs without ropes.'

Nick couldn't leave it there. Not enough information. Not enough facts. And he wouldn't allow Hugh – or anyone – to get away with sloppy investigation. 'Was there *any* evidence that suggested foul play?'

'Couldn't find anything definitive. He was pretty banged up, died of his injuries before they could get a chopper in to him. But if you'd seen her afterwards – she was too controlled. Not like a normal woman would be. My gut says she could have done it. And we have to explore every possibility.'

As he walked to the front of the room with Hugh to lead the briefing, Nick's gut insisted she didn't commit either crime. But how could he know for sure, without going over both cases, finding evidence? He'd spent hours with her today, gained a strong impression of an intelligent, dedicated professional. Yet she'd argued herself that impressions could be biased.

He liked her, dammit, respected her – but was he creating a false image of her, based on his own assumptions, and on what he wanted to believe?

❦

She had to concentrate hard on the drive home along the narrow dirt road. The current affairs program on the radio did little to distract her thoughts, and the image of the victim's face, framed by the body bag, kept floating into her mind, blurring with her memories and becoming Leon's.

By the time she parked beside the homestead, fatigue and reaction had set in and her whole body shook, cold despite the heat. She stumbled through her back door, dropped the keys on the kitchen table and went straight to the bedroom. Stripping off her uniform, she crawled under the blanket, clutching the pillow to her, letting the tears flow as she hadn't let them since the night, years ago, she'd huddled on a narrow rock ledge cradling Leon in her arms, crying in the driving rain while the storm raged around them and his life ebbed away.

FOUR

The reality of remote policing hit home as Nick surveyed the officers assembled for the briefing. Hugh and the detective constable from Homicide, Shelley Brock, would likely only be here for a couple of days, to lend expertise and support to the critical early stages of the investigation. If they didn't close the case in forty-eight hours, he'd only have the officers available in the local region, and most of them were in front of him: a dozen uniformed police from Strathnairn and outlying stations pulled off general duties, and Aaron Georgiou, a keen young detective with good instincts but inexperienced in crimes other than domestic violence, assault and stock theft.

With his new colleagues still to trust him, Nick let Hugh take the lead in the briefing, using the opportunity to observe the reactions of the team, assess their contributions, get a solid feel for the people he'd be working with.

Those who hadn't seen the victim at the scene paled as Hugh flicked through the graphic photos projected on the large screen, and there were more than a few muttered swear words. But when Hugh finally showed an image of the victim's face – for some Hugh-logic reason, he'd left that until last – one of the constables swore more loudly and rose to his feet.

'I think I know who he is,' he said. 'Picked him up a year or so back for DUI and marijuana possession, when I worked at Tamworth. Mitchell, I think his name was. Travis Mitchell. He'd been DUI before, so he got a six-month sentence. Nice enough young bloke, but a bit wild, and not too bright with it.'

Nick went to the whiteboard and wrote the name, the first real lead. Before Hugh could pass responsibility for looking into it to Brock, Nick forestalled him. 'Can you follow that up – it's Carruthers, isn't it? I think the CSOs got a partial print from the vic's burned hand. See if it matches Mitchell's prints from his records. And since he's in the system, there should be a next-of-kin record and, if we're lucky, a current address for him.'

He scrawled the constable's name as the action officer beside Mitchell's name on the whiteboard and set down the pen, returning to where he'd propped on the edge of the table. Hugh threw him a decidedly unamused look, but didn't object out loud. To object would be to acknowledge a threat to his leadership, and they both knew it. It had been one of the first lessons Nick had taught him, almost twenty years ago.

He'd given Hugh the lead on this one, but only because he chose to do so, for the benefit of the investigation, and he'd simply take it back the moment he needed to.

Hugh steered the briefing through the key issues and allocated tasks – mostly standard general enquiries, fishing expeditions, since they had so little to go on. He didn't make the mistake of naming Jo as a person of interest. Scarcely mentioned her at all, in fact. Either a wise decision in a small, possibly partisan community, or because he planned to keep his suspicions to himself until he had some evidence.

When it came to the point of identifying local drug dealers to question, Hugh received blank stares from most in the room.

Aaron shot Nick a glance before he volunteered an explanation. 'There's not much in the way of drugs out here,' he said. 'Not illegal ones, anyway. Alcohol is a much bigger problem. There's a bit of dope, but it's mostly low key. There's occasional methamphetamines and party drugs, but young people tend to bring their own back from the city. Some heroin along the truck routes, but that's pretty much it. I haven't heard anything about coke in the district.'

Nick doodled some figures on his notepad. Strathnairn, the largest town in the district, had a population of barely seven thousand. Add in a couple of other towns like Goodabri, a handful of small communities and a thinly spread agricultural population, and it still made fewer than fifteen thousand people in an area of thousands of square kilometres. Not a large or potentially profitable market for drug dealing. Not to mention the difficulties of running an illegal operation where secrecy would be hard for a local to maintain, when every second person in the street probably knew their name and at least half their history.

The cocaine they'd found was a small quantity, less than five grams in each of the twelve packs. Not a significant drop, just enough for a small private party, or for a minnow dealer.

Nick figured that if the biker had left it there for the vandals' party, something had to have gone wrong with the deal. And something had definitely gone very wrong for a young man, perhaps Travis Mitchell, who'd dabbled in drugs and served time in prison.

But they were still no nearer to finding out the identity of the biker, or of the vandals who'd smashed up the camping ground. Until they had some more leads, he was working blind.

☙

Curled up on her bed, Jo woke abruptly from a deep sleep. Evening light slanted across the room, with the apricot tinge of sunset.

The soft creak of something treading on the timber back veranda sounded again – the noise that had woken her.

Still groggy from sleep, rattled by the emotional exhaustion of her breakdown, she delved for the security of logic and tried to concentrate on the noise. It could be a possum or a roo, or a dog. A wallaby had polished off the potted herbs she'd had out there, just last week.

But they'd have tripped the rear security light, and there was only the fading sunlight shining into the room. No light coming from her bedside clock, either, or from the computer desk in the corner, where the printer, wireless router and external hard-drive usually glowed like a Christmas tree.

Pushing aside the pillow she'd been hugging in her sleep,

she slid off the bed to the floor and dragged her discarded clothes closer.

Creak.

If it was someone, rather than something, then she'd rather they believed she wasn't alone. If whoever was out there expected the house to be empty, the sound of voices might frighten them off.

Despite the constriction in her throat, she forced a laugh into her voice and said, 'No, I'm *not* coming back to bed.' Clothes in hand, she rose to her feet, slipped out the door and into the corridor, mumbling a protest in a passably low tone.

'Yes, the power's off again,' she called back to her imaginary lover. 'And I'm starving, so it looks like you're on barbecue duty again tonight.'

In the bathroom, she fumbled as she pulled on her rumpled uniform shirt and trousers, checking the pockets for her phone and keys.

Phone, but no keys. Kitchen table – maybe that's where she'd left them. *Damn.* Kitchen, with the curtains wide open at the large window, looking out over the back veranda.

Creak.

Okay, so the sound of voices hadn't discouraged her visitor. What next?

Normally, she'd simply go out and confront someone poking around. That was part of her job, and she'd dealt with all types – lost hikers, itinerants looking for a place to sleep, roo shooters scouting the landscape, young louts on the lookout for mischief – time and again, even alone and at night.

But tonight, with a man in the morgue and his murderers still on the loose, she'd be cautious.

With mobile phone reception more reliable at the front of the house than at the back, she walked as quietly as she could down the corridor to the room the National Parks staff used as a storeroom and general office. French doors leading on to the front veranda and spare keys for the service truck in the desk drawer gave her an exit strategy if she needed one. A heavy metal torch from the storage shelves could serve as both a light and a weapon.

Trying to breathe evenly to steady her heartbeat, she stood to the side of the window, watching out through the gap between the light curtain and the glass. The sunset glow had faded away, but nothing moved in the twilight shadows in the front yard, and she could hear no sounds other than the frogs croaking down at the river and the low, pulsing *oom-oom* of the frogmouth that lived in the grove of eucalypts over the fence.

She flicked through the contact list on her phone for the Goodabri police station. Not usually staffed twenty-four hours, but with the ops centre nearby maybe someone would be there, or the phone forwarded through.

Catching sight of headlights through the trees, she paused with her finger on the dial button. Definitely coming this way; the vehicle turned in at the driveway entrance and slowed to cross the cattle grid at the fence line.

In the glare of the headlights she couldn't identify the vehicle until it pulled around to park in front of the house.

She breathed easier. A service ute, and fellow ranger Erin Taylor driving it. Jo pushed open the French door and crossed the veranda to meet her.

'Mal sent me,' Erin announced cheerily as she opened the driver's door. 'I'm under orders to ensure you're okay, make sure you're fed and stay overnight if you want me to.'

She'd half-expected Mal to phone or call in this evening, and blessed his sense in sending Erin instead. Practical, down-to-earth Erin would not fuss over her, or panic in the current situation.

'Your timing is great. Not only am I starving, but the power's out and I think there's someone wandering around the backyard.'

'Shit. Have you phoned the cops?'

'I was just about to.' She rapidly reconsidered options. 'But now you're here, I think I'll phone Mal and tell him we're going to take a look, and if we don't phone back in ten minutes, to call the police station. It could just be that the fuse tripped and the wallaby came back for more herbs.'

'Good plan.' Erin grabbed a torch from behind the front seat and started unhooking the tonneau cover on the back of the ute. 'But phone Simon rather than Mal – if one of our colleagues is going to come charging out here in a white ute to save us, I'd prefer it was Simon.' She lifted out a crowbar, gave it an experimental swing and grinned. 'Not, of course, that we actually need saving. Let's go and scare off your rampaging wallaby.'

Her apprehension lightened, Jo tossed the phone to her.

'You phone Simon. I know you want to.'

But as Erin made the call to the third ranger in their team, Jo focused beyond her voice, on the sounds around, listening for anything that didn't belong.

With Simon duly alerted, and determined to ride to their rescue whether they needed it or not, they walked through the house, making noise and chatting as they went, flashing the torches around the rapidly darkening rooms. Jo much preferred to scare away an intruder than to confront one.

Nothing moved on the back veranda or in the yard beyond it, except for a possum, scrambling up one of the ancient fruit trees near the dilapidated chook shed.

'Maybe that's your culprit,' Erin said.

Jo gave a slight nod, but didn't for a moment believe it. She'd grown up in the country, knew the difference between a human footstep and a possum's. And she'd become familiar with that possum since she'd moved in here; it regularly climbed up veranda posts, scrabbled along the roof, breathed its rattling possum breathing outside the windows, but it had never made the timber boards of the veranda creak.

She waved her light towards the corner of the house. 'I'll check the fuse box.'

The hard ground under the fuse box grew little in the way of grass, and there was too little dust to see any discernible marks. But she covered her fingers with a handkerchief, just in case, when she lifted the lid and ran the light across the switches inside. All three power circuits sat just below 'on'.

Tripped by a power surge? All three of them? It might be possible; power supplies out here could be erratic. But she kept the handkerchief covering her fingers as she flicked each switch properly off, then back to 'on', to protect any fingerprints that might be there.

In the distance, above the croaking of the frogs and the possum's hissing, she heard an engine kick to life and she looked across the paddock beyond the homestead in time to see a single headlight swing away and speed off down the road.

FIVE

He drove to Newcastle through the night, music blasting from the speakers to keep him awake, stopping for strong black coffee at the few twenty-four-hour truck stops on the way.

At five in the morning he pulled into a motel on the edge of town, aiming to grab three hours' sleep before the scheduled nine o'clock autopsy. But sleep didn't come easily, and he stared at the ceiling, too many unsettling thoughts circling in his brain to switch off. The bitterness of his partner's betrayal, and the whispered rumours about his own loyalty from his new colleagues . . . a brutal murder, with no leads . . . Hugh, never easy to deal with . . . and a woman whose eyes he couldn't get out of his mind . . .

He rolled over, pummelled his pillow into softness, and buried his head in it.

When his alarm jerked him out of a dream at eight, he'd been back in that brothel in Melbourne, pain ripping through his body, a bloodied gun in his hand, and two bodies beside him. But in this dream the bodies weren't those of Terry Costello and the mistress of his mob target; they wore the faces of Hugh and Jo.

A cold shower made him alert but did little to improve his mood.

While he dressed he checked his emails. One from Malcolm Stewart with the names of the couple in the caravan he flicked on to Aaron, with instructions to follow up and find them. A brief message from Hugh confirmed that the partial fingerprint from the victim was a match with Travis Mitchell, twenty-two years old, three months out of prison, no fixed address.

Running out of time, he shut down the laptop and headed out the door. At least he had a confirmed name to take to the coroner's office.

Being able to refer to the victim by name did not make the autopsy any easier. Nick had attended many, knew the process, the smells and the sights, but they'd never, ever become easy to watch. In this one, the violence that had been disturbing when the victim was clothed became harrowing when the full extent was laid naked.

But he fulfilled his responsibility to observe as the forensic pathologist and her assistant did what had to be done efficiently and with respect, and he answered questions as to the crime scene and the sequence of events following the body's discovery to aid the doctor's analysis. She confirmed that the majority of injuries were inflicted prior to death, their nature clearly amounting to torture, before the final, fatal gunshot wound to the head. Nick found himself hoping that the toxicology reports would reveal ingestion of significant amounts of alcohol or other numbing drugs.

By the time it was finished, they were all grim. The doctor stripped off her mask and hat at the edge of the room, and leaned back against the wall, ashen-faced.

'I have a son around his age,' she said. 'That was as bad as—' She broke off, stood up straight. 'Let me check the records. I'll meet you in the conference room in ten minutes.'

The furnishings and warm timber tones of the conference room made for more pleasant surroundings than the sterilised stainless steel of the autopsy lab, but the scent of death clung in his nose, and the sunshine and chirping of birds outside the window grated against the harsh reality of death he had been witness to and the anger growing inside him.

The doctor returned in a little over ten minutes, handing him a file with photos and documents.

'That's the original file, but I can email you a copy. He's a John Doe, found in bushland near Coffs Harbour four weeks ago. Estimated date of death around three weeks before that. A difficult examination, because of the decomposition, but you may want to follow up with the investigating officer. There are similarities, including an amputation and the manner of it. Although this victim lost a foot, not a hand.'

Nick flicked through the pages, stopping at the list of those present at the autopsy when a name leapt off the page: Detective Senior Sergeant Hugh Dalton.

Hugh, who'd shown the images of their victim on the screen at the briefing last night and neglected to mention a similar case. Who'd labelled Jo Lockwood a likely suspect.

Just what was Hugh's game?

'Thanks, I will need a copy of this report,' he told the doctor. 'And there's another one, coronial findings from a few years back, that I need to get hold of, too.'

Not unusual for Hugh to run his own agenda; he'd never been a strong team player. But since they had scarcely seen each other in the past few years – hadn't worked directly together for even longer – Nick was determined to keep on top of every facet of this case. And as Hugh had suggested Jo's involvement, that included finding out about the death of her fiancé.

'I don't know the name, but perhaps you might remember it – he was a National Parks ranger, involved in a search in the Barrington Tops.'

'Yes, I remember that one. Rossetti. Leon Rossetti. I examined the scene and performed the autopsy. He was struck by a falling tree limb during a storm and fell thirty metres down the face of a bluff. What's your interest in that case?'

Unwilling to voice Hugh's intimations, Nick carefully kept to the bare, factual minimum. 'The ranger who found Mitchell yesterday was also with Rossetti when he died.'

The pathologist raised an eyebrow. 'His fiancée? If you're implying a possible involvement in Rossetti's death, as I reported to the coroner, Rossetti's injuries were consistent with her statement and the scene I observed. Rescue services were not available, due to the storm, so she climbed down to him alone, with only a basic rope fastened to a tree. I saw it there – one hell of a scary climb, even in sunshine.'

'Could Rossetti have survived, if he'd been airlifted to hospital immediately?'

'He survived the initial fall, but even if he'd been in an intensive care unit within the hour, he might not have lived. As you'd expect from such a fall, there were skull, spinal, thoracic and limb fractures and significant internal bleeding. It's a wonder that he lasted some hours, but there was nothing his fiancée could have done, in the circumstances.' She paused, steepling her fingers in contemplation. 'I doubt he was aware of it, but I hope it was some comfort to her that he didn't die alone.'

His top priority had to be returning to Goodabri, so he packed the report she printed for him in with his laptop, to read later. Nothing she'd said suggested any basis for Hugh's suspicions. Which left three possibilities: that Hugh knew something the pathologist and Coroner didn't; that his cynicism had skewed his judgement; or that he was playing some kind of game.

Nick suspected the latter. He just wished Hugh hadn't dragged Jo into it.

ॐ

Describing a face she had only seen partially obscured by a motorbike helmet, and from a distance without the helmet, challenged Jo's memory for detail. In the small office off the main incident room, the artist patiently manipulated graphics on the computer screen, prompted her with questions and options, and at the end of an hour they had an image that resembled Jo's memory of the face she'd seen two days ago, and in her dreams last night. The physical shape, skin tone, dark-brown eye colour and cropped black hair were as close as she could recall; what she couldn't adequately describe for a static image was the unemotional, shuttered expression, the lack of warmth or response in his eyes.

The memory of that cool, unchanging gaze had woken her numerous times in the night, and a cheerful breakfast with Erin and Simon in another dry, hot morning had not erased the chill in her spine or the prickling sense of being watched.

In the tiny bathroom at the rear of the makeshift ops centre, she splashed cold water on her face.

'Get a grip,' she told her reflection in the mirror. 'Plenty of people ride bikes in the park.'

The power *did* go out occasionally, a wallaby would forage where it had found tasty green food before, and the biker she'd spoken with the other day might simply rate high on the autism spectrum, with a brain not wired for instant empathy.

And she had paperwork piling up in the office next door, deadlines to meet and no desire to lose another day of work.

Glancing back into the main room, she could not see Hugh Dalton. Probably still outside, giving a media statement to the small crowd of television and newspaper reporters.

The annoyance at seeing her own face on the evening news still rankled. Dalton hadn't mentioned her by name in his carefully worded statement yesterday afternoon, but with little solid information to go on, a local reporter had filled in a few seconds' airtime with an image of her taken at the park opening last week. She'd had to field anxious phone calls from her mother and her brother after they'd seen the news. This morning's *Strathnairn Standard* had also carried the story, but now that the name of the victim had been released, there was only passing mention of her.

The 'Closed' sign on the front door of the National Parks office hadn't dissuaded a number of people from knocking and rattling the handle this morning. She'd have to keep a low profile today, using the rear entrance, skulking in the back office, out of sight and hearing from a media mob hungry for any morsel of information to fill out a so-far thin story.

Slipping out the back door of the police building, she encountered Aaron Georgiou coming in. As with many of the regional police officers, she'd met him a few times, through liaison meetings between the services, a bushfire preparedness exercise last month and the occasional social gathering. She liked Aaron; he reminded her of her younger brother, although Aaron was more serious and showed her far more deference than Todd ever did.

'Have you got another minute, Jo? I have a quick question for you.'

'Sure. If you don't mind coming in.' She unlocked the door of her building and ushered him inside, locking the door behind them. Despite the rough-and-ready nature of this temporary office, at least it was her territory.

He accepted her offer of a chair in her sparsely furnished work room and took out his notebook. 'That couple you saw on Tuesday – the Baxters, according to the camping permit Mal gave us – did they happen to mention which way they were headed? The sarge wants me to track them down.'

'They said they were planning to stop in the Bunya Mountains on their way to Noosa.' They'd been a friendly, pleasant couple, obviously devoted to each other, so the brief conversation she'd had with them stood out in her memory. 'Their names are

Tom and Shirley. They were driving a newish-model white LandCruiser and towing a large caravan – a Jayco, I think.'

'That's a fantastic help. Now at least I've got a general direction.'

'Try the Bunya National Park office.' She did a quick search on her computer. 'If they're in the park, the office should be able to find them. Here's the phone number.' She read the number from the screen and he noted it in his notebook.

'Thanks, Jo. I'll call them.'

Her chair squeaked as she leaned back. 'He really suspects the motorcyclist is involved somehow, doesn't he? Detective Matheson, I mean.'

Aaron tucked his notebook away in his shirt pocket, his young face sombre.

'I guess so. That's why he wants to talk to the Baxters. He's worked a stack of investigations involving drug rings and violent crime, including undercover jobs. He's familiar with how they're organised, how they operate, how they think. So I trust his instincts.'

Undercover jobs – that explained Nick's control, the power she'd sensed in him, his ability to switch from serious to friendly, to wear different faces. And that left her wondering who the real Nick was, under the careful control.

A detective who suspected the motorcyclist of involvement in one or both crimes carried out in the park, and was allocating resources to investigate that lead; that much she knew for certain.

'Aaron, you should know . . . it may be nothing at all, but I might have had an uninvited visitor yesterday evening. On a motorbike.'

'Shit, Jo. Why didn't you report it?'

'Nothing definitive to report. Some strange sounds, a power failure, and the sound of a bike in the distance. Erin Taylor arrived and we had a look around together, but there was no-one there.'

He dragged a hand through his hair, clearly worried. 'I'll tell the sarge when he gets back from Newcastle.'

So, he would tell Nick, not Hugh Dalton. The Sydney detective must have higher-priority suspects than a biker seen twelve hours or more before the crime. Like her. But Aaron at least didn't seem to share those suspicions.

'If you see or hear anything else unusual, Jo, call us straightaway. I don't like thinking of you out there alone.' He paused in the doorway, cleared his throat. 'Look, I know you might not feel you know any of us here yet, but believe me, people respect you, and we'd rather a dozen false alarms than . . . well, than anything else.'

As she closed the door behind him, Aaron's friendly concern touched her, and his efforts to assure her of her acceptance in the community. Four months wasn't long to be in a rural area, especially since she wasn't much good at making connections outside work. Although the division's main office was in Strathnairn, she went there only a couple of times a week, in between her duties in the various parks, establishing the new park and setting up this building for its role as temporary visitor information centre until the new Goodabri centre was built. She worked with a great team in Erin, Simon, Mal and the field staff, but they all worked out of the Strathnairn office, and she sometimes went days without seeing them.

She liked people, but being alone much of the time suited her nature. More so since Leon's death.

Flicking the overhead fan up to its highest setting, she returned to her desk. She had plenty of work to bury herself in to distract her thoughts from yesterday's events, and a quiet office with no interruptions to allow her to focus on crossing items off her To Do list. A funding submission to double-check and submit before five p.m. Wildlife survey data to incorporate into a report for the Minister, due by the end of the week. A plan for upgrading the fire trails to be finalised for next week. The summer family activity program to proofread before it went to the printer. Determined to catch up, she concentrated solidly for hours.

By late afternoon she had reached the summer family program. She stared at the list of activities. In just over a week, schools would be finished for the year and the busy summer season underway. Camping grounds across the four National Parks they managed would be filled with families, daytrippers would drive out from nearby towns, and the rangers and field staff would be flat out from dawn past dusk until the new school year started in February.

She checked the date on her computer. Eight days until the first weekend of the school holidays. Eight days before she was scheduled to take a twilight spotlighting walk along the gorge track from Gumtree Flat. Always popular with families, and usually she loved taking them – excited kids watching for possums, sugar gliders and bats, and their parents, almost as wide-eyed.

But unless the police caught the murderers before then, she'd be on edge, worried about safety, apprehensive about what they might find.

Had Travis Mitchell been part of the group of vandals, or an innocent camper caught up in their violence? Twenty-two years old, according to the news reports – younger than her brother. Younger than Aaron Georgiou. A man who should have had a long life ahead of him, instead of a terrifying, agonising death.

Her chest tightened to a painful lump, sorrow and despair swirling murky shadows in her mind. *No.* No, she would *not* permit gloomy thoughts to take over, to take her back to the desolation of depression she had worked so hard to escape. She pushed her chair back, crossed the office to the kitchenette and filled a glass with water from the cooler.

No wallowing. She'd allowed herself a good cry last night, the release of tension. Getting stuck in negative patterns of thought wouldn't help herself or anyone.

The back door slammed, and footsteps sounded down the corridor. Jo glanced at her watch – quarter to five, almost the end of the work day.

'It's just me,' Erin's voice announced, seconds before she appeared in the doorway. 'Everything all right?'

Jo leaned against the windowsill, not quite able to paste a smile on her face.

'I'm okay.' She drank a couple of mouthfuls of water, pressed the cool glass against her cheek. 'Diversion therapy just failed there for a moment.'

'Sucks when that happens and you remember, doesn't it?'

Typical Erin: no tiptoeing around, just down-to-earth understanding.

'Yep.' Not a topic she wanted to dwell on right now, so she switched the subject. 'I thought you were at that tourism planning conference in Tenterfield today.'

'I was.' With a wry grin, Erin helped herself to juice from the fridge. 'I escaped.'

'That exciting?'

'Oh, if we'd played buzzword bingo, I'd have filled my card before morning tea.'

'I'm glad it was you and not me. So you're here because . . . ?' No real need to ask the question. To check on her, naturally. Erin knew about Leon's death, and although she didn't tiptoe around her, she cared enough to worry, assuming Jo's solitary life meant still-active grief. Maybe it did. Jo wasn't too sure anymore.

'Thought I'd pop in on the way back to 'Nairn,' Erin said breezily. 'It's Thommo's farewell tonight. Are you coming? You're welcome to stay at my place if you don't want to drive back home.'

A crowded pub, farewelling the popular captain of the Strathnairn volunteer emergency service? Her head throbbed just thinking about it.

'I think I'll pike out of that one tonight, Erin. I've got a rescued sugar glider to release, and after that I'm planning on an early night.'

Glass halfway to her lips, Erin frowned at her. 'Where are you releasing it? Can it wait until tomorrow and I'll go with you?'

'The wildlife carer dropped it off this afternoon. There's no sense giving it the trauma of carting it around for another day, when it's not far out of my way and I can just release it before I go home. It's no drama.'

It wasn't. Couldn't be a problem. She'd gone over it again and again since the wildlife carer had emailed this afternoon.

Erin gnawed on her lip, unconvinced. 'What if someone follows you?'

Jo drained her glass of water, rinsed it out at the sink. Sensible. They all just needed to be logical and sensible.

'It's not far off the road, Erin. If someone follows then I'll see them. I've got the radio and the phone. But honestly, I see no reason for anyone to target me. Just because some kid on a trail bike decided to poke around the homestead last night doesn't mean I should cower inside and not do my job.'

Even a mere seven hours in the office had her restless, longing to be outdoors again. She hated the idea that fear should force her into hiding behind locked doors. The mystery biker from the camping ground could well be in Tibooburra or Bourke or even Thargomindah by now, enjoying a cold beer in an outback pub, oblivious to any crimes that had occurred.

'Do you want Simon and me to come and stay at your place tonight?' Erin asked. 'The cops have finished with the crime scene, so Mal wants us to go out to do the clean-up first thing in the morning. It's just as easy to do that from your place.'

Your place. But not her place, in reality. Staff quarters and work depot, a base for major projects in the area, and only a temporary home for her.

Jo kept her face neutral as she dried her glass and put it away in the cupboard. 'Of course you're welcome anytime you want to come, for work reasons or not.' No lie there – Erin was easy company and a good friend, and observing the deepening friendship between her and Simon made Jo happy for them both, even if they hadn't quite worked it all out themselves.

Time for another gentle nudge, perhaps. With an air of pretended innocence, she said, 'But if you're going to be partying tonight, wouldn't you be better off staying at Simon's? You can walk to his place from the pub, so you could relax and have a few drinks, instead of staying sober to drive back here.'

Erin blushed an attractive shade of pink. 'But—'

'But nothing. You know what you want, and I'm betting he wants the same.' She paused to regard her friend, deciding how much to say, remembering the goals and dreams she'd waited too long to grasp, lost in Leon's unexpected death. 'Don't do nothing and maybe regret it later, Erin. Simon's a good bloke. You can trust him.'

'Yeah, I know that.' Erin paced towards the window, changed her mind and propped on the edge of the table instead. 'Speaking of trust, what did you think of the new detective?'

'Nick?' The change of subject – and the sudden shift in thought from Leon to Nick – took an unsettling moment for her brain to process. 'Highly competent, I'd say. Professional, tough. Not one to tolerate fools. Why?'

'I was at the pub Tuesday night after rescue-squad training. A few of the boys in blue joined our table, and there was some talk. Remember that police shooting, a couple of months back, in Melbourne? A copper was killed and some underworld thug's girlfriend. An undercover cop was the only survivor, and the only witness.'

A vague memory lurked in her mind, devoid of detail. 'I heard about it, but didn't pay much attention. Seems they're always shooting each other, down there.'

'Yep. Anyway, the undercover guy's name was suppressed, but apparently it was Matheson, seconded to the Victoria Police.' Erin dropped her voice, as if concerned they could hear her next door. 'And some of the local boys think the official enquiry that cleared him was a whitewash.'

That she hadn't expected. 'Funny that they'd talk about it in the pub,' she wondered aloud. 'Don't police usually stick together over that kind of thing?'

'Well, they weren't shouting it from the treetops. I just happened to be at the end of the table where the muttering was loudest. I was a bit surprised, too – the blokes are usually pretty tight-lipped – but the close-ranks-and-protect-the-brotherhood loyalty doesn't appear to apply to Matheson. And the words "corruption" and "murder" were thrown around.'

Aaron had mentioned the undercover work, and she could imagine Nick passing as a convincing criminal – not a thug, but a sharp, intelligent mastermind behind complex crimes, able to act any part required.

In his own role, he showed little softness, despite his unfailing courtesy towards her. Tough and uncompromising. If he chose to walk on the wrong side of the law, he'd be a dangerous man.

She pushed that image from her mind. He was a police officer, a detective; she'd have to trust in the system and her instincts, and he'd given her no reason to believe that trust misplaced.

There had to be more to the story. There always was. Police faced dangerous situations and had to make split-second decisions every day. The suspicions about him might be a sign of the occasional tensions between regional and newly arrived city cops, and possibly held as much substance as the whispered accusations against her, after Leon's death.

ॐ

He reached Uralla around seven, and pulled in to a late-night service station and café on the edge of the town. Despite little in the way of appetite, he bought a couple of muesli bars and a Coke, his body needing the break from driving and the caffeine as much as the food. With a good two hours still to go, he didn't plan on blacking out at the wheel from fatigue and lack of sustenance, and there'd be few places open on the roads between Uralla and Goodabri.

He chose a corner table, his back to the wall, with a clear view of the other tables and the area outside through the windows. Old habits died hard.

He'd taken the back road from Newcastle, winding up through the mountains. A quicker route than the highway, but with little phone reception, so his phone had beeped with voicemail notifications as he'd approached Uralla and come in range of a phone tower.

Two messages. He cracked open the soft-drink bottle and drank some while he listened to them. Hugh's response to the voicemail he'd left earlier was typically casual and brief.

'We never turned up anything on that John Doe in Coffs, mate. No leads, no witnesses, nothing. The case is pretty much dead in

the water. Or the bush, so to speak. I'm following up on Mitchell's connections. I bet we'll get something from his prison mates.'

Aaron's message consisted of a brief but concise recap of the day's developments, the last on the list – the news about Jo Lockwood's possible intruder – making Nick grip the phone tighter.

An intruder, so soon after a murder – he didn't like those kinds of coincidences. Hugh had been bloody careless, letting slip to the media who had found the body, and although Nick couldn't see how it could result in a threat to Jo, it worried him nonetheless.

He deleted the message, took another mouthful of Coke and was about to check his emails when the phone buzzed. Aaron's number.

'Sarge, glad I've caught you.'

The relief in Aaron's voice set Nick's radar for bad news on alert. 'What's up?'

'I've just heard from the Queensland police.' There was a brief pause while he swallowed, but he continued, 'Going by the rego and the car description, they're pretty certain the vics found in a burned-out caravan this morning are the Baxters, the couple that Jo spoke with the other day.'

Nick set the bottle down slowly on the table. 'Two vics?'

'Yes. Both of them, in bed. Won't be certain until the autopsy, but the detective I spoke with reckons it's suspicious. Gas bottles don't usually explode these days.'

No, they don't. Not at night, with an elderly couple tucked up in bed.

He stuffed the muesli bars into his pocket, picked up his drink and headed for the door, the phone still at his ear. 'Any witnesses?'

'None. It was an isolated camping area. They were the only ones there.'

Not the only ones, Nick would have bet. Someone else had been there. Someone who had killed them. Money and thrills aside, there weren't a lot of reasons to kill an elderly couple. But they'd been in the National Park on the day Travis Mitchell was murdered. They'd spoken to a motorcyclist who might be linked to drugs. So had Jo – and she'd had an intruder last night, on a bike.

'Aaron, get on to Jo Lockwood. Send a couple of uniforms out to her place, or go yourself. Make sure she's not alone, anywhere.'

'I already tried to phone her, Sarge. There's no answer on her mobile or at home.'

'Keep trying. Keep trying until you find her and make sure she's safe. Then keep her that way. I'll be there in ninety minutes.'

SIX

The sun, close to setting, cast a red–gold glow across the landscape. Jo left her truck under a tree by the creek, taking only her backpack and the small covered cage holding the sugar glider.

She walked along the road a short distance, then up the ridge that formed the border of the park. To the east lay bush and rough granite hills, too rough to farm, small creeks cutting through rocky valleys.

To the west the hill sloped away more gently, and there the land had been cleared a century ago for grazing, leaving only small pockets of timber. The thousands of trees Jack McCulloch had planted in green corridors over the past forty years would not be fully grown, with the hollows necessary for many birds and mammals, for another twenty or thirty years. But the bush was slowly regenerating, the old forest and the new seeding young trees and gradually encroaching on the shearers' quarters and shearing shed, deserted since Jack switched from sheep to cattle many years ago.

The homestead itself lay a kilometre away, deserted, too, now that Jack was in the nursing home, with no-one to pass the property on to. He'd sold off his stock, leased some of the land, couldn't yet bring himself to sell the whole property and the homestead that had been in his family for four generations. Jo knew the heartache of that; a run of bad years and her father's terminal illness had seen her own family forced to make a similar decision when she was seventeen. She felt for Jack, hoped the property would see new owners who cared for the land and continued his family's stewardship.

But for now McCulloch Downs was empty, save for a few cattle on agistment, and with the park on one side and the quiet paddocks on the other, she walked along the fence line at the top of the ridge for half a kilometre, to where she'd found the dehydrated glider at the bottom of a tree a couple of weeks ago. After recuperating in the care of the local wildlife rescue service, his best chance of survival lay in release here, where he came from.

The sun had set, the cloudless western sky deepening to a deep mauve. A gold glow peeked over the ridges to the east. Although she knew the basic science of atmospheric effects and refracted light, the huge golden orb of a full moon rising never ceased to bring her pleasure. She took the few minutes to simply stand, watching it, the cage resting at her feet. Belatedly she remembered her camera in her backpack, and, setting the exposure for the dusky light, she framed a few shots of the moon silhouetting the trees on the next ridge.

When moonlight spilled around her, she knelt by the cage on the ground and slowly opened the small door. Using her knee as a makeshift tripod, she steadied the camera, capturing a couple of images of the sugar glider's striped head as it cautiously poked a nose out into the fresh air, but gave up trying to photograph it as the glider made a sudden dash for the nearest tree, and scampered up the trunk.

And there it was, done, a wild creature returned to its habitat, to the natural cycles of life among the trees. Always satisfying, one of the many pleasures of her job.

'I hope you find your family, little fella, and live a long life with lots of offspring,' she murmured.

Buoyed by the beauty of the evening, she began to make her way back to the truck, the rough track clear enough in the moonlight so that although she took a torch from her backpack, she didn't turn it on.

The sounds of nocturnal creatures stirring accompanied her; rustlings among the leaves, the swoop of a microbat in front of her, and the reverberating call of a tawny frogmouth, a short distance ahead. As she approached what appeared to be the stump of a limb on a branch it transformed into a bird, the frogmouth gliding away from her, down the ridge.

Being out alone in the dark, miles from anywhere, normally didn't spook her. She didn't believe in ghosts, the native animals posed little threat, and statistically she was far safer out here than on a city street.

But tonight she moved more quickly, wary, eyes and ears alert for anything that didn't belong. Only two hundred more metres to walk, then down the hill to the creek and her truck, and she could head home for a late meal, a shower and bed.

She heard the oncoming vehicle before she saw its headlights through the trees to the west. Her pulse rate lost its regular rhythm, pounded erratically. Only a handful of people lived along the dirt road between the tiny community of Derringvale and Goodabri, and it was hardly a short cut to anywhere. It could be a local, travelling back to the Goodabri area, although there was a quicker route from Strathnairn. Hoons out for a drive? Kangaroo shooters, perhaps?

Her truck would be obvious once they crested the rise and headed downhill again, but maybe they'd assume it had broken down or been deserted. Phone, wallet, keys, camera – yes, she had most things of value with her in her backpack.

She wouldn't let anyone know she was there unless she knew exactly who they were. Having to be so cautious sat uncomfortably with her, rubbing against the grain of a lifetime of country living. It was the Australian bush, dammit, not the back streets of some city.

But instead of coming up the hill, the car slowed, turning off the road near the derelict shearers' quarters, about a hundred metres from where she stood.

Now *that* didn't make sense. Why would anyone go there, especially at night? The place had been picked clean by antique hunters years ago.

The vehicle – a ute – pulled up in front of the shearing shed, leaving headlights blazing at the building while the driver climbed the old wooden steps and went inside.

Keeping in the shadows of the trees, Jo moved closer, about fifty metres from the shed, while the man was out of view. It technically wasn't National Parks property, but out here, with large properties covering thousands of hectares, neighbours kept an eye on things for each other.

While some of the blokes who wandered the bush might camp for a night or two in the many old shearers' quarters that dotted the countryside, Jo knew from yarning with them that the larger, draughtier, lanolin-soaked woolsheds weren't a preferred camping spot. So a ute swinging in to park so confidently by the shed in the dark didn't . . . well, it didn't *feel* right.

She tugged her camera out of her backpack and made sure the flash was turned off. Steadying it on a tree stump, kneeling behind it so she stayed out of view, she zoomed in on the illuminated area between the ute and the shed. When the man came out again and hurried down the steps, the headlights cast his face in good light, and she snapped several frames.

She cursed the flutter of nerves that made her hand shake but continued to photograph, despite the poorer light beside the ute, as he quickly undid the tonneau cover on the back and slid something long – about a metre, maybe wrapped in cloth – from the tray. He glanced several times to the west, as if keeping a watch out for another vehicle on the road.

Whatever he was doing, Jo doubted there could be an entirely innocent explanation. Maybe it was some sort of prank, or maybe he was hiding stolen goods, but with a man murdered just two days ago, and a stash of cocaine found, she kept clicking photos, and stayed out of sight.

He came out after a couple of minutes, taking the stairs two at a time, before getting in the ute and driving back the way he'd come, away from the ridge concealing her truck.

Jo breathed deeply again, and waited until his headlights had disappeared from view before she walked down to the shearing shed.

It was Jack McCulloch's private property, but she had a good relationship with him, had visited him a number of times in the nursing home to talk about the history of the area, and she doubted he'd mind her trespassing in the circumstances, to check things over.

The timber steps creaked as she walked up them, and the corrugated-iron door into the shed opened with a squeak, rubbing against the floorboards. Moonlight streamed into the shed through the door and through the propped-open corro vents along one wall.

The wool press and the skirting tables were long gone, but the pens waited, empty, where they'd once fed sheep to the shearers on the boards. She counted eight shearing stands, some of the old flywheels above still draped with electric cord. Behind where the shearers had stood, the chutes they'd pushed the shorn sheep down to the pens outside were draped with spiders' webs.

She shone her torch into the darker corners, where the moonlight did not reach. A stack of empty pallets leaned against one wall, some draped with old hessian wool sacks. The only signs of recent disturbance she could see in the shed were scuff marks in the dust around those pallets.

Whatever the guy had brought in had to be among the pallets. There was nowhere else to hide anything in the open shed. She pulled aside the wool sacks. The pallets were stacked haphazardly, some upright, some flat between them. But underneath the top flat one, the shine of metal glinted in the torchlight, and she shifted the pallet aside.

A large steel lockbox, the kind that most of the farmers and workers in the region had fitted on the back of their utes and trucks for tools and equipment. She had one herself, although this one was older, battered, and the latches had no padlocks.

Who would go to the trouble of stowing a large tool box in an empty woolshed, and hiding things in it?

Drugs, perhaps. Or reptiles or birds for smuggling. Or it could be . . . no, what he'd carried hadn't been big enough to be a body. Unless . . . She tried to veer her mind away from that thought.

Damned unlikely, but the possibility would haunt her if she didn't find out. And if it were reptiles or birds, then that was her responsibility, and the sooner they were freed the more chance they had of survival. The illegal wildlife trade was lucrative, increasing – and often deadly for the creatures. On other occasions she'd found animals stuffed in socks, sealed in cardboard tubes, and in boxes and tins, drugged, dehydrated, dying.

She doubted there'd be snakes loose in the box, but just in case – and to protect any fingerprints – she pulled on the leather work gloves she always carried in her backpack before she carefully lifted the lid.

A frayed poly feed bag covered the contents. She raised a corner of it, then more.

Nothing slithered or wriggled, and the torch light glinted on cold metal.

She exhaled a long, slow breath. Not reptiles, not birds, not drugs.

Weapons. At least two semi-automatic rifles, a pump-action rifle, and a couple of handguns visible in the top layers. She touched nothing, just shone the light around to get an estimate of the size of the box. Large enough to have more weapons beneath what she could see.

She swore under her breath. A cache this size, of this type, meant serious criminal business, not an amateur collection or a hiding place for someone's unlicensed guns.

She took her phone from her pocket – as she expected out here, no signal. And this wasn't something she was going to report on an open radio channel. Without moving anything, swapping her phone for her camera, she took a couple of shots, using the torch to provide light, then she replaced the feed bag and closed the lid of the box.

But as she slid the pallet back on top of it, she heard the rumble of an engine, and the glow from headlights shone in through the open door.

If the vehicle went straight past, it would be okay . . .

The engine changed down a gear or two, the vehicle slowing, the rumble sounding more like a large truck than a ute or a car as it turned on to the rough track to the shed.

Shit, shit, shit.

She huffed out a frustrated breath while she mentally raced through her options. She'd faced down illegal hunters in the past, confronted licensed shooters who'd strayed into the park, all just part of the job. But with murder, drugs and now weapons, she'd be stupid to take the risk without back-up.

She stuffed the torch into her pack, dragged the wool sacks back across the pallets, and crossed the floor quickly to the most distant shearing stand. Pushing her pack in front of her, she crawled into the sheep chute, dropping down out of sight under the woolshed, crouching in the darkness as the truck parked beside the shed. Doors slammed, and at least two pairs of heavy footsteps climbing the stairs sent vibrations through the timber building.

The moonlight didn't reach here, and she groped through the blackness and spider webs, easing her way past the old sheep pens, closer to the footsteps above. They'd gone straight to the stack of pallets, clearly not worrying about noise as they dragged them out of the way.

The thump of a pallet falling to the floor covered the gasp she couldn't quite stifle when something ripped into her upper arm with a sharp pain, cutting through her shirt and her skin. A nail, sticking out where one of the sheep pens had fallen apart. The wet warmth of blood trickled down her arm. She unhooked her shirt sleeve, pressed it against the wound, and stayed still, listening to the men's conversation.

'Is it there?'

'Yeah. They're all there. He found it in time.'

'Just as fucking well. Otherwise he'd have gone the same way as his stupid fucking mate.'

'Yeah.'

Jo crouched in the dark, fist against her mouth to stifle any sound. Travis Mitchell. Were they talking about him?

'Trying to rip off the boss. What a fucking fool.'

Metal scraped against the wooden floor. 'Yeah. Stop squawking and grab the other end. We ain't got all bloody night. Buyer'll be waiting and we don't want to fuck this up.'

Her heart pounded so sharply it almost hurt. She forcibly slowed her breathing, stayed entirely motionless, while they made their way back across the shed and down the stairs. She abandoned the brief idea of trying to photograph the truck's rego plates. Stay out of sight, stay safe, stay alive. If they didn't know she was here, they couldn't hurt her.

She didn't move until they'd loaded the box, reversed and swung back on to the track, headlights well away from her direction. Slipping to the edge of the shed, she stayed behind one of the thick support posts, noting what she could of the size and shape of the truck as it drove away in the moonlight.

When they were out of sight she emerged, her limbs shaking. She gulped in lungfuls of the night air, and then made her unsteady legs work well enough to run from the woolshed, back into the bush on the ridge.

SEVEN

The phone on the dashboard lit up, and seeing the number, he punched *answer* before it finished its first buzz.

'Jo! Where are you? Are you okay?' His headlights made ghostly shadows of the trees lining the dirt road ahead. With the few houses of Goodabri just behind him, it was still another ten minutes to the Riverbank homestead.

'I'm fine.' The breathless catch in her voice belied the words. 'Listen, there's an empty cattle truck heading west on the Derringvale Road with a stack of weapons.'

Derringvale – where was Derringvale? He tried to picture the map. North of Strathnairn. Maybe forty minutes west of Goodabri.

She hurried on. 'There are rifles, semi-autos, pump-action and handguns. It will probably be at the Derringvale Junction in less than fifteen minutes. If you can get a patrol up there you might be able to catch them. There are two men in the truck – and I think they're connected to the murder.'

He swore under his breath. 'Where the hell are you, Jo? You're not with them?' The thought of her huddling in the back of a truck with weapons and murderers made his mouth dry.

'No, they didn't see me. I'm near the McCulloch Downs woolshed, where the guns were hidden. It's off the Derringvale Road, about fifteen k's from Goodabri.'

He slammed down a couple of gears, veered to one side and spun the wheels as he did a U-turn on the dirt road, back towards the road he hoped led to Derringvale.

Fifteen kilometres from Goodabri. From his recollection of the map, there was nothing between the two towns, except grazing properties and the southern end of the National Park. And Jo was out there, probably alone.

'Stay on the line, Jo. I'll radio for any cars out that way. I'm on my way to you now.'

He put the call in on the radio, heard two cars respond from north of Derringvale. Depending on which way the truck turned at the junction, they might or might not catch it. Too far away himself to catch up with the truck, Jo's safety became his first priority.

'Jo, if I take the road that goes out past the Goodabri race course, is that the right road to get to where you are?'

'Yes.' She paused a moment, then asked, surprise in her tone, 'How come you're out there?'

'Looking for you.' His actions, his orders, would be the same for any witness potentially at risk – but not the worry eating at his control, and the frustration of the past hours, not knowing.

That was new, a level of anxiety he hadn't felt since his youth, looking out for his siblings. 'You haven't answered your phone for almost two hours.'

'Not much phone signal out this way. I've only just seen the messages.' Concern sharpened her voice. 'What's happened? Is everyone all right?'

'Yes.' Everyone but the Baxters, and she probably wasn't thinking of them just now. 'I'll fill you in when I get there. Are you somewhere safe?'

'Yes. Really. I'm up on a ridge in the one spot there's phone reception, perfectly safe, and I can see for miles around in the moonlight. If you put your emergency lights on as you approach, I'll know it's you. You're coming from Goodabri?'

'Yes. Just turning onto the Derringvale Road now. I'll be a few minutes yet.'

'You'll see my work truck when you get to Eight Mile Creek. Go past it, over the ridge, and the old woolshed is on your left. I'll meet you there. My battery's getting low, so I'm going to hang up now. I'll see you soon.'

The minutes, and the kilometres, seemed to go inexorably slowly, even though he took the dirt road as fast as he dared in the darkness. He turned on the unmarked car's police lights when he crossed Five Mile Creek, the strobing blue and red flashing from the grill casting eerie flickers on the road ahead.

At Eight Mile Creek her truck sat on the side of the road, dark and deserted. Over the rise and out of the park, the farmland spread before him, well lit under a full silver moon, the woolshed and its outbuildings easy to see among a small cluster of trees.

He'd forgotten how bright a full moon could be when there were no other lights competing with it. Bright enough to cast shadows, bright enough to see without a torch.

Bright enough that when he'd parked beside the woolshed and switched off the headlights, he could see her sitting on a fence post, waiting for him. She slipped off the post and walked towards him, the soft, pearly moonlight silhouetting her, slim and lithe, her head haloed by wisps of windblown hair that had escaped from her ponytail, almost ethereal.

Dammit, where had that thought come from? It wasn't like him. Fatigue, worry and relief must be scrambling his brain. He dealt in facts, not fairytales.

And she was no goddess or spirit, but an entirely down-to-earth woman, her uniform trousers grimy at the knees, a dark stain on one sleeve and blood trickling down her arm.

'You're hurt. What happened?'

She glanced at her arm and gave an unconcerned shrug. 'Just scraped my arm on a nail. I washed it, but if you have a first-aid kit, it could do with a little more disinfectant than the couple of wipes I had.'

'There's a kit in the car. While I clean it up, you can fill me in on events.'

She sat on the woolshed steps, and he switched the headlights back on to give more light.

'I warn you,' she said, as he joined her with the kit. 'Tonight's perfume is Eau de Woolshed, featuring base notes of well-rotted sheep manure, with subtle highlights of old lanolin. I'd take shallow breaths if I were you.'

Despite her attempt to make light of things, he could see the fine lines of strain around her eyes, the effort to smile, the weariness in her shoulders. She must have been worn out, because she let him examine the wound on the back of her upper arm instead of trying to do it herself. Her shirt sleeve had ripped, and the ragged cut, a couple of inches long, still seeped blood.

He sat on the step behind her, first-aid supplies in easy reach beside him. Beneath the whiffs of Eau de Woolshed he caught the scent of something lightly floral, and he had to drag his brain away from dwelling on the smooth skin under his fingers and the elegant curve of neck and shoulder to concentrate on crime and his responsibilities to investigate it. 'What the hell happened, Jo? Erin Taylor said you were going to release an animal and then head home. That was hours ago.'

'That plan worked fine until the "head home" part.'

He worked silently while she explained, briefly and concisely, what she'd witnessed. No drama in the telling, although her jaw tightened and the muscles in her neck tensed as she spoke of waiting for long minutes in the sheep pens under the woolshed while the two men were inside. She'd been scared, well aware of the danger.

'I'm sorry, I don't have a description or photos of the truck or the guys who took the guns. Hiding seemed the wisest course of action, in the circumstances.'

He carefully taped a dressing over the wound, making himself breathe in and out, slowly. If she had been discovered . . .

If she'd been discovered, she'd likely be dead by now. Whether or not the comments she'd overhead referred to Mitchell's murder, crims who dealt in quantities of illegal weapons did not leave witnesses alive to report the matter. It would have been easy – too easy – to commit murder here in this isolated place and to conceal a body where it might never be found.

The notion of Jo dead – or worse, tortured as Mitchell had been – tested Nick's control, and he averted his face, packing up the first-aid kit to avoid exposing the unaccustomed, inexplicable emotion.

Plan, act, protect. Emotion had no place in what he had to do.

'If you're able to drive,' he told her, as he carried the kit back to the car, 'I'll take you to your truck, and then I'll follow you back to your place. I'll organise a couple of officers to protect you there tonight.'

'Protect me?' She pushed herself up off the step. 'These guys don't know I was there. I'm in no danger from them.'

'That's not the main reason I'm worried.' He didn't beat around the bush. 'Jo, a couple were murdered last night in Queensland. Set up to look like a gas-bottle explosion in their caravan, but the detective I spoke with is fairly certain they were shot at close range first. They're still to be formally identified, but it's likely they're—'

Her face paled as she interrupted him. 'Tom and Shirley Baxter.'

'Yes. The car and the van are registered to Tom Baxter.'

Biting her lip, she turned away, her breathing ragged as if she were holding back tears. 'Their daughter's due to have a baby soon,' she said after a moment. 'They were thrilled about becoming grandparents.'

How many times had he heard something like that? A new baby, a new job, retirement – always a reason why the dead should not be dead. And yet they were.

'It's never fair, Jo,' he said, cursing himself for the empty platitude. Sixteen years of policing and he still had no useful words to offer.

She dragged the heel of her hand over her eyes and gave him an apologetic glance. 'Sorry. It's not as though I actually knew them. But they seemed a lovely couple, very happy together. The way it should be.'

The way it should be . . . He hadn't read her as a romantic, yet out of all that had happened, this was one of the few events to crumple her composure.

She blinked again, tight and slow to gain control. Within seconds she'd focused on the issues, the practical implications. 'You're worried that the motorcyclist is connected. The Baxters saw him, probably spoke with him, and now they're dead.'

'Yes. Aaron told me about your visitor last night. If the men you overheard tonight are connected with the murder – I think it's likely – then chances are "the boss" they spoke of has a number of people working for him.' A number of people killing ·for him, as they'd killed Mitchell. Nick's gut instinct shouted that the motorcyclist could well be the 'boss'. 'We can't take any risks, Jo. You saw him too. You can identify him and place him at the scene. I want you under protection at all times until we have some more answers.'

Her face set, she nodded without arguing, and when he held the passenger door of his car open for her she got in without hesitation. He drove her the short distance to her truck and then followed close behind her along the winding dirt roads until they reached the homestead.

And all the way, he turned the facts of the case over in his mind, searching for answers. Three murders, drugs, weapons, an unidentified motorcyclist and an identified, but dead, ex-con. An ex-con who'd stolen a rifle, tried to cheat his boss? That could add up – losing a hand was a traditional punishment for theft. But that was only one piece of a larger puzzle, and he still had to work out how to fit all of the pieces together.

❦

The corrugated iron of the homestead roof shone in the moonlight as she approached, the house itself still and dark, a familiar haven. Not much prospect of the quiet, early night she'd hoped for, though, with all that had happened to distract her, and the likelihood of strangers guarding her.

A police car waited in the driveway, but it was Aaron, not a stranger, standing beside it.

'Hi, Jo,' he greeted her through the window. 'Nick radioed ahead that you were on the way, and asked me to meet you both here. I've checked the garage and around the house, and there's no sign of intruders.'

He'd left room for her to drive past his car to park in the garage. Dropping her head on the steering wheel for a moment after she'd switched off the engine, she tried to gather enough courage and mental energy to face the challenge ahead. If she'd discovered Travis Mitchell's body days or weeks after his death, there would have been no clear date of death, nothing to connect him with any visitors to the park. But she'd discovered him within hours, while recent events and visitors were still fresh in her mind, and potentially in the minds of others.

As much as she hated the thought of being under guard in her own home, she didn't need convincing that the risk was real. The Baxters were dead, murdered, and if she hadn't woken up yesterday afternoon, if Erin hadn't arrived, she might not be sitting here now.

And she shouldn't be sitting here, but getting out and going inside . . .

Nick waited for her just inside the garage, and when she took her backpack and the cooler box out of the back of the truck, he picked up the esky.

'I can carry it,' she protested.

'So can I,' he answered mildly.

Not much point insisting on her independence in the circumstances, especially over such a small thing.

She led the way along the back veranda to the kitchen door. As she unlocked it, Nick and Aaron both moved to enter before her, hands hovering near their guns. Both serious, both intent on their duty, working silently together as if they'd done this a thousand times before.

While they checked the house for intruders, she dumped her backpack on a chair, flicked the electric kettle on and grabbed mugs, tea and coffee from a shelf. Easy, practical tasks that almost kept her thoughts from the reality of having police officers with guns in her home.

'I don't know about you guys,' she said when they returned, 'but I'm hanging out for a cup of tea. And a shower.' *And five minutes' peace and quiet to get myself together.* 'You'll probably both be glad if I have one. Help yourselves to coffee and anything else you want. There are some bacon and cheese scrolls in the freezer if you're hungry. I'll be back by the time the tea's brewed.'

She fled to the privacy of her bedroom, the sound of voices following her as the two men began to patrol around outside the house. She should have joined them, showed them the layout and the sheds, instead of walking out on them and hiding. She just couldn't . . .

Yes, you can, she told herself. Shower, change and go back into the kitchen. Composed and ready to deal with the situation. In control.

Less than ten minutes later, out of the shower, she brushed the last of the spiders' webs out of her wet hair, and pulled on cargo pants and a T-shirt.

Ready to return to the others, she put a hand on the door knob. In control. Mostly. Scared and tired and worried and still grappling with shock about the Baxters, but composed enough that she wouldn't fall to pieces on anyone.

'I reckon the sheds are the danger spot, this one in particular,' Aaron was saying as she approached the kitchen. 'Anybody could sneak down the hillside at night – or even in daylight – and hide until they find an opportunity.'

Her bare feet made no sound on the timber floor. Nick was the first to see her come through the door, looking up from the hand-drawn diagram lying on the table, as if he'd caught her movement in his peripheral vision.

She thought she saw an instant of surprise widen his eyes, but maybe she'd imagined it, for he acknowledged her return with a bare nod before including her in the conversation.

'The sheds – can they be locked?'

'The large machinery shed, yes,' she answered. 'But the tool shed doesn't have much of a lock on it. We don't keep anything valuable in there.'

She pulled up one of the vacant chairs, looking quickly over the diagram of the homestead buildings as she reached for the teapot and the mug waiting for her. They'd got the layout of the place pretty right, even after only a few minutes' survey.

'If we park the tractor right in front of the tool-shed door, no-one would be able to get inside. The door opens outwards,' she explained.

But that only solved a small part of the problem. The diagram only reflected the buildings. The reality of the situation was more complex, with extensive wooded areas to the north and west, reaching up the hill behind the homestead.

'How would you do it, if you were a crim?' Aaron asked Nick, and then flushed. 'Sorry, Sarge, I didn't mean . . .'

The undercurrent in Aaron's flush and Nick's impassive expression brought the rumours Erin had mentioned to mind, but he answered the question with only a trace of dry coolness in his tone. 'A sniper shot from the hillside back here, assuming there's tree cover. And assuming a simple elimination of the target is the objective.'

And there was something in that stony face that said he could do it – wait motionless in the bush, watch for the target, take precise aim, pull the trigger.

A simple elimination of the target . . . The stark, emotionless words referred not to a kangaroo, or a wild dog or boar, but to her.

EIGHT

He'd scared her, and he'd meant to. He wanted Jo to understand just how easy – too easy – it would be for someone determined to kill her. Acting alone, the sniper shot would be the simplest. But if the killer didn't care about attracting attention and collateral damage, and had assistance and weaponry, then nowhere would be safe. A raid with several guys and semi-automatics blazing, and they could all be dead within minutes.

Although few groups would be brazen enough to run that kind of attack, signs pointed towards the possibility. The mob violence of Mitchell's death indicated that a group already bound by murder existed in the area; the weapons Jo had found, if connected, gave them firepower.

He shoved away the image of this peaceful country kitchen strafed by gunfire, the red pottery teapot shattering, Jo falling, blood-spattered and lifeless.

He couldn't let that happen, had to keep her safe.

'Are there still rooms at the hotel in Goodabri, Aaron?'

'No. The Goodabri Show is on this weekend. I booked the last two rooms for Dalton and Brock.'

How could he protect Jo with the few resources the district commander, Keith Murdoch, had given him? Overtime for just one officer to stay with her. Plus himself, because he'd be damned if he left her and something happened.

He didn't have many options. 'I'll call Hugh. You should be able to stay in Shelley Brock's room.'

Jo didn't object, but her nod lacked enthusiasm. As he scrolled for Hugh's number on his mobile, she said, 'Reception's scratchy out here. Use the landline.' She indicated the phone on the wall as she rose from the table. 'While you're doing that, I'll get my laptop and download tonight's photos.'

Aaron's chair scraped as he stood. 'I'll go round the house, check the doors and windows are secure.'

Nick nodded his approval. Thorough and dedicated, Aaron, with more experience, would make an excellent detective. Unlike some he'd worked with.

'You can't put her in with Shelley, mate,' Hugh said when Nick outlined his request. 'She's . . .' The hesitation gave him away. 'She's pretty buggered. Didn't get much sleep last night. And there's only one bed in her room.'

Which Hugh was sharing. The self-satisfied amusement and innuendo made that obvious. Leaning against the wall by the phone, Nick gritted his teeth in silence. Hugh had always had plenty of lovers, but a junior officer, on a job, broke both rules and ethics. With Jo returning to the room with her laptop, he couldn't respond in the blunt terms that immediately came to mind.

'That's . . . *unfortunate*,' he said, his coolness loading the word with censure.

Hugh merely laughed. 'Jealous? Oh, well, you can keep your Doctor Lockwood company tonight.'

He made an effort to restrain his anger. 'I didn't hear that, Hugh. I'll see you at the briefing in the morning.'

He cut the connection, swearing silently. Damn Hugh and his cowboy attitude. He'd always been a good cop, despite his propensity to skate around the edge of proper procedure. But now alarm bells were ringing, loud and clear, in Nick's mind. Sometime, in the past couple of years since he'd spent any time with him, Hugh's idiosyncrasies had become more pronounced. If that was affecting his professional judgement, Nick would have to act.

Jo glanced up from plugging the laptop into a socket. 'Is there a problem?'

Even without hearing Hugh's side, she couldn't have missed the tension in the phone conversation. Or Nick's abrupt end to it, jamming the handset into its cradle.

Too aware of her ability to read him, he returned to the table and his rapidly cooling mug of coffee. 'The plan to have you stay in Shelley Brock's hotel room isn't going to work. Is there other accommodation in Goodabri or nearby?'

'There are a couple of very basic cabins at the caravan park.' She flipped open the computer and booted it. 'But it's right next to the showground, and all the showies are already there, to set up for tomorrow. Showies are mostly fine, but I'd feel safer here.'

No argument from him on that. A showground full of itinerant sideshow workers that could at times attract a rough element didn't constitute 'safety' in his definition. He made a mental note to check if Travis Mitchell had any connections with the sideshow circuit.

Jo rested her chin on her palm, watching him over the screen. 'Nick, I know this homestead. I know the house, the outbuildings, the land around it – even in the dark. The home-ground advantage has to count for something, and your colleagues at Goodabri are only ten minutes away. It's as safe as any other place I can think of in this area.'

He could take her into Strathnairn – but to where? The motel he was staying in fronted the highway on the edge of town, with bushland behind it. No more secure than this. And he didn't know the town well enough yet to be familiar with the other motels.

Aaron's footsteps sounded along the corridor, and he stifled a yawn in the doorway. 'Everything's secure. There are decent locks on all the doors and windows, Sarge.'

Locks wouldn't stop bullets, but they'd slow down an assault, give at least a few seconds' warning. With two armed officers, and Jo's familiarity with the environs, it would have to be enough.

Running low on alternatives, he made up his mind and looked squarely at Jo. 'You can stay here, with police protection, for tonight, Jo. I'll remain on watch, and I'll see if I can call a female officer in as well.'

Relief in her eyes, she smiled slightly. 'It's the twenty-first century, Nick,' she said. 'I'm sure your female colleagues have more important things to do than play chaperone.'

'I'll take a watch, too,' Aaron offered. 'That way we can sleep in shifts.'

'Shouldn't you and Aaron be off-duty? It's getting late, and you've been on the go all day.'

He swallowed another mouthful of coffee, the coolness dulling the caffeine kick in his brain. Off-duty? The job took as long as it took. The rhythm of work and sleep underscored his life. After ten years living immersed in undercover roles, little else remained.

'Unless you have an objection, I'm staying,' Nick said.

Nothing in her body language or expression suggested discomfort. She'd relaxed as soon as he'd said she could stay at the homestead.

'I live way the other side of Strathnairn, Jo,' Aaron said. 'Not much point driving all that way when I'd only get a couple of hours' sleep before I have to come back. So it's actually easier to stay here.'

'You can use the bunks in the room opposite mine,' Jo said. 'Make yourselves at home. It's not much, but you should be comfortable enough. We could all do with some sleep. I'm planning to head to bed, just as soon as I download these photos for you.'

Sleep would be a long time coming, if at all. On the pretext of getting his own laptop from the car, Nick stepped out into the night, pausing on the veranda to survey the moonlit grounds, listening for movement. A possum scrambled over the fence, away from him, and some kind of owl hooted nearby. Otherwise it was quiet and still – a stark contrast to the constant city sounds he'd become used to.

In the car, he radioed in, requesting a patrol to cruise nearby roads, and relaying enough of his plans that anyone listening in would know that Jo was not unprotected and alone.

Alone. Other than colleagues, she'd made no mention of friends, or family, or a lover. She lived by herself out here in the bush, yet with her easy manner and occasional light teasing she didn't give the impression of a recluse or even an introvert.

She'd only lived a few months in the district, so perhaps close friendships were still to come. Or maybe she still grieved for Leonardo Rossetti.

He slid the report from the coroner's office into his laptop case before he picked up the overnight bag he'd taken to Newcastle. He would read the report tonight, find out if there was any evidence at all for Hugh's suspicions.

No point denying it, curiosity drove him more than doubt. Curiosity about Jo, and the man she'd loved, as much as the circumstances of his death. He needed to untangle the interests of the case and his attraction to Jo. Go back into the kitchen, set up his laptop and work.

Only a few more minutes, and she'd probably go to her room and close the door.

Only a few more minutes, and the hyper-awareness that tensed his body would ease, once he no longer had her in such close proximity. A witness, under his protection – that put her even further off limits than a colleague.

Intellectually, he knew it. But ever since she'd walked back into the homestead kitchen after her shower, her hair loose about her shoulders, the masculine khaki shirt replaced by the simple T-shirt that clung softly to her curves . . . ever since then, the low-level awareness of her had ratcheted up multiple notches, and his subconscious kept taunting him with how good it might feel to brush his fingers over her cheek, to touch the smoothness of her skin, and to simply put his arms around her and hold her body close to his.

⌘

The curtains she'd never before drawn across the kitchen window deprived potential snipers from a line of sight, but they also deprived Jo of her customary view across the back yard. Bright, 1970s-style gold, orange and brown circles blurred in front of her eyes instead of the moonlit silhouettes of trees and sheds.

A wave of claustrophobia threatened, her pulse kicking up, her brain telling her to move. Stupid, stupid, that the room so familiar to her seemed so small, dark and stuffy with the windows covered.

She turned her back to the window. *Breathe.* She couldn't feed the fear and adrenaline. Calm thoughts, a mug of chamomile tea, and some distraction, and she would hopefully unwind enough to sleep. Nick and Aaron were here, and she would be safe.

With her focus firmly on the kettle, not the window, she refilled it and set it to re-boil.

Aaron's muted voice, out on the veranda phoning his housemate, altered tone as he exchanged a few comments with Nick, before Nick came back inside carrying a laptop and an overnight bag. The fluorescent lights cast harsh shadows on his face, accentuating the lines of worry around his eyes. Not a man who smiled a great deal, despite the seeming ease of yesterday's not-quite-playboy grin. Did the weight of duty ever lift enough for him to relax and put his own needs first? Did he have a partner, a wife, a friend to support him through the tough times?

She pushed that thought away. No business of hers what he did off-duty, how he dealt with the stresses of his job. But making his burden as light as possible by being positive and uncomplaining was well within her power.

'I've put pillows and bedding on the bunks in the spare room for you and Aaron. The bedding's basic camping stuff – we're not a luxury resort,' she added, keeping her tone cheerful. 'There is, however, decent coffee and tea.'

He relaxed enough for the side of his mouth to quirk. 'That ranks it several stars above many places I've stayed. Decent coffee is usually only a luxury.'

'Help yourself any time you want, it's in the cupboard.'

'Thank you, I will. I could do with another caffeine shot to keep me going.'

Always that quiet courtesy from him, respect for her in his understated good manners.

He rinsed the cold grounds from the plunger and tossed in several heaped scoops of fresh coffee. He wasn't intending to sleep anytime soon, apparently. Perhaps if she went to her room and he thought she was sleeping, he might relax his guard a little.

The photo download complete, she quickly clicked through the images. She'd almost forgotten the sugar glider – it seemed days, rather than hours, since she'd released it – but she'd lucked on a good shot of it escaping the cage.

The photos that followed didn't make her smile. Some of the images of the man going into the woolshed were blurred, or underexposed. A couple were clear, including one where she'd caught him with the zoom, almost face-on, his features lit by his car headlights.

The two she'd snapped of the weapons were reasonably well exposed, at least where the circle of torchlight fell on them. She made a copy of both images, adjusting the exposure and contrast settings to make the shapes of the guns beyond the central lit area clearer.

Aaron returned, calling out to identify himself before lightly rapping on the locked front door. Nick rose to let him in, and Jo watched him check through the blinds before opening the door.

Cautious, not taking any risks with their safety. Her safety.

Hopefully the images might help the case move forward.

'You'll want to see these, Nick,' she said, before he returned to his chair.

He stood behind her, looking over her shoulder, Aaron beside him.

'You can't see it so well in this image, but this one—' She indicated the area on the screen, 'It was definitely a pump-action, and you can see the two semi-autos.'

'Looks like a couple of handguns underneath. That could well be the magazine of another semi-auto.' Crowded as they were around the table, his arm inadvertently brushed her shoulder as he pointed, and she stared at the screen, drawing on all her willpower to ignore the wave of awareness and the jumbled mix of reactions to his nearness.

He moved away, pouring another mug of coffee as he asked, 'How big did you say the box was?'

'Over a metre long, a good half a metre wide and deep. You can see it's pretty full. There's at least a dozen, maybe more weapons in there.'

'Quite a haul,' Aaron commented. 'We've had a few reports of stolen rifles in the past four months or so, but not that many.'

'I saw the open files,' Nick said. 'No-one's going to report an illegal weapon missing, though, and I'm guessing some of these aren't legal. Jo, is there much hunting around the area? Do you know any of the professional shooters?'

'We had a feral-goat-control campaign in the new park not long after I came here, so I can give you names and contact details of some of the professionals. Mal will know more. I don't know much about the recreational hunters. They often come from outside the area. If you can find this guy, though, you'll find out where he got at least one of the guns.'

She flicked back a couple of images, so that the man she'd seen filled the screen. Young, maybe late teens or early twenties, he had a round, boyish face that should have been grinning. Instead, the tightness in his expression, the furtive, slightly sideways glance, suggested worry, or fear.

'Shit,' Aaron swore behind her. 'I think I know who he is. Can I . . . ?'

She made way for him, and he sat at the laptop, studying the image on the screen.

Nick drank a mouthful of coffee while he waited. Not exactly patiently – he fixed his attention on the screen, too – but without pushing Aaron for more information immediately.

Aaron dragged a hand through his hair as he faced his boss. 'Jesus, Sarge, I can't be a hundred per cent sure, but . . . the detective before you – Garry Coulter – I saw him at the pub not long before he died, with a guy he said was his nephew. Don't know his name, though, the sarge never introduced him. But I'm fairly certain it's this bloke. They weren't happy – looked like they'd been arguing. Come to think of it, Gazza was pretty stressed, all round that time. Something was worrying him.'

'He was stressed? How did he die?' Nick asked sharply.

'Car accident.' Aaron's face drained of colour. 'On the Derringvale Road, not far from McCulloch's woolshed. He must have fallen asleep at the wheel or something. Rammed into a tree on a straight section of the road. Car was burned out before he was found.'

Jo clasped her hands around her mug. Where the hell was that herbal calm?

'It could just be a coincidence.' Who was she trying to convince? Herself? Certainly, a moment of distraction, a nano-sleep, or a swerve to avoid an animal could all so easily result in a deadly accident on rural roads. She'd not met Coulter, but his nephew was involved with the stolen weapons, and Coulter had died close to the place they were hidden. She didn't like the chances of coincidence.

Beside her, Nick's stillness radiated tension.

'Aaron, we need to look for connections,' he said after a moment. 'We've got rifle thefts going back nine weeks or so, and Coulter died about six weeks ago. We'll review the accident investigation and his case notes, and we need to find the nephew.'

The draught from the overhead fan blew cold on her neck and shoulders, and she stepped away from the stream of air.

'Your safety is a top priority, Jo,' Nick said quietly, as though he'd seen her involuntary shiver and guessed her train of thought. 'I'll ensure that you're protected at all times until we've arrested the perpetrators.'

'Thank you.' He deserved the courtesy of her gratitude, even if the last thing she wanted was to go into hiding, denied her normal life, without her space and independence. But there were at least three deaths already – four, if Garry Coulter's death was suspicious – and she would do whatever she could to avoid adding to the tally.

NINE

The beeping of his phone alarm dragged Nick from a deep sleep. Groping for the phone, forcing his eyes open, recognition of his surroundings took his brain a sluggish half-second. Six-thirty. Sitting on a bunk, having attempted to stop himself from falling into a deep sleep, a couple of pillows cushioning the bars between his back and the wall. No sign of Aaron, only Jo passing the open door of the room, in a blue cotton robe, her hair loose over her shoulders.

A cramp shot through his bad thigh as he too-quickly swung his legs to the floor, so that he had to dig the heel of his hand again and again into the muscle to release it.

So much for being ready to defend Jo in an instant. So much for showing no weakness.

Jo was either tactfully giving him privacy as he woke, or she hadn't glanced through the door as she passed, so she didn't see his moment of near-helplessness.

The sound of running water from the bathroom down the corridor answered the question of Aaron's whereabouts.

Standing, he adjusted his weapon belt over the jeans and T-shirt he'd worn to sleep in, and went into the kitchen.

'Morning,' Jo greeted him with a smile, spooning tea into the ever-present red teapot. 'I won't ask if you slept well, because Aaron said you didn't wake him to take over until after three.'

'I had enough to keep me going.'

Not that he'd drifted off immediately, despite his exhaustion, his thoughts too preoccupied to easily silence. It hadn't just been the unanswered questions about the crimes. While on watch last night he'd read the coroner's report into Leonardo Rossetti's death.

Despite the coroner's careful, objective language, the events described were chilling, and had haunted his dreams when he'd finally slept. Two ten-year-old boys missing in rugged country. A desperate twelve-hour search by volunteer emergency services, police and National Parks staff before forecast wild storms arrived, and the hard decision to call off the search at dusk. Stranded by flash flooding and downed trees, Jo and her fiancé had hiked to higher ground, Rossetti going to the edge of the bluff to check for any sign of the kids in the valley below. In the gale-force winds, a falling tree branch had struck him hard, knocking him over the edge. With no chance of a rescue team until daylight, Jo had climbed down to him, stayed with him on a narrow ledge all night while his internal injuries slowly killed him.

Despite Hugh's proclaimed suspicions, it was *that* action that convinced Nick of her innocence. A murderer wouldn't put themselves at significant risk, climbing down a cliff face in a ferocious storm, to stay with an injured person for hours. That could only have been an act of dedication. Or of love.

He could scarcely imagine how harrowing it must have been for her. What Hugh interpreted as coldness Nick recognised as control, a personal armour protecting deep emotions. Even her humour served as protection, keeping those emotions private. Not unlike himself.

Her strength, intelligence and courage, both physical and emotional, impressed him. Attracted him, if he was honest. Invaded his thoughts and his dreams. Made him envious of a dead man.

Hell, he needed to get some mental distance. Sane, professional distance.

Oblivious to his wayward thoughts, at ease in her own environment, Jo reached for the container in the cupboard and asked over her shoulder, 'How would you like your morning coffee?'

'By the litre.' Okay, so friendly humour probably didn't count as professional distance – but with Jo, it came more naturally than detachment. He opened his laptop, in the vain hope that distraction might work better.

'Not a morning person, huh?'

'I cope.' Late nights, early mornings, lack of sleep – he coped with it all on a regular basis. Everything except sharing his waking moments with an interesting, beautiful, out-of-bounds woman. Definitely out of practice at that.

Emails. He'd check his emails, drink his coffee, wash, shave and dress, and arrange protection for her for the rest of the day.

'I presume I won't be working out in the field today?' she asked, bringing over his coffee.

'Not today.' He ran through some logistics in his head. 'As long as there are other staff around, either in your office or our operations room, you could work indoors.'

She gave an exaggerated grimace. 'Oh, good. I just love days filled with paperwork.' Her light-hearted tone made it more self-deprecating joke than complaint. 'Which would be why,' she added, 'even though I was stuck there all yesterday, there's still enough on my desk to keep me busy for a week.'

'You and me both. I'd far rather be out catching the bad guys than compiling statistical reports.'

Standing by the table, sipping her tea, the blue Japanese-style fabric of her robe shaping softly over her lithe, feminine curves, Jo seemed more at ease than he felt. With a small smile, she commented, 'Well, since I won't get my life back until you get this lot of bad guys, I'm all in favour of you ditching the reports for now.'

Since he wouldn't get his equilibrium and effortless detachment back until she was no longer in close proximity, ditching everything but the investigation worked for him.

⁂

None of them had eaten dinner the night before, but with Nick and Aaron due at an early briefing in Goodabri there was little time for a hearty breakfast. Jo grabbed some fruit bread out of the freezer and set Aaron to toasting it while she dressed in a clean uniform and brushed her hair.

An electric razor hummed in the bathroom, and the acrid

smell of burned toast wafted from the kitchen. Almost like an ordinary morning, when members of her team stayed overnight. Except these were police officers, not rangers, and while Aaron buttered toast his handgun sat securely in its holster on his hip.

When Nick returned to the kitchen, shaved and changed back into business trousers and white shirt, his grim expression held no hint of relaxation or the humour he had shown just minutes earlier.

'We'll need to get there early,' he said, shutting down his laptop. 'I'll have your building checked out before you go in, Jo, and I'll find a female officer to stay with you today.'

Despite the butter and marmalade, her toast tasted dry in her mouth. She hadn't objected to working in her office, with the police next door, but someone staying with her and cluttering up her space all day? She washed her mouthful down with luke-warm tea. 'Is that really necessary? When there are cops just next door?'

He watched her, as if assessing how much of a fight she would put up, and replied evenly, 'Most of them will be out on the job during the day. So, yes, I think it's important that there's at least one officer assigned specifically to you.'

Damn. She could understand the rationale, but she didn't look forward to it.

She pushed a plate of toast towards him. 'Eat some. You won't be much use to anyone if you collapse from lack of food.'

He ate on his feet, packing away his laptop, retrieving his overnight bag from the bunk room. He finished his second piece of toast as they walked to his car, while he gave instructions to Aaron to follow them in.

He was silent in the car, preoccupied with his thoughts, and she might have let him remain that way if it weren't for the restlessness of her own mind, and the need to focus on *something* other than that unease.

'You don't ever stop for long, do you? You know, for incidentals like food and sleep.'

He threw her a quick glance. 'Not when there are murderers, guns and drugs out there.'

'But aren't there always murderers, guns and drugs out there?'

He slowed for the turn into Goodabri, the indicator clicking loudly in the silence, his profile sharp and unsmiling. 'Yes,' he said after a moment. 'There always are. Too many.'

They drove without talking through the quiet, early-morning streets of Goodabri, with fifteen minutes to spare before the briefing.

He turned into the lane behind the shop buildings, and through the open gate into the shared yard. Surrounded by a less-than-sturdy timber paling fence, the yard had a derelict wooden shed, a gravelled area for five or six cars to park, and a patch of grass that had long ago ceased to be either lawn or green.

The small crowd of police officers on the grass set her pulse drumming, until she saw that they were cheering on a pair of fighters.

'What the . . . ?' Nick muttered, his attention half on them as he pulled in to park close to the door of her office.

She had a better view from her side of the car. 'It's Hugh Dalton. And Nate Harrison. But it's okay – they're grinning.'

Nick swore and slammed his car door, and Jo kept pace with him as he strode across to the group. The six officers watching the tussle made way for them, just as Nate threw Hugh to the ground and held him there.

Lying on the ground, Hugh laughed. 'Good one, Harrison.' With a quick jerk of his body and a punch, he dislodged Harrison, sent him crashing to the ground, and then rolled away and stood up, brushing dead grass off his shirt. 'Hiya, Nick. Thought we'd start the day with a short training session, get the metabolism going, since Harrison here was bragging at the pub last night that he's a black belt in Tae Kwon Do.'

Nick didn't smile, coolness in his hard face and his cross-armed stance. 'You must be losing your skills, Hugh, if he dropped you.'

'Nah, I was just letting him think he had me.'

A few of the watchers snickered, but Jo couldn't discern in that confident grin whether he spoke the truth or was simply saving face. A testosterone-fuelled performance, either way, with the competitive mood spreading – already infecting those watching, keen for excitement.

Still performing the alpha-male role, still grinning, Dalton turned to his opponent, already back on his feet. 'Hey, Harrison, I bet you a hundred bucks you can't drop Nick.'

Harrison's eyes lit up. 'You serious, Sarge?'

Nick's coolness dropped to arctic chill. 'I'm not playing games, Hugh. We've got work to do.'

'Are you getting past it, Nick? The body not what it used to be? Too old?' Hugh's mock concern had to be intended to taunt.

Nick didn't blink, didn't react at all. 'Too busy. Carruthers, you and I will check the Parks office is safe before Jo goes in.' He turned on his heel and walked away.

She saw Matt Carruthers' hesitation, heard Hugh's chuckle, but she followed Nick, only a couple of steps behind. Two quick footfalls on the dry ground, a catch of breath, and a flash of blue uniform passed her, lunging at Nick.

Her warning shout faded in her throat, already too late.

Nick's reactions, far quicker than hers, had Nate Harrison flipped onto his back on the ground in what seemed a single, smooth move.

Nate swore; Hugh and the others laughed. Nick silently held out a hand to Nate, helped him to his feet.

Hugh joined them, clapping Nate on the back, all masculine mateship. 'I may have neglected to mention, Harrison, that Nick has cupboards stuffed with black belts and dan scrolls, and is feared by street fighters from Cairns to Hobart. So I'll waive the hundred bucks you owe me. Okay, everyone, fun's over. Briefing starts in four minutes. Carruthers, Harrison, make sure Doctor Lockwood's office is clear, and do it quickly.'

Jo watched Hugh stride away. Interesting how he'd done that – switched effortlessly from one-of-the-guys to commander, from irresponsible larrikin to dedicated officer. How he'd managed the whole scene so that Nick's new colleagues had witnessed his skills, and strengths, in action, yet none of them – not even Harrison – came out of it looking a fool. Interesting, too, the tension between Hugh and Nick, Hugh's competitiveness, Nick's impassiveness.

Not quite impassive. As he took his laptop from the back of the car and locked the doors, the hard line of his mouth and jaw hinted at temper and displeasure.

'A cupboard full of black belts and dan scrolls?' she asked as he joined her again.

He shook his head. 'I only kept the few that matter.'

The few that matter . . . Matt and Nate swung out the door of her building, announcing it all clear, before she could find words to ask what mattered to him and why.

But as he held the door open for her, he added, his voice flat, 'I've been fighting since I was a kid, Jo. I had to be good at it. It's not something I'm proud of.'

He turned away abruptly and walked into the adjacent building, without waiting for her response or looking at her again.

She shut the door behind her, locked it and leaned against it, her thoughts whirling, trying to process all those new facets of Nick and piece them together with what she knew already.

A complex, layered man, practised at concealing his emotions – yep, that summed up Nick Matheson. But her initial instincts, days ago, hadn't been far wrong, and perhaps his physical fighting skills shouldn't have surprised her. He did, after all, have a superb body, lean and fit and muscled, even though she was doing her damnedest not to notice it. Or to think about it.

She pushed herself away from the door and went into her office. As she switched on her computer and waited for it to boot, the fight scene replayed in her mind, and two points stood out clearly: Nick had no taste for violence, and had bested Nate without hurting him at all; and Nick and Hugh had a long history, and not necessarily a happy one.

She shook her head in frustration as if that physical act might dislodge the stubborn thoughts. The relationship between Nick and Hugh was no business of hers. *Nick* was no business of hers. They might have been thrown together the past couple of days due to the investigation, but her involvement would be over, soon enough, and all she needed to do in the meantime was cooperate when requested, a professional, responsible citizen.

The very last thing she needed in her life was a complex, intense man who could disturb – shatter – the emotional balance she'd finally found.

༜

Hugh started the briefing as Nick walked in to the ops room and he propped on a table at the back and studied him while he gave the rundown of the previous day's developments and events.

On the surface Hugh seemed unchanged, with the same brash energy he'd had twenty years ago as a wily, smart-mouthed kid on Newcastle's toughest streets, only lightly smoothed after fifteen years of policing. The whole scene outside had been typically Hugh.

But under that confident surface Nick could discern cracks. Dark smudges under his eyes. Tiny hesitations in his speech. An edge of brittleness in his top-cop performance, and, most telling, his frequent micro-glances towards Nick.

The Hugh of old was skilled enough to avoid acknowledging a rival. Two years Hugh's senior, responsible for him, Nick had channelled the kid's naturally competitive streak by challenging him, fighting him, letting Hugh compete with him. A tradition of competition Hugh had continued into adulthood, into the police service, a constant in their relationship. Like this morning.

So Hugh's inability to conceal the hyper-awareness in a setting as familiar as a case briefing was a dead giveaway that something was up.

Nervousness? Lack of confidence? Complex though this case might be, Hugh had worked plenty of tough ones in the past.

Hiding something? Nick scanned the room. Shelley Brock sat in the middle, a couple of local cops on either side. Interesting that she'd placed herself there, and not at the front near Hugh. Even more interesting that she kept her face down, apparently concentrating on her notes, her shoulders rigid. When Hugh ran through the list, allocating tasks, he gave her a couple of things to follow up, but carefully avoided looking at her.

Whatever had happened between them in the night hadn't left them happy lovers.

'Which brings us,' Hugh was saying, 'to the matter of the weapons cache allegedly discovered last night by Jo Lockwood. According to her statement, she saw it loaded into a truck and driven away from a shearing shed on the Derringvale Road.' He tapped the location on the large map on the wall, and Nick gave him credit for his research. All part of being seen to be in control, of being on top of the details. 'Unfortunately, neither of the patrol cars in the general area was able to pick up the truck. I'll take Jo out to the woolshed again this morning, go through what happened and see if we can find anything else in daylight.'

Now he did look directly at Nick, the challenge clear, watching for a response. Nick didn't give him one. Objecting would play straight into Hugh's game, whatever it was. And logically he had no grounds to object. Instead, he smoothly took control again, strolling to the front of the room, plugging a USB drive into the laptop projecting onto the screen.

He clicked through the file folders as he spoke. 'Jo was able to take some photographs of a man who deposited what was likely a rifle into the cache shortly before two others arrived and removed it. Aaron saw the photos last night, and thinks the suspect might have local connections.'

He scanned the group for reaction as the image filled the screen. Most showed no signs of recognition. Nate Harrison stared pointedly out the window. Matthew Carruthers frowned, but said nothing.

'Carruthers?' Nick prompted.

'I might be wrong, Sarge.'

'And you might be right. Spill it, Carruthers.'

Reluctantly he shifted in his seat, glanced around at his colleagues. 'Thing is, Sarge, he looks like Garry Coulter's nephew. Garry was here before you. I saw the lad come in a few times. Bit on the wild side he was, and Gazza was worried. Not much of one to talk about private stuff, was Gazza, but I think the lad had been inside.'

Strike two. Aaron had been correct – identity confirmed. Almost. 'Do you know his name, where he lives?'

Carruthers cleared his throat. 'I think he might have stayed for a couple of weeks. I heard Gazza complaining a few times that he was a bloody layabout, bludging off him the whole time. He buggered off before the funeral. Took some of Garry's stuff, too, I reckon. Can't prove it, though. His name is Bradley. Bradley Coulter.'

Nick wrote the name up on the whiteboard, his thoughts racing to connect the few facts they had. Another ex-con, like Travis Mitchell. But it seemed prison hadn't reformed Bradley Coulter. Nick had seen a hundred similar stories – young men preferring a fast buck and an easy life to working a legal job.

Hugh took advantage of his momentary silence to move to the lead again. 'What about other family?' he asked. 'Did Coulter have a wife? Kids?'

Nate Harrison snorted. 'His missus ran off with another bloke six months ago. Didn't even bother coming for the funeral. She's selling the house, doesn't want anything of his, except his money.'

Nick brought the focus back to wrapping up the briefing. 'From the conversation Jo overhead last night, we have strong reason to believe that the people handling the weapons are connected to the murder of Travis Mitchell. So we'll follow all lines of enquiry. Carruthers, get hold of Bradley Coulter's record. Find out if he could have met Mitchell in prison.' Nick's gut said they had. If they could find the links, follow them, they'd get to the answers. 'If Coulter's on probation, get on to the probation officer and see if they have an address. Brock, track down Mrs Coulter. See if she knows anything about Bradley, where he might be.' He half-expected an objection from Hugh, but there was none.

'Harrison, you'd know some of the professional shooters around here?' A guess based on some knowledge of small-town culture, but confirmed by Harrison's nod. Good. He'd give him a task that implied trust, and no rancour from the incident this morning. 'They'll have an idea about activities in the nearby parks and forests. See if they've heard any rumours about missing weapons, rifles for sale, that kind of thing.'

He continued, assigning tasks, and the briefing finished within a few minutes.

Hugh held a media conference immediately afterwards, a task Nick left to him by choice, although it meant he had no opportunity to speak with him. He had nothing solid to confront Hugh with, only a growing, uneasy feeling that Hugh was no longer on top of his game. It happened to some cops. The pressures of the job created physical and emotional tensions that at times left scars. Some cops made it through the bad times and stayed good cops. Some didn't.

∝

With the low rumble of voices drifting through the wall from the operations centre next door, and a police constable sitting at the kitchen table, Jo battled to concentrate on statistical reports.

Squeak. Her old chair protested her restless movement, for the umpteenth time. *Squeak.* She pushed back from the desk, crossed the corridor to the kitchen.

'That chair is driving me crazy,' she said to Dee Edwards, her minder. 'Probably you as well.'

As she pulled open the door of the general storage cupboard and reached in to hunt for oil, a sharp knock sounded on the back door.

'Stay there,' Dee ordered, her hand already on her Glock.

Jo bit her lip. Crazy what her life had become, locked into her building, half-hiding in a cupboard, while a police officer answered the door for her. She closed her fingers around the small oil can. Not much of a weapon, household oil, and the chances of anyone attacking her so close to the police had to be minuscule, but the flight-or-fight response kicked in, and she had nowhere to run.

She relaxed her grip on the can at the sound of Nick's voice and Dee's cheery request for permission to duck back next door, now that he was there.

His gaze ran a quick sweep of the kitchen as he came in. Practised, as if he expected danger in every room he entered.

Dark eyes studied her. 'Everything all right?'

She fell back on her determination to remain professionally friendly, and her old standby for uneasiness – humour. 'Yes. Other than a terminal case of boredom. Dee's pretending an interest in microbats,' she nodded at the booklet on the table, 'but I don't think she'll make an enthusiast.'

He might have smiled, for all of a millisecond. 'Hugh Dalton wants you to accompany him to the woolshed, to go over the scene there again. But there's no requirement, Jo – you don't have to go if you don't want to.'

Getting out of the office appealed more than staying in. But spending time with Hugh Dalton would likely raise other issues – namely Hugh's suspicions about her past – and she didn't want them clouding this case. Better to get everything out in the open.

She took a breath. 'I didn't recognise him the other day, but it seems we've crossed paths before,' she said. She left that as an opening, wondering if he'd discussed it with Hugh.

Nick inclined his head slightly. 'He did mention it.'

She swallowed. Hugh had *mentioned it*. The very tactfulness suggested Hugh had *mentioned* a whole lot about the case. Just to Nick, or to all of them?

Cold anger stilled her body. She looked directly at Nick. No running, no fighting, just standing firm. 'He seems to believe I pushed my fiancé off a cliff. He also implied I was involved in Travis Mitchell's murder. So, am I on your list of suspects, too, or is he just naturally suspicious?'

He took a moment to consider his answer, but not for an instant did he avoid her gaze. Honesty – or at least a good semblance of it. But he'd worked undercover, had to be a good actor.

'Hugh's a good detective,' he said, evenly. 'He's suspicious of everyone, and that makes him look in places others might discount. Police work is adversarial by nature – it usually comes down to us trying to get crims to say what they don't want to say – and a lot of effective cops thrive on that. Hugh's one of them.'

Okay, so there wasn't anything defensive about the explanation, and it made logical sense. Adversarial by nature – yes, she'd seen that in Hugh. She could find a way to deal with him. Probably.

'As for my list of suspects for Mitchell's murder,' Nick continued, careful and deliberate, 'I keep an open mind because everything is possible, so yes, you're on it.'

Ouch. Not what she wanted to hear.

'Along with everyone else within a four-hundred kilometre radius,' he added. That almost, but never quite a smile softened his blunt honesty. 'But I do have you ranked somewhere down near the dingo.'

It took a moment for his meaning to sink in. She blew out a breath. 'I guess that's a relief. For me and the dingo. At least, based on what I saw, the autopsy should clear the dingo.'

She knew more than most people what a wild dog could do. There'd been nothing, even in the brief look she'd had, that suggested any carnivore had mutilated Mitchell's body.

Nick nodded. 'Final analysis and reports are still to come, but I was at the examination yesterday and the pathologist found no evidence of canine interference.'

'You were there?' Of course he'd been there – that's why he'd gone to Newcastle. She just hadn't considered what that involved. Observing while a pathologist investigated all of those injuries, seeking answers. She had to swallow again. 'It must have been rough.'

He looked away, briefly closed his eyes. 'They always are,' he said.

And there was something in that moment of unguardedness, the admission of vulnerability, that told her he spoke the truth.

TEN

Garry Coulter's house, in a quiet street in Strathnairn, stood out from its neighbours only because of the overgrown garden, the closed curtains and the For Sale sign on the front fence. Nick knocked on the door for form's sake, but no sound came from inside.

'What was Coulter like?' he asked Aaron, as they walked around to check the back.

'Quiet, mostly. A bit old-fashioned, you know, as a detective, but a decent enough bloke.'

Old-fashioned? Yes, that fitted with the records Coulter had left. Only the bare minimum online, but a fair few notes, in hard-to-decipher handwriting.

In the backyard, vegetable plants lay brown and dead in square, wood-bordered plots, under a shade-cloth covered frame to protect them from the worst of the sun. A corner of the shade-cloth, loosened from the frame, flapped in the breeze.

Near the back door, the lid of the garbage bin sat crookedly, sunlight glinting on the neck of a beer bottle, preventing it from closing. Through the open gap, Nick could see other bottles piled in haphazardly.

'Was Coulter a drinker?' he asked Aaron.

'Not much of one, at least that I saw. A social beer or two, that's all.'

Nick pulled on latex gloves, and raised the lid of the bin. There were dozens of beer bottles tossed inside. Beside the garbage bin, the rectangular box for recyclables was also full, but when he lifted the lid of that, the mix of soft drink bottles and household plastics were neatly packed for maximum space efficiency.

Everything he'd seen of Coulter, except that pile of beer bottles, suggested a desire for order. Handwritten file notes, all on the same size paper, in date sequence. Straight, regimented garden beds. Mineral water bottles on one side of a box, fruit juice on the other.

The beer bottles didn't simply not fit the garbage bin, they didn't fit the man.

He went up the three cement steps to the back entrance. The closed fly-screen door shadowed the main, wooden door, but when he looked closely he saw beyond the screen the split in the wood, around the lock. The door itself sat slightly ajar.

The hunch that had brought him here – the fact of an empty house, and a possibly homeless ex-con who knew it well – might just have proved worth following.

'There's been a break-in,' he told Aaron. 'Phone the real

estate agent. Find out the last time anyone was here, whether they know about it.'

'I know Mrs C had everything of value put into storage, not long after the funeral,' Aaron said, pulling his phone out. 'So there shouldn't be much to steal. The agent should have an inventory of what's here, though.'

With clear evidence of a crime having been committed, Nick could legally enter the house. He pushed the door open cautiously. The warm, slightly musty air of a closed-up building hit his nostrils, and he listened for any sound before he went into the laundry. The older-style washing machine mustn't have been of sufficient value for Mrs Coulter to want, but it was clean and undamaged.

His senses alert, Nick mentally catalogued all he saw. An unpretentious 1960s weatherboard house, on the inside as well as the outside. Lino floors in the laundry led into the kitchen, but a quick scan showed nothing obvious disturbed, only a couple of the chairs sitting at an angle to the simple wooden table. Unlikely that Coulter had left them that way.

The lino gave way to grey carpet in the empty living room. From the indentations in the carpet pile Nick could visualise the layout – coffee table and side tables, sofa and chairs facing a long cupboard, probably an entertainment unit, and bookshelves against a couple of the walls.

In the master bedroom, the furniture remained – Mrs Coulter obviously hadn't wanted the marital bed. The matching ensemble of timber bedhead, chests of drawers and wardrobes was not the most fashionable but was in good condition, the bed neatly made with a plain blue bedspread drawn over the pillows. The wardrobe still held Coulter's clothes – a collection of white shirts, navy trousers, jeans and moleskins – and a couple of shelves of linen and towels.

The screen door thwacked against the frame as Aaron entered, and Nick left the bedroom to meet him in the passageway.

'The agent says no-one's been here for more than a week,' Aaron reported. 'There was no sign of forced entry then. He's on his way over to inspect the damage.'

'There's not much I can see so far, but there's the other bedrooms still to check.'

One bedroom was empty, the marks of a desk and possibly filing cabinets pressed into the carpet pile. But in the last bedroom they found a different story. An unmade single bed, the covers strewn as though by a restless sleeper. A couple of pillows and a blanket on the floor suggested a second, makeshift bed. The mirror on a chest of drawers had been removed from its framework, and lay propped on the chest, along with several empty beer bottles.

The sickly smell of something rotting hit Nick's nostrils, and he walked into the room, around the far side of the bed. Half a dozen beer bottles lay on the floor, alongside two pizza boxes. He crouched down, lifted the lid on one of them. Two wedges of pizza remained, congealed cheese growing a green mould over stinking pepperoni and ham.

'It's only a few days old, by the looks of it,' he said to Aaron. 'We'll need to call the CSOs in here, see if they can pick up anything to ID Bradley Coulter, and whoever was with him.'

'You definitely think it's Bradley?'

'Yes.' Nick considered it almost a certainty. 'Other than the broken lock, there's no vandalism. He's used this room, presumably where he stayed before, not the others. Is the agent bringing the inventory? We'll need to see what, if anything, is missing.'

'Yes, he is. Apparently, the Salvos are booked to come and clear out the rest of the stuff on Monday.'

Nick studied the room, looking for hints to the young man who'd stayed there. No personal belongings, no clothes in the wardrobe. He'd moved out, even if he did return to camp occasionally. Had he left the district around the time of his uncle's death, only returning some days ago? Or had he just been staying elsewhere in the interim?

As Nick went to the door, his blurred reflection in the mirror propped on the chest of drawers caught his eye. Lines of fine dust marred the surface; fine *white* dust. He knew those types of dust patterns. Another quick scan of the room showed nothing more suspicious, but when he returned to the pizza boxes and raised the lid on the second one, he found the evidence: two small plastic bags, fine white powder clinging to them, and a couple of plastic straws.

He left Aaron at the house to wait for a uniformed officer to guard the scene until the forensic specialists arrived, and drove across town to the Strathnairn police station. He needed to get Coulter's files, go through those handwritten notes in detail. And he needed to update the district commander, inform him what they'd found at the house of the deceased officer.

Unanswered questions chased around in his mind on the drive. Would the drugs at the house match the drugs found at the lookout? Those still puzzled him; if they'd been for the mob at the camping ground, why had they still been there? If they'd been left for someone else, then who? Just how many criminals were using Jo's National Park for their activities?

Jo. Thoughts of her never seemed far away. As he'd left Goodabri earlier, he'd seen Hugh's car also leaving, Dee Edwards in the car as well as Jo. With another woman present, Hugh would surely behave professionally towards Jo, not aggressively. He had no doubts about Jo's ability to handle him if he stepped out of line; she was confident, assertive, and experienced at law enforcement within the National Parks context. More than a match for Hugh. Nick wouldn't have let the plan go ahead otherwise.

But still he wondered how she was going, where she was now.

In his office, he booted up his computer and added the recent events to his personal notes – the murder of the Baxters, the weapons cache, the drug evidence they'd just found at Coulter's house. Under the heading 'Suspects', he included the two images they had – the police artist's image from Jo's description and her photos of Bradley Coulter. He also added Garry Coulter's death to the event list, with a question mark: Accident? Murder? Suicide?

Then he printed out his notes, and went to report to the district commander, Inspector Keith Murdoch.

He'd met the Inspector on his first day, had a few short conversations with him since, was still forming his impression of the man. A busy man, certainly, with a district station and multiple small satellite stations under his command. On his way out to a meeting, Murdoch granted him five minutes.

'Tread carefully there, Matheson.' Murdoch tapped a finger against the name of Nick's predecessor on the notes, after Nick had provided a brief summary. 'Coulter was a well-respected officer here.'

Nick regarded him evenly, held his ground. 'I gathered that. But he left at least five unsolved gun thefts, and now there's evidence linking his nephew to possibly stolen weapons and perhaps even to murder. That raises questions I can't ignore.'

Murdoch nodded, unruffled by Nick's assertiveness. 'I'm not suggesting you ignore them. Simply that you understand that some of his colleagues may be resentful of any suggestion from you that questions his character.'

'I'm here to investigate crime, not to win a popularity contest.'

'Respect is part of effective teamwork, Matheson.' He handed back the notes. 'By all means, review his open cases, and the accident investigation. Keep me informed of progress. If Coulter made mistakes, or was compromised by his nephew's actions, I'd like to know first. I can't back you up if I don't have all the facts.'

As an indication of trust, it was strong enough, but Nick accepted the reminder; he needed the rest of the team on his side as far as possible. Tact in dealing with the questions surrounding Coulter had to be part of his strategy.

Back in his office, he checked his emails and skimmed through a couple of forensic reports that had arrived. The lab in Newcastle had found little on Travis Mitchell's clothing; a couple of partial prints on the belt tourniquet, but no matches in the database for them. The examination of the cocaine had found it was high-grade, not cut with other substances. They'd lifted a couple of prints, again not matched to anything on file. Not many answers there – yet.

He was about to click the file closed when a line caught his eye. *Ten small resealable plastic bags each containing approximately five grams . . .*

No. Not ten bags. He'd counted them himself, up on the hill where Jo had found them. There'd been twelve bags contained in the larger bag. Twelve, not ten, that he'd handed to one of the CSOs once he'd returned to the camping ground, to go into the locked evidence bag. With the forensic pathologist on the phone, they'd been too busy, then, to complete the drug evidence log. He knew Hugh had looked at it later; he'd seen him talking with a CSO, drugs in hand, and had assumed they'd logged it then.

So when had those two bags of coke gone missing? He'd have to follow the trail back – from the lab, to the officer who'd logged the evidence, to the forensic team on site, to Hugh.

Don't let it be Hugh. That he'd even formed the wish in his thoughts felt like a betrayal.

He'd have to report the missing drugs to Murdoch. Let Murdoch set the investigation up according to procedure. Official processes would determine at what point in the evidence chain they'd gone missing.

He had his hand on the desk phone to call Murdoch when Aaron swung into the office.

'The truck that took the weapons has been found. Dumped on a road east of Derringvale. At least some of the guns are still there. Dalton is on his way there now.'

Dalton. With Jo. Nick grabbed his car keys. 'So are we.'

Hugh Dalton played the cool, alpha cop confidently enough, and no longer treated her with outright suspicion, but once in a while as Jo showed him the woolshed and described the events she noticed a momentary lapse in concentration, a slow response, an abrupt transition between one question and the next, as though he'd lost his train of thought.

Granted, he had to have plenty on his mind, with a murder investigation and stolen weapons, but where Nick translated his concerns into focused, direct action, Hugh seemed to lack that focus.

In the car, travelling to the lane near Derringvale where the truck had been found, Hugh carried on a lightly flirtatious conversation with Dee Edwards.

Watching from the back seat, Jo didn't discern signs of genuine interest from either party. More likely the cheeky innuendos and easy manner were his habitual style in talking with women. Not unusual for a good-looking, fit, confident man in his thirties. She'd met plenty of the type.

Not that he tried any of that charm on her. He might flirt with his colleagues, but she apparently held no attraction for him. A mutual feeling.

When his phone rang, the relaxed charm evaporated. He slipped the earpiece on before answering and from where she sat, Jo saw his knuckles turn white on the steering wheel.

His brusque responses to his caller gave little clue of the topic of the call. 'Yes. No.' He glanced at her in the rear-vision mirror. 'Not possible.'

Not possible to discuss a police issue with a civilian in earshot? That would make sense. But it didn't explain the tension in his hands, the flare of his nostrils as he exhaled a pent-up breath, or the clipped words, delivered with barely restrained force.

'I'll sort it out.' He disconnected abruptly, and his eyes found hers again in the mirror. Rather than ignoring it to check the road behind, this time his direct, second-long consideration stayed on her, anger or some similar emotion narrowing his eyes.

She broke the eye contact, looked out the window at the passing landscape. The stresses of the past days were making her paranoid. He'd probably just been arguing with a wife or girlfriend over some domestic matter. That would fit the tone and content of the brief conversation.

In an hour or so they'd be back in Goodabri, and her involvement in the case would be mostly over, other than whatever actions Nick recommended for her safety. She could go to the office and concentrate on her job.

She tried to still her uneasiness by mentally listing the tasks she'd tackle this afternoon. Updating fire-management strategies could absorb some hours. Outside the car, the strong sunlight accentuated the summer dryness, the yellow–brown of shrivelled paddocks, the dust blowing in the wind. A few seasons of above-average rainfall had driven significant growth of grasses, undergrowth and trees throughout the region, but the wet cycle had finished months ago, and an early, hot summer had already transformed most of that growth into dry fuel. The fire trails in the new park needed more work, clearing overgrown areas, widening in some places, and signage.

Yes, she'd finish writing up those recommendations today. As soon as she was done with the police.

With that practical decision made, she paid attention again to the view outside the window.

'Church Lane is coming up on the right,' she told Hugh. 'Just around the bend.'

'Looks like a road to nowhere,' he muttered, slowing to make the turn.

'It only goes as far as the river. In the eighteen-hundreds there was a large sheep station down there that supported a small community. A huge flood in 1893 pretty much wiped it all out.'

Except for the deserted stone church, which sat on higher ground a hundred metres from the river, the cattle truck she'd seen last night on the grass behind it.

Hugh parked on the road a short distance behind a couple of other police cars. He paused briefly, staring at the scene before saying abruptly, 'Come with me, Doctor Lockwood, so you can identify the box and the weapons. Dee, find out if that lot have an ID on the truck rego yet.'

Outside the airconditioned car, the dry heat sucked at Jo's skin, and she jammed her hat well down on her head so the wind couldn't catch it.

At the faded sign in front of the church listing the monthly services, the detective stopped suddenly, a harsh, humourless laugh breaking from him.

'Saint Patrick's,' he muttered to himself. 'That'd be bloody right.' With no further comment he strode on, not looking to see if Jo followed. To add to his strange behaviour, in the short distance through the dry grass around to the back of the church, she saw his hand go to the holster on his belt, then jerk away, twice.

Unease slowed her steps. He was wired tight, tension radiating from him. Maybe this situation reminded him of some past trauma. An officer who'd served in Homicide for some years had probably been in tight corners at times. She knew too well how memories could haunt, how a small trigger could bring them flooding back, strong and real, even years after the event. But officers had already cleared this site, and with at least four other cops less than fifty metres away, they had to be safe. She had to be safe.

The tailgate of the truck was open, the loading ramp down, but other than the remnant odour of cow shit, it was empty.

'Is this the vehicle you saw?' Hugh asked.

'I'm pretty certain. Same type, same colour, same kind of trailer.'

Drag marks down the ramp and in the dust led around the other side of the truck, where the box lay open on the ground, its battered metal glinting in the bright sun.

But she paused before joining Hugh beside it, studying the tracks in the dust.

Tact might be the best option. 'You'll have seen the bike tracks here?' He hadn't of course, but he glanced back with a vague nod. 'Two motorbikes, is my guess,' she continued. 'Carrying their own getaway transport, I suppose. Or maybe they were stolen, too.'

He ignored her suggestion, kneeling by the box and staring into it. The guns absorbed his attention. 'You said there were semi-autos and a pump action in here?'

'Yes. Nick has copies of the photos I took.'

'Yeah, well, there's not now.' He regarded her for a long moment. She heard another car arrive, a door slam, and saw Hugh glance past her towards the road before he gave a weird grin and said, 'I don't suppose *you* took those rifles, did you, Doctor Lockwood?'

Irritation with him bloomed into full-on anger, pulsing in her head. 'Photos were all I took, Detective Dalton.' She struggled to keep her voice even, the words scraping in her throat. 'I suggest you concentrate on finding the felons out there who are now well armed.'

He rose to his feet, his gaze scanning along the tree-lined river below them. 'Yes,' he said, almost absently, without looking at her. 'Get someone to give you a lift back to Goodabri, Doctor Lockwood.'

No word of thanks for her cooperation, no attempt to delegate an officer to drive her.

Furious at his lack of common courtesy, she spun on her heel and strode away.

⚮

Jo came around the front of the truck at such a pace that Nick caught her by the shoulders to cushion their impact. As he steadied her, he registered the warmth of her shirt fabric, the firm muscle beneath his hands, and the anger blazing in her eyes. She had a temper, and wasn't trying to hide it.

'Sorry.' She found her balance, and stepped back a pace. 'That man is a pain in the neck.'

'Hugh?'

'Yes. The semi-automatics aren't there, and he accused me of taking them.'

Damn Hugh and his games. And damn the need to show a united front and support him. 'You've been with me since last night,' he said. 'That's a pretty solid alibi.'

She hesitated, glanced back at the truck, and dropped her voice. 'Look, it's not my business, but Hugh's behaviour this morning . . . well, it's been erratic. Made me wonder if he's not coping well with some kind of recent trauma. If he was a colleague of mine, I'd be worried.'

Oh, Nick was worried, all right. More worried about Hugh than he'd been since the scrawny street kid had befriended Patrick and became another responsibility to protect. But memories couldn't help him now, and Hugh had long ago ceased needing his protection. If Hugh had taken the cocaine, if he was crooked, there's no way he could protect him.

'I'll keep an eye out.' A mild, even-toned response that betrayed none of his concern. Playing a role again, concealing his thoughts. He grasped at the small matter in which he could be more himself with Jo. 'I shouldn't be long here. If you want to wait, I'll give you a lift back to Goodabri.'

'Thanks. I'd appreciate it.' She nodded towards a scattering of old gravestones under a large tree behind the church. 'I'll wait in the shade over there. Might cool down my temper.'

Her wry, self-aware smile stayed in his mind as he turned away and walked around the side of the truck . . . and vanished when he found himself looking down the barrel of a rifle.

He stilled, focusing on Hugh's eyes, his awareness encompassing man, hand and rifle. 'What got into you, Hugh?'

Hugh laughed, the rifle dipping slightly lower as he relaxed the aim. 'Just testing your reflexes. I don't think you're quite the man you used to be, Nick. Your hand didn't move near your gun at all.'

'You used to be a better cop, Hugh.'

'So did you. Or so I thought. Until you murdered Terry Costello and that woman in Melbourne.'

That Hugh – *Hugh*, of all people – could accuse him twisted like a knife in his chest. But then, didn't he have his own doubts about Hugh?

He kept a carefully neutral face. 'Is that what you think? That I murdered them?'

Hugh shrugged, as casually as if they were discussing the weather. 'Your fingerprints were on her gun. The one that killed Costello. There's rumours you were screwing her. You visited her brothel often enough.'

Hugh had laughed naturally a few moments ago, but now his smirk came tardily, tacked on at the end. A performance, and not a smooth one, with the rifle still pointed loosely in Nick's direction. What the hell was going on in Hugh's head? He'd play it easy, neither defensive nor aggressive, until he could work it out. The truck screened them from the view of the other officers; he needed to resolve things before the situation exploded.

'You know how it is with undercover ops. My role was as a security contractor, providing bouncers, bodyguards and security systems for the brothel. Besides, the mistress of the head of an organised-crime syndicate is really not my type.'

'I'm not sure you have a "type", Nick. You've been living like a monk for years. Although you do seem taken with Jo. Noticed that the other day, at the camping ground. I don't blame you. Cute butt.'

Control. He needed to retain it, not hand it to Hugh by responding to his provocations. The sun shone hot on them both, and sweat glistened on Hugh's face. The hand he dashed under his nostrils wiped away a trickle of blood.

Nick held steady, but he subtly shifted his weight on to his good leg, ready to spring. 'Put the rifle down, Hugh. You're a better man than this.'

'No, I'm not. I never have been.' His bitter laugh ended with a crack.

Regret, conscience – whatever it was, that fracture in Hugh's bravado gave Nick a sliver of faith to hold on to. 'Is it just the drugs? Or are you in deeper than that?'

'Oh, I'm a good six feet in. I'm not as strong as you, Nick. I screwed up, and now they're jerking the strings. I've got no choices left. I hope you had fun with Jo last night, mate, 'cause I'm supposed to shoot her. Should I do it, Nick?' He raised his voice, injecting it with anger. 'Would that get you to show some fucking emotion for once?'

Nick launched himself as Hugh gripped the rifle tighter and swung it in Jo's direction.

He knocked the rifle out of Hugh's hands before they both hit the ground, hard, and pain almost paralysed him. The rifle fell wide, but instead of twisting towards it, Hugh took advantage of Nick's weakness to dislodge his weight.

'Took you bloody long enough,' Hugh said while they grappled on the ground, a wild, crazy grin distorting his features. 'Keep fighting. When there's enough witnesses, shoot me.'

Nick turned the moment of disadvantage – being flat on his back – into advantage, using the leverage of the ground and the strength in his limbs to throw Hugh sideways, twisting the opposite direction himself and springing to his feet.

I'm supposed to shoot her . . . Whatever Hugh was planning, whatever this performance was about, his comments were warnings, not threats.

The Hugh of old was still there, and Nick had to trust him enough to go with his plan for now, make the fight last long enough to keep them all alive.

They circled slowly, watching for any break, any signal of intent. Instincts on full alert, Nick pinned Hugh with his eyes, asserting his control.

'Just like old times in the dojo, isn't it?' Hugh mocked.

'More like on the street. Dojos have rules. I suspect you're not planning to follow any of them.'

Footsteps pounded, and his peripheral vision caught blurs of khaki and blue near the truck. Without taking his eyes from his prey, he called out, 'Stay back, all of you. That's an order.'

Hugh attacked, feinting a cutting chop with his right hand while his left foot kicked into Nick's thigh. Nick caught his arm, turning the energy of the thrust into leverage to unbalance Hugh and throw him to the ground.

Hugh rolled to his feet in an instant, came at him again, raining blows and kicks that he had to work fast to block, again and again and again. Full-body contact fighting, hard and rough and powerful, a dangerous mix of martial arts and raw street brawling. Not quite back to condition after his injuries, Nick caught a couple of punches to his head, but with a lifetime of experience he shook those off, not slowing down.

Spinning away to come at him once more, this time Hugh leapt in with a sharp kick that caught Nick's injured thigh, eroding his balance, weakening his defensive throw so that they locked together, each immoveable.

'Almost time to go for your gun, Nick,' Hugh murmured, before he threw himself into a somersault to the ground, as if Nick had thrown him, and rolled, drawing a blade from an ankle holster as he did.

'Sarge!' Aaron called. 'He's got a knife.'

Nick spared a quick glance away from Hugh. Aaron and four others were fanning out, surrounding them, weapons drawn. Apparently Hugh's intention, and exactly what Nick had hoped to avoid. Hadn't they seen that he'd made no attempt to draw his own gun? He'd have to, now, so that they wouldn't think him defenceless and fire to protect him.

'Don't anyone shoot. It's under control. Hugh, drop the knife. We'll sort this out.' With no intention of firing it he drew his own weapon, holding the gun by his side, pointing to the ground.

'Sorry, Nick. Can't be sorted any other way.' Hugh locked eyes with Nick, a tumult of emotions behind them. He raised his arm with the knife, began to move in with a wide, easy to read, swiping movement.

But even as Nick braced his left arm to deflect the strike, shots sounded in quick succession, Hugh's body jerked twice and crashed to the ground, while a flock of birds screeched and screeched in the distance.

ELEVEN

Aaron had pushed her behind the truck when they'd drawn their weapons, but in the seconds after those shots Jo cautiously emerged, taking in the scene quickly. Nick kneeling beside the fallen Hugh, yelling for an ambulance. Aaron running to him. The other officers, guns in their hands, casting questioning glances at their colleagues.

Down at the river, the corellas circled in a mass cloud of white noise but below them she caught a dark shadow moving, filtered sunlight through the trees glinting a reflection.

A bullet ricocheted off the steel truck frame, inches from her.

'Shooter by the river!' she yelled, ducking back behind the truck.

'Everyone down!' she heard Nick roar.

She hunkered behind the rear wheels of the truck, out of the line of sight of the sniper. But through the gap under the truck she could just see Nick, and part of Hugh's prone body, and she held her breath as Nick and Aaron rose to their feet, carrying Hugh between them.

Just metres from the truck, the church offered better cover, and the wooden door into the vestry was aged and cracking.

Calling for them to follow, she made a run for it across the open ground, ramming the door with her shoulder to break the old lock, pushing the splintered timber open with them only a step behind her.

The tiny vestry had too little space, but the door into the main church stood open, swallows flittering among the ceiling beams, the seats stacked at the side, unused for many years, covered in dust and bird droppings.

Blood soaked Hugh's stomach and chest, dripping into a pool on the floor even as Nick and Aaron gently lowered him. Critical wounds. Fear and worry rushed round her thoughts, memories overlaying them, threatening panic, and in the incoherent whirl she sent a silent wish to Saint Patrick for a miracle. She didn't believe in saints, but if there'd ever been a benevolent presence in this place, Hugh sure as heck needed it.

Nick immediately knelt beside Hugh, his already bloodied hands pressing against the two wounds. 'We need a rescue chopper, Aaron. Then call for back-up, and make sure no-one takes stupid risks. If you can get a fix on the snipers, good. Pursue if you can.'

Concentrating on action to quell her rising fear, she rapidly unbuttoned and slipped off the shirt she wore over her crop-top and folded it roughly into a pad. She dropped to her knees in Aaron's place, sliding the pad under Nick's hand onto the abdominal wound and applying pressure.

Hugh groaned, the sound gurgling in his throat, and Nick gripped his hand. 'I'm here, mate. The ambulance is coming.'

Jo knew better than both men that the ambulance was at least half an hour from Strathnairn, the rescue helicopter a similar time away in Tamworth. With her free hand she checked Hugh's pulse: uneven, barely there. His skin was pale, his abdomen distended beneath her hand, and his blood already soaked her folded shirt.

Internal bleeding, and quite likely damaged organs. Even if Saint Patrick lent a hand, the chances of paramedics and equipment arriving in time were slim.

She closed her eyes to steady the panic threatening again. Hugh, not Leon. *Not Leon.* No storms, no long, agonising wait for help that couldn't come. She *could* stay with Hugh, *could* comfort him. She *could* stay here with Nick, and be strong.

Nick. Despite the sounds of shouts and revving cars outside, he made no move to leave, his hand still gripping Hugh's, concern cracking his usual impassive mask. She'd thought them only colleagues, until that out-of-the-blue fight erupted. None of it made sense to her. The violence of the fight contrasted sharply with Nick's concern now, and that linked grip. Whatever the history between them, Hugh mattered to Nick. She closed her hand over both of theirs in silent support.

Hugh tried to move, moaning as pain twisted his face.

'Hold still, mate,' Nick urged, all his focus on the injured man. 'Won't be long and you'll have some pain killers.'

'No . . . have to . . . could have saved them, Nick . . . my fault . . . Christie was meeting *me* . . .'

'I've always known that, Hugh.' Nick spoke quietly, with a gentleness that belied his usual distance. 'It doesn't matter.'

Hugh's eyes flickered open, searching for Nick's, his breathing increasingly ragged. 'Grace . . . see her sometimes . . . but they know . . . they think . . . that's why . . . I *had* to. For Grace.'

Whatever Hugh's words meant, they were a shock to Nick, his face paling.

'Someone's threatening *Grace*? Who is it?'

'Files . . .' Hugh's breath came now in slow, shallow gasps. 'Pat's birthday . . . you have to . . .' The voice faded, eyes drifted closed, air expelling from his lungs. Seconds passed before he drew in another shallow breath. 'Failed . . . you . . . brother . . .'

'No, Hugh. You made good.' The steadiness of Nick's deep voice wavered again. 'More than made good.'

Jo felt for a pulse, found nothing, and there was no movement in Hugh's chest, no more breaths.

'Shit, no.' Nick yanked open Hugh's shirt, began compressions, and Jo moved to Hugh's head, training kicking in to administer mouth-to-mouth. *Don't think, just do. Breathe, count. Breathe, count.* They established a rhythm, cycled through it several times, but Hugh lay motionless and silent.

Beaten, her own breath uneven as she fought back tears and failed, Jo sat back on her heels. 'He's gone, Nick. I'm so sorry.'

'Yes.' It was a long moment before Nick closed Hugh's shirt over his bloodied skin, and he grasped his hand one last time before laying it on his chest and letting go.

Thoughts raced and jumbled around in his head, defying any order or sense. He pushed himself to his feet, paced a few steps away, stared at the peeling white paint on the wall in front of him, his chest painfully tight.

Hugh was dead. He'd tried to *orchestrate* his own death, might well have succeeded in his plan, but someone else shot him first, silencing him. Someone out there, beyond the river.

Hugh's partially revealed secrets left too much unexplained. Nick needed to sort out his thoughts, take charge of the whirl of emotions muddying logic.

Anger with himself – he acknowledged that. He tried to still his shaking hands as he wiped the worst of the blood from them with his handkerchief, but the metaphorical blood remained. He'd failed Hugh. Should have paid more attention, made more of an effort to keep in touch. He would have for Pat, if his brother had still been alive. But he'd let Hugh flounder, unsupported, when Hugh had no-one else but him.

Christie . . . Yes, he'd always known about Hugh and his sister, known she'd come to meet him the day she died. It's why he'd sent Pat to gatecrash the date, worried about the intensity of their heady teenage attraction. *His* fault Pat had died with Christie in that hail of bullets, moments before Hugh arrived. Not Hugh's fault.

But Grace – what had Hugh meant, that he'd been seeing Grace? She was a doctor, in Queensland – Nick knew that much about his youngest sister, although he'd not contacted her since he was eighteen. For her sake. For her safety, he disappeared from her life, to protect the last of his shattered family.

The young Hugh had always had a strong core of loyalty, and a fondness for Grace, but they hadn't spoken of her in years.

Had Hugh sought her out, or had Grace found him? Either way, protecting Grace might go some way towards explaining Hugh's erratic actions. But who had threatened her, and held that over Hugh? Was she really in danger? And where was the connection with this case?

A feather-touch on his shoulder alerted him to Jo's presence beside him, compassion and questions in her eyes. Of course she had to be wondering, curious about Hugh's behaviour, the fight, his last words. Nick wished he had answers for her.

'He was a friend of my brother's.' Gravel in his throat made him stop. *Get a grip. Take control.*

'You don't have to explain to me, Nick.'

He did have to. Had to acknowledge aloud each of them, even if they could no longer hear it. 'He was a homeless kid who helped Pat in a street fight one day. They stuck together after that. Christie . . .' After all this time, he should be able to say her name naturally, without revealing the pain. 'Christiana was my sister. She and Pat were killed, murdered almost nineteen years ago.'

'I'm so sorry, Nick.' Not just customary words repeated by rote. She understood loss, her unwavering eyes holding the echo of her own grief.

Emotion an indulgence he couldn't afford, he dismissed her empathy, and his lingering sense of failure, with a brief shake of his head. 'It was a long time ago.'

He should explain about Grace, couldn't think of adequate words. 'Grace is my youngest sister. I haven't seen her since she was twelve. I don't know what Hugh meant about her.'

He couldn't see how Grace could be in danger, couldn't make sense of any of it. But, Grace in danger or not, he had to solve it – the whole complex case – before anyone else died. His job, his responsibility. Memories were irrelevant.

Movement outside the cobweb-draped window caught his eye – a probationary constable securing crime-scene tape to a fence post. A blowfly buzzed into the church, diving for Hugh, and Jo moved quickly to wave it away.

'I'll stay here with him,' she offered, with only a slight waver in her voice, 'if you need to go out there.'

Leave *her* alone with the body of the man they'd been unable to save? Despite her courage, her determined composure, he would not put her through that.

He pulled out his phone. The death of an officer required a formal investigation – especially when other officers had weapons drawn. He had procedures to follow, notifications to make.

And when that was done, he needed to find out who had fired the bullets from near the river. Three bullets. He'd heard all three, seen the last ricochet off the truck, just inches from Jo.

The bastard had murdered Hugh, and tried to murder Jo.

TWELVE

Nick turned his back to her, thumbing a couple of buttons on his phone, briskly asking for the Strathnairn commander when the call went through. Unemotional, in control, he reported the facts of Hugh's death.

Standing uselessly in the middle of the empty church beside the dead man, Jo had no idea what to do next. Nick didn't need her. Hugh didn't need her. Her hands too sticky with Hugh's blood, she couldn't thrust them in her pockets or tuck loose strands of her hair back from her face. Couldn't *do* anything, except concentrate on keeping it all together, resisting the urge to give in to an emotional and physical reaction to the situation. What use would that be to anyone? She had to support Nick, not be a burden.

She made herself stand by Hugh's side and look at him. In death, without the animation of his macho behaviour, Hugh appeared almost boyish. In his thirties, around her own age, maybe a year or two older. Too young to have died. Like Leon, who'd died at barely thirty, with so much achieved, and so much potential unrealised. Whereas Hugh had died believing himself a failure.

Dull, empty blue eyes stared, unmoving. Nothing remained of the street kid who'd gone to the defence of another youth, of the confident man who'd played the flirt. Nothing remained but memories, questions, and the grief Nick had been unable to completely hide.

Hugh's last words made little sense to her, despite Nick's explanation of the family connection. Files, coercion, a threat to Grace – even added to Hugh's erratic behaviour and the bizarre fight with Nick, all she came up with was confusion. Confusion, and apprehension.

'As soon as the situation's in hand here, I'll have Jo Lockwood escorted back to Strathnairn.' Nick faced her as he mentioned her name, dark eyes holding hers. 'We'll need to organise protection for her. Yes, it's warranted. There was a clear attempt on her life.'

Despite the baking heat in the building, she had to clench her hands to stop them shaking. That third shot from the sniper had almost hit her. She'd seen him, caught the reflection off his telescopic sight, because nobody else had been in the direct line between them. Either the sniper had misfired, or he'd been aiming at her and missed. She wanted to believe the first option – a wild shot, an attempt to drive them under cover to enable his escape – but Nick's certainty rammed reality home. The sniper had killed Hugh, then turned his sights on her.

'What's going on, Nick?' she demanded as soon as he finished his call. 'Did you understand what Hugh meant?'

'Not much of it. Yet. You said he was acting strangely this morning, Jo. Did he say or do anything in particular that made you think that?'

Just about everything he'd done was strange, but she zoomed in on specifics. 'There was a phone call that seemed to rattle him. He was very short with the caller. Just a few words. He said, "No, not possible." And then he said he'd "sort it". It's just an impression, but he looked at me in the rear-vision mirror and I had the feeling that I was what he'd "sort".'

Nick swore under his breath.

She recalled the start of the fight, the raised voices that had made her turn, the sight of Nick throwing himself at Hugh, and the rifle falling to the ground. The rifle that had been pointed towards her.

'He was going to kill me, wasn't he? He would have shot me.'

Nick gave a slow shake of his head. 'No. He warned me so that I'd stop him. He had no intention of pulling the trigger, Jo.'

The sweat trickling down the back of her neck tracked a chilling path, spreading along her spine. She shrugged her shoulders, rolled her head to dislodge the uneasy sensation.

'Will you be able to find out who made that last call?'

'I'll ask for his phone to be checked, although it was probably a blocked number. But this is a crime scene now, and since I'm involved, I won't touch anything more. There'll be an internal investigation team arriving within a couple of hours. They'll want statements and interviews. They'll want to speak with you, too.'

'They're not going to blame you, though? The evidence must be clear enough that he provoked the fight, and that the sniper shot him?'

Nick stilled, watching her, and weighing his words before answering. 'They'll know quickly enough that I didn't pull the trigger. However, as I was brawling with a fellow officer when he was shot, there's bound to be suspicion and questions, about my relationship with him, and our involvement in the case. I'm new here, and I've been an undercover specialist for almost ten years, the last job ending badly. That doesn't lead to a whole lot of trust between police officers. But you're under no obligation, Jo. You've had a stressful few days. You don't have to talk with them if you don't want to.'

No obligation? Her obligation, as he had put it, went deeper than simply telling the truth about the scene she had witnessed. Nick had torn the rifle from Hugh's hands. She owed Nick her life.

~

'You were behind the truck, you said. So you didn't actually see who fired the shots, did you, Doctor Lockwood?'

Jo sipped water from her glass and mentally counted to three to steady her temper before she answered. 'I also said that I heard rifle shots, fired from a distance, not a handgun less than five metres from me.' She eyed the detective senior constable from the Critical Incident team. 'Do you not understand that there's a distinct difference in sound?'

Raised eyebrows acknowledged his surprise, but then he smiled, with more of the condescension that had driven her mad half the afternoon. 'Not everybody knows enough about firearms to recognise the difference. Especially when the situation is tense.'

Did he think she spent her days hugging koalas? She clasped her hands around the glass and drew on her stretched patience to set about educating him. 'My job involves enforcing the laws banning firearms in the National Park, and also coordinating regular campaigns against feral animals. I'm more than familiar with firearms, and estimating direction and distance in a range of landscapes. The shots that killed Detective Dalton were fired from the river. I'm sure everyone present will tell you the same thing.'

'We have to be thorough, make sure nothing is missed. So, you know some of the local shooters? Have you seen anything out of the ordinary or suspicious lately?'

She raised an eyebrow. 'Apart from a vandalised camping ground, a dead body, cocaine and weapons stashes and a murdered detective? No, I can't say I have.' Not a particularly helpful response to the question, that burst of sarcasm, but in her overtired state it eased her annoyance more effectively than a polite answer.

Apparently not an entirely insensitive clod, he laid down his pen and started to gather his notes together. 'You've had a tough few days. Your information has been very helpful. Thank you.'

Her muscles stiff from over an hour in the uncomfortable plastic chair, she rose to her feet slowly, rubbing the ache in her neck, the sudden change in his approach leaving her uncertain how to respond. 'What happens from here? Do you need a formal statement from me?'

He held the door open for her. 'We've got more interviews to conduct. I'll contact you tomorrow if we need a statement.'

She would have asked about Nick, but before she found words the detective had ushered her down the short corridor to the reception area and left her there with no more than another brief word of thanks.

Where to now? The abrupt ending to the interview had denied her the chance to find out more about how this situation affected her from here, and she stared out the glass doors, trying to gather coherent thoughts as she watched the slanting sunlight glow on the low hills behind Strathnairn.

An afternoon in Strathnairn police station hadn't been part of her plan for the day. Being stranded in Strathnairn without her vehicle definitely wasn't in any plan. Pretty much any chances of planning anything had been shot to hell when she'd found Travis Mitchell's body the other day.

Should she try to organise a ride back to the homestead, or find a place to stay overnight in Strathnairn? Where would she be safe? The seriousness of the threat against her loomed in her mind, but she pushed it down while she focused on practical matters. No-one, other than Nick, had expressed concern about her safety, but she hadn't seen Nick since they'd arrived at the station hours ago, and she hadn't seen Aaron – who seemed to be the only officer *not* treating Nick like a leper – since leaving the old church.

Despite Nick's matter-of-fact explanation, she didn't comprehend enough about police culture to interpret the undercurrents, suspicions and tight-lipped attitudes of most of the cops this afternoon. Her observations and instincts about Nick couldn't be *that* far wrong, surely? On one level he frightened her, but not in a way that made her doubt his integrity; she had never once felt unsafe with him. Perhaps it was her response to him that frightened her.

The door behind her opened again, and she turned at the sound, the small hope it might be Nick or Aaron flickering out in an instant. Shelley Brock carried her overnight bag in one hand, a pair of dark glasses in the other.

'Jo.' Shelley stopped beside her, lowered her bag to the floor and slid the glasses into place on top of her head, making no attempt to mask her red-rimmed eyes. 'Have you got a moment?'

A tête-a-tête with Shelley Brock? They'd had hardly exchanged more than a couple of words until now. Off following some other lead this morning, Shelley had only arrived at the church just as Jo was leaving, and she'd barely spared Jo a glance in her distress for Hugh. But the woman had lost a colleague, a friend, perhaps more, and Jo well knew the agony and desolation that was just beginning.

'Sure, Shelley.'

'I wanted to thank you . . .' Shelley began, taking a moment to blink back tears. 'I heard you did CPR. Thank you for trying to save him.'

'Nick and I just did what anyone would do. I'm very sorry for your loss, Shelley.' Stupid words, useless words. Words she'd heard recited by too many people. 'You and Hugh were close?'

Shelley gave a bitter half-laugh, half-sob. 'If "close" is a euphemism for "lovers", well, it's not much of a secret that we sometimes were. I don't think he let anyone get close to him; not really. Certainly not me. He made that clear, last night. But he was so full of life, of energy . . .' She screwed her eyes shut for a moment, sniffed, on the edge of falling apart. 'I couldn't help falling for that.'

'Of course not,' replied Jo, at a loss for anything else to say. She'd fallen for a similar man herself. Lived with him, loved him, had planned to marry him. Until he'd died, just as suddenly as Hugh, leaving her adrift and alone.

Shelley straightened her shoulders, a mask of determination settling on her face. 'Yeah, and aren't I a bloody fool? Anyway, I've got to get out of here, but . . . well, thank you. I'm sorry you've been caught up in this mess. But you can trust Nick to get it sorted out. Hugh thought the world of him.'

If Hugh really thought the world of Nick, then what had the fight been about? More questions without answers.

'Do you know where Nick is?' Jo asked.

'In with the boss, apparently. Oh, and Jo, can I ask you a favour? For Hugh?' She looked directly into Jo's eyes. 'For Nick?' She tugged an envelope from a side pocket on her laptop bag.

A car horn tooted, and she glanced out anxiously, then back to Jo. 'That's my taxi. Look, I found this in my laptop bag this morning. Hugh's bag is the same as mine, so maybe he confused them. I think it's some notes about an old case he was writing up last night, but I think he would have wanted Nick to see them first. I've got to go. Can you see that he gets them safely? Thanks, Jo.'

She handed the envelope to Jo and whirled out. The squarish, masculine handwriting in heavy black pen, stark against the white paper read: *Nick Matheson. Personal and Confidential.*

Personal and confidential notes about an old case? In a handwritten envelope? Goodabri might be off the beaten track, but it had Next G internet, and the pub had free wireless, so why hadn't Hugh emailed the notes to Nick?

'*Files* . . .' Hugh had said, in his last breathless moments. For all Shelley's belief he'd simply mixed up their bags, she hadn't been privy to that final conversation between the two men.

Footsteps sounded along the linoleum floor, and Jo turned the envelope in her hands, making her decision. She wouldn't go anywhere until she'd seen Nick and handed it directly to him.

ॐ

After repeated interviews during the afternoon, Murdoch's directive to go home came as no great surprise, but Nick wasn't prepared to accept it without objection.

'Are you ordering me off-duty? Or suspending me?'

The challenge didn't ruffle his superior's easy manner. Murdoch played it relaxed, leaned back in his desk chair and gave him a straight answer. 'No, I'm not. But you've worked five days straight since you started on Monday, including a night drive to Newcastle and overnight protection duties. And you lost a long-time colleague today. You probably need some down time.'

'I need to investigate several linked murders. These first days are critical.'

A lesser man would have bridled at the disagreement, and at the deliberate avoidance of the customary 'sir' from a subordinate, but Murdoch showed no sign of annoyance or anger. An excellent actor, or a man comfortable enough with his command to treat a detective as an equal? Perhaps elements of both. Everything Nick had seen so far of his new boss suggested the man was no fool. Probably as sharp as a street knife, under that comfortable persona.

'The Critical Incident team will give me a preliminary report this evening. Brock is returning to Sydney this afternoon, on compassionate leave, but there are two more detectives on their way from Homicide. I expect the CI team to hand over to Homicide, and you'll cooperate fully with them on both Mitchell's and Dalton's murders, as the cases likely overlap.'

'I've told the CI team everything I know for a fact.' A careful truth, not a lie. But he wasn't prepared to have strangers dig into Hugh's life until he'd found a few answers himself. Hugh had said he was in trouble, and there was the missing cocaine – but accusations of corruption could sometimes see a dead cop carry the can for everything, and little investigation beyond that. He wouldn't let that happen to Hugh.

Murdoch strolled to the window and ran a perfunctory glance over the view outside before turning so that the sunlight silhouetted him, the sharp contrast casting his face into shadow, obscuring his expression. A textbook interrogation technique.

'Do those "facts" include the reasons why Dalton appeared to be deliberately provoking you?'

Not a fool at all. Either he'd been watching the interviews, or someone from the CI team had briefed him.

Still sitting in the chair in front of the desk, Nick purposely relaxed, lounged back, despite the upright, symbolically more powerful stance Murdoch had taken.

'I don't know –' Nick stressed the word slightly – 'the answer to that.'

'Then give me your educated guess.' An order, not a request. From his commanding officer, who had the power to suspend him, deny him access to the investigation and police resources.

The fact that he hadn't done it, yet, indicated that Nick could trust his judgement, to a degree.

He chose his words with care. 'It's possible that Hugh may have been acting under coercion. But I don't believe it was his intention to harm anyone.'

'Is that why you didn't fire when he came at you with a knife? Or has the incident in Melbourne affected your reactions?'

Of course he would ask that, as any responsible commander should. 'No, it hasn't. Hugh and I trained in various martial arts together for many years. I know how he fights, and today he wasn't really serious. He deliberately swung the knife in a move any twelve-year-old with a week's training could block.'

'I'd still like to know why a man of Dalton's experience would appear to threaten a fellow armed officer when surrounded by others with weapons drawn.'

A reasonable query, calmly made. Murdoch knew how to apply pressure.

Nick leaned forward, elbows on his knees, relying on honesty to build the tenuous sense of trust between him and Murdoch. 'I need some more time to think it through, sir. All I have so far are fragments, and I have to work out how they go together.'

Murdoch strolled back to his desk, reaching for a pen as he sat. 'We'll have a briefing with the additional detectives at Goodabri at eight this evening. Go home and get some rest after that, and report your progress to me tomorrow morning.'

A reprieve, of sorts. But he heard the unspoken message: he'd better come up with some answers by morning. He intended to – he had a case to solve, and Jo's safety to ensure.

'Thank you. About protection for Jo Lockwood, sir. Do you have a preference for which officers I allocate?'

Murdoch rolled the pen between his fingers, taking his time to respond, his gaze unwavering. 'Matheson, the reality is that with five officers pulled off the roster for CI debriefing, and a crime scene in the middle of nowhere to preserve, we simply don't have sufficient staff. I suggest you arrange for her to stay with a friend or colleague. The National Parks team here are reliable and practical. If she's somewhere in town, a patrol can check every hour or so.'

A patrol every hour or so? Nick didn't waste breath arguing. Facts couldn't be changed; Strathnairn had limited resources, and he'd just have to deal with it, find his own way to keep Jo safe.

But first he had to find her.

He came across Matt Carruthers in the corridor outside Murdoch's office.

'Jo?' Carruthers answered his query. 'I saw her in reception, a while back.'

He found her standing by the window, staring out. Tense, like some kind of caged animal, longing for escape. Who could blame her? They'd disrupted her day, her week, and even though she had kept it together today, the emotional strain had to be difficult for her.

She must have heard the door, or seen his reflection in the window. Without any haste she turned to face him, studying him as he approached, lightly tapping a white envelope against her fingers.

Since he'd last seen her she'd changed out of her blood-stained crop-top into a T-shirt. A simple one, but the low neck, fitted shape and pastel colour brought back to mind the image of her toned skin beneath. Irrelevant. Definitely irrelevant.

'Everything okay?' she asked.

That her first concern should be for him didn't sit well with him when he was the cop and she a civilian who'd been through more these past couple of days than anyone should. And then to be left here to wait in the sterility of the police station, all stainless steel and white linoleum and coldness.

'Yes. Sorry to keep you waiting so long. Standard procedure takes a while to work through. I hope you've been treated well?'

'Perfectly fine.' She held out the envelope to him. 'I need to give you this.'

An envelope with Hugh's handwriting on it.

She glanced at the reception desk, stepped closer to him. 'Shelley had to leave before you'd finished your meetings,' she said, quietly. 'Apparently their laptop cases are similar, and Hugh *accidentally* put this in hers, not his own.' Her eyes didn't waver from his. 'She left it with me; asked me to make sure you got it.'

Nick turned the envelope in his hands, both keen and reluctant to open it. *Files*, Hugh had said. And he'd 'misplaced' this envelope so that it wasn't among his personal belongings and computer records that the CI team would go through. Convenient. Very convenient. But a deliberate action on Hugh's part, or a true mistake?

Jo's thoughts must be running along the same lines as his. And she'd made sure the envelope reached him.

'Thanks, Jo,' he said simply. She nodded.

Voices out in the corridor – Carruthers, Aaron – came closer, passed by without pausing.

Nick folded the envelope. Later. He'd read it later. 'We need to get you somewhere safe, Jo.'

She accepted the change of subject without comment. 'That's pretty much in hand. I had a phone call a few minutes ago, and apparently a number of my colleagues have been planning. Simon and a couple of the field staff have been out at the homestead today doing some maintenance work. They'll be cutting firebreaks tomorrow around the place, and so they're prepared to stay overnight. Erin's heading out there, too. Unless you object, I'll go home tonight.'

A possible solution – at least for tonight. She'd be among friends, and less than ten minutes from the police station at Goodabri. 'Are they people you can rely on? Sensible?'

'Yes, absolutely. Erin and Simon are both rangers, and are also involved in volunteer emergency services. Simon's a gentle giant at heart, but his size would scare off a few thugs. Robbo and Bruce are field staff and can pretty much turn their hand to anything. With three or four vehicles out front and five of us inside, it should be a solid enough deterrent, shouldn't it?'

There would be six inside. Until he knew more, he would not leave her without police protection.

He checked his watch – just past six. Plenty of time to get to the homestead and then out to Goodabri before eight. 'I'll take you home. I'll probably call back after tonight's briefing is over. If you don't mind, I can bunk down on the floor.'

She didn't appear to mind the suggestion, just raised an amused eyebrow, in that relaxed, teasing way of hers that he'd glimpsed sometimes. 'Don't you have a home to go to, Detective?'

A home? No. Places with a few belongings and pieces of furniture had never equalled a home. 'I'm still staying in a motel. Finding a place to rent isn't as important as ensuring your safety.'

Her head tilted slightly, studying his face, she said, 'Thank you.'

Sincere gratitude, delivered simply, and for a moment it almost floored him.

'It's my job, Jo.'

No longer joking, she challenged him. 'To be on duty for seventy-two hours straight?'

Damn. Cool cop with his colleagues, tough cop with law-breakers, courteous cop with members of the public – after years playing a ruthless criminal bastard, he'd slipped back into his police roles easily enough. But she had expressed more concern, more recognition of him as a person, than anyone had for a long time, and his repertoire of roles came up empty. Protector, yes, but circumstance had thrown them together, more than usual. Friend? How could he be a friend to her? He'd forgone friends years ago, not prepared to risk anyone being hurt by the violence he had to immerse himself in. He wasn't sure he even knew *how* to be a friend anymore.

'I do what needs to be done.' To soften it, acknowledge her concern, he added, 'I've had some sleep, both nights. Enough to get by.'

'Good.' She managed a smile. 'But let me know if you need me to drive, so you can catch a nap on the way to Riverbank.'

He needed to drive. To keep his eyes on the road, and not on her.

She sat beside him in the car, silent until he'd pulled out of the police station car park and around a couple of corners on to the main street. He heard her slow intake of breath, and in the corner of his vision he could see candid hazel eyes steady on him.

'I wasn't asked for details of what Hugh said in the church, and I didn't offer them,' she said. 'I figured that was personal, between the two of you. I just told them he was barely conscious. I'm not entirely sure why, and maybe I'm a fool, but I'm trusting you, Nick. I hope that isn't one enormous mistake.'

That explained why they hadn't grilled him about Hugh's dying words. Because Jo hadn't revealed them. If they'd asked her, she wouldn't have lied – he understood that about her – but she had decided to leave it up to his judgement what to reveal.

Jo trusted him, when his colleagues still regarded him with suspicion and doubt.

He had to clear his throat before he spoke. 'I'm grateful, Jo. I didn't tell them much because I need some time to piece the full truth together. I know you've got more than enough reason to doubt him, but whatever his failings, whatever he got caught up in, Hugh was a decent man at heart. I hope his letter gives me some answers to what happened.'

'I hope so, too – for all our sakes.'

She fell silent again, rested her head back against the head rest and closed her eyes.

He thought about the envelope as he slowed the car to turn on to the highway.

One glance at the familiar untidy scrawl against the white paper and he'd almost heard Hugh's laconic tone, saying his name, one last time. Now he saw in his mind's eye not the grown man, the detective, but the skinny, half-starved feral kid, surviving on cheek and attitude. An additional responsibility that he'd accepted, because the lad's fierce loyalty to Pat and Christie and Grace had earned him more than his share of fights, bruises and bloodied noses. And because Hugh, the irrepressible clown, had made them laugh, when his siblings, with their father in prison and mother gravely ill, had little enough to laugh about.

A few pages, Hugh had left him, judging by the thickness of the packet. Hardly 'files', but he had to hope there'd be enough information to lead to a break in the case, a solid direction to investigate.

He had to trust Hugh, despite the questions and shadows over his behaviour.

He had to trust Hugh, in the same way that Jo trusted him, despite her unanswered questions.

He'd return her trust by sharing as much of the information with her as he could. Just as soon as he made sense of it all.

THIRTEEN

The low sunlight cast long tree shadows, a constant flickering of bright light and shade across the road that strained her vision.

Closing her eyes, trying to relax, failed; her mind too occupied with the events of the day and the image of Nick, staring stony-faced at the road.

Sometime during the day, he'd changed his bloodied clothes for the navy blue search-and-rescue uniform. Fighting with Hugh, he'd been more than warrior enough, even in the civilised business clothes; now the dark uniform T-shirt shaped lean, hard muscle, a potent reminder of potential force and energy.

A complex man, Nick Matheson. Intelligent, courteous, intellectually and physically powerful . . . and an excellent actor, in control of all his outward expressions of emotion.

Yet she trusted him. If the interviewing detective had specifically asked her what Hugh had said, she'd have had to tell him. Although her personal code of ethics could accept –

just – the omission, an outright lie would have been a different matter. She'd have needed a lot more than instinct to justify that.

Instinct? No, she had more reason than that to trust Nick. His commitment to duty, to start with; he'd scarcely stopped since he'd arrived at the murder scene on Wednesday. His concern for her safety – even to the point of risking his own life to knock down a man with a gun aimed at her. And the glimpses she'd caught of powerful feeling beneath the controlled demeanour. Those facts all added up to a man with a strong core of integrity and dedication.

She wondered about his family; the siblings who had died, the sister he hadn't seen for years, the violence he'd hinted at in his youth. More than enough sorrow in those events alone to give a man reasons to build a wall around his emotions. But he'd also worked undercover, for a long time, it seemed. What did that do to a man? The roles he had to play, the kinds of people he had to live with, the things he had to do to survive? Not questions she could easily ask, not just now, despite the tentative friendship their shared experiences in the past few days had brought.

Neither of them bothered with small talk, letting the silence sit between them. There was only the rumble of the engine, the occasional sound of a passing car, and the clicking of the indicator as he slowed to turn off the highway on to the short-cut road to Goodabri.

'This is the right road, isn't it?' he asked.

'Yes,' she replied, then added almost without thinking, 'Watch out for kangaroos. There can be a fair few around, this time of day.'

'I will.'

The quietly spoken agreement made her realise how few *facts* she knew about him. 'I assumed you were a city type. My apologies if I got that wrong, and I just told a country boy the obvious.'

The silence returned for a moment before he answered. 'I've worked in all sorts of places.'

An answer, but not an answer. And no invitation to probe. She didn't press him for more details. If he'd wanted to tell her where he came from, he could have. He probably had far too much on his mind to engage in idle chat. Whereas she could have done with distraction from the worry of things she could do little about.

Distraction came when they arrived at Riverbank. Her workmates were still on the job, clearing the last of the old, straggling hedge from the garden perimeter, cutting dangerous low limbs off the eucalypt trees.

Not just cleared of fire hazards; cleared of hiding places. Little now obstructed the view between the homestead and the paddocks beyond the dirt road.

One of the work trucks was already loaded high with garden waste. Beside it, Rob and Bruce watched the car approach up the drive, visibly relaxing when they recognised her. As Nick parked in front of the garage, Erin came round from the back of the homestead, whipper-snipper in hand.

The heat hit Jo the moment she stepped out of the air-conditioned car, and in an odd way she was grateful for it. Alive, and back in familiar surroundings. If not alone, then with people she could relax with.

Erin greeted her with a concerned once-over, disguised with a grin.

'Good timing,' she said. 'We're just finishing up. Simon will have food on the table in thirty minutes. If you hurry, you can have first shower, before we hard-working types use all the hot water.'

A shower and food. Definitely good ideas. She'd had no appetite for the sandwiches offered at the police station, but that was hours ago.

Erin gave Nick the once-over, too, but in an altogether different way. Part protective-lioness, part twinkle-in-the-eye.

Jo introduced them, and they shook hands. Nick polite, serious, as though he hadn't noticed Erin's appreciative gleam.

Erin gestured towards the house. 'Simon's in the kitchen. Head on in and I'll join you in a few minutes.' Tucking the whipper-snipper under her arm, she strode away.

'Will you stay for something to eat, Nick?' Jo asked. 'It's been a long time since breakfast, and Simon always makes enough to feed a platoon.'

He glanced at his watch, and nodded. 'I will, thanks. I'll get my laptop.'

The rich, hearty aroma of Simon's Bolognese sauce wafted out through the screen door, setting her stomach rumbling even before she'd stepped inside. She paused in the hallway.

'You'll want some quiet to read Hugh's letter. Use the office. No-one will disturb you. I'll knock when dinner's ready.'

'Thanks, Jo.' He looked, for a moment, like a man who'd been on the go for three days straight. 'I'll have to eat and run, though. The briefing's in Goodabri at eight.'

No rest for him yet, apparently.

'Use whatever you need in the office. Phone, internet – the wireless password is "Riverbank".'

She closed the office door and left him, giving him the little privacy she could. It was all she *could* do, just now, and the inactivity and lack of control over her own life and decisions gnawed at her, a constant restlessness and whirring of frustration in her thoughts mingling with the growing fear that she had been trying to ignore all afternoon.

In her bedroom, she stood in the centre of the room, suddenly so tired she could scarcely think straight. Simon clattered pots and whistled in the kitchen, Robbo and Bruce talked out on the veranda as they sharpened the chainsaw, and the whipper-snipper buzzed in the direction of the small shed.

All of them doing their almost-normal work, while her routine had been thrown topsy-turvy.

A shower. Although she'd had a good scrub with disinfectant at the police station and changed into a fresh T-shirt, the memory of a dying man's blood spattered on her body couldn't be easily washed away.

Hugh's blood. Hugh, lying dead on the floor of the church . . . She felt the shock of reaction finally hit, wrapped her arms around her body to stop the trembling radiating out from her centre, rocked backwards and forwards on her feet and tried desperately to hold back the tears that burned her eyes.

Damn, she couldn't break down now. Couldn't, wouldn't. Had to hold everything together. She sucked in air, concentrated on deepening, slowing, her rapid shallow breathing, biting her lip so that she'd breathe through her nose, not her mouth.

Counting her breaths, blocking out wild thoughts with the steadily building numbers.

She'd reached a hundred and thirty before the trembling slowed right down.

Her still hands shook when she unclasped them, and she had to think to make them undo the band holding back her hair.

She needed to move, act, do *something* other than rock in useless whimpering.

A shower, clean clothes, a meal, and she would be functional again. Mostly. And then . . . ? She'd have to think about what she could effectively *do* towards solving these crimes. She knew the landscape. She'd built up a reasonable amount of trust and respect with the locals. She had to be able to contribute *something*.

Considerate of the others, she didn't spend long under the shower, despite the temptation. But she shampooed her hair, and she unwrapped the rose-scented soap her mother had sent last Christmas and lathered her skin with it.

Despite that feminine indulgence, she pulled on a linen shirt from the wardrobe and buttoned it up over a pair of comfortable, cotton trousers, slipping her feet into flat leather sandals.

As she combed her hair, Simon gave a general call-out that food would be ready in five.

The office door remained closed, all quiet beyond it. She knocked, opened the door when he said to come in.

On the desk, the pages of the letter lay face down. Nick stood by the window, his face hidden from her as he looked out between the gap in the curtains.

She remained just inside the doorway, partly to block the sight-lines of anyone passing, partly to give him space. Partly to give herself and her fragile emotions some distance from him. No sign of his usual impassive expression in the brief glimpse around as she'd come in.

'Dinner's almost ready. I'll bring some food in if you want some more time,' she said gently.

'No. It's okay.' He exhaled a long, slow breath and faced her, keeping some space between them. Weariness clouded his dark eyes, took the edge off the intensity of his usual control. 'He wanted to die. Believed he deserved it. The fight – it was to give me a reason to shoot him.'

'But you didn't,' she said softly. Words for Nick, not the furious words she'd have flung at Hugh, if she could have. How dare he try to force that decision, that responsibility, onto Nick? Reading the letter must have been harrowing.

She let her comment rest in the silence, didn't push him. If he needed to talk, she'd listen. If he needed something more – physical contact, a touch, a hug – then hell, she could do with the same thing herself. If not, so be it. Witnessing death together created a shared experience, the beginnings of a friendship, but they still hardly knew each other.

'No, I didn't. But I failed him, nonetheless.' His mouth a grim line, he scooped the pages of the letter together, folded them along the original fold lines.

Conversation over. He had experience with sudden death, doubtless had his own ways of dealing with his emotional reactions.

He fitted the folded pages back into the envelope and slid between them a small plastic bag containing a micro memory card.

He caught her glance at it. 'The files Hugh mentioned. He said everything he knows is on there. I just have to find a card adaptor so that I can read it.'

That problem could be easily solved. 'I have one,' she told him. 'My GPS uses a micro SD card. I'll get it for you.'

She deliberately didn't probe – about the letter, about what might be on the files, about anything. He had a heck of a lot more to deal with than her, and he'd tell her anything she needed to know, when he'd had time to process it.

She trusted him on that.

∂

By the time you read this, I'll probably be either dead or in a cell. If you shot me yourself, then everything's gone the way I wanted it to. If you didn't, by the time you get to the end of this, you'll wish you had.

Hugh's opening lines stuck in Nick's head, playing relentlessly over and over and over, charging his anger further with each repetition. Anger with Hugh, for a thousand reasons. For even thinking that he'd fire to kill him. For trying to put him in that position. For keeping secrets. For becoming so entangled that he could see no way out and *wanted* to die.

But the heat of his anger with Hugh had nothing on the searing anger at himself.

If he'd kept in more frequent contact with Hugh, he might still be alive. In protective custody, perhaps, but not lying cold in a morgue. If he'd contacted Hugh once his own case was over, he might have uncovered his problems: the desperate cocaine use, the blackmailing scum who'd supplied him and the bastard they'd sold their information on to. He knew from the inside how those networks operated: target a cop on the edge of a breakdown, gather information to hold over them. If he'd known Hugh was in deep, he could have acted. The bastard behind the John Doe murder in Coffs Harbour might have been arrested, and Travis Mitchell might still be alive. Grace would be safe. Jo would be safe.

Failure sat heavily in his chest.

He seriously considered making some excuse, avoiding the shared meal, but it would be a long night and he needed to eat. His hurried breakfast toast, here in this kitchen with Aaron and Jo, seemed a whole lot longer than thirteen hours ago.

He wasn't sure what he'd expected of this meal – maybe a camp-out mood, beer and frivolity. But no, these were professionals, taking their task seriously, determined to assist a colleague and friend in need, and although there were some jokes and teasing, the underlying mood when they all sat around the table was sober.

Simon's culinary skills matched his professional confidence and leadership, and the two other men, while quick to give cheek, deferred to him in a good-natured way. Despite Erin's sassy scrutiny when they'd met, her attention – when it wasn't on Jo – was all for Simon. An interest that the man returned, although there was little overt about it, as if he was ill-at-ease with his own attraction.

And that, Nick could relate to. Across the table from him, Jo joined in the conversation as warm damper and steaming bowls of spaghetti Bolognese were passed around, comfortable in the company but with the underlying tension of the situation showing in her quiet manner and the strain around her eyes.

A close-knit team, who genuinely liked and cared about each other. And who were all, in no subtle way, assessing him.

Once they'd finished serving and started eating, Jo unfolded a map in front of her on the table.

'Let's think about this. Three incidents in the past few days, all between Derringvale and this point in the park, which can be accessed off the Derringvale Road. We all drive along that route often.' She glanced up at Nick to add in explanation, 'There's another park on the other side of Derringvale, to the north-west. Now, if we all go over the past couple of weeks, think about who's been out in any of the parks, any incidents or unusual happenings, anything even vaguely out of the ordinary, then we might come up with something that can help the police.'

Nick nodded his agreement, inwardly respecting Jo even more for pushing her own fears aside to focus on ways to move the investigation forward. These people knew the district well, both on-road and off-road, and interacted with a variety of people, out and about. 'Good idea. That photo you took of Bradley Coulter last night, Jo – pass it around. Travis Mitchell's sister supplied a photo of him, taken a few weeks ago. I'd like to know if any of you have seen either of them, and if so, when and where.'

He took out his phone, started scrolling through emails with one hand while hurriedly eating a few more mouthfuls with the other. When he found the email with the image of Travis, he passed the phone to Simon, on his right. Simon took a few moments to study the picture, and handed it to Erin.

Erin's fork stopped halfway to her mouth, hit the bowl again with a clatter.

'Him. Yes. I know him. I'm sure it's him. Robbo, take a look.'

The phone shook in her hand as she passed it across the table, but she pulled herself together enough to explain.

'A few months back, maybe July? It wasn't long before you came here, Jo. Anyway, Nick, sometimes we get groups from the low-security prison out doing projects for us. It's a government-organised program. They've got their own specially equipped van, and they stay on site. That guy was part of a group that re-did the fencing along the southern boundary of the park. I was liaison for that project and I remember him, because he was forever trying to chat me up.'

'Yeah, it's him all right,' Rob agreed. 'Brash young hoon, full of himself. Not much of a worker.'

Her face pale, Jo pushed the map closer to Nick. 'The southern boundary of the park crosses the Derringvale Road at Eight Mile Creek, near the McCulloch woolshed. Then it roughly parallels the road west –' she stretched to trace a path on the paper with her finger – 'to here, where it turns north. Not far across the river from Church Lane.'

She watched him to ensure he grasped the significance.

He did. 'Travis Mitchell knew at least two of the three crime sites. But he died at the first one.' So others had known those two sites – and their abandoned buildings – well enough to make plans to use them.

She followed his line of thought as if he'd spoken it aloud. 'Plenty of people would know the Derringvale Road. Locals, regular travellers from the north-west to Goodabri or beyond. Some people head down Church Lane to fish in the river. But it's still a possible link, isn't it?'

'Yes. We're following up Mitchell's contacts in prison. I'll make sure we find out who else was on that work gang. Thanks for that lead, Erin.'

'I'll get the photos of Bradley Coulter in a minute,' Jo said. 'In case he was one of that crew, too.'

Rob passed his phone back to him, and Nick registered the time on the display. 'I'll have to get moving. I expect to come back later on – I'll use the police lights on the car as I approach. In the meantime, if you can, as Jo suggested, go over any recent events, that would be useful.'

Travis Mitchell's previous visit to the district added another sliver of information to the hazy, incomplete picture. Hugh's letter had added a little more, and answers, if there were any, might well be in the files.

Jo left the kitchen with him to get the card adaptor, silent beside him when she had every right and plenty of cause to demand explanations. But to explain to her meant to reveal more of himself than anyone, other than Hugh, had ever known.

He'd do everything in his power to keep her safe, but by the time she read Hugh's letter, and he explained the history between them, she would know that he'd failed, repeatedly, to protect those for whom he was responsible. He doubted he would hold on to the fragile beginnings of trust she had placed in him.

He'd give her the letter and let her make her own choice, fully informed.

When she brought in the card adaptor, he held out the letter to her. 'I'll answer your questions after you've read it.'

She brushed it away. 'It's personal, Nick. Between you and Hugh.'

Personal, yes. And there was one paragraph in there, with no bearing on the case, that he'd rather she didn't read. But he could hardly take scissors to it.

'You were there when he died. You heard what he said. That must have raised questions in your mind. You need the truth so you can decide whether to keep trusting me with your life.'

He placed it on the desk, took his laptop and left the room without looking back at her, without knowing whether she'd picked it up or not.

The last of the day's light was fading as he drove towards Goodabri, the narrow road darkening with shadows, the moon not yet rising.

Alone for the first time since he'd read the letter, its implications occupied his thoughts, and he could visualise the words on the pages, hear them in his head as clearly as if Hugh spoke beside him.

I never told you about me and Christie, because you and your father could be right scary bastards, and I knew she deserved better than me.

Hugh had blamed himself for Pat's and Christie's deaths, when the real blame lay with the criminal mob their father had become mixed up with on the docks, and the shifting loyalties and betrayals when they'd come under police and government scrutiny.

Nick could all too easily imagine his father's reputation terrorising the young Hugh into silence. It didn't matter that the reputation exceeded reality. Archie Matheson had been a fighter, an unbeaten champion of no rules, no holds barred back-street fighting that nobody dared cross. Fear had beaten more people than his fists – exactly the way he intended. Until the crime bosses framed him for an assault he didn't commit, and he'd gone to prison.

When it came to reputation management, Nick had learned from his father's example. A survival skill, not one that made him proud. But he'd learned it young, and he'd used it, as deliberately and as ruthlessly as his father had, to protect his siblings.

He couldn't recall Hugh ever visiting their father in prison, but he'd have heard enough on the streets to fear him. And although their father had never abused or intentionally terrorised his kids, he'd probably grilled Christie about boyfriends on her visits, all protective father, despite being behind bars.

But Hugh hadn't been the danger, and Christie and Pat had paid the price for their father's decision to give critical evidence for the prosecution in the high-profile murder trial of mob boss Victor Zinchenko. Their father had been relatively safe, in solitary confinement – but two of his children had been gunned down at a bus-stop, in a drive-by shooting.

Nick hadn't understood, until he'd read those handwritten pages, how deeply Christie's loss had affected Hugh.

Even now, I still can't get her out of my head. The psychs would

*probably have a field day with that. They'd have a full-on fucking
festival with all the shit in my head.*

Typically Hugh, that sardonic black humour, and yet . . .
And yet a call for help, for comprehension, beneath it.

A call he was too damn late to do anything about.

❦

Jo closed her bedroom door to shut out the noise – Rob and
Bruce unrolling sleeping bags in the bunk room, Erin and
Simon talking quietly while they washed dishes – and curled
up in her large wicker chair, reluctantly opening the envelope.

A confession of sorts, the raw honesty of the letter told her
as much about Nick as it did about Hugh. Hard to read, not
because of the untidy, inconsistent lettering, but because of the
raw emotion layered beneath the self-deprecating tone.

Some of the references went over her head, but with the
bare bones Nick had told her about his siblings, and what she
knew of both men, she made sense of most of it. The 'too-
young' Hugh, hiding his relationship with Christie because
'she deserved better than me', almost broken by her death. The
longing that had seen him visit Grace time and again after she'd
contacted him a year ago, because he 'wanted that time back,
before Christie and Pat were killed'.

No wonder Nick had looked so shaken, his control cracking,
when she'd gone into the office earlier.

Hugh's respect for Nick came through strongly.

*I still wish, sometimes, that I'd died instead of them. You
probably do, too. But you kept me out of the gutter, and you and
the police force gave me a purpose to keep going.*

But there came the confession of a worn-out cop who'd seen 'too many drive-by shootings' and found alcohol and sex no longer enough to allow him to forget. A line of cocaine, a dealer who sold that information to others, and 'my life hasn't been my own since'.

He feared for Grace, trusted Nick would ensure her safety. *You're her brother . . .*

She very nearly folded the pages back up, the rest unread. When she read the next sentences, a part of her wished she had.

. . . will you ever get your own life together? I've never seen you look at a woman the way you look at Jo. I didn't really think she was guilty of anything – I was just trying to prod some response from you. If she's right for you, don't throw it away on some rubbish notion of duty . . . The undercover shit is eating you alive.

She forced a long, deep breath, telling herself not to put much credence in the observations of someone in such an unstable state of mind.

She closed her eyes briefly, shut out the scrawl and the confusion it was creating in her. Regardless of whether Hugh was right or way off base, this stuff was too personal, too intrusive into Nick's private life. She understood he wanted her to read it because she'd witnessed those last words of Hugh's, but he couldn't have been comfortable about this.

She began the last page – case-related, a reference to the 'John Doe up the coast' being connected, and the admission he'd been ordered to compromise the Mitchell investigation.

Eliminating her had been one of his orders, presumably. Her skin cold, her fingers stiff, she could scarcely hold the paper any longer as she skimmed the last lines.

If I've done any decent, worthwhile things in my life, they're because of you. The screwed-up shit is purely my own doing.

The writing blurred before her eyes, her chest tight.

What she'd seen of Hugh, and now what she'd read, began to fit together into a whole that made sense. A man who wore a confident, devil-may-care mask to conceal a soul scarred, traumatised; compromised by a stupid action, weighed down by guilt, and desperate to escape it and see things made right. Desperate enough to plan to force a situation in which Nick would shoot him . . . *because that would be quicker and more fitting than what the bastard's minions would do to me.*

Hands shaking again, she dropped the letter onto her desk, went into the bathroom, splashing cold water onto her face, staring at herself in the mirror as water dripped to the basin.

Eyes wide, skin pale, breathing shallow . . . *shit*, she had to master herself, stop the panic from taking over again.

She was safe here, and despite hating the confinement, the drawn curtains, the lack of freedom, she wasn't going to do anything to put herself in danger.

She'd seen what they'd done to Travis.

She would focus on helping Nick; the sooner he sorted out this case the sooner she would be safe, free, and then she could think about everything else. She would go through the camping permits records. She would go through her photos. She would compile everything the others remembered into a list, a map, and look for links. If there was anything she could find to help Nick's investigation, he'd have it before morning.

FOURTEEN

The dark, empty streets of Goodabri contrasted with the Ferris-wheel lights and the noise from the showground at the edge of town, where most of the locals had congregated. Only a few cars stood in front of the pub; other than that, the main street was quiet, except for the cars parked around the temporary incident base. More than he expected.

With only ten minutes to spare before the briefing started, and Hugh's files to look over, he avoided time-wasting conversation by staying in the car, connecting Jo's card adaptor to his laptop and inserting the micro-card.

He found a single, encrypted folder.

Hugh had written in the letter: *Everything I've got so far is in the files. What happened on Pat's birthday will get you into them.*

What happened on Pat's birthday . . . He remembered. Jesus, he remembered, couldn't forget. The day that should have been

Pat's sixteenth birthday, a month after they'd died, riddled with bullets. An empty, grief-filled day.

He'd worked, worked for fourteen hours straight, two shifts on a demolition crew, carting and stacking and tearing apart anything of value in an old factory, working himself to exhaustion to forget . . . so when the police came to question him, it had taken a while for the news of the Zinchenko brothers' deaths in a car-bomb explosion to sink in. The Zinchenko brothers, widely suspected of being the ones who'd killed Pat and Christie, in revenge for Archie Matheson's evidence against Victor Zinchenko.

The box on the screen prompted him for a password.

Another line in Hugh's letter became meaningful.

What happened on Pat's birthday will get you into them. And if you're wondering about that, the answer is yes.

Grinding his teeth, he typed 'revenge'. Nothing happened. He typed 'explosion', 'car bomb', even, thinking of Hugh's warped sense of humour, variations on 'kaboom'. None of them worked.

How would Hugh define it? He'd taken no pleasure, made no black jokes, simply said, as exhausted and dispirited as Nick was, 'That's justice, isn't it?'

Not revenge. *Justice.* Nick didn't agree with the means, could never have condoned it and was damned glad he'd never known, but he could at least understand the young Hugh's actions, when the law had been helpless to act.

Nick typed the word, giving it a capital letter, and the folder opened.

Files . . . yes, Hugh definitely had made records. More than a dozen sub-folders, with notes, images, audio and video recordings.

With little time to spare, Nick copied the folders across to his laptop.

Inside, the main room bustled with people rearranging tables, desks and computers, making more space for those gathered. Some he knew – officers who should have been off-duty, like Matt Carruthers, Dee Edwards and Aaron Georgiou. Murdoch stood at the front of the room, in discussion with two officers in plain clothes. The additional detectives, Nick assumed.

Murdoch beckoned him, and one of the two detectives turned as he approached. Leah Haddad. Her dark hair cut short, no longer quite as skinny as she'd been, and a wedding ring on her finger.

She greeted him with genuine warmth, and a handshake that lasted a fraction longer than necessary.

'It's been a while, Nick. And I would have preferred better circumstances.'

Sixteen years since basic training. Twelve years since they'd worked together in Cooma. And ten years since they'd posed as a couple on the north coast, and arrested a drug-dealing cruise-boat operator. They'd crossed paths briefly a few times since then, but never for long.

'It's good to see you, Leah.' He meant it. Dedicated, ambitious, and hardworking, she had a reputation for getting things done. 'Last I heard, you were in Wollongong.'

'Still am, officially. But I was seconded to Homicide in Sydney three months ago.' She regarded him with concern. 'I heard about the Melbourne business. Is everything all right for you?'

He nodded, grateful for her unspoken vote of trust. She knew undercover ops, had done a stint in the specialist unit and had plenty of connections. Even with most of the details of the Melbourne case still suppressed for operational reasons, she would have her ways of finding out information.

Murdoch called the room to order and began the briefing as Nick expected, with the introduction of Leah and her partner, some respectful comments about the shock of Hugh's death and a summary of the CI team's preliminary report, the forensic evidence confirming their witness statements that a sniper's bullets had killed Hugh.

'Please note that Detective Dalton's name must not be released to the media until his next of kin are informed. Unfortunately, his nominated next-of-kin contact is currently on a London-to-Sydney flight and is unaware of his passing. My counterpart at HQ will meet her at the airport in the morning.'

Her, Nick noted. But not Shelley. Most of Hugh's affairs lasted no more than a few weeks. The only things he'd stayed committed to were his career and his martial-arts training.

Until Grace had come back into his life.

She hadn't answered the phone when Nick had tried calling from Jo's place . . . possibly because she was on a London-to-Sydney flight. Grace used her adoptive parents' surname, not Matheson, so Murdoch wouldn't have connected her to Nick.

'Funeral arrangements will be advised in due course,' Murdoch continued, and although his gaze swept the room, encompassing them all, it finished on Nick, with an unspoken question. A police officer killed in the line of duty traditionally received a full police funeral with honours. Nick gave a very small shake of his head, a gesture only Murdoch would notice and understand.

There would be no such honours for Hugh. The confessions in his letter would have to come out. They might avoid publicity, but Murdoch and others had to be informed.

Murdoch went on smoothly, 'I've accepted the CI team's preliminary recommendations, and as there appears to be a clear connection between Dalton's murder, the stolen weapons and possibly Travis Mitchell's murder, I'm authorising Nick Matheson to continue heading up the investigation, liaising with Detective Haddad. Matheson, I'll hand over to you now.'

Not a popular decision, judging by some of the glances exchanged as he strode the few paces to face the gathering. The shooting death of a second police officer in his presence in the space of three months would only add fuel to the conspiracy theories. But he'd never earn trust or respect from them if he let that sway him.

On the whiteboard, in Hugh's scrawled writing, the tasks allocated at the briefing that morning remained. The routine of working through those, getting reports, following up, would keep them all focused and on task.

'Let's start with Garry Coulter's nephew. We suspect he spent a night or two at his uncle's house in Strathnairn recently. Any progress on his background and current whereabouts?'

'I did some digging this arvo,' Aaron said. 'Bradley James Coulter was sentenced in Sydney last year to nine months for a break and enter. He served the last three months at Glen Innes – it's a minimum-security facility. He's been out since August.'

Nick nodded. 'That's a lead. Mitchell was on a prison work crew in the National Park in July. They did fencing from here,' he traced the line on the map, between the pins designating the crime scenes, 'to here. Find out from Corrective Services the name of every man in that work crew, and exactly where they went while they were there.'

'Will do. I don't have another address for Coulter yet. His driver's licence lists an address in Sydney that was demolished six months ago. Corrective Services has the same one.'

'Finding Bradley Coulter is a priority. Contact Social Security. Do whatever you need to.' Confident Aaron would handle all that, he moved to the next item on his mental list. 'The truck this morning – who ran the rego?'

'I did,' Dee Edwards responded. 'Plates had been changed, so it took a while to find the real rego details. It was reported stolen from a property west of Moree yesterday. The owner came back from a few days in hospital to find his shed broken into, and the truck and two farm bikes gone.'

A truck and two farm bikes. Transport for stolen goods and getaway in one job.

'Who went after the sniper? What do we have on him?'

'Not much, Sarge,' Carruthers answered. 'He rode off on a bike straightaway, across the paddock. Not a powerful bike – the engine sounded a bit dodgy, but he was pushing it hard over rough ground. No helmet, brown hair, brown T-shirt, but other than that I don't think any of us got a good look at him.'

Nick knew the rest of the story, from the hurried updates he'd gleaned at the church. By the time they'd got to the cars, and over the river, the sniper had had too much of a head start.

Aaron had organised road blocks on the surrounding roads, but there'd been no sign of the biker.

Brown hair and brown T-shirt could describe around sixty per cent of the male population of the district. But that description and the dodgy bike engine didn't match the biker Jo had seen the day before Mitchell was murdered.

'Forensics were still processing the site late this afternoon,' Murdoch said. 'They've promised an initial report in the morning.'

Nick read between the lines. If there'd been anything significant – like a dropped rifle, or a piece of clothing or a drink bottle potentially swarming with DNA – forensics would have reported it immediately. Fingerprints on the truck or the remaining guns might be their best hope.

That and good old-fashioned police work. 'Right – Travis was young, and so is Bradley Coulter. It's Friday night. Divide up the pubs – here, Derringvale, Strathnairn and any other communities in the district – take a copy of their photos, and the composite of the man Jo Lockwood saw, and show them around. Find out who's seen them, when, who they were with – names, descriptions, whatever you can get.' He remembered the bright lights at the showground. 'Ask around at the Show, too. Locals and stall holders, especially around the sideshows. If you find Coulter, arrest him and notify me immediately.'

He dismissed them, and Aaron took over handing out photographs and coordinating teams for pub visits.

'You haven't got much to go on yet, have you?' Leah challenged lightly when he joined her and Murdoch at the back of the room.

Although she'd taken a back seat in this briefing, her challenge confirmed that her ambitious nature hadn't changed, and she wouldn't be content playing second fiddle for long. She would want to make it her case, her success.

He only wanted what he'd always wanted – to get criminal scum off the streets, preferably while keeping his name and his face out of the media. So he'd take her contribution, use her skills, work with her to solve the case, and she could have the credit and the media appearances.

'We have a name and a face for one suspect, and a face for another. When we find Coulter, we'll have more. If you've got other leads to follow, I'd be happy to hear them.'

'The one notable omission from your lines of enquiry is into Hugh Dalton himself. Why was he targeted? Why not you or any of the others?'

That question couldn't be answered in a room full of police. Word would get out eventually, but it should be through official statements. He waved Leah and Murdoch into a small office and pulled the door closed behind him.

He could not protect Hugh. Hugh must have understood that, must have expected it, the moment he'd left the letter in Shelley's laptop bag.

But it still felt like a betrayal to say to his commander, to say to a senior detective from Homicide, damning words that could never be taken back. 'Hugh was compromised, initially blackmailed about his drug use, but he'd been acting under coercion for a while. With someone he cared about threatened, I think he got to the point he could see only one way out. He set up that confrontation, intending to provoke his own death, because he refused to eliminate Jo Lockwood as ordered.'

Leah whistled. Murdoch propped on the edge of the desk, arms folded. 'You're sure about that, Matheson? You have evidence?'

'Yes. He said a few things during the fight. And before he came in this morning he arranged for a memory card containing files to get to me; I received it late this afternoon. It seems he wanted it all over, one way or another, today.'

'Why not just hand himself in?' Leah asked.

'Because that wouldn't have protected his . . . his friend. If they thought he was spilling information, she would be endangered. I believe he saw an opportunity to escape an untenable situation, and took it, making it look – more or less effectively – that he'd been thwarted in an attempt to kill Jo. Arguing with me, coming at me with a knife, almost guaranteed that one of us would fire at him.'

'But the sniper at the river silenced him first,' Murdoch observed. 'Where is his friend? We'll need to protect her.'

Hugh's 'friend'. Neither sister nor lover, but the word 'friend' seemed inadequate for the deep longing revealed by the letter. *She's beautiful, Nick, and sane and gentle and so like Christie I kept going up to Brisbane to see her . . . I swear I didn't touch her, but I couldn't keep away.*

Certainty settled in his gut. 'I don't know for sure where she is. But if his next-of-kin contact is Grace Anderson, then that's her.'

'Yes. None of us in Sydney knows her, though. He went out with various women, but he didn't speak of her. Do you know who she is?' Leah asked.

'Yes.' He couldn't let them see the effort it took to speak as if it didn't matter to him. 'She's my sister. Hugh knew her when he was a teenager, and has been in contact with her recently.'

'Your sister?' Leah queried, eyes sharpening on him. 'I shared a house on a job with you for two months, and you never mentioned a sister. I thought you had no family.'

He'd never mentioned a great many things to her, despite the intimacy of pretending to be a couple, and long hours of close proximity.

But he needed to ward off any suggestion that Grace's connection to him compromised his involvement in the case. He needed to stay involved to keep her safe.

'I haven't seen her since I was eighteen and authorised her adoption by her foster carers,' he said, blunt and hard and factual in spite of, maybe because of, how much it hurt. 'She was twelve. I doubt we'd even recognise each other.'

&

Jo studied the maps spread on the table, and compared the highlighter dots to the list on the notepad. Outside, the three men did another tour of the grounds, flashlights casting occasional arcs around the edge of the curtains. At the kitchen counter, Erin added ice to a jug of water. The draft from the overhead fan tugged at the edge of the notepad paper as Jo turned to the second page, and checked off the remaining points on the list.

'Are you seeing what I'm seeing, Erin?'

Erin brought over the jug and a couple of glasses and sat down again.

'I'm seeing a lot of fluoro-coloured dots on photocopied maps. Isn't that what I'm supposed to be seeing?'

'If you were going to commit a crime in this park, or hide something, where would you do it?'

'I don't know. Somewhere isolated, I guess. The old hut on Johnson's Fire Trail. The hollow tree at Sandy Creek. The rock overhang at Diggers Falls. There's plenty of places off the beaten track.'

'Exactly. Each of those places is marked on a park map, even the old state forest map. You can get to them all with a two-wheel-drive. But none of them have facilities yet, and they're off the main park loops.'

'And none of them,' Erin said, finding each place with her finger, 'have fluoro dots on them.'

'Every instance of loutish behaviour we've recalled, every BMW bike rider, every overnight party we've cleaned up after, has been in one of the other parks, or in one of the two camping grounds the prison crew used in July.'

Erin leaned back in her chair, sipping water, her eyes still on the map. 'If they're all the same lot, they don't know this park well, do they?'

'No, they don't. More like tourists passing through than local bush lads. If you were going to murder someone, why risk doing it in such a public place? Leaving the body so close was a risk, too – it might not have been found soon, but it would have been eventually. Anybody who knows the area at all could think of a heap of places it wouldn't be found. I mean, people hiding garbage can be more creative than that.'

A yawn cut her short, and she screwed up her eyes, sucking in oxygen.

'You should get some sleep, Jo.'

'No, not yet. I'll wait until Nick gets back at least. He'll want to see this.' And she wasn't likely to sleep much, anyway, so she might as well stay up.

'Interesting guy, your Nick,' Erin observed.

Frustration and tiredness made her irritable, despite the relative innocence of Erin's comment.

'There's no "my" Nick about it, Erin. He's a workaholic cop doing his job.' *I've never seen you look at a woman the way you look at Jo* . . . Damn Hugh for sticking that into her head. Nick knew she had read it, and now it would hang between them, like whatever else it was that was developing. But still, she had no reason to be cranky with Erin. 'Just don't go imagining something that isn't there, okay?'

'Sorry. I'm just a romantic at heart, and I'd like to see you have a happy-ever-after.'

'I had a happy-for-five-years, which is more than a lot of people get.'

'Would you get involved with someone again? Or was Leon your one and only?'

Damn. If they were going to talk about this, she needed alcohol. Or chocolate. Since she had to keep her head about her, chocolate would have to do.

She tugged open the fridge door and rummaged in the back for the block she'd bought a few days ago.

Erin misread her silence. 'Sorry, Jo. None of my business. You must still miss him.'

Yes, she still missed him. Sometimes. His ready grin, his bear hugs, his full-on energy. But sometimes days passed now without memories catching her unawares. And as she said to Erin, 'It's okay,' she accepted that it was. Really. All of it. Even the days passing without thinking of him.

She broke off a row of chocolate and tossed the rest to her friend. 'As for being my one and only, I don't know that I believe in the soul-mate, one-true-love destiny thing. There's more than seven billion people on the planet. If there were only one for each person out of all those billions, the statistical chance of finding them is pretty low.'

Erin snorted while chewing her chocolate. 'Trust you to bring love down to logic and statistics, Doctor Lockwood.'

'Oh, love's rarely logical. Pheromones and anxiety and ego can royally derail logic and sense.' And loneliness. Yes, that could do it, too. 'But I'm telling you, Erin . . .' She smiled, spoke lightly, as if it were just a bit of play. 'If I get involved with someone again, it will be a guy with a nice, safe occupation, and even safer hobbies. A stamp-collecting music teacher, maybe.' Not a man who thrived on the adrenaline rush of extreme exploration in the wilderness, caving and white-water rafting and abseiling and hang-gliding. And definitely not a man who knew violence and crime and who on any day could be shot in the line of duty. The thought of losing anyone again, of the abyss of emptiness, terrified her.

Before Erin could respond, the thump of footsteps sounded on the veranda as Bruce, Simon and Rob returned from a security check outside. Under their cheerful smiles they all cast her less-than-subtle glances, each assessing her, checking her, concerned for her, doing what they could to keep her safe and calm.

She moved towards the kettle. 'Coffee, anyone? I'm afraid all the chocolate is gone.'

'Not for me, thanks, Jo,' Simon said. 'I'm going to catch a bit of shut-eye for a few hours. Boz and Rob are planning to stay up and watch the cricket. I'll get up again around two.'

Like Nick and Aaron last night, they'd sorted it out between them. Keeping watch over her.

'You go and get some sleep, too, Erin,' she said as she filled the kettle. 'I'll be awake for a fair while yet. I've got some photos to look through.'

Hundreds of images she'd taken of camping grounds, viewing spots and walking trails, potentially to use in brochures and on the website. The chance that she'd inadvertently photographed any of the perpetrators was a very slim one, but she had to do whatever she could. She had to stay busy, fill her mind with something other than thoughts about who was targeting her, and what she would say to Nick when he returned.

෴

The moon hung almost directly overhead, bright in the night sky, as he drove along the gravel road towards the homestead.

After midnight. Another day gone, and he wasn't much closer to cracking this case. But now with Hugh's information, he had some idea of the type of ruthless, violent bastard behind the murders of Travis Mitchell and the Coffs Harbour John Doe.

The type of man who could order multiple murders – two youths, an elderly couple, a police officer, a National Parks ranger – without blinking an eye. The type of man who would punish those who failed to follow orders. The type of man Nick had pretended to be for the past two years.

Hugh only knew a surname – Ramirez – and suspected a South American drug connection, perhaps an attempt to establish one of the cartels in Australia, but he had little hard evidence. Nick had added the two images in Hugh's files to the artist's sketch of the man Jo had seen, and emailed the lot to Interpol for a facial recognition scanning. There might be an answer in the morning.

The dark shadow of a car parked at the homestead gate became eerie as it started to strobe red and blue lights at his approach. He flicked his lights on in response and pulled up beside it.

'It's all quiet here, Sarge.' Nate Harrison, pulling a long shift. 'Now you're here, I have to head back to town, make sure the crowd at the Show go home without trouble. I'll come back out later, check on things again.'

'Did Inspector Murdoch send you?'

'Yes. He said to swing by here a few times, keep an eye on the area.'

Nick left the police lights on as he drove slowly up to the homestead. A curtain flicked at the living-room window, then another at the bunk-room window. The automatic security lights switched on, then the stronger veranda light, illuminating the area in front of the main door where he parked. Out of the car, he paused so he could be clearly seen.

The front door swung open and Bruce waved him inside.

'That your mate at the gate heading off?' he asked, without waiting for an answer. 'Only thing moving out there's been a possum. Over near the fence, though, so it didn't even trip the security lights. Jo's in the kitchen, if you're looking for her.'

Nick glanced into the living room as he passed. Rob still stood at the edge of the window, and the television showed the cricket test match, with the sound muted. An empty crisp packet, two coffee mugs and soft drink bottles were on the side table. No evidence of any alcohol, despite Australian sport-watching traditions. A couple of decent, responsible blokes taking their self-appointed role seriously.

In the ten paces to the kitchen door, he mentally braced himself for Jo's questions. She'd have plenty, after reading Hugh's letter.

At the end of the kitchen table, she looked up from her laptop screen as he entered. She had let her hair fall loose, and the overhead fan wafted strands gently around her face. Above her strong cheek bones, dark smudges of tiredness underlined her eyes, but the smile she gave him, though subdued, had both warmth and welcome.

He smothered the instinct to smile back. He needed to put distance between them, keep it that way. Show her she had no reason to be concerned about Hugh's unfortunate comment.

'Any news?' she asked.

Not enough and too much. 'Nothing definitive. I'm still working through the files.'

Laying his laptop on the table, he opened an image on the screen.

'Have a good look at this and tell me if it's the man you saw.'

He took a glass from the dish drainer and poured some water from the tap, leaning against the kitchen bench while she studied the image.

'Yes, I think it is. It's very like him. This was in Hugh's files?'

Not the answer he wanted to hear. He had to concentrate to swallow the water past the tightness in his throat.

'Yes. His name is Ramirez. He's the ruthless, violent bastard Hugh wrote about, the one pulling the strings. Possibly with connections to a South American drug cartel. Hugh believed he's behind another murder, a few months ago.'

'The John Doe he referred to, on the coast?'

'Yes. A similar case to Travis.'

She grimaced. 'Poor bugger. One's bad enough. Two . . .'

'Hugh believed there may be more. So do I. There are a few young men missing who match the profile. Jo, I don't want to scare you, but if Ramirez *is* part of one of the South American cartels, then he's extremely dangerous. They're moving into Australia, and their methods are brutal. If you can ID Ramirez, you're a problem for him. Hugh was ordered to eliminate you. With Grace under threat, he ran out of options.'

She shoved back her chair and circled a few paces around in the corner between the table and the wall, like a trapped animal with nowhere to go.

He stayed by the bench, letting it take some weight from his aching leg, but more importantly, keeping a physical distance from her. He didn't know how long he could avoid the more personal conversation, but sticking to the case for now gave him some emotional distance, which he needed if he was going to answer the tougher questions.

She came to rest against the wall, hands in her pockets, facing him across the table. 'Jesus, Nick, you do know how to make a bad day worse. Did Hugh have definite proof against Ramirez? Do you?'

'Not yet. But I'll find it, Jo. I know criminals, organised crime, gangs, and how they operate. So did Hugh. From long before either of us joined the police. That's why I've been doing the undercover work for so long.' He drew in a silent breath, and said the truth bluntly, with no padding or preamble to diminish the ugliness. 'I grew up on the docks in Newcastle. My father worked there during the last years of organised crime in the Painters and Dockers Union, when the police were cracking down and the turf wars were bloody and violent. My father was a fighter. When I was twelve, he went to prison for six years for aggravated assault, for some standover work he did for his union mates.'

The only thing confession did was leave a bad taste in his mouth. That, and a frown on the face of a woman he respected.

The fan overhead swung around and around with an uneven *fwap, fwap. Fwap, fwap.*

'That must have been hard on your family,' she said finally.

'Yes. My mother was ill. When she died, I couldn't look after the girls – I was sixteen – so they went into foster care. Teenage boys are hard to place in foster care, so I made sure Pat and Hugh and I managed the house and routine fine, and Community Services let us stay at home. Easier for everyone.'

'What happened to Christie and Pat? How did they die?' she asked finally.

'My father gave evidence against Victor Zinchenko, one of the crime bosses.' A mouthful of water made no difference to the shards of glass in his throat. Show no weakness. Report the facts. Tell her, say aloud, what he had not spoken of for years. 'Pat had just met Christie off a bus, when a car sped past and sprayed them with bullets. They both died instantly.'

'Oh, Nick.'

She offered no platitudes, but he had to look away from the horror and hurt and sympathy in her eyes.

He would have preferred platitudes.

He drained his glass as if it were hard liquor, wished it was. He couldn't act as though it didn't matter to him. Even if he could, she wouldn't have believed it. He sought for the anger within. Anger for Pat, who should have had computers to exercise his geek brain and a future in programming or mathematics or something. Anger for Christie's lively, generous soul, a girl who never made womanhood. Anger now for Hugh.

The sudden buzz of the phone on the wall made them both start.

'Who the . . . ?' Jo muttered, reaching for it, answering it as Rob and Bruce pounded in from the other room.

'Yes, Mal.' She held up a hand to silence them, and Nick loosened the instinctive grip he'd taken on his Glock. 'Shit. Okay, where? Off Blackberry Road? Yes, we'll bring the truck from here. We'll be on our way in five.'

She was on the move the moment she replaced the handset. 'There are several fires on Blackberry Road. Get your gear and the tanker, guys. Mal's sending Craig and his crew out there with the Strathnairn truck. I'll wake the others and get my gear.'

Fires? And she intended to go out, into the wild, to fight them. Logical thought left him as he moved to intercept her at the door, his hand on her arm. 'No. Jo—'

Their eyes met, and she gave his hand a brief squeeze before shoving it aside. 'This is my job, Nick. They're forecasting strong westerlies, high temps and firestorm conditions by morning. If we don't get these fires under control before then, we're all in deep shit.'

FIFTEEN

Her brain whirling madly, jumping about from one thing to another, she hurried down the passage to knock on the bunk-room door. Too much happening, tonight. His revelations. His closed, controlled, denial of emotion. His insistence on protecting her. Her mental checklist of things to gather before she left. Things she needed to tell him, about the case, about his pain, her pain. About the distance he insisted they keep from each other, giving her no say at all.

Too much to say, too little time.

After a brisk knock, a call-out at the door and Simon's confirmation, she turned towards her own room, her fingers already on the buttons of her shirt.

Nick faced her in the passage, tall and tough and all cop in his uniform, the weapons belt bulky on his hips. 'It isn't safe, Jo.'

'Of course it isn't safe,' she said over her shoulder, aware he followed her a few steps and stopped in the doorway. She yanked off her shirt, reached for a merino T-shirt. 'Did you think of "safe" when you carried Hugh into the church with a sniper around?' She didn't wait for an answer, kept talking while she stripped off her light trousers and pulled on her firefighting uniform. 'We can't wait until tomorrow, or there'll be far more people at risk. There's a lot of dry timber between Blackberry Road and Goodabri.'

He spoke firmly. 'You should be protected. Not out there in the open in the dark.'

She sat on the edge of the bed to pull on thick socks. 'There'll be plenty of us, all in uniform fire gear. If anyone's stupid enough to chase a fire to come after me, they won't be able to pick me from the others, especially in the dark.'

'But if he wears fire gear too, you won't recognise a killer. I'll follow you out there in my car.'

He was right about the first part, but she knew the parks staff, the Rural Fire Service crews and the State Forests team. His second statement concerned her more. Tugging at the laces on her boots, she spoke bluntly. 'You'd need a vehicle with better clearance on those tracks. And unless you've done advanced fire-fighting training, or have your chainsaw licence, then you belong on a fire ground as little as I belong in a police shootout.'

She sighed, her bluntness falling away under his steely glare. 'You have to trust me, Nick. I know fires, and they scare me more than human killers. There's three, possibly four fires out there already. No lightning tonight, not much of a breeze to spread spot fires – it's most likely deliberate. If you can get some patrols out on the roads, there's a chance of catching the idiot. Not to mention any other bad guys lurking.'

She watched his usually unreadable face work through several responses before he finally nodded. 'I'll get on to it. We'll get some road blocks up and patrol the access roads. I presume Blackberry Road is on a map?'

'Yes.' She stuffed keys in her pocket, grabbed the satellite phone and GPS, caught sight of Hugh's letter on her desk and handed it to Nick. 'Regarding the other case, I've left some notes on the table – all places we've seen evidence of hoons in the past couple of months. Some instances of illegal shooting, vandalism, that kind of thing. The only ones in this park are in the southern end of it. They're marked on the map. There are also some photos printed out that I took for brochures. They may be nothing, but there are some bikes, vehicles and young men in them. None I recognised.'

He took the letter and hesitated an instant before replying. 'Good. I'll have someone look at them.'

He moved aside as she passed through the doorway, and with the adrenaline starting to pump through her arteries and her sheer relief at being active, doing *something* after days of passivity, she grinned up at him. 'Go catch me a firebug, Detective.'

Along with the State Forest land, National Parks had acquired a Forestry department dual-cab fire-fighting tanker, and Bruce and Rob had it out of the shed, ready to go. By the time she'd grabbed her protective jacket and helmet from her own vehicle, Nick was stowing his laptop in his car, and Simon and Erin were on their way from the house.

The trouble with fires on the east side of Blackberry Road, fanned by a westerly breeze, was getting safe access to them. Sandwiched between Bruce and Rob in the truck on the fifteen kilometre trip out, Jo compared the printed map to her recent GPS recording of the area's tracks and fire trails.

'I've only been on these roads a couple of times since the handover. I don't suppose any of you guys are more familiar with them?'

They topped a ridge, out of the trees, and Bruce stopped the truck while they surveyed the fires, visible in the distance among the trees and smoke. Three, Jo figured, a kilometre or so apart, each already covering more than a hectare. But not crowning yet. Manageable. Probably.

She reached for the radio and reported the situation concisely to the fire communication centre. As leader of the first crew to arrive, standard procedure made her Incident Controller. 'Strathnairn One Alpha, this is East Ridge Control in Riverbank One Alpha. You guys take the first fire, near the Blackberry Road corner. We'll go along the East Ridge fire trail and tackle the second. The third's close to the river, might slow down there. Firecom, we'll need RFS and Forestry crews on alert. If the fires aren't easily containable, they'll spread out of the park.'

'RFS Goodabri Two Alpha leaving base now,' an RFS crew responded. 'Where do you want us, Control?'

Three crews for three fires. That evened up the odds. And the RFS crew could go to the fire closest to the park boundary. 'Goodabri Two Alpha, take the north end of Blackberry Road, at the junction with the river,' she instructed. 'Report in when you get there.'

The East Ridge fire trail wound along the crest of a low line of hills, with dry scrub and rough, rocky ground on either side. Here and there, they caught flickers of red flame, eerie in the dark night.

'Stop here, Bruce,' Jo said, comparing her GPS data to the shadowed landscape. 'We'll follow this old fence line and have a look on foot.'

She and Simon walked in a couple of hundred metres, their boots crunching on thick layers of dry leaves, bark and grasses on the scattered rocks, the ground too rugged to drive the truck across.

'It's crossed the creek,' Simon said, pointing to a tongue of flame visible among the trees, still some distance off.

'Creek's as dry as a bone, has been for weeks, and it's too tiny here to halt anything.' The breeze stirred a branch overhead, and she checked the wind direction, relative to the lights of the truck behind her. The fire front ran roughly parallel to the trail, the breeze driving it directly to it. 'Best bet's probably to back burn up to the fire trail. That will make a decent firebreak.'

'I agree, Captain.'

Simon's grin flashed in the moonlight, a show of support she appreciated.

'Let's get started, then, before the wind picks up any more.'

Heat, smoke, the garish light of flames dancing in the night, the rumble of the pump and the crackling voices on the radio made up the entirety of her world for the next few hours. Hard physical and mental work, hauling hoses, clearing scrub, keeping track of fire and people and constantly assessing, planning, acting and reassessing.

Not the worst fire she'd fought – there had been plenty hotter, wilder and more dangerous than this one – but an overwhelming weariness dragged at her body by the time the firefront reached the firebreak, around sunrise.

With the sun came the heat, and the breeze strengthening to wind blowing ash, smoke and glowing cinders as they worked to extinguish the last of the flames and embers.

Stopping for a few minutes to check in with the other crews, she sat on the step of the truck, gulping water from a bottle in one hand, the radio in her other.

She watched her team as she listened to each crew report. Rob and Simon hosed down stumps to her right; to her left, Erin raked debris away from the base of a tree, and Bruce . . . She caught sight of him just as he staggered backwards a step, raised his hand near his chest, and toppled face first to the ground.

Heart attack, she thought as she raced across the blackened ground with the first-aid pack. He'd been looking grey and tired.

She reached him at the same time Erin did, and let loose a string of desperate swear words as she rolled him over and yanked open his jacket. His T-shirt, like hers, was soaked with sweat, but when she pushed it up, blood stained his skin, seeping from a hole beneath his ribs.

༄

The old guy they'd picked up with a lighter and thirty dollars in his pocket and a few clothes in his swag wouldn't give his name, and emphatically denied that he had anything to do with lighting fires. Nick believed him on that. He didn't believe that he'd seen no-one else in the vicinity.

His judgement distracted, he'd come down too heavy on the man initially, thinking him guilty before realising that he was already spooked by something even scarier than an aggressive cop. So, he'd handed him over to Aaron.

Now, with a hot pie fresh from the bakery across the road, and some soft drink, he went back into the small office they were using as an interview room.

The man had been living rough, and although they'd already given him sandwiches and tea, his eyes lit up at the sight of the pie.

Nick straddled a chair and faced the guy. He couldn't hold him much longer without a formal charge, and there wouldn't be anything to charge him with. Time to be the good cop. 'Listen, mate, I'm sorry I was tough on you when I picked you up. The thing is, I've got friends out there fighting those fires, and I was angry that some pyromaniac idiot had put them in danger. But it wasn't you, was it?'

The man blew on the hot pie filling, and gave a minute shake of the head.

'I believe you.'

He was good at concealing his emotions, but the small inhalation of breath gave him away, and the determined focus on the pie that didn't hide the relief in his eyes.

Nick had run images of recent missing adults, and found no match. From the look of the old bloke's well-worn clothes – patched moleskins, checked shirt and battered hat and boots – he'd seen a lot of miles; one of the men who still travelled the back roads permanently, camping out, working odd jobs here and there for a few dollars or a meal. A man who may have seen more than the dust beneath his feet.

'You haven't committed any crime, so I don't need to know your name or anything about you. As soon as you've finished eating, you can walk out that door. But look, mate, before you go, you might be able to help me with something.' He took up the small stack of photos from the folder he'd brought in. 'I think these people might have been camping out in the bush. Have you seen any of them lately?'

He placed the photo of Travis Mitchell, alive, on the table. The man pretended to concentrate on the escaping filling of his pie, tried not to look at the photo, but after a moment, his eyes flicked towards it. No recognition.

Nick placed the second image on the table. Bradley Coulter. This time, the man's glance skidded across to the photo twice. Recognition? Maybe. He wasn't sure.

The third image – Hugh's photo of Ramirez – drew more of a reaction than the other two, the instant shake of the head too vehement a denial.

Fear.

Fear in the difficulty swallowing a small mouthful of food. Fear in the briefly closed eyes and in the fingers grasping the pie so tight gravy squeezed out.

'I need to find this man. We know he rides a motorbike sometimes – a BMW. I think you've seen him, and he worries you. Is that right?'

No response, at first. Then a sniff. 'He's been around. Over near Derringvale a week or two back. Some blokes I yarned with up at Rocky Creek in the forest reckoned he'd been out there with some lads, shooting. That'll have been a week ago, maybe. There's a cave I sometimes camp in. He was near there this afternoon, by the creek with a mate. Saw them from across the creek. He saw me, and he pointed a rifle and told me to get lost. I scarpered. He's mad, that bloke.'

'What time was that?'

'Couple of hours before sunset, maybe. I walked through the scrub. Didn't want to meet any of his lads on the road.'

'If I get a map can you show me where the cave is?'

'Yeah. Reckon I can. But don't tell him I told you, when you catch him. Don't want any of his lads coming after me.'

'I won't.'

When Nick brought the map in, the man fumbled for his glasses in his pocket and propped them on his nose, studying the map carefully to get his bearings.

'Just give me a minute,' he mumbled, adjusting his glasses. 'Here. Must be round here. Yes. The creek here, where Blackberry Road ends.'

Ramirez. Blackberry Road.

'Nick.' Leah knocked lightly on the open door, grim faced. 'A moment?'

She would only interrupt for an emergency. Preoccupied, he excused himself to the old man, and followed Leah to the main room, where she handed him headphones. 'There's been a call in to Crime Stoppers you need to hear.'

He put on the headphones as she started the audio file on her computer.

A male voice, racing, speed and desperation giving it a high tone, the words strung together in a rush, ignoring the operator's questions.

'We shouldn't have done it. The drugs screwed our heads . . . really weird stuff, sick and weird and wired and I don't know if I remember straight. She's screaming still, in my head. It wasn't right, what we did. She didn't know anything. She begged and begged but we didn't stop. Mitchell deserved it but she didn't. You have to stop him. He'll do it again. He'll make us do it. You've got to stop him. You've got to—'

The call ended abruptly on a swear word, the silence afterwards chilling. With what they knew of Mitchell's death, Nick wouldn't bet much on the caller's chances. Or those of the woman he'd been speaking about.

His gut clenched tight. 'What time was the call?'

Leah wrapped the cord around the headphones with slow, deliberate movements. 'About eleven last night. Crime Stoppers didn't have much to go on, they thought it might be a crank call, until somebody cross-referenced the name. They sent it to us just a few minutes ago.'

'Can they pinpoint the call origin?'

'Not exactly. But a mobile phone, somewhere in this general area.'

Ramirez had been seen near where the fires started, with at least one other man. And a woman, by the sounds of it, had been raped, probably worse, sometime before eleven last night.

Ramirez was on Blackberry Road before Jo had gone out there, he reminded himself. Hours before. And he'd been listening to the fire service radio channel half the night, had heard her voice, calm, professional, capable in her job.

The uneasiness winding around his spine wasn't listening to logic.

218

Around him, the hum of conversation ebbed and flowed as the night shift handed over to day shift and officers arrived and left. The police radio at one end of the room continued the normal incidents for a Saturday morning in a regional area, but the portable radio on his desk kept at least half of Nick's attention.

'Firecom, this is Riverbank One.' Nick stopped breathing, focusing totally on the radio. A male voice, not Jo. Simon? 'Emergency sitrep. Request ambulance and police assistance. Repeat, ambulance *and* police. One injury.'

Emergency sitrep. Ambulance and – he'd emphasised the 'and' – police. One injury. But who the hell was injured? Why was Simon, not Jo, reporting?

A serious injury requiring urgent attention would be Code Red. But Simon had called an emergency, the code for life-threatening danger to the unit. And they'd only need police if . . . He snatched up keys, radio and phone, and ordered everyone in the room, 'East Ridge fire trail. I want every available vehicle heading up there now. Jo Lockwood's fire crew is in life-threatening danger, from something other than fire. Somebody's –' *Please don't let it be Jo. Not Jo* – 'already injured.'

&

They all crouched, partially protected by a low pile of rocks, Simon and Rob half-supporting Bruce while Jo wrapped a bandage firmly around his abdomen over a thick dressing pad. Bruce's blood smeared the surgical gloves she'd taken precious moments to pull on, to protect the wound from the ash and grime that coated her hands. Red against the opaque white on her fingers, it still reminded her too much of yesterday. Twice in two days . . .

Think, she inwardly screamed. Breathe and think how she'd get them safely out of this situation. Help would be at least twenty minutes away.

'The shot came from the north,' Jo told the others. 'We need to get Bruce into the truck, and get out of here.'

'I can walk,' Bruce muttered.

'Not fifty metres on rough ground with a trigger-happy sniper, mate,' Simon said. 'You all stay here, with your heads down. I should be able to get the truck pretty close in, probably to just over there. That will give us cover to load up.'

A good plan, but as captain it was her responsibility to take risks, not his. And she was the most likely target. 'Simon, you can't—'

'I can. Ex-army, remember?' His wry grin softened the way he took charge. 'I've had years of practice in evading snipers. Keep your heads low, and be ready to move as soon as the truck's in position.'

He didn't wait for an okay, but spun up onto his feet and bolted to the truck, his yellow jacket vivid against the scorched ground.

'He's been in Iraq and Afghanistan,' Erin said, flat and toneless, her gaze fixed on Simon, yanking the door open and leaping up into the cab.

Jo blew a breath out, sucked another long breath in. He still had to drive across rough ground, among rocks, tree stumps and fallen logs, with the driver's side north-facing, leaving him exposed to the sniper.

Iraq and Afghanistan. He didn't talk much about his army service. Not generally. Not to her. He was friendly, reliable, solid . . . and elusive when it came to his private thoughts. Interesting that Erin knew something about it.

He'd better not get himself injured or killed. The two of them deserved a chance to resolve whatever was keeping them apart. Whatever she had to do to ensure it, she would do. No matter the risk to herself.

Bruce groaned, tried to move and muttered a curse.

'Hold still, Bruce. Won't be long before we have you out of here.'

Nick had said similar words to Hugh. There had to be a better outcome this time. Had to be. She couldn't do it again, couldn't bear it if . . . No, Bruce had only one wound, to the side, hopefully missing critical organs. As long as he didn't bleed out internally, he had a chance.

Simon brought the truck to a stop about five metres away, keeping out of the sniper's gunsights by clambering across the front seat and out the passenger door.

Together they lifted Bruce and transferred him with some difficulty to lie on the back seat of the truck. Jo hated moving him, but they had little choice.

'Rob, you stay on the floor in the back with him,' Jo said. 'As long as we don't crash, you'll be safer there, and you can watch him. Erin, you too.' She continued, right over their protests. 'Rob, you've got a wife and kids to get home safe to. Erin, if he needs CPR, you can do it.'

She hoisted the first-aid pack in after them, and swung up into the front seat after Simon.

'Head down,' Simon said, shoving the truck into gear.

She grabbed the radio mike off its hook and spoke into it while bent over almost double to keep below window level, one hand against the dashboard to steady herself as the truck lurched across towards the track. 'Firecom, this is Riverbank One. Emergency sitrep. We are evacuating and will rendezvous with ambulance and police at Becketts Corner. Request rescue helicopter for medical evacuation. Repeat, rescue helicopter for medical evacuation required. Read back.'

Firecom repeated the request to confirm receipt, and Jo breathed a little easier. The rescue chopper could fly Bruce directly to a Tamworth or Newcastle hospital – or to Sydney, if they deemed it necessary. Strathnairn Hospital was smaller, with fewer specialists, and too far away by road.

As they approached the fire trail, two loud bangs hit in quick succession off her side of the truck.

Simon swore. 'Hold on, everyone.'

He put his foot down harder and swung the truck onto the trail, hitting it with a thump that banged Jo's chin hard against her knees.

The shots had come from the north; they were now heading south along the trail, the gunman behind them.

She clicked the radio button on. 'Riverbank One to all East Ridge units. Strathnairn One, withdraw to staging area at Becketts Corner. Goodabri Two Alpha, return to base via Cattlemans Creek Road. Do not, repeat *do not*, proceed along East Ridge Trail or Blackberry Road. Rifle shots fired and unit directly targeted in this area. Firecom, please advise sitrep to police.'

More than likely, the police were already listening in. Nick might be listening. She didn't think he was the type of man to say 'I told you so' out loud, but he had to be thinking it. She'd weighed up the risks, made her decision. Would Bruce have been wounded if she hadn't been there? Her gut coiled tightly at the thought, until logic argued that it was impossible to know at this stage. She'd probably have been an easy target, on the radio by the truck, but the sniper had shot Bruce, not her. What kind of rationale was that? Unless he'd planned to pick the others off, one by one, leaving her alone . . . No. They had to get away. *Would* get away.

The truck leaned as Simon rounded a sharp bend, and she sat up straight, the vehicle now out of the line of sight of the shooter. In among the trees she caught glimpses of grey–brown smoke in the sky.

'You didn't mention the smoke ahead.'

'Nope,' Simon said. 'I don't think it's near the trail. Must be a spot from the first fire.'

'The wind's a westerly. The first fire is south.'

'Yeah.'

She kept a watch for it, scouring the fractured views as they twisted and turned along the tree-lined crest road, trying to pinpoint the location.

'Might be one of the gullies,' she said.

'Yeah, I think so, too.'

A couple of gullies ran west–east, carved out of the ridge they drove along. The wind would funnel any fire straight up a gully.

'How much water have we got left?'

'A little over eight hundred litres. Enough.'

Enough to protect them for a short while in a mild burn-over. Mild being a relative term. If the wind picked up any further, if the temperature kept climbing, there would be nothing mild about this fire.

But they couldn't stop, couldn't go back. Bruce's breathing was becoming more laboured.

The road dipped, the top of the ridge to their left an impenetrable rock cliff. She could see the location of the fire now.

'It is in one of the gullies, but it looks like it's not up to the road. We'll be right,' Jo said, as much to encourage herself as those in the back.

Smoke curled over the road, filling the air as they came closer, and Simon slowed the vehicle.

'Keep a watch on the fire, Jo. I have to concentrate on staying on the road.'

The rocky bluff formed a wall to their left, dotted with trees, shrubs and grasses. To their right, off the narrow track, the gully sloped away steeply.

With the binoculars, Jo managed to discern some flames through the smoke. 'The fire front is about five hundred metres away.'

Simon threw her a relieved grin. 'No worries, then.'

Nothing to stop the fire from rushing up and cresting the ridge. But they'd be through before then. Ten, fifteen minutes later, it would have been a different story.

Crossing the head of the gully, Simon rounded a bend . . . and slammed on the brakes.

Rob shouted, Erin gasped and Jo braced herself as the truck skidded slightly in the gravel. They came to a stop a metre from a large eucalypt tree, fallen across the road, the trunk a good two metres in diameter, branches and leaves thick around it.

No way around the tree, no way over it. They'd have to cut it up with chainsaws.

And they'd have to do it before the fire reached them.

SIXTEEN

At the staging area at Becketts Corner, the Strathnairn National Parks fire truck arrived at the same time as the third police vehicle from Goodabri.

Nick had an ordinance survey map spread on the car bonnet, the large sheet giving a much clearer idea of the area than the small screen of his GPS. A huge area of wilderness for a killer to hide in, and only two access roads into it.

'Is Blackberry Road clear of fire?' he asked the firefighters. 'Can I send police cars right along it?'

'Yes,' one of them said. 'They need to stay alert, in case the wind changes or the bastard bug lights more, but all three fires are mopped up.'

'Carruthers and Edwards, you take Blackberry Road. Georgiou and I will take the fire trail. We'll meet up down here—' He broke off as the portable radio gave its warning hiss before Jo's voice came through.

'Firecom, East Ridge Control emergency sitrep. Road blocked by fallen tree at grid . . .' A voice in the background spoke, and then she repeated the map grid numbers. 'Medium fire approaching along gully approx four hundred metres west of position. We will attempt to clear the road for ten minutes, then withdraw approximately five hundred metres north.'

'Jesus,' someone muttered.

The wind tugged at the map under Nick's clenched hands. The same wind sending a fire towards a trapped crew. Towards Jo. His initial relief at hearing her voice earlier evaporated, leaving only cold dread. He couldn't battle a fire. Couldn't threaten it, throw it to the ground, shoot it.

A yellow-clad arm reached over the map for the radio.

'Firecom, this is Strathnairn One. We will proceed to assist Riverbank One.'

Nick took the radio from the ranger's hand. Disregarding protocol, he depressed the button and spoke. 'East Ridge Control, police assistance proceeding from north, ETA twenty-five minutes, and from south, ETA ten minutes.'

He couldn't battle fire, but he might be able to protect her – protect the crew – from other dangers.

'All units proceed with extreme caution,' Jo ordered, her voice sharp with a rough edge of desperation. 'Obstacle intentional, not natural. I suspect at least two malicious individuals, north and south. Repeat, danger north *and* south.'

Obstacle intentional. Some bastard had felled the tree *on purpose* to trap them.

'Carruthers, Edwards, get onto the trail from the north, make sure it's clear and escort them out that way if necessary.'

The long way around, more than thirty kilometres; they'd take a while to get there. If Jo and her crew decided to risk escaping back that way, they'd not only be running the gauntlet of the sniper, they would be taking a wounded man needing urgent medical attention much further from it. A tough choice for them to make.

'If you see anyone on the trail,' he added, 'arrest them. Do whatever you need to do to apprehend them.' Looking as grim as he felt, Carruthers and Edwards nodded in understanding.

He folded the map up roughly. 'Aaron, we'll follow the tanker in from the south. When the ambulance arrives, it should come after us as far as it's safe.'

The whole way down the narrow dirt track through the dry, scrubby bush, Nick kept immediately behind the tanker, willing it to go faster, letting loose a string of swear words when smoke obscured visibility, slowing them down further.

The minutes ticked away, and the fear they'd get there too late pounded against the thin thread of his control.

Choking smoke, ash and burning leaves swirled all around, and the growing rumble of the fire and the roar of the wind almost drowned out Simon's chainsaw. The fallen ironbark – felled at the base by someone else's saw – was huge and tough, its many branches obstructing the road as effectively as the trunk itself.

A cough racked Jo's burning lungs as she and Erin dragged each end of a three-metre branch off the road.

Flames licked at the base of a tree fifty metres away.

No more time.

'Tell them to quit,' she shouted to Erin. 'We're getting out of here.'

At the truck, she sprang up into the driver's seat and started the engine.

'How are you doing there, Bruce?' she asked, talking for reassurance rather than expecting an answer, twisting around to see into the back. His chest rose and fell slowly. 'You just keep breathing, Bruce. You're going to be fine. No other outcome is permitted. You got that clear?'

His closed eyes flickered behind his eyelids, mouth twitched a fraction. 'Nag, nag,' he muttered.

Conscious, coherent, and attempting humour – all good signs.

The flashing lights of the Strathnairn truck approached through the smoke on the other side of the tree, shadowy figures moving in front of it. Simon, Erin and Rob were all closer to it than to her. But no way could they get Bruce out of her truck and over the hurdle of the tree in time.

'Strathnairn One, position not defensible. Take three Riverbank crew and withdraw immediately,' she ordered over the radio. 'I will retreat approximately five hundred metres north.'

'Jo, you can't—'

Craig? Simon? The call broke off with an oath as a fireball swept up the slope, exploding the pile of cut-off branches near the road into a wall of searing flames.

She repeated her instructions loudly. 'This is East Ridge Control in Riverbank One ordering immediate evacuation in nearest vehicle.'

She thrust the truck into reverse, straining to see anything of the track behind her in the swirling smoke. She began edging backwards anyway, using the rocky wall of the bluff to one side as a guide to the track's location. Glancing continually between the rear-vision mirror, the bluff and the fire, she caught sight of a figure in a yellow jacket and helmet running through the smoke. She stopped and he leaped up onto the truck's running board, yanking the door open.

Nick, not Simon. *Nick*.

'They're all on the other truck,' he said. 'Go.'

The radio crackled. 'Control, we have three Riverbank crew on board. Evacuating now.'

Nick breathed heavily beside her.

Anger and relief battled it out in her mind, neither winning. As she started reversing again, she let him have the anger. 'What the *hell* did you think you were doing? Don't you know what fire can do? You could have been killed or badly burned. You were damned lucky.'

'Yes. I *was* lucky.' Calm, steady, not arguing. When she turned to see past him to the mirror, he was watching her, and answered her, eye-to-eye. 'I was thinking that I couldn't let you do this alone.'

As if she didn't have enough to unsettle her already, his straightforward honesty erased her anger but threw her brain into confusion. No, she didn't want to do this alone. Any of it. As for Nick . . . she focused on edging the tanker backwards, checking the driver's side mirror, the rear-vision mirror, anywhere but him.

'How's Bruce?' he asked, after a moment.

'Breathing,' came the rasping reply from the back.

Breathing. Just. But he'd made it this far and she had to believe that he'd be okay. Probably. As long as she could get them out of danger. As long as the maniac shooter wasn't waiting just down the road. As long as the ambulance or the rescue helicopter made it in time.

'Get over the back and keep him alive,' she murmured to Nick.

Twenty metres in front of the truck a wall of flame poured over the dirt road, lighting the straggling bushes on the bluff, the heat and wind surging it upwards and outwards. Her foot heavier on the accelerator, she reversed as fast as she dared.

⁑

Despite his height and size, Nick managed to climb over into the back of the cab without hitting Bruce, prone on the seat. Crammed into the small space between the seats, he began an assessment – pulse faint and thready, breathing shallow and uneven, complexion pale and skin cool to the touch.

Not good. But not desperate yet, either. He'd lasted half an hour or more since the shooting. Blood soaked the wound dressing, and still seeped from his side, but not in any volume. Although in his late fifties, his physical fitness had to give him more of a chance.

'It bloody hurts,' Bruce muttered, as Nick examined the wound.

'I know. I've done a couple of these myself. They hurt like hell.' And, crouched awkwardly as he was, the shredded muscle of his thigh still throbbed with pain, almost three months on.

The truck slowed to a stop. The little he could see outside the window showed blue sky and sunshine visible through the thinning smoke.

'I can turn around here,' Jo said over her shoulder. 'Just as well, because I hate reversing.'

Half a kilometre or more in a large vehicle down a narrow hillside track with severely limited vision – no easy task for anyone. Yet that had been her only words of complaint. Staying with Bruce and the tanker in the face of fire and snipers, then making that dangerous backwards drive, had taken courage and sheer guts. No ordinary woman, Jo Lockwood.

The three-point turn accomplished efficiently, they moved forward at a faster speed. 'We're out of that fire range, guys,' Jo said. 'You can breathe easier.'

'Riverbank One, this is Firecom,' the radio interrupted her. 'Emergency rescue helicopter is en route, ETA ten minutes. They will attempt landing four hundred metres south of Diggers Creek junction.' A grid reference followed, and Jo passed a map over the seat to him before she answered.

'Wilco, Firecom. ETA thirteen minutes. Confirming grid—' She recited the numbers, while Nick quickly found the place on the map. Beyond where Bruce had been shot. Closer to where Carruthers and Edwards would join the fire trail.

With his portable radio tuned to the police channel, he instructed the other two vehicles to rendezvous with them there.

'It's a cleared paddock,' Jo explained when he'd finished. 'Probably the closest decent landing place. The chopper must have already been out this way, to get here so quickly. It's based in Tamworth, serves the whole north-west region.'

Bruce had drifted into unconsciousness again, and Nick kept fingers on his pulse, willing it to keep beating.

'Not long now, Bruce. The paramedics will have pain killers for you.' Déjà vu. Yet he had far greater hope now than yesterday with Hugh. Hugh had died, probably bled out, within minutes. Bruce had only one wound, to the side, and if any major organs or arteries had been hit he'd have been dead already.

The strain on Jo had to be immense, but she kept driving, kept going as she'd done throughout the night and morning, and not once in any of her radio calls or his brief conversations with her did he detect panic or loss of composure.

The distinct sound of a helicopter rose over the rumble of the engine.

'There she is, doing a flyover,' Jo said. 'Only a minute or two and we're there, Bruce.'

Bruce made no sign he'd heard.

Within three minutes Nick surrendered his place in the cab to a paramedic. Within five they had Bruce out, on a gurney, fitting a cannula for a saline drip.

Jo remained in the truck, reporting in. Superfluous to the medical needs, and aware they were in a large open paddock edged by thick bush, Nick scanned the land around.

'Did you see any vehicles, bikes or people as you flew over?' he asked the helicopter pilot.

'Your blokes, coming in from the north. They're not far away. Bloke on a quad bike, heading west cross-country, probably a couple of klicks from here. Other side of that other road – Blackberry, is it?'

Nick nodded, processing the information. A quad bike heading west across country – a needle in a haystack without air surveillance, and he'd not be able to get that into the air in time. He knew the rough lie of the land from here – much of the park to the west and north, and only a few roads and tracks through the scrub and farmland for a hundred kilometres in those directions.

On a quad bike a rider could easily carry a chainsaw and a rifle, maybe could have travelled between the site of the shooting and the place where the tree had been felled. There could be two of them, but the fact that this one was travelling west, away from them, eased a fraction of Nick's concern. He radioed instructions for nearby cars to be on the lookout and pursue.

Jo's door opened, and she swung down to the ground, wavering slightly as she landed so that she had to steady herself with a grip on the door frame.

Nick held out a hand to her. 'You okay?'

'Yes.' She made a brave effort at a smile. 'Just a shaky leg there for a moment.'

Shaky leg, and reaction to the stress setting in, if he read the tenseness in her body right. But she walked steadily enough over to where the paramedic worked on Bruce, gave details of his name and age, and the circumstances of the injury.

'Where will you take him?' she asked.

'The John Hunter Hospital in Newcastle,' the medic told her. 'I know it's further for his family, but until we know what injuries there are, it's better that he has access to a good range of specialists.'

'I'll let his wife know. They've got a daughter in Maitland.' She took hold of Bruce's hand. 'Did you hear that, Bruce? I'll phone Mary. I'm sure she'll be down with you as soon as she can. And you'll probably get to see Rachel and your scamp of a grandson in a day or so.'

Maybe Bruce didn't hear her reassuring words, maybe he did. Nick had vague memories of his own state by the time the ambulance arrived after he'd been shot in Melbourne; in too much pain, too groggy to open his eyes, too weak from blood loss to move, just aware of movement and voices and one kind, direct voice who'd spoken to him by name, as if he was there. He had no idea if he'd actually responded, or only thought he had.

Jo moved aside so the paramedics could transfer Bruce into the helicopter. The sun, moving up in the sky, beat down on them, the freshness of the early morning long gone, and she took off her helmet and shrugged out of her firefighter's jacket, tossing them on the seat of the truck.

Long hours of hard, physical work and perspiration made her T-shirt cling to her, and strands of damp hair stuck on the sides of her face and neck, mixing with ash and smoke grime.

The sooty, sweaty dirt did nothing but highlight the strength of character in her face, and her beauty, authentic and sincere. No pretence, no being anything she wasn't.

Unlike him.

His chest as tight as if he'd been shot again, he took off the jacket he'd borrowed from Simon in those mad, desperate seconds before the fire struck, concentrating on folding it neatly and avoiding watching Jo's throat as she gulped water from a bottle.

But when she offered the bottle to him, her hand trembled noticeably.

'Sit down,' he said, taking the bottle before she dropped it.

She perched on the step of the truck, the shakes setting in. She hugged her arms around herself in a fruitless attempt to stop them.

'Sorry. Reaction, I guess.' Her teeth chattered but she tried to grin regardless. 'Can't imagine why.'

He played along with the gentle humour. 'A murder attempt, an injured friend, a couple of bushfires, a too-close call, and all before breakfast – nope, nothing there to stress anyone.'

Behind him, the rotors on the helicopter started to whirr and he heard car engines approaching on the track. He spared only a quick glance to check they were the police cars.

Another shudder racked her, but still she tried to joke. 'Actually, the driving backwards was the worst. My spatial sense is lousy.'

He wanted to touch her. One of those reassuring touches on the arm, the hand, that she gave so naturally to him and to others. Hell, he wanted to take her into his arms and hold her until she stopped shaking.

He did neither, just pulled some words from the mass of unfamiliar thoughts crowding his mind.

'You did an amazing job, Jo.'

Her head jerked up, all humour gone. 'No, Nick, I didn't. I came out here despite your warning not to. And now Bruce is being flown to hospital.'

He *had* warned her not to go. But how much of that had been about legitimate operational considerations, and how much about his personal fears for her? And how much of the motivation for his mad dash over the fallen tree, past the burning debris, had been a rational decision to protect a witness and an injured man from snipers, rather than pure desperate need to be with her?

'You made a professional decision based on facts and probability. I had no right to try to stop you. There was no evidence, no firm reason, to assume a specific danger for you.' Not then. He had plenty now.

'Yeah, well, firm reasons or not, Bruce was shot instead of me.'

'I'm not convinced you were the target.' Worried, yes. Convinced, no. 'Bruce is close on six foot tall, and a big man. Even in fire gear, it would be hard to mistake him for you. Even assuming it's the same group, they may not have known you were out here.'

'Oh, come on, Nick – anyone tuned to the radio channel knew. I was broadcasting my position, right down to grid references, all night.'

'Without mentioning your name. They'd have to be pretty close to the local community to know who captains which tanker. Other than Bradley Coulter, we've got nothing so far that suggests they have local connections.'

She fell silent, but not necessarily in agreement.

The chopper's rotors spun at high speed, sending a hail of dust and dry grass over them as it rose off the ground and moved forward, making a graceful curve as it gained height to fly over the two police cars pulling up nearby.

Nick waited with Jo in the shade and relative protection of the fire tanker while Carruthers and Edwards came across to join them.

Their first question was, 'Who was hurt?'

A blunt reminder for Nick that everyone knew almost everyone here. With no phone reception and no names used over the radio, it had to have been hard on the locals to know one of the crew had been injured, but not which one.

Jo rose to her feet. 'Bruce Lockyer. He was shot.'

Carruthers swore. 'Bozza. Shit. How bad?'

'They're taking him to Newcastle.' She didn't elaborate. On a scale of severity, Newcastle ranked just behind Sydney. That said enough.

Beside him, she wavered a little on her feet. She had to be close to the end of her endurance. If he was honest about it, so was he.

'We'll take you home, Jo. It's probably best if you pack some things and stay somewhere safer in Strathnairn for a few days.'

She nodded wordlessly, and climbed back into the tanker to collect her gear.

He beckoned his colleagues a few metres away. 'Dee, I need you to drive us back to Jo's place and then to Strathnairn. We'll leave the tanker here to be picked up later. Matt, there's a site down by the river that needs to be checked. That man we picked up earlier saw our key suspect, Ramirez, and another man there yesterday afternoon, and a report to Crime Stoppers suggests a sexual assault took place in this area – I suspect in the same place. Meet Aaron there, and be careful.'

As soon as she was seated in the back of the police vehicle, Jo used the satellite phone to call Malcolm in the comms centre.

'Simon's spoken with you? Good. They're taking Bruce to the John Hunter. Can you phone Mary and let her know? She'd probably rather hear it from you than me. But look, tell her that he was aware and talking some of the time. Joking, in fact. Yes. Thanks, Mal. I'm going to take a few days off. Seems wisest in the circumstances. I'll give you a call on Monday.'

He looked over from the front when she finished the call, but she'd let her head fall back against the seat and closed her eyes. Not resting; creases tightened around her eyes and she bit her lip, drawing in a deep breath, then another. She fought for composure, and he gave her silence and space to find it.

With Dee driving, the radio a familiar, non-urgent chatter in the background, and his phone without a signal, he closed his own eyes, trying to still the thoughts racing around and around.

He needed order, and clarity, and unemotional strategies and decisions.

Order? As soon as he had Jo somewhere protected in Strathnairn, he'd find Leah, Murdoch and a large whiteboard, and they'd map out everything, including the information from Hugh's files and this morning's events. Then they'd prioritise, plan, and allocate teams for a multi-pronged strategy.

Clarity? He let his instinct feel around what he knew, and what Hugh had gathered. Ramirez was building a gang. Drawing together restless, unemployed, disconnected young men. Rewarding them with drugs and money. Binding them with violence. Making them punish those who transgressed, symbolically and viciously. According to Hugh's sources, the John Doe had tried to run – and lost a foot. What about Mitchell? A hand cut off for what? Stealing? A nervous Coulter adding a gun to the cache at the last minute fitted that scenario.

Ramirez manipulated them, owned them, watched them carry out his orders – and thus left no DNA or fingerprints of his own. And they may have gang-raped a woman last night.

Immediately he thought of Jo, of her vulnerability, and he jerked open his eyes. Unemotional strategies? No. Where Jo was concerned, he could not be unemotional.

There had been a time when he'd gone out with women, had friends, occasional lovers. Then he'd gone into covert operations full-time, living lies for ten years, these past few constantly walking a thin and dangerous line between playing cold-blooded, controlling, immoral bastards, and actually becoming one. With his cover potentially blown in the aftermath of the Melbourne job, he'd asked to return to normal duties. But he knew there never had been, never would be, any vestige of 'normal' within himself.

So, he would do nothing about his feelings for Jo other than protect her, by doing his job. She'd loved a good man, probably still grieved for him, and she deserved far better than a cop who'd forgotten the little he'd ever known about how to function in ordinary society without donning a mask and hiding behind a lie.

Dee turned through the homestead gate. The old house with its white-painted timberwork verandas shone in the bright sunlight. A rambling country home, with small birds flittering through the bushes, serene and peaceful.

The bushfire and shooting priorities had reduced the number of patrols during the night and morning, and despite the undisturbed appearance, he planned to be cautious.

'Check around the back,' he told Dee. 'I'll go with Jo through the front.'

Jo got out of the car, her face set, closed, her voice lacking emotion as she said, 'It won't take me long to pack.'

She was almost stumbling as she walked beside him across the grass. But still she pushed herself on.

Now they were within range, his phone beeped with multiple text messages and he slowed, his attention split between it and Jo.

He'd missed three calls. He opened the text from Leah, and stopped dead as he read it.

Brock not home in Sydney. Airline says not on flight. No message, no response on phone.

Already at the door, Jo unlocked it, pushed it open, and he called for her to wait, sprinting across the drive and up the steps after her.

She was at her bedroom door when the scent hit him. Faint, but that distinctive mix of urine, shit, blood and death.

She pushed open the door as he reached her. Frozen, rigid, a strangled cry dragged from her throat.

'No!'

She turned, straight into him, burying her face in his chest, banging her head, her clenched fist against him in desperate denial, sobbing 'No, no, no, no,' with each hit.

He held her tightly against him, keeping her from looking again, from seeing Bradley Coulter's battered and bloodied corpse sitting on her bed, tied to the wrought-iron bedhead, her camera hanging around his neck, his eye sockets a mangled, bloody mess where his eyes had been.

SEVENTEEN

In the shower room in Strathnairn police station, Jo stripped off her grimy, stinking clothes and stepped under the water, turning it hotter, letting it pour over her to warm her and wash away the cold shivers that kept racking her body. Uncaring how many litres of water she used, she stayed there. Eventually warm enough to think, she squeezed soap from the dispenser into her hands, scrubbed and scrubbed her hair and her body to be free of soot and dirt and the taint of death.

Nothing could scrub her memory of the nightmare of Bradley's corpse on her bed.

The soap dispenser empty, she leaned her forehead against the tiles beside it, suds swirling down the drain at her feet.

Breathe. Control. Let emotion drain away like the suds. *Breathe. Control.* Hold it together.

Someone tapped on the door, and Dee called, 'Are you okay in there, Jo?'

'Yes.' The word scraped in her throat.

'I've left some clothes just here for you. Sorry, it's only my gym gear. But it's clean.'

'Thank you.' She made an effort, pushed herself away from the wall. 'I'll be out in a minute.'

White T-shirt, navy track suit. Jo pulled them on, the warmth of the clothes doing nothing to stop her shivering in the airconditioned bathroom. With wet paper towel, she wiped dust and soot off her boots before lacing them up over Dee's cotton socks, then stuffed her clothes into the plastic bag Dee had left for her.

In front of the mirror, she finger-combed her wet hair into some semblance of order, and stared at her haggard reflection. Dark smudges under eyes still red from stinging smoke. Or maybe from crying.

She had to make sure she didn't fall to pieces again. Almost everything after walking into her bedroom blurred in her memory, only a few things remaining clear. Nick's strength, holding her up when her knees buckled, steering her from the house, keeping a supportive arm around her when she dry-retched into the garden, protecting her head with his hand as he guided her into the rear seat of the car.

And she remembered the harshness of his voice as he'd called for back-up.

He'd stayed at Riverbank, sending her to Strathnairn and safety with Dee as soon as others arrived. She didn't know how long he'd be out there, whether she'd see him again today, or who would be advising her of the next steps from here.

Squaring her shoulders, she opened the door and went to find out.

***

'Bloody hell,' Leah said, joining him in the doorway of Jo's room. 'They sure did a job on him, didn't they?'

'Yes,' Nick agreed. 'That phone call last night – it might have been him. The timing fits. And that could be a phone in his pocket.'

'CSOs can check it. But yes, it's likely.'

He'd seen all there was to see, but he didn't move away from the doorway. What they'd done to Coulter angered him, but what they'd done to Jo affected him at least as much, maybe more.

They'd not completely trashed her room, but they'd tossed things off her bed, searched to find her camera and scarves to tie Coulter to the bedhead, and left drawers and wardrobe open. A vicious, nauseating invasion of her space, her privacy, and a warning and threat to her safety.

The blue robe she'd worn the other morning lay crumpled on the floor, a large dusty boot print dirtying the bamboo pattern. An image that would haunt him, as if they'd trampled on, violated, Jo herself.

They would, if he couldn't protect her from them.

He had to find them, before they found her. Had to push his feelings aside and get on with his job, work with his colleagues to track down and catch the bastards.

'I've notified the coroner's office and called in the forensic team,' he told Leah. 'They're on their way, should be here in an hour or so.'

'Good. He didn't die here, by the looks of it.'

'No.' He'd made his observations already. There'd have been more signs of struggle, more blood, if they'd killed him here. 'There's dirt and leaves on his clothes, and on him. See his hands? He clawed in the dirt.'

'We're looking for another crime scene, then.' She turned away, and they moved to the fresher air outside. 'Have you heard from Aaron yet?'

'A radio report that they're searching the bushland near the river, close to where one of the fires started.' Frustrated by the necessary inaction of waiting, he leaned his elbows on the railing, pointing his phone in different directions, searching for a signal.

Leah propped against the veranda rail beside him. 'I'm worried about Shelley. If you told me that she could be in on this, if you thought she was compromised somehow, like Hugh was, I'd have more hope for her.'

'I doubt it.' He'd already considered that, dismissed it. Shelley had passed Hugh's letter on; not the action of an accomplice, or an enemy.

'Maybe she's just run home to her mother,' Leah suggested, grasping at straws.

'Would you? She's young, ambitious, just earned her detective badge.' Like Leah herself had been, years ago.

Leah sighed. 'No, I was too driven to run home. It would have been an unforgivable weakness. But I wasn't one to fall in love, either, and Shelley was. I had lunch with her last week.'

Neither of them voiced the other possibility, but confirmation of it came within minutes: the radio notification a coded request for back-up, the text message from Aaron that beeped onto Nick's phone moments later more precise.

Homicide located. GPS coords following. Prelim ID DC Shelley Brock.

A heaviness weighing in his chest, he passed the phone to Leah, staring at the tree shadows on the lawn as she read it, his thoughts echoing her bitter, defeated swear word, repeated again and again.

'Do you want to go, or stay with this one?' he asked her. She'd known Shelley, worked with her, even if only for a few weeks.

'I'll go.' The catch in her voice didn't stop her. 'I owe it to her, Nick. But you've done all that's needed here – the uniforms can wait for forensics. You're dead on your feet, so I'll drive. We'll have to go via Goodabri, though – I need to phone my boss, and you'll need to inform Murdoch. And get some caffeine.'

In the ten minutes at the Goodabri incident room, Nick reported Shelley's death to Murdoch in Strathnairn, scalded his tongue on strong black coffee, and left a message with the witness protection unit requesting protection arrangements for Jo.

'You think she's that much at risk?' Leah asked as they returned to the car.

'Yes. I think the sniper shooting this morning, and Coulter's corpse, are both specific warnings to her – they know she can ID Ramirez, and they want her to know fear before they take her. So until we arrest them all, I want her well away from here, in witness protection.'

'Probably wise. She won't thank you for it, though.'

No, Jo wouldn't thank him. She'd been restless enough confined to her office, and her home, for just a couple of days. Days, weeks, perhaps even months inside a rented apartment in another town or city, far from the bush she loved, denied contact with friends and family, with nothing meaningful to do – she'd hate every moment of it.

She'd probably end up hating him.

But when he saw what they'd done to Shelley before dragging her body into the bush not far from the river, he knew Jo's hatred would be a price he'd willingly pay a thousand times over to ensure her safety.

⁂

The interview room was daunting enough even though Dee left the door open, Jo hadn't done anything wrong and she knew she was welcome to wander to the meal room and the bathrooms whenever she wanted to. She couldn't imagine being closed in here for hours and being questioned about a crime. She didn't want to imagine it.

She'd done every Sudoku puzzle in the stack of old magazines Dee had left, and at least half the crosswords. She also knew more about the personal lives of famous people she'd scarcely heard of than most people knew about hers.

But she kept ploughing through the articles, desperately trying to keep her mind off the horror in her bedroom, never quite succeeding. Hours ticked away, and although Dee kept stopping by with upbeat words, Nick hadn't returned, and the station was eerily quiet, only a few staff remaining.

Her mood improved slightly when she heard Erin's voice with Dee's in the corridor, and she was out the door in seconds.

Erin dropped the duffel bag she carried and gave her a hug. 'I'm so glad you're all right,' she said. 'What a shit of a day for you.'

'I'm okay. But yes, a shitty day.' An understatement of epic proportions.

'Nick just called,' Dee said. 'He's on his way back now. He'll be here in half an hour or so.'

This time, Dee's smile was forced, and she hurried away without any further comment, leaving Jo wondering what had upset her.

Erin handed her the duffle bag. 'I gather you couldn't bring anything from your place, so I went shopping for you. Clothes, PJs, toiletries, phone charger and . . .' She drew a small plastic bag out of a side pocket and waved it like a trophy, 'Leaf tea and infuser.'

Jo had to blink away tears. Erin had solved one immediate problem for her; even if she could have retrieved some of her own clothes, the thought of wearing anything that had been in her bedroom made her skin crawl. 'You're an angel, Erin. Thank you.'

Erin grinned cheekily. 'Don't thank me until you see what I chose. I went for plain and functional – well, except for the PJs; I thought you needed a little bit of spoiling – but all the receipts are in there, so if you don't like anything, I can return it.'

'When I can get to a computer, I'll transfer some money to repay you. I've only got my driver's licence and ten dollars on me.' Another logistical problem to deal with. She'd have to ask Nick if her wallet was still in her room, or if it had been stolen. Where she'd be staying the next few days, how to access her money, replacing cards and documentation if necessary, salvaging some belongings and finding a new place to live without nightmare reminders . . . all issues she'd have to deal with, soon. Before she could get on with her life again. Assuming the twisted, murdering bastard criminals were arrested so that she *could* get on with her life again.

The nausea that had plagued her all afternoon made her gut do another somersault.

'Come into the break room,' she said to Erin. 'I'll make a cuppa. Unless you have a bottle of Scotch in here,' she added, 'in which case we'll drink it.'

Unlike the interview room, the staff break room had windows to the outside world, a few armchairs as well as the standard-issue table seating, and some photographs decorating the white walls. A fraction less sterile and claustrophobic, and the armchairs definitely more comfortable for her weary body.

Erin stayed fifteen minutes, and in quiet conversation, mutually avoiding the worst of it, they caught up on some of the happenings of the day. Mal was driving Mary to Newcastle; they expected news of Bruce's condition this evening some time, after surgery.

When Erin left, Jo drew her knees up and curled in the armchair, closing her eyes and breathing deeply, slowly, to calm her mind. Positive, constructive thoughts would get her through. She could, *would* cope with everything. She had the support of friends, dedicated police officers investigating the case, and chances were they'd remove the threat to her soon.

She'd find another place to live and settle into the district properly; instead of marking time at the homestead, she'd make her own home.

⚜

From the doorway, Nick saw her dozing in the chair, arms around her tucked-up legs, head resting against the cushion. Safe and whole, and peaceful, at least for now. He needed to keep her that way.

She'd had an exhausting and traumatic night and day, and he would not disturb her much-needed rest to tell her about Shelley.

He pulled the door closed quietly, flipped the sign to 'Meeting in Progress' and continued down the corridor to brief Murdoch on what they had found.

Accepting the chair Murdoch offered in front of the desk, he gave a concise report on the visible injuries he and Leah had observed.

Murdoch didn't interrupt, and he stayed silent for a long moment when Nick finished, his forehead resting on steepled fingers. 'There are days I hate this job,' he finally looked up and said. 'She must have suffered a great deal.'

Nick's mouth felt like sandpaper. 'Yes.' Even without full forensic examination, that much had been grimly obvious. 'From the phone call, it sounds like there was a group of them, and they were demanding information from her.'

He could almost see Murdoch's thought processes, racing through the possibilities and implications. 'We can presume they knew of the relationship between Dalton and Brock and that's why she was targeted. How well known was Dalton's connection with you?'

'Not very. We were in the same intake for basic training in Goulburn, but after that we were posted to different areas. I trained with him at a dojo sometimes when I was working out of Sydney, but other than some shared history, we don't really have a lot in common. Until this week, I hadn't seen him for a couple of years.'

'What if Brock told them about his letter to you? Would she have revealed that?'

He considered it briefly. 'If they were asking questions like that, then yes, it's likely. I don't believe that she understood the significance of it, and she didn't know me.' So she'd have had no reason to endure pain to protect him. His gut tightened at the thought that she might have tried.

Murdoch paced to the window. 'If they even suspect that Dalton passed information to you, that would make you a target.'

'Possibly.' It didn't rate high in his concerns. At any moment in the past ten years his cover could have been blown and he'd have been a dead man. 'There's no evidence of it.'

'Nevertheless, with two murdered police in two days, we're not going to take chances. You need to be rested and alert, so I'm ordering you off-duty, Nick.'

'I can't go yet. I still have to arrange—'

Murdoch overrode his protest. 'You *can* go off-duty and you *will*.'

A direct order Nick would have to obey. Or find some way around.

'I value your dedication, Nick,' his commander continued, resuming his place at the desk, back ramrod straight and tone formal, 'but I will not have you risk your health and safety or that of your colleagues, or the public. You are not working alone on this case. You will remain off-duty for at least twelve hours and you will get some rest.'

Nick didn't object. No use denying that he *was* exhausted. If he'd been sharper, he'd have handled Murdoch better, not pushed him into pulling rank.

'We still need to arrange protection for Jo Lockwood, sir. I can't get her into witness protection until at least tomorrow.'

'There isn't a safe house available in the region at present for Jo. However, as this case has now become a major incident, there are additional officers from Sydney and the region and twenty trainees from Goulburn due to arrive shortly. They'll be accommodated in the Police Youth Club. It will be basic, but I think it's the safest solution for Jo to stay there with them tonight. Given the possible threat to you, it might be wise for you to stay there, too.'

Nick nodded in agreement, his decision made before Murdoch had voiced the suggestion. Whether intentionally or not, the Inspector had given him what he needed – relative peace of mind about Jo's safety overnight, and enough assistance in protecting her that he could allow himself a few hours' sleep.

Assuming he could switch his mental activity a notch or two below frenetic in order to let himself sleep.

Murdoch's phone rang, and Nick rose to leave but the Inspector signalled him to stay as he answered it. A senior officer, going by the number of 'sirs' Murdoch used.

'That was Assistant Commissioner Fraser,' Murdoch said when he'd finished the brief call. 'He's confirmed the establishment of a formal Strike Force to investigate the murders of Brock and Dalton. There's a media release going out now announcing it, and HQ is flying up a DCI to lead it. Goodabri doesn't have sufficient resources, so we'll move the incident centre back here.'

The decision came as no surprise. He'd discussed the likelihood with Leah already. Two murdered detectives made it a high-profile, priority case. Although it meant he'd no longer have charge, the additional resources a declared Strike Force brought might make the investigation quicker.

They needed it resolved quickly. *He* needed it resolved quickly. The escalation of violence overnight – the torture and murder of both Bradley and Shelley within a few hours of each other – suggested a significant psychological shift in the gang. The bodies of Travis Mitchell and the John Doe had been hidden; but for the dingo and Jo's observation skills, Travis would not have been discovered for weeks or months. Not so with Shelley and Coulter.

Ramirez had cultivated in his gang a taste for torture and murder, an addiction to that power and contempt for the police.

What alarmed Nick most – what set every muscle in his body tense for action – was that the placement of Coulter's tortured, blinded remains in Jo's bedroom was a clear and confident message that they intended to do exactly the same thing to her.

EIGHTEEN

The trouble with drifting to sleep wasn't so much the sleeping, but the waking. Bad dreams danced in her subconscious until she jerked awake; nightmare images of faces with empty eye sockets laughing at her from the depths of a fire.

Over-used muscles had stiffened while she dozed, protesting when she pushed herself out of the armchair and hobbled to the sink. She splashed her face with cold water and drank two glasses of it, the cold liquid refreshing the staleness in her mouth.

Someone had closed the door, so the break room was empty, but she could hear a few voices down the corridor somewhere, and went to find out if Nick had returned, and if there was any news.

She was just a few steps down the hallway when Nick walked out of a room and saw her. His attempt at a smile didn't work, overwhelmed by the tightness in his face as he motioned her to follow him into his office. He offered her a chair and waited until she was seated before drawing his own chair up to the desk.

'I'm sorry I kept you waiting so long this afternoon. And I'm sorry that I have more bad news to give. I don't know if you've heard, but Shelley Brock didn't get onto the plane last night.'

Her heart had sunk at 'more bad news'; at mention of Shelley's name dread tightened fingers around it. 'She's not all right, is she?'

'No.' His voice hardened, his dark eyes clouded, world weary. 'Her body was found this afternoon, near where one of the fires started. Her death . . . it wasn't quick, Jo. Forensic and autopsy reports will take a while, but what we saw is indicative of multiple injuries, and multiple sexual assaults.'

The chill settled in her bones again, and those fingers dug into her chest, made it hard to breathe. He hadn't used the blunt, more emotive terms. Gang rape. Torture. Murder.

Her brain couldn't, wouldn't accept it. Her voice shook. 'I saw her. Spoke with her. About Hugh. She loved him even though he couldn't love her. The taxi arrived out the front and she dashed out, saying she was late.'

She clutched her arms around herself, tried to resist the urge to rock back and forth. She wanted to be held, to draw strength from him, but he sat behind the desk, unmoving. Not unmoved. Something beyond the clamour of her selfish need registered the whites of his knuckles clenched around a pen, and his eyes. Eyes that had seen Shelley in death. Could still see her.

She had to pull herself together. Deal with it, be strong and help him, not drain from him. What could she remember that might help?

'She thanked me for trying CPR. She said I could trust you, that Hugh thought the world of you. Then she remembered the letter just as she rushed out the door. I didn't see the taxi driver.' She was babbling, and nothing of use. 'I'm sorry.'

'The taxi was left behind the depot. But we can't contact the driver who was rostered.' He exhaled a slow breath, as if trying to temper frustration.

What could she say to support him?

'This isn't a densely populated region, Nick. You're going to get a break soon. Someone will know something, have seen someone. Even if they've been camping out in the wilds, they'll have to buy supplies somewhere. People around here often remember strangers.'

'We'll start publicising the photos we have of Ramirez and Coulter and Mitchell. If we can find out who they've been hanging out with, that will help.'

'And it will help if I get out of your way and lie low for a while. Where do you recommend I go?'

'There are additional police arriving this evening, including a bus-load of cadets from Goulburn. They'll be accommodated at the Police Youth Club. I want you to stay there as well, for tonight, Jo. It won't be luxury accommodation, but it will be safe.'

Mats on the floor with a bunch of young trainees. She could do that. 'I don't need luxury. You said for tonight. What about tomorrow?'

'I'm making arrangements for you to go to a safe house under police protection for a while.'

The determined edge in his tone put her on alert. No consultation, just a decision made for her. Not his usual style with her. 'Can you define "a while"?'

He held her gaze, unflinching. 'Until it's safe.'

'Why don't I just go and stay with my mother in Sydney for a few days? Her apartment block has good security.'

'No. Under no circumstances contact your mother, Jo. Or anyone else in your family, or friends. No-one. No phone calls, emails, nothing.'

The severity of his orders scared her. 'Are you talking about witness protection?'

'Yes.'

'I can't just disappear, Nick,' she argued. 'I have friends. A family. I speak to my mother at least once a week. If I vanish, she and my brother will assume the worst.' Her mother would be sick with worry, her brother would be pounding on the police station counter, demanding action and answers.

He tapped his pen against the desk a couple of times, taking a moment before replying. 'You could phone one of them from here. Tell them you might be out of contact for a week or so. Give them Inspector Murdoch's name as a contact. He'll be able to pass on any urgent messages.'

She sighed, too tired to argue. 'Thank you. I guess I'll need to switch off my mobile.'

'Yes, and keep it off. Better still, leave it here. And I mean it about no email or internet, Jo. Your laptop wasn't on the table where you left it. You have to assume they'll have access to sites you regularly visit, your usernames and passwords, and that anything you do electronically could be tracked.'

Panic overtook tiredness for a moment, her family in her thoughts. But it dissipated slowly as she worked through the implications. Other than email addresses, she kept her family's contact details in her head, not on her laptop. And none of them used email addresses with identifying surnames. Her mother scarcely used email at all, preferring phone contact. Todd might be on social networks, but Jo had steered clear of them.

Nevertheless, she'd ask Todd to go and stay with their mother for a few days.

That contingency planned for, she considered her own situation. No access to her belongings, no contacts, no work, no internet.

She tried to smile, but didn't quite succeed. 'I'm going to be bored stupid, aren't I? Any chance of some books to read?'

'I'll arrange some for you. What would you like?'

She preferred to browse, to take time deciding about books, but he had a multiple murder case to work on and she'd taken up enough of his time. She thought quickly. 'Maybe something chunky that will keep me going for a bit? Science, philosophy, history? Or perhaps a novel or two – but nothing gruesome or depressing, please. Cheerful ones. Where the good guys win and everyone lives happily ever after. I think I'm going to need to believe that.'

ᘔ

He'd been twelve, the first time he'd stepped into a Police Youth Club. Twelve, self-conscious in the unfamiliar karate uniform, angry, and convinced he didn't belong, that they'd toss him out after a good beating as soon as they discovered he was Archie Matheson's son.

He carried that same tension between his shoulderblades twenty-five years on, walking into the Strathnairn Police Youth Club. In his youth, he'd come to belong, to trust in individuals, to bring his siblings into the classes and safety of the local club. But the taint of the places he'd been since then, the bars, drug warehouses and clubs where people fought to maim and kill, the things he knew that no youth should know, the things he'd seen, pretended to be . . . he'd come full circle, and no longer belonged.

In the main hall, a half-dozen young kids in martial arts uniforms hauled gym mats from a storage room, dragging them into low piles. Nick scanned the layout of the place; change rooms and a fitness centre to one side, and stairs leading to a second storey above, looking over the main hall, with maybe an office or two and an activity room. A sign near the entrance indicated that squash courts were on the other side of the central block. A kitchen at the rear of the hall. Three exits, that he could see: the front one they'd come through, a side door and a back door out of the kitchen.

A man wearing traditional white uniform and a dark blue *hakama* carried a broom through the breezeway between the change rooms, his attention on the kids. The shaft of envy hitting his gut at the sight of the formal pleated trousers of the Aikido uniform he'd once worn took Nick by surprise. So did the flood of memories when the man registered their presence and glanced across, recognition dawning in his eyes at the same moment Nick placed his face.

In a subtle transformation of focus and purpose, David Thomson laid down his broom, straightened his back, and bowed. 'Sensei! Welcome. I'd heard you were in town, wondered when you'd have time to visit.'

Out of the corner of his eye, Nick caught the enquiring glance Jo cast him. Behind David, his young students scrambled into a crooked line, not quite sure what was going on, or of etiquette, but one of the bigger students bowed so the others followed suit.

Nick almost froze. He'd been a different person when he'd taught David in Sydney. Eleven years younger, inspired after six months training at the head dojo in Tokyo, and optimistic that he could, maybe, make a difference. Something stirred in his gut – yearning, nostalgia, he wasn't sure what it was – but despite the grimy uniform he'd been wearing for days, and the preoccupations and worries crowding his thoughts, he returned his former student's bow as if he too stood, grounded and balanced, in a *hakama*.

Respect for them, not for himself. The man he'd become over the past ten years made a mockery of the principles he'd once tried to live by.

'David. It's been a long time.' He indicated the class, watching with curious, wide-open eyes. 'So, you're teaching now.'

David grinned, coming forward to shake his hand warmly, as easy and as carefree as Nick remembered him. 'Yes, I moved up here a couple of years ago. There was no-one else, so I started teaching. I still aspire to your discipline and skill, Sensei.' He held out his hand to Jo. 'You must be Jo. Keith Murdoch said you'd be coming over. I'm David, the centre manager, and occasional Aikido instructor. Nick was my teacher, some years ago when we both lived in Sydney. I hope he will be again.'

'I haven't trained properly for a while, David. I'm very rusty.' And unfit. Not so much in body, because he'd trained hard in other fighting forms until his recent injuries slowed him down. But unfit in mind, in spirit.

Before David could utter an invitation to train with him, Nick changed the subject and asked directly, 'Do you mind if I take a look around? I need to ensure that Jo will be secure here.'

David gave little sign he'd noticed the lack of courtesy. 'Of course. I've been told to expect about thirty officers and cadets. They should all fit down here. There's an empty office upstairs. If you'd like some privacy, Jo, you're welcome to use that.'

'Thank you,' Jo said, and Nick thought he detected some relief in the words. She'd been remarkably uncomplaining, all along. Yet this upheaval of her normal life, the very threat to it, had to be unsettling in the extreme. Instead of somewhere quiet and peaceful to retreat to, he was throwing her in with a mob of strangers.

The office, although small, was uncluttered and recently renovated, with fresh paint and carpet, blinds on the internal windows, a desk and filing cabinet in a corner. And a solid lock on the door.

'I'd take this, if I were you,' he suggested to Jo.

She nodded. 'It might be quieter. And I'm more used to being alone.'

The upper level overlooked the hall on one side and squash courts on the other, with seating for spectators. In the first court, a couple of men had just finished a game. The second was empty. He walked along the balcony to check the last courts. They'd been converted into one room, the floor fitted with a large mat centred in the space, and a portrait of Aikido founder Morihei Ueshiba on the far wall.

Up here in the viewing area, he had not technically entered the dojo space, yet he had to consciously restrain the instinctive bow that etiquette and habit required.

Perhaps Jo had seen his instinctive movement. 'You used to teach Aikido?' she probed.

'I've taught a lot of different forms of fighting. Many of them incompatible with Aikido's minimal-harm principles.' Not relevant to the situation now. Not a priority to consider the reasons for the unsettling nostalgia. He changed the subject briskly. 'There's a fourth exit down there, past the last squash court door. I'll check to make sure it's alarmed.' And he'd sleep upstairs, near the office she'd be in. Four exits were good from a fire safety perspective; four *entrances*, one of them away from the main hall area, were less safe from a protection perspective.

Voices came from downstairs, and within a few minutes the hall was busy with police cadets and their duffel bags. Some Rotary Club members arrived with a portable barbecue, which they set up out the front of the building, and a couple of cars of officers from other areas arrived shortly after. With over twenty armed police in the building, and four apparently reliable and dedicated Rotarians in their sixties nearby, Nick considered it safe to leave Jo for a short while.

In the motel room he'd scarcely seen this week, he quickly peeled off his dirty clothes, washing them under the shower as he cleansed sweat, ash and dirt from his body. He wrung his clothes out and draped them over the shower screen; in the harsh summer heat, they'd likely be dry by the morning.

Stacked in the corner of the room, the four removalists' boxes he'd brought from the storage unit in Sydney contained the limited elements of the life he led between undercover jobs. Not much. He rummaged in a different box for the clothes he'd bought after his release from hospital, and dragged on jeans and T-shirt.

Showered, dressed and shaved, he felt marginally better than dead beat. Preparing for whatever the next few days might bring, he packed an overnight bag, and then he ripped open the tape on one of the storage boxes. Books, Jo had asked for, but the shops in Strathnairn closed by five on a Saturday afternoon, and few were open on Sunday. He hadn't labelled the boxes properly, could hardly remember packing them over twelve months ago, but there were books somewhere.

Coffee maker and basic kitchen equipment. No, not that box. When he opened the second box, the memories he'd been struggling to supress all evening surged back. On top, wrapped in tissue paper and still in its precise folds, lay the indigo *hakama* he'd put away years ago. Hardening his heart, he put it and his dojo clothes to one side.

Under his Aikido books and the few texts he'd kept from his university studies, he found the small pile of paperback books he'd lugged from one rented apartment to another until he'd finally put them in storage. Some Terry Pratchett novels that had belonged to Pat. A couple of Ursula Le Guin books that Christie had struggled with on first read but declared 'awesome' after the second.

He drew out one of Grace's *Little House on the Prairie* books and flicked through a few pages, the black-and-white illustrations meticulously coloured-in with pencil blurring in front of his eyes before he snapped it closed it again and replaced it in the box with his mother's Bible and the theological texts she'd bought in her search for answers.

Not much left of his family, and all of it from a used book store.

But he didn't have time to remember, and what good would it do, anyway? He packed the Pratchett and Le Guin books into his bag for Jo, and on the spur of the moment he added in his Aikido uniform. Rebuilding his physical fitness made sense. He didn't allow himself to consider anything more than that.

He had a job to do, killers to arrest and charge and a witness to protect. Being ordered off-duty wouldn't stop him doing it.

༪

One of the things Jo appreciated about smaller towns was the way people simply pitched in when need arose. In most communities, the Rotary or a similar service club could start up a barbecue, chop up salads and feed steak sandwiches to thirty or more hungry police officers with little notice.

With nothing else to do, and feeling out of place among the young cadets, Jo offered to help in the kitchen. The rhythm of slicing lettuces and tomatoes, buttering bread, and the easy, getting-to-know-you chat with Rotarians Helen and Frank distracted her thoughts from darker subjects, at least for a while. Maybe someone had told them why she was there, because they never asked, and they avoided any mention of the murders.

They found common interests easily enough, mostly to do with the land and environment. By the time they'd cleaned up, she had invitations to speak at one of the local LandCare groups about her PhD research on microbats, and to visit Frank's garden of local native plants. Fairly typical of the welcome and genuine interest in her work that she'd experienced in the last four months from the locals. She liked the town and the broader community, could see herself staying some years here.

Assuming the killers were caught. Why the hell did she keep remembering that caveat, and the threat to her?

Out in the main hall, Keith Murdoch and a dark-haired woman – one of the Sydney detectives, someone had said – were setting up a computer projector for a briefing. After being introduced to Detective Leah Haddad and invited by Murdoch to attend the briefing, Jo found a place at the back of the room and leaned against the wall. Not that she wanted to hear and see graphic details – she had enough fodder for a lifetime of nightmares in her head already – but if her life and the lives of others were at risk, the more information she had, the safer she might be.

Nick came in through the side door during Murdoch's introduction, standing to the side and scanning the group. Looking for her, she realised, as he made his way across the room and stood beside her, his attention, after a fleeting, drawn smile at her, on the briefing. But she was glad he was there, by her side.

Murdoch acknowledged her in his outline of the key events, and she felt herself flush as most people turned to take a look at her. Some curious, some with sympathy, some just impersonally processing relevant information about the what, who, where

and how of the crimes. She might as well be wearing a label –
Exhibit 1: National Parks Ranger.

Yep, that would be the National Parks ranger who regretted
changing her roster and going in to work on Wednesday. On
Tuesday, too, come to think of it. If she hadn't seen Ramirez,
she might have avoided the bullseye on her forehead.

She studied her boots while images of the murder victims
were screened. Gutless of her, but she couldn't quite rally the
scientific neutrality to view them unemotionally. Not when the
killers apparently planned to do the same kinds of things to her.

Nick touched her shoulder, murmured, 'You okay?'

'Yes,' she whispered back, trying for lightness. 'I never did
like horror movies.'

Being stuck in a real-life one was even worse.

There was little in the briefing she didn't already know –
until Leah Haddad mentioned the old man, and where he'd
been picked up. In the middle of everything else today, she
hadn't heard about that.

'One of the sites we'll have you cadets search tomorrow is
here,' Leah said, using a laser pointer on the projected map.
'According to an informant, our chief suspect was here yesterday
afternoon. It's only a few hundred metres from where Detective
Brock was found.'

'Older gentleman, with a white beard and a gruff manner?'
Jo asked Nick in an undertone.

'Yes. Do you know him?'

She nodded. 'Met him in that area a few weeks ago. Nice
old guy – a bushie from way back.'

She'd shared a cuppa and a long yarn with the old man, deep in the bush, learning about the district from his rich knowledge of history and stories. If he was out there, alone, he'd be almost defenceless against thugs.

'Leah arranged a lift for him to Strathnairn,' Nick added quietly, as if he read her concern. 'He'll stay in town for a few days.'

One weight off her mind, at least.

'The bus will leave for the search site at six in the morning,' Leah was saying. 'You need an early start, because it's over an hour out to the site, and it's going to be hot later in the day. Jo, if you wouldn't mind, can you tell us something about the terrain and if there's anything they should be wary of?'

A little more notice would have been good, but this was her work, her expertise and she appreciated that recognition. Far better than being a witness or a target.

She walked through the assembled police to the front, and accepted the laser pointer from Leah. The projected topographical map detailed familiar ground. 'The river in that area is close to the north-east boundary of the National Park. The other side of Cattlemans Creek Road is State Forest. In the park, there is a series of low granite hills with creeks in between that flow into the Nyland River. However, none of the creeks are flowing at the moment, and the river is very low. The river flats aren't very wide at this point, and there are low, rocky rises on either side. Be aware that there are a few old mine shafts in this area of Diggers Creek, but that's a little way up from the junction where you'll be working.'

She drew breath and swallowed, wishing she'd grabbed a bottle of water earlier. 'As far as other things to be wary of

– it's going to be stinking hot tomorrow. Drink plenty of water tonight, so you're fully hydrated, and take several litres *each* tomorrow. Also, because we had a wet winter, there's a lot of dry grass and undergrowth, and it's a bumper year for snakes. I appreciate that as you're looking for evidence you'll be watching the ground in front of you, but please do take extra care, particularly among the debris from last year's floods. Most of the snakes here are highly venomous, and you'll be a long way from medical care.'

At least they'd be properly dressed for it, in solid boots, long trousers and protective gloves. But she'd check with the supervising officer that their first-aid kit included long, wide bandages suitable for snake bites.

She got caught after the briefing was over, answering more questions than expected from the cadet's supervisor, so that when she looked around for Nick she couldn't see him. With those in the hall starting to arrange gym mats and preparing to settle for the night, she found a small mat for herself and carried it upstairs.

Nick stood near the office door, his bag at his feet, staring at the phone in his hand so intently that he didn't hear her approach.

'Nick?'

He looked up swiftly, too swiftly to conceal the pain darkening his eyes.

'What's wrong, Nick?'

He shook his head as if to clear it. 'A message from my sister.'

NINETEEN

Murdoch's text message simply read: *Grace Anderson trying to contact you –* and a mobile phone number.

But there was nothing simple about it. Nothing simple in the mix of raw emotion assaulting him. Emotion he'd convinced himself he'd left behind, dealt with, close on two decades ago.

Definitely nothing simple about dialling that number and talking to Grace. When he'd dialled her home number last night, emotion dulled by sheer adrenaline overload, even then he'd been ashamedly relieved when she hadn't answered.

Facts. Straightforward facts. 'My youngest sister, Grace, is trying to contact me.'

Jo waited, watching him, as if she expected more. Of course she expected more. That one sentence hardly explained anything. Anyone but Jo and he'd have left it there. Wouldn't have even revealed that much. But he needed her to understand. Needed, perhaps, to draw on her strength.

'I told you I haven't seen her since I was eighteen.' *Breathe, control, focus.*

He expected her to ask why. Instead, after a long moment, she said, 'That must have been hard for you.'

Hard? He'd done what he'd had to do, for Grace's safety. No regrets. The cost to him – the emptiness, the sorrow – had been bearable, for her sake.

Never show weakness. He'd blown that rule multiple times, with Jo. But to earn trust, he had to give trust, and he trusted her. She knew almost the worst of him already, and she hadn't judged him harshly.

He had to steady himself before calling Grace. Perhaps explaining to Jo, putting spoken words to the tumult of memories and emotions and arguments in his head, would give him clarity and the emotional composure to make the call. Maybe Grace already understood how willingly he'd ripped a hole in his heart to protect her. Maybe Jo needed to understand how far he'd go to protect those he cared about.

'Let's go over here where it's quiet, and I'll explain.' He walked away from the noise and the curious eyes of those below, to the balcony overlooking the squash courts, his mood drawing him along the railing to where they looked into the dojo. The lights from the main hall hardly reached here, only a few security lights glowing in the dimness.

Arms resting on the railing, Jo shoulder-to-shoulder beside him, he began. 'The day Christie and Pat were killed, I was visiting my father in prison. He'd called me in to tell me he planned to give evidence. Vinchenko was powerful, influential, and my father feared reprisals. Word must have already got out,

270

though, and I was too late. I identified their bodies there at the bus stop. Then I went to Grace's foster home. I hadn't been entirely happy with the carers, and I knew she was putting on a brave face. Anyway, I packed some clothes for her, and took her as far away from Newcastle as I could afford train and bus tickets for.'

She'd cuddled into him the whole way, crying a little, sleeping a little, small and fragile under his arm. Trusting him completely, reliant on him to protect because his father hadn't.

Facts, not emotion. 'I left her with the Child Protection office in Toowoomba and told them it was too dangerous for her to stay in Newcastle, to find somewhere safe for her. They did. I made sure she was happy before I signed the papers allowing her adoption by her foster parents a year later.'

'Were you close to her?' Jo asked quietly.

'Close?' he repeated. Yes, 'close' probably described the powerful mix of affection and love and fraternal protectiveness he'd felt for his sister. 'She was the youngest by several years, small for her age, a tiny doll of a girl. We were all close. When our father went to prison, we Matheson kids became targets. We stuck together and we looked after her. But Grace was the most vulnerable of us, and after the others died, I had to get her out of there.'

He cleared the roughness in his throat. He'd been staring ahead into the dusky dojo as he spoke, aware of Jo's presence, telling his story to her, yet not quite courageous enough to watch her response.

Within his field of vision, her hand, tanned and calloused from outdoor work, lean and strong, closed over his.

271

'I've never had to deal with the kind of violence and loss you've experienced, Nick. I've never had to make such difficult decisions. Nobody should have to, especially not a teenager. You haven't seen her since you consented to her adoption?'

He took her hand in his, brushed his fingers gently over hers, over the back of her hand, as if the connection with her decency could ground him and counter the violence of his life. And then he drew his hands away, abruptly, as if it had been no more than a mere touch between friends.

'No, I haven't seen her. For a long time I couldn't be sure that there was no threat. Grudges last a long time in that kind of culture.' Instead of connecting with hers, his hands gripped the cool metal of the railing. 'When I started working undercover, my background and the fact that I had no close family or friends made me a suitable person to infiltrate gangs and underworld mobs. So I kept it that way.'

She turned to face him. 'You're a remarkable man, Nick.'

'No, I'm not. Two of my siblings are dead. Three, if you count Hugh.' He was never sure if he did, in fact, count Hugh as a sibling. 'And now Hugh has involved Grace in this nightmare.'

Jo sighed, and said gently, 'So, go call your sister, Nick. If you need a friend afterwards, you know where to find me.' She brushed his cheek with her lips, as easily as Christie and Grace used to, and walked away, leaving him alone.

The screen on his phone glowed in the dim light, and his finger hovered over Grace's number. One touch, and he'd be dialling it. Just as soon as his pulse stopped battering his ear drum.

The drumming banged some sense back into him. He would dial it. But not on this phone. Not on a phone connected to him where the contact might be traced. The fewer people who knew of her relationship to him, the better.

He went downstairs, borrowed a cadet's phone and took it to the privacy of the unused squash court.

Grace answered immediately, as if she'd had her phone in her hand. A woman's voice, not a girl's, but retaining the hint of a lilt like their mother's.

'It's Nick, Grace.' The words came out almost even.

'Nick! God, is it really you? Are you all right? They told me about Hugh. But I don't have your number, and the Inspector wouldn't tell me anything about you. Are you okay?'

'I'm fine. It's good to hear your voice, Grace. I'm . . .' he trailed off, then forced himself back on track. 'How did you know where I am?'

'Hugh phoned me, days ago. He was in a strange mood, he said something about your new job, something about arranging it. Sometimes I can't tell when he's joking and when he's not, and it worried me. He hasn't let me get in touch with you, Nick, even though I wanted to. He said you couldn't contact me.'

Hugh had *arranged* his posting here? It couldn't be possible. Or could it? There'd been a distinct lack of available positions on offer when he'd spoken to HR. Hugh wasn't the only officer in the police force who disregarded rules and policies at times, preferring the informal network of mates and favours. Something else to look into, later.

'Were you there? When he was shot? Are you all right?'

'I was there.' He swallowed, and narrowed in to the most significant issue. 'He was worried about you, Grace. About your safety. So I'm worried about you. Where are you? In Brisbane?'

'No. I flew into Sydney this morning, and they met me and told me about Hugh. I'm going to stay in Sydney for a few days. His lawyer is here, and his apartment, and there will be things that need doing.'

His brain raced through options, possibilities, strategies. He had contacts in Sydney, police and others who owed him a good turn. 'Don't stay in his apartment. Stay in a quality hotel, somewhere secure at least for tonight. I'll pay for it, if you're short of funds. And I'll arrange someone to stay with you.'

'I'm not in his apartment. I don't know how much he told you, Nick, but we weren't lovers. Never were. Anyway, he had a new girlfriend. One of his colleagues.'

Nick kneaded the tension in the back of his neck. 'I know. Shelley Brock. Listen, Grace, she was murdered last night.' He heard his sister's gasp, hated scaring her. 'I don't know if there's a danger for you, but he spent time with you, and if they are harming people who were close to him . . . I need you to take extreme care. Tell me where you're staying, and I'll ensure there's extra protection there.'

Whether they'd been lovers or not, according to Hugh, Ramirez and his gang had believed it. Even with Hugh's death, Nick couldn't be sure the danger had passed.

He noted the name of the hotel and her room number. Not far from a dojo he knew well. He could have people he trusted watch her floor tonight.

'I'll be careful, Nick,' Grace promised. 'And you have to be, too. It's past time I saw you again. There's so much more to say. I've missed you.'

'I've always missed you.' Saying it aloud, at last, dissolved some of the hard lump in his throat. 'I'm sorry, Grace. I only ever wanted you to be safe.'

She sighed, not bothering to stop the tears showing in her voice. 'I know that. I understand. There's nothing to forgive, never has been. I'll see you soon, okay?'

'Yes.' He disconnected the phone. He'd lived too much of his life unsure about tomorrows. And he still couldn't promise his sister that he'd see her again.

⌘

Jo lay on a gym mat on the floor in the corner of the office and contemplated the ceiling. Downstairs, most of the police were sleeping, a few talking in low murmurs audible under the hum of the airconditioning.

Silk pyjamas, Erin had bought her. Soft and smooth and sensuous on the skin, and oh, so unsuitable for sleeping on a gym mat with thirty cadets nearby. She smiled at the thought of them. Maybe sometime soon she'd pamper herself and wear them, but not tonight. She'd changed, instead, into a camisole and cotton pants lighter and cooler than Dee's track pants.

Nick had been in a while ago. He brought her some books, gave her a brief summary of his conversation with his sister and said he'd be working for a while. Then he'd wished her goodnight and walked away, closed, distant, as if they hadn't shared anything at all. Worrying about the case perhaps, all detective.

She'd tried to read for a while but couldn't concentrate.

She might as well close her eyes, focus her mind on relaxing and try to sleep.

Breathe in. Relax. Breathe in. Relax. Don't think of bodies, or fires. Don't think of the pain in Nick's eyes. Think of beautiful things, peaceful things. Early morning sunlight shafting through trees. A little joey kangaroo, small and fuzzy, peeking at the world from its mother's pouch, warm and safe. Safe. Protected. Nick's arms around her. Strength. Comfort.

She woke suddenly, striking out at a nightmare, panic driving her heart rate fast and confusion clouding her thoughts about where she was until she recognised the room, different in the darkness with only ghostly, dull shadows from the security lights and the moon shining through the skylights.

She checked her watch. Just past midnight. Her heart rate still raced and the images from her dream still lurked, only barely in the background. She needed to wake up properly, clear them from her head, before she could rest again.

Muscular aches dug tentacles deep into her legs, shoulders and spine as she rolled over, almost making her groan aloud. Damn, but the after-effects of hard fire-fighting could *hurt*.

She'd have to stretch before she totally seized up. She had the space in this office, nothing and no-one to trip over. Standing, she reached upwards, bent slowly over to touch her toes. At least half of her muscles protested. Another gentle stretch upwards . . . she looked through the internal windows. Nick's bag was out there, and the mat he'd found. His boots stood beside his bag, neat and straight. But he wasn't there.

She swore under her breath. He needed sleep even more than she did. He'd been walking around looking like a ghost for days. And she would feel better, safer, knowing he was nearby.

She went in search of him, but didn't have to go far. Small sounds came from the martial arts room: the brush of bare feet on a mat, deep, even breaths.

The skylight above him shed enough illumination into the room for her to see him from the balcony. The full, pleated trousers of his Aikido uniform swished softly as he worked through an exercise with a wooden staff in the semi-darkness. Graceful. Powerful.

His back to her, he didn't see her, and she sat in the shadows, watching silently, as all her impressions and experiences of him swirled gradually around like the staff he swung, and began to form into a cohesive, multifaceted whole. She'd thought his police uniform and gun belt made him look like a warrior. But compared to this, they were . . . *ordinary*.

He finished the routine, bowed from the kneeling position and then sat, motionless, for some time – she didn't know how long – before he began the exercise again.

This time, something had changed. The grace and power were qualitatively different, both smoother and more intense. Incredible masculine beauty, strength and harmony distilled into a precisely contained but unbroken flow, each movement effortlessly following the last, the whole perfectly balanced.

She had no doubt that armed only with a wooden staff he could be lethal – if he chose. But she also had no doubt that at every moment of every movement, he had complete control over where and how the staff moved, where and when it started and stopped.

She'd never understood, until these moments watching him, why traditional martial-arts training and discipline were so respected and awed.

Despite all that he'd suffered and lost, she saw no anger, no aggression. Self-discipline, self-control, internal strength, rather than enforced power over others.

That strength of mind, honour and dedication earned even more of her respect.

More than her respect, if she was honest with herself.

His guarded reserve couldn't be more different to Leon's outgoing, easy way with everyone, his boundless energy and enthusiasm. But in all the ways that mattered to her, in that solid, central core of respect and commitment to others, they were similar.

All her efforts to keep emotionally distant had failed, and the attraction to him – far more than physical – could no longer be denied.

But the power of it frightened her.

༪

Nick completed the kata, the wooden staff smooth and solid in his grip, the mat cool and springy under his bare feet.

He returned to the kneeling position and bowed to the portrait of O Sensei, the great teacher and founder of the art, with gratitude for the discipline and the awareness, and for the strength and balance they gave him.

In the last time through the kata, the discordance in his mind and body had eased. He had found his centre of calm, of clarity and determination, a certainty that he'd not felt since before the undercover work, since the six months he'd spent, at twenty-five, in intensive training at the head dojo in Tokyo.

He could protect, would protect. That was the heart of who he was, who he'd been since he was twelve years old and had stepped up to look after his family after his father's imprisonment.

He had no illusions that right always prevailed, but if he hadn't always succeeded, it had not been for lack of commitment.

The doubts that had assailed him these past few days dissipated and settled into their proper perspective, and the fatigue in his body became just that: fatigue from lack of sleep, not nerve and muscular weakness from a poisonous biochemical cocktail of emotional and physical stresses.

He would sleep for a few hours, and then he would be better equipped to find, confront and neutralise the current threats. And when that was achieved, he would consider his future.

The undercover shit is eating you alive.

The memory of the letter sounded in his mind as if Hugh was there, saying the words. And Hugh was right – the half-life he'd led for almost a decade, his own life subjugated to the roles he'd played, had sucked him dry. He'd been right to request a return to normal duties. He'd have to make sure it stayed that way, so that he could finally *be* Nick Matheson.

As he climbed the stairs, a figure rose from the bench seats on the balcony. Jo. He knew her profile, the easy way she moved, her slim body softly shaped by some light clothing, white in the dusky light.

She came forward to meet him. 'I think I've just seen the real you,' she said quietly. 'And I think I'm beginning to understand who you are.'

Her presence should have disturbed the equilibrium he'd found, but it didn't. He gave that a small test.

'I've spent much of the past decade playing different people, Jo,' he said, his voice low. 'Why do you think this isn't just another performance?'

She answered him slowly. 'Consistency. Authenticity. And the fact that you seemed . . .' She tilted her head, searching for a word. 'Whole, I guess. At peace with yourself.'

Whole and at peace? 'I'm working on it,' he said. 'I've missed Aikido. I studied it seriously for some years, but while I was undercover I couldn't practise it openly. When I couldn't sleep, I thought I'd start to fix that.'

She reached out a hand, fingers brushing against the side of his face. Brief, gentle, and he didn't move away from it. Had no desire to move away. 'Seems to me you've fixed something. Will you sleep now?'

'I think so.' The sense of peace still infused him, but sleep . . . No, he wanted more than sleep. 'How about you? Couldn't sleep?'

'I had bad dreams.' She gave a small, rueful smile. 'My subconscious can see right through my pretence of bravery.'

'You've had one hell of a few days, Jo.'

'Yep. I'm trying to keep calm and rational about it, but underneath . . . well, underneath I'm scared. I'm not keen on the whole possibly dying thing.' She tried to smile again, but the strain made it waver, and she bit her lip, still trying to keep it in place.

And that was the end of him. He'd been fighting his feelings for her since that first day. But to deny that, to deny her, would be a lie, and he was through with living lies.

He drew her into his arms, and she came easily, rested her forehead against his shoulders, her fingers splayed on the cloth over his chest. When she'd turned into his hold earlier today, she'd been in shock, traumatised, and he could have been anyone she trusted. She might not even remember it. But this time was different.

He held her close, rested his face against her hair, aware of every point of touch, of her body against his, the curve of her shoulders and the small of her back under his hands, the soft fabric of her camisole scarcely concealing the warmth of her skin.

Aware, too, of his responsibility, and her need for reassurance. He tried to give her a solid foundation for some hope. 'You're not the only one who's scared, Jo, and I can't promise happy endings for everything. But these thugs are making mistakes. We're going to track them down quickly. I can promise that you'll be under police protection until we do.'

'Thank you.'

She didn't move, stayed in his arms, and he could feel, hear, her deep regular breaths as she struggled for calm.

He matched his breathing to hers. Authenticity, she'd said. Wholeness. He couldn't be authentic and whole if he hid from his emotions.

'I'd give my life to keep you safe, Jo.'

She drew her face away just far enough to look up at him. 'I know that, Nick.' Holding his gaze, she brushed her lips against his, once, and again.

Sensual, yes, but more than that. Intimate. Trusting. Honest.

He'd played so many roles over the past decade, had sex when the job required it, always in character, hard and hot and often controlling and never gentle and definitely never emotionally intimate or honest.

Never himself.

In the semi-darkness he held her close, and he returned her trust, allowed her to know his vulnerability, with soft tastes of her lips, her mouth, the line of her jaw, the pulse at her temple. Her body pressed against his, lithe and soft yet strong, fuelled a longing for something more than the physical release of sex. More intimate, more giving than simple sex.

They paused eventually, their breathing ragged, and Jo tucked her head into his shoulder, one hand resting on his waist.

He didn't need the awareness of the timber floor, cool and firm, under his bare feet, to have the sense of being grounded. Here, holding Jo, he was in the right place, steady and grounded and completely himself.

She lifted her head, raw honesty in her eyes, in the solemnity of her voice. 'I told Erin I wouldn't get involved with a man who might get himself killed. That terrifies me, Nick. When

Leon died, grief – it eroded everything I was for a long while. I was petrified I'd lose myself.'

The ground beneath his sense of certainty tilted. Jo. *Her* needs, not his. 'But you didn't lose yourself.'

'Not entirely. Not forever. Not something I want to go through again, though.'

Still holding her close against his pounding heart, he loosened his jacket, and taking her hand, guided it to the puckered skin between his lower ribs where Terry Costello's bullet had ripped into him. His voice felt just as rough as he said, 'I can't promise not to die, Jo.'

He half-expected her to recoil, but her fingers on his skin were feather light, with a gentleness that soothed the still-healing nerves around the wound. Then she covered it with her palm, protecting, and her eyes met his.

'I don't know what's between us, Nick, or where it's going. The intensity scares me. But I won't deny it. I want you. I want you to stay with me tonight. No promises, no assumptions, no complications. Just stay with me.'

He grazed her mouth with his, closed his eyes to absorb every sense, every taste, touch, impression of her hands, her mouth beneath his, her body with his. Heat and need and longing roared to life within him, and his focus narrowed. Just Jo. Nothing but Jo and the craving to be with her, to give himself to her, completely.

❦

That a man so strong, so hardened, could be so gentle scarcely surprised her. That she could want him so intensely did.

Firm muscles flexed under her hands. Back, shoulders, waist and chest. Hips against hers. A hard body, powerful, but not threatening. She tasted, explored, his mouth, his face, the hunger for connection acute, his hands on her skin drawing her deeper, further into pure need.

Somewhere, downstairs, someone coughed a few times, awareness of the sound only slowly registering in her brain as Nick stilled, alert.

Upstairs, in the shadows, they could not be seen, but without speaking she took his hand and drew him towards the darkened office, where the blinds on the windows would provide privacy.

His hand still in hers he stopped by his bag, crouching for just a moment as he reached into it and found something, a small rustle of plastic in his hand as he rose again.

She smiled in the semi-darkness. Protection, in all its forms.

She clicked the lock closed on the door. Moonlight drifting through the skylight fell on him, tall and rock steady.

His breathing rasped quietly, as uneven as hers.

With his fingertips, he slowly traced a fiery sensual path down the side of her face, her throat, lightly over her breast to her waist, and she trembled, stepping into his arms again for the closeness she ached for.

While his hands slid up from her waist and slipped the camisole over her head, making nerves come alive in every inch of skin, she pushed his jacket open, pressed her lips against his chest, trailed fingers around his hips where the *hakama* tied.

'You're a little formally dressed, Nick,' she murmured. 'I want to touch you. All of you. Skin to skin.'

With a gentle hand he lifted her head, let her see the desire in his face. 'We will,' he said, and lowered his mouth to hers.

Need seared through her as his left hand closed over her breast, and she claimed his mouth again, hungry for him, for every sensation, desperate to give him the same sublime pleasure he gave her.

His fingers teasing her breast obliterating coherent thought, she fumbled with the ties on his *hakama*, but with his other hand he brushed hers aside, nimbly dealing with the knots.

'Wait,' he said against her mouth. 'Don't move.'

He stepped back only far enough to remove the *hakama*, but his intense, all-encompassing focus never left her.

Her heart full, she pushed the jacket off his shoulders, laid her hands on his chest; warm skin, firm flesh, the scars he carried, and all of it, all of him, hers for this brief time. Hers to share with, to gift with her care and honour and love.

'I want you, Nick. Completely.'

The last of their clothes fell to the floor, and the mat pressed cool against her back, but Nick's face filled her vision as his touch overwhelmed her senses. His eyes, dark and deep, locked on hers as she drew him in to her, again and again and again, until he threw his head back and let go his control and his release, deep and strong, triggered wave after wave of exquisite sensation.

When it finally faded enough for thought to return, he rolled her into his arms, holding her close, his lips against her temple.

❧

Nick stayed with her, and she slept cradled against him on the mat. Her subconscious must have been either exhausted or reassured, because when she woke it was slowly, when he moved in his sleep. A long time since she'd shared a bed, listened to a man's breathing beside her, felt his body warm against hers.

No promises, she'd said. No complications. And two unattached adults physically attracted to each other should be able to have sex without it becoming a 'complication'.

But what they had shared was more than just sex. They'd made love, shared love, given each other love and tenderness and acceptance.

Definitely not *uncomplicated*.

She was falling hard for him – had fallen already – and she knew he'd do everything he could to keep her safe from external threats. But could she be safe with him, afterwards? A dangerous job, a traumatic background. If she allowed herself to be close to him, how would she cope if he was killed on duty? How would she cope if the trauma of his past became too much for him, and he went off the rails, like Hugh? Or if he gave up and walked away one day, put a gun to his head and pulled the trigger?

Nick brushed a thumb against her temple, kissed her forehead lightly. 'Go back to sleep,' he murmured drowsily. 'You're safe with me.'

There was no way he could have read her thoughts. But she closed her eyes again, felt her mind relaxing despite the irrationality of it. He wasn't Leon. And she was stronger than the young woman she'd been years ago. They just had to stay alive through this crisis. The rest she would find a way to deal with, in the future.

When she woke again, he was gone. The muted daylight of early morning glimmered through the skylight and a steady hum of voices and noises drifted from downstairs. Not quite six o'clock.

She selected jeans and a T-shirt from the clothes Erin had bought her and dressed quickly.

The cadets were loading onto the bus as she went downstairs, the other officers in varying states of readiness for the day ahead, some clutching paper coffee mugs. Through the open front doors, the smell of bacon wafted in from the Rotary barbecue.

Nick had his laptop open on a table at the back of the room, a coffee cup beside it, but he paced nearby, speaking on his phone, and any peace he might have found last night had vanished. Too far away to hear his words above the noise of the television, she could see the conversation consisted of intense, urgent, short exchanges.

Frank brought in a platter of bacon-and-egg rolls, and she accepted one from him although she had little appetite. Given the uncertainty of the day ahead, taking advantage of breakfast to shore up her energy levels made sense. But as she juggled eating it without egg dripping on her T-shirt, she kept an eye on Nick. He finished that call and made another – he must have left a message for it was only brief.

He came across the room to meet her, all detective, with no evidence of the lover she'd been close to in the night.

'Can you be ready to leave in five minutes? I'm going to take you back to the police station. It'll be more secure than here today.'

'I can be ready in two. What's happened?'

'I'll tell you in the car. If you can bring down my gear, I'll pick you up at the back entrance in a couple of minutes.'

She flew up the stairs, put the books Nick had loaned her in her bag, picked up his and was back down again, waiting by the kitchen door when he reversed out of the parking area and swung around to pick her up.

On the short, two-block trip, he kept his eyes on the road, tense and alert, as he briefly explained.

'That was Interpol on the phone just now. They've confirmed, from both fingerprints and facial recognition analysis on the photograph, that the man you saw on the bike is Eduardo Guerrera Ramirez. The Ramirez family runs one of the major Mexican drug cartels.'

Mexican cartels. She read the news, knew of the ongoing violence in Mexico and drug wars in other parts of South America, had felt sorrow for the terrible cost inflicted on ordinary, decent Mexicans by the drug lords and their cartels. 'They're here, in Australia?'

'Yes, they've been coming in recent years because prices are high here and it's lucrative compared to other places. I've seen a lot of different organised-crime groups. Many of them can be very violent, but it's mostly towards their rivals. In Mexico cartels have enormous influence, through corruption, intimidation and fear. Anyone inconvenient is eliminated. What concerns the Australian police is that the cartels are bringing those same attitudes and practices here.'

He turned the car into the police station parking area and swiped his access ID to open the security gate. While it gradually opened, he turned to her. 'Jo, I can't overstate the risks. I've told you before how dangerous Ramirez is. You're the only one who can place him at the scene of Mitchell's murder. I know it's going to be hard on you, but you need to stay in witness protection for as long as it takes to get him and all his associates locked away.'

TWENTY

After escorting Jo to his office, Nick found Murdoch had already arrived, despite the early hour. Clean shaven and parade-ground straight, only his tightly drawn, pallid face reflected the strain.

'I saw the Interpol email you forwarded,' he said. 'Have you spoken with them?'

'Yes.' Although Murdoch indicated the chair, Nick remained standing, too wired to sit. 'They're sending a report on Ramirez with the information they have. The family cartel supplies the drugs but he runs more as a lone wolf. Modus operandi may be similar to when he set up operations in Canada: targeting regional areas for cocaine transportation routes, attracting a gang of disaffected youths by promising money and drugs, training them up in violence and intimidation. It seems to fit the pattern here.'

Murdoch didn't disagree outright – just worked through some of the questions he had aloud. 'There's not much of a market out here. And we haven't seen an increase in drug-related crime. A reduction, in fact, since the Mafia bust a few months ago, south of here.'

'I doubt much is intended for this district. I'm guessing they're bringing it in somewhere along the Queensland or Northern Territory coasts, and using inland roads to shift it to the southern states. But I'm also guessing – hoping – that the operation is still in its set-up phase. The Federal Police haven't got a file on him, and according to Interpol he was last sighted in Vancouver in July. The John Doe up near Coffs died in late September.'

In the midst of his increasing concern, Nick held on to that sliver of hope. If it was early in the establishment of the local mob, they might have a chance of catching them before the web had spread too far. Ramirez might not have earned the fierce loyalty that would make the ring hard to crack – or that would make his associates remain dangerous to Jo, and other witnesses after they arrested Ramirez. If, if, if . . . He needed that hope, because the thought of Jo hidden away for months or years terrified him.

Murdoch pulled up a window on his computer. 'Some reports have come in from Crime Stoppers since the photos were released to the media last night. I'll forward them on to you and Haddad. I've just scanned through them – a few likely sightings, some descriptions of men with them, and there might be a location – there's a report of a shooting party staying in an old hut, north of Derringvale.'

'I'll get Leah to follow them up. I'm going to take Jo Lockwood away today, and I'd like an escort car at least as far as the New England Highway.' Over an hour away, that would see them escorted out of the district and, he hoped, away from any immediate threat. 'Witness protection officers will meet us further south at Singleton, and arrange a safe house and police protection for her. I'll be back later tonight.'

He didn't mention Grace, and Murdoch didn't ask him about her. Nick would arrange whatever she needed for safety.

'Keep in touch with Haddad during the day, Matheson—'

There was a sharp rap on the door, and Leah poked her head in without waiting for an invitation. 'You need to come and see this news report now, sir. You too, Nick. Some idiot is trying to stir up trouble.'

Someone had turned up the sound on the television in the break room, so Nick heard the newsreader's overly dramatic voice, heard his own name even before he saw the screen. When the dozen or so officers watching it stepped aside for him, his own face filled the screen, in the years-old newspaper article hinting at his dismissal from the police force – the story that had been planted to build his cover as a corrupt former cop, to ease his entry into the underworld.

In fewer than three minutes, the newsreader breathlessly twisted together a handful of facts with rumour and outright lies, citing the 'ongoing investigation' into the Melbourne incident, Nick's aliases and 'well-known links' with organised crime, and quoted speculation from unnamed police sources that he'd been too convincing as a criminal not to be one, that he'd been fighting with Hugh immediately before his death, managing to imply, without actually saying it, that he was involved in the murders of Hugh and Shelley.

The whole piece implied an inept local investigation, relying on a corrupt cop – *him* – and hence doomed to failure.

Murdoch jabbed off the power button on the television, his usually composed face reddening with rage.

Nick's anger ran deeper, colder. He turned and grimly surveyed his colleagues. Most were locals, just come on duty for the day shift, gathering for a 6.45 a.m. task allocation. Some shifted uncomfortably on their feet, one or two edging to the door. A couple of them returned his glare with a coolness that could have been contempt. A few avoided looking at him at all. Aaron fumed silently, scanning the group himself, looking for guilt.

'Nobody leave,' Murdoch commanded those near the door. 'That was the most atrocious and blatantly irresponsible piece of pseudo-journalism I have ever seen. I will be in contact with headquarters the moment I return to my office, and you can be sure that the Commissioner will immediately lodge a formal complaint with the broadcaster.'

Murdoch scanned the room, his anger still evident in the veins pulsing at his temple. 'I will also recommend that the Ethics Branch launch an immediate investigation into the leaking of sensitive operational information to the media. This is a very serious matter, and anyone who is found to have transgressed the rules will face disciplinary procedures.'

Being identified as an undercover officer on national television was serious enough – the permanent end of his covert work. Having his name, face and aliases publicised gave a whole lot of criminals he'd crossed exact directions to find him. Not that it would have been impossible before – the underworld had access to technologies most police could only dream about – but it made it much simpler.

Murdoch wiped his forehead with a handkerchief. 'Detective Senior Sergeant Matheson has served the New South Wales Police Force for more than fifteen years in a distinguished and decorated career, often at significant personal cost. He has my complete confidence and support.'

Significant personal cost? Oh, yes. And the cost had just gone way up. Any thoughts he might have dared last night about a possible relationship with Jo were now smashed. He'd told her he couldn't promise not to die on the job, but he'd figured that returning to normal duties at least reduced the risks. Not so now. She'd lost enough, with Rossetti's death. He could never ask her to run the risk of that kind of grief again. And he could never put her in the position of being harmed in order for someone to get to him.

So that one night, the few hours together, would be all he'd share with her. And this afternoon, witness protection officers would take her away, for days or weeks or months, and he might never see her again. A wave of harsh, bitter anger threatened to consume him.

Murdoch marched back to his office but Nick stayed, giving each of the assembled officers a hard stare, seeking any sign of guilt or contempt. 'Somebody leaked that information about my fight with Hugh. That wasn't in any media statements. And someone knows someone who had already put together a dossier with details of my jobs and aliases. And somebody – probably the same somebody – then contacted the journalist or producer of that news show and fed them a story of half-truths and lies. And that somebody better damn well pray that when the hitmen start coming for me, they don't take out anyone else in the spray of bullets.'

His gut a hard ball of despair and loss, he pushed past them out of the room. Leah followed him, and although he didn't acknowledge her she caught up the couple of paces to stride beside him.

'I hope you actually manage politeness with your new colleagues sometimes, Nick. Because that was an impressive deployment of your I-know-ten-ways-to-kill-you-with-my-little-finger glare.'

'I'm not in the mood to laugh it off, Leah. You know the implications as well as I do.'

'I do. And you're going to need your colleagues to back you up, so you might try trusting them and treating them as though you're on the same side.'

'Trust?' He stopped walking and spun around to face her. Some of the others had left the break room and were following at a cautious distance. He didn't care. 'I trusted my partner in Melbourne, Leah. Terry Costello was supposed to be my back-up. Instead I found he was blackmailing and raping the target's mistress. That was just before he blew my cover and shot me. And I trusted the covert unit at HQ, but now details of the past few years' jobs and aliases are on the breakfast news. So, I'm not inclined to trust *anyone* right now. Including you.'

It had flickered through his mind that she might be responsible. She knew something about his work, knew about this case and could potentially have had the contacts to find the rest. If ambition had corrupted her, or maybe some threat . . .

Instinct said no, but perhaps he just couldn't bear to consider the possibility of another betrayal.

As he turned to continue down the corridor, he saw Jo, standing in the doorway of his office where he'd left her.

She'd likely heard a fair amount of that. Good, because she needed to know the truth.

Although his mind raced with possible strategies to deal with the new threats, concern for her overrode all of them. Eliminating any threat to Jo – and to Grace – had to be his first priority. He just needed to stay alive long enough to see it through. And he had to ensure that no-one ever suspected his feelings for Jo. He could not risk her becoming a target to get to him.

Details of the past few years' jobs and aliases are on the breakfast news.

She'd heard the hurried footsteps a few minutes ago, the growl of raised voices from the break room. But she'd not heard enough to grasp what had happened until she'd come to the door and heard Nick's words.

The icy expression on his face stayed in place as he strode the fifteen metres down the corridor to her. He waved her inside, closed the door, and leaned against it. His face tightening, he closed his eyes for the length of a breath in and out.

She had never seen him reveal that much stress.

'Your aliases were on the *news*?' Impossible. She had to have misheard, misunderstood.

She listened, horror constricting her heart, as he repeated details of the news broadcast.

'But they can't do that. There are journalistic standards—'

'Oh, I'm sure there'll be a retraction and an apology before the end of the day. A couple of heads may even roll. But the effect won't change.' He sank into his chair at the desk, dragged his hands through his hair. 'The segment will have been downloaded plenty of times already and will be in wide circulation among criminal organisations by lunchtime.'

Who would, now they could connect his aliases with a real name, know exactly where to find him.

She stood by the window, staring out while she tried to control her voice enough to ask, 'What will you do?'

He came to the window, gently guided her away from it and closed the blinds, shutting out the early summer sunlight. And any peering eyes. 'I'll take you away from here as planned. Then I'll come back and find Ramirez and his mob.'

'But shouldn't you go into witness protection yourself?'

He shook his head wearily. 'It's like you and the bushfire the other night, Jo. This is my job, my responsibility. I have skills and knowledge that might help solve the case. So I'm coming back here to do that.'

'Where they can find you.' She looked directly into his eyes, and he didn't look away.

'Yes.'

'I hate the thought of that.' Anger began to burn through the numbness. Anger at everything, at Ramirez and Judases and the whole situation that was tearing her heart apart. She wanted to cry, couldn't cry. She wanted to fall apart on him but she had to stay strong and in control. But she also had to be honest. 'Dammit, Nick, I know we said no complications, but my head and my heart aren't in agreement. I hate the thought of you dealing with this alone. Of *us* dealing with this alone. I'm afraid for you and I'm afraid for me.'

Afraid of falling apart, of the chasm of grief. Afraid – terrified – of losing herself and sense and meaning.

He didn't answer immediately. Didn't hold her and lie to her that it would be all right. He paced across the small office, back again, stood just beyond touching distance from her, his hands thrust deeply into his pockets.

He swallowed. 'We're both doing a lousy job of "no complications", aren't we?' Without waiting even a breath for an answer, he went on, 'Jo, I'm going to walk out that door shortly, and from that moment I will treat you as nothing more than an acquaintance, a responsibility. Maybe even an inconvenient one. I want you to know . . . I need you to know that it will be a lie. The closeness we shared means more to me than I can explain. But for your safety, no-one must guess or even suspect it.'

I'd give my life to keep you safe, Jo.

New layers of meaning sank in. He wouldn't just throw himself in front of a bullet for her. If she was held hostage or threatened, he would give himself up for her.

Except that she would not allow that to happen.

'I understand, Nick. But you need to understand this: for your safety, I will lie, cheat, steal, kill, or die if necessary. I will also follow all precautions and I'll stay in police protection for as long as it takes. I will not allow anyone to use me to get to you.'

He reached out a hand, stepped forward. 'Jo—'

She'd go to pieces if he touched her, and she desperately needed to stay strong, for them both. She moved aside, away from him. 'Nick, please,' she protested. 'Since we're both doing a lousy job on "no promises", as well, we'd better avoid making any assumptions about why that is, and any further complications, and just get on with the pretence. Please.'

He nodded wordlessly, turned away. About to open the door, he paused. 'I'm sorry,' he said quietly. Then, his shoulders straightened, his head lifted higher, and he breathed in deeply, once.

As he stepped out of his office, he looked back at her, and there was nothing of the man who'd caressed her with tenderness and held her gently in the night. Only a crisp, cool professional. 'We'll be leaving within the hour, Jo,' he said firmly but politely. 'As I mentioned, all your basic expenses will be covered. You may switch your phone on while you are still in the police station in order to get any necessary data off it, but you must switch it to airplane mode before you turn it off, and then leave it off.'

'That's already done.' Turning off her emotions was far harder. As she walked out the door in front of him, she forced some impatience into her tone and added, 'I'm well aware of the traceability of phone signals. I've also turned off location services and disabled the GPS functions.'

'Good. You can wait in the interview room you used yesterday. I'll have someone come and get you when we're ready to leave.'

Aaron emerged from a nearby room and Nick immediately turned away from her as if he'd already mentally dismissed her. 'Aaron, I need you to follow up some Crime Stoppers reports ASAP. I'll forward you the details now.'

In the interview room she pulled up a chair to the table and dropped her head on her folded arms. An empty room, nothing to do but think.

She'd better get used to that.

Without work, without contact with friends or family, without Nick . . . without access to her research materials or scientific journal databases, just shut into a small apartment all day every day, she'd have to find *something* to do to occupy the time. Something other than finding out if Bo and Hope had ever managed to stick together on *Days of Our Lives*. If her minders could bring her books, she could catch up on some of the classics she'd never read. Or maybe they could bring her yarn and knitting needles, and she could knit squares into blankets. Or get adventurous and try socks.

For an independent woman accustomed to running her own life, it would be a challenge. But she'd cope, somehow. She had to, because it was as much about Nick's safety as her own.

Bordered by trees, with dry paddocks beyond, the road ran mostly straight east, now and then curving in a ninety-degree bend to zigzag around century-old property boundaries. Nate Harrison and one of the junior constables were the escort – they wouldn't have been Nick's choice, but resources were short and they had to go to Tenterfield, anyway.

Nick kept a hundred metres behind the escort car and they travelled together at the speed limit. There was little other traffic around, only the occasional car from the opposite direction.

Jo hadn't said a word since they'd left Strathnairn. She stared determinedly out the window, hands gripped together on her lap.

He could have pushed some conversation, but what would be the point? Nothing could be changed, and to add anything else to what they'd already said to each other would cause nothing but pain.

About forty kilometres out from Strathnairn, a mob of cattle spread across the road, ambling along, forcing him to slow to a crawl. They should have had warning signs out, but in the dry, dusty summer there were plenty of mobs of cattle moving up and down the stock routes, some of the drovers more efficient than others in placing the signs. On another day, he might have thought it peaceful, the placid beasts mooching along in the sunshine.

The escort car inched through the mob, making slightly better speed, drawing further ahead. The road curved here, a sharp bend around a huddle of old deserted farm buildings.

A couple of guys on farm bikes rode without helmets on the verge alongside the mob, and two kelpie-like dogs raced with them, barking madly, spooking a group of half-grown calves into running directly in front of his car.

Nick had to jam on the brakes to avoid them. The escort car disappeared around the bend, sight of them obscured by trees and the old buildings, and his gut instinct kicked in with a warning adrenaline shot.

'Nick,' Jo said, low and urgent. 'This isn't right. Those guys don't know the first thing about cattle. Neither do the dogs.'

TWENTY-ONE

Alarm bells jangling loud in his head, Nick checked the rear-vision mirror, about to yank the gear into reverse. Stock milled across the road behind him, and an old, large four-wheel drive approached, driving up the centre of the road, nudging cattle out of its way. Not a farmer.

He radioed an emergency order for the escort car, and blasted on the car horn to scare the cattle, but another four-wheel drive roared from behind a farm building out onto the road ahead.

He yelled at Jo to get down as a figure with a rifle leaned out of the four-wheel drive ahead, spraying the cattle with bullets. Several fell. The rest, panicked now, raced towards him, and accelerating into a mob of panicked, half-ton cattle made as much sense as ramming into a tree.

Ahead, the vehicle and the two motorbikes blocked the road. Behind him, the other four-wheel drive – an old Patrol – had stopped in the middle of the road, blocking any escape that way, and the driver sprayed another round of bullets into the mob. More cattle fell, blocking the road.

Jo hunkered low, but she twisted her head to see him. 'That's the missing semi-autos, by the sounds of it.'

'Probably. There are six men: two in each vehicle and two on bikes. The escort car should be here any moment. Stay in the car and stay low. I'll try to bluff them until the others get here.'

The cattle were mostly past them now. The live ones. The dead and dying created a road hazard, and the two guys on bikes wove around them to come closer.

Where the hell was Harrison? They couldn't have driven more than a few hundred metres ahead, had to have heard his radio call – and the gunfire.

If any civilians were about to drive into this it could become a bloodbath. Guys who dropped cattle for fun probably didn't care much who else they hit.

Jo reached for the radio. 'I'll turn the sound down, but keep calling on it,' she whispered. 'Be careful.'

'There's a second gun under the seat. Any chance you get to escape, Jo, do it. If I can get them into position, I can deal with them. If you see me scratch my head, blast the horn as a distraction for a second.'

He left the keys in the ignition, engine idling. Taking his Glock from its holster, he opened the door slowly, letting them see the weapon. Closing the door, he left the weapon casually on the roof of the car as if it were a statement of trust.

'Rather messy, guys.' He strolled forward as they rode to within a couple of metres of him, everything in his stance, his expression, his language reflecting an unhurried, amused, hardened criminal. Exactly the kind of role he'd played for years. 'Hasn't Ramirez trained you lot better than this?'

Late teens or early twenties at best. Glancing uncertainly at each other, the one in a heavy-metal T-shirt drew a pistol. Nick couldn't see a weapon on the other but that only meant he didn't have a rifle. Knife, pistol, nunchakus – a range of deadly weapons could be at his waist under the sleeveless checked shirt or in his boots. Thirty metres ahead, the occupants of the Pajero walked towards him, carrying rifles. One dark, average height, mid-twenties, black leather vest; the other with a shaved head, arms covered in tattoos, and a steroid-assisted build.

Still no sign of the escort car.

'What have you done with Harrison?' he continued. 'You know, if he's in on this, we could have saved a lot of fucking bother.'

They weren't convinced yet, but he was unsettling them. Good. Their uncertainty gave him a slight edge.

One against six. To have any hope, he needed them closer together, needed those semi-autos within reach. And he had to get them further away from Jo.

'Your mates are going to meet with a little trouble,' heavy-metal guy with the pistol gloated. 'Couple of blown-out tyres or something like that.'

So Harrison was involved. No help there. He just hoped they had the sense to keep any civilians away.

He shrugged. 'Waste of fucking effort if you ask me. I was bringing the woman to Ramirez anyway. Although shit knows what he wants with the hysterical, complaining bitch. Besides,

I've compromised her already, so no way will she be a credible witness against him.'

From behind him he heard a shout in disgust and a complaint about 'fucking cow shit'. Keeping his attention on the four in front of him, three of them now definitely confused, he threw up his hands in disbelief.

'Jesus, you don't fucking get it, do you? My cover was royally fucked this morning. I thought that might have been Harrison's doing, but maybe he's not that bright. I did the righteous indignation shit, bought a few hours, but I figure it's time to pull the plug on that lark and fuck off to Canada.'

He took a few steps closer to them, thumbs hooked into his pockets, casual and relaxed. On the surface. Underneath, he recalculated the odds. He almost had them believing. The two on bikes, yes. Younger, slightly awe-struck by his unflustered attitude, they'd be slower to react. Not so much Leather and Shiny on foot beside them, with rifles still pointing his way. Pump action and semi-auto. The two from the Patrol behind – one a little older, one younger – had come around his side of the car, not Jo's side. An advantage, because it kept them in range. But not one he could make use of, yet.

'Anyway,' he continued his casual chat, buying time, 'since Ramirez is starting up here, I can give him some gold tips about who's who and who's rotten. Trade him for the same info on the Canucks.'

'That's enough bullshit.' Leather, pump-action man stepped forward, but not close enough. 'The boss wants to see you both. Alive. At least for now.' Trace of an accent. A grin reading as a clear threat. 'But he sure ain't planning to fucking trade or pay for what he wants from you.'

Alive. That one word improved the odds. Nick shifted his weight to spring and frowned in pretended puzzlement as he scratched his head.

The explosion of a shot shattered the windscreen to the left behind him, hit Leather, and in the moment of distraction, Nick dropped the young guy on his right with a vicious uppercut to his neck, sidestepped and tossed the older one as he charged, used the momentum to kick the bike out from under checked-shirt biker, and grabbed the muzzle of the rifle as Shiny swung it, ducking under and pushing with the force of the swing up and out so that the round went into the air and Shiny went onto his back.

Another shot had toppled the other biker. A third shot went wide and as he heard a car door and a harsh, 'Drop it, bitch,' Nick spun around to check on Jo and grab his gun if he could. The far side back door open, a seventh man – where the hell had he come from? – held a pistol to the back of her head.

For one heart-seizing moment he thought she wouldn't obey the order to drop the gun, that she'd fire at her target before the thug blew her head apart.

He raised his hands high in surrender, and she read his message, letting the gun fall forward onto the dashboard.

Two of the guys he'd put down, Shiny and checked-shirt, were scrambling to their feet, swearing, Shiny already lifting his rifle. The first he'd hit, the young one from the Patrol, was still half out of it, and his mate was rising slowly. Not experienced fighters, except maybe Shiny, if it took them seconds to recover from a fall. The two Jo had shot, Leather and the heavy-metal biker, bled on the ground, the biker writhing and groaning.

Five seconds it had taken, maybe ten, and with that element of surprise they'd almost won. If Ramirez wanted them alive, then there might be another chance, other chances. He had to believe it, and be ready. But as he watched in silent fear and rage as the seventh man dragged Jo from the car, a handful of her hair twisted in his hand, gun in his other hand close to her head, Nick vowed that he'd find that chance before they did to Jo what they'd done to Shelley – even if, as a last resort, he had to kill her first to prevent her suffering.

∞

She fought, kicking, yelling, striking out at the body behind her, partly an instinctive response to the blinding pain in her head, partly in desperate hope that the distraction might give Nick an opportunity to fight some more.

She thudded out of the car to the ground, but her captor hauled her up by her hair, the moment of relief when he let it go obliterated in the punishing back hand across the face, so hard she hit the ground again, gasping for air, her head screaming, and hating every breath that caused such agony.

'Restrain them and load them,' a harsh voice ordered, above her, around her, right inside her skull. 'We've taken too long here.'

'What about these guys?'

'Put the kid in the Pajero.' He pronounced it in the Spanish way, not the Australian. 'Finish and leave the others.'

Her eyes closed, she lay still, ear against the ground, and as the pain in her head faded to a shriek she became aware of a vibration, a faint, low rumble somewhere underneath her pounding pulse and the distant braying of cattle. Either her head was about to explode, or she could hear an oncoming vehicle. Police? *Please, please, let it be the police.*

Another short, sharp sound registered, loud in one ear, a dull thud in the other. Then another.

Finish and leave the others.

Nausea swamped her, and she pushed herself up just enough to vomit into the dirt. Shooting armed men in self-defence as she'd done was one thing; they'd given her little choice. But callously shooting unarmed, injured comrades instead of helping them, or leaving them where others might help them – that was another thing entirely. Violence and brutality, not mercy.

She struggled to her hands and knees, tried to open her eyes but the bright sunlight made her head swim, and when she gasped for air, a nauseating mix of cow shit, blood, heat and dust hit the back of her throat and made her throw up again.

'Get a move on!' the voice shouted.

Rough hands hauled her to her feet, and it was all she could do to stay upright, her body shaking. She forced her eyes open to find Nick.

The man with the shaved head smashed Nick's face into the car roof as her captor pushed her against the other side of the car, his grip tight around her neck so she couldn't move. Nick's eyes opened, looking straight into hers. Aware. Focused. So there had to be a reason why he wasn't fighting now, why he let the man hold him there while another bound his hands behind him with plastic restraints.

Taking her cue from him, she let them cuff her hands behind her back, and endured the groping search for weapons before they pushed her towards the Patrol. Nick's captor yanked Nick around to face him, and she heard the thuds of hard punches into his gut, his grunts, and Shaved Head's order to walk.

The wild leap of hope when she saw the approaching car dived into sickening disappointment when she realised it was a beat-up utility, with two men who greeted the others. At the rear of the Patrol, her captor taped her mouth and dragged a dark hood over her head, pulling the drawstring closed around her neck. She fought to breathe through the instant panic, writhed as hands lifted her at the waist and half-threw, half-shoved her into the cargo area behind the back seat. Her shoulder rammed into something sharp and hard, spearing pain into her spine and head, her cry smothered by the tape.

She tried to wriggle into the corner, to draw her legs up close. They were bringing Nick now, their movements hurried, voices in the distance urging speed, doors slamming, engines revving.

'Get the fuck in,' Shaved Head barked, with another thud of fist on flesh.

Her legs were jostled, bumped as they pushed Nick in, and she curled in tighter, her back against the side wall of the car, trying to give him space.

The door slammed shut on them, the engine of the Patrol started and two other doors shut.

Her head throbbed, her mouth tasted of bile and her instinct fought against the hot blackness of the hood, but she could not let herself cry, because if she clogged up her nose she would suffocate.

She had to calm herself, try to still the spinning in her head and be ready for whatever came.

Nick's boots nudged hers, slid beside them, his leg pressing gently against hers. Deliberate contact.

Unable to see him, talk to him, touch him other than in this one way, she found the gesture comforting, reassuring, and she uncurled her legs enough to increase the contact.

She concentrated on breathing, on lowering her pounding pulse rate, on being aware of surroundings and sounds. They'd done a U-turn, back towards Strathnairn, and were travelling fast. The men in the car had hardly spoken.

A right turn on to a dirt road, a sharp bend to the left. She knew where they were. Now she could start counting time and measuring how far they went.

ᐭ

They travelled for perhaps an hour, mostly on dirt roads, rough and jarring on the hard floor of a vehicle that needed new shock absorbers, made worse by a driver who travelled too fast, with no respect for the vehicle or the road.

The men didn't talk much, but when they did Nick listened to their voices, their words, their manner. The dark-haired, dark-eyed, accented man who'd held the gun to Jo's head might be Mexican, and he carried some authority. Not as much as 'the boss'. He growled at the driver to slow down on two occasions, received a mumbled apology and a slight reduction in speed in response.

The driver, the man who looked around thirty, tried to cover his nervousness and didn't succeed. He wondered aloud how 'the kid' was. No answer. Reckoned they'd got away with it pretty well, hadn't they? A noncommittal grunt in reply.

The driver persisted. 'If it wasn't for the bloody bitch – who'd have thought she'd be such a good shot?'

'Shut the fuck up, Gibson,' the other guy growled.

Nick pressed his leg against Jo's, and she responded with an answering pressure.

Gibson would be an easy target. Back on the road, he'd charged blindly, been thrown easily and fallen hard. Later, he'd hesitated on the order to shoot the two wounded men, screwed his eyes shut when he did it. New to the gang, Nick figured. Excited by the promise but starting to worry about the cost.

Nick ran through his assessment of the others again. Nine of them initially. Seven now, including the kid, who might well be concussed. The Mexican and Gibson in the Patrol with a handgun and a semi-auto; Shiny and the kid in the Pajero, with a semi-auto and the pump-action; Checked Shirt on a bike, and since Nick had heard two bikes overtake them, one of the guys from the ute must have picked up Heavy Metal's bike – and, presumably, his gun. Which left one guy in the ute.

Shiny was dangerous, a brute who took pleasure from violence. Probably had already served time for a violent crime, not in minimum security. Checked Shirt was cocky, and pissed off that he'd been tossed from his bike so easily. The kid and the two guys from the ute he didn't know enough about, yet.

The vehicle slowed, and the Mexican mumbled something as he clambered out. They edged forward a few metres, stopped again, and the Mexican climbed back in. A gate. They bumped for a little over rough ground, bushes scraping against the vehicle's side. North of Strathnairn, he figured from what he could tell of the direction they'd taken. North-east or north-west, he wasn't sure.

They stopped again, and swung around in reverse. The men left them, slamming doors but not locking them, and within minutes the temperature in the vehicle began to rise. It had been warm enough before, but parked in hot sunshine without airconditioning, he soon felt sweat dripping down his neck, soaking his shirt.

Jo pressed her leg against his. She would know as well as he did that if they weren't let out of the literally baking heat soon, they'd be too weak to function, let alone to take advantage of any opportunities. People died in less than half an hour locked in cars like this.

Voices. The uneven, medium-pitched engines of the farm bikes. Footsteps crunching on gravel.

The back door yanked open, a rush of warm air on his shirt marginally cooler than the air inside.

'Put them out the back and give them some water.' The Mexican's voice, some distance away. 'But don't rough them up. He wants them in good shape.'

Despite the instructions, the arms that yanked him out weren't gentle, and unable to see, Nick stumbled finding his feet and rammed his bad thigh against the towbar, sending blazing pain down his leg.

Jo's exit was just as quick, and she staggered against him. But here the air was fresh, although hot; they were outside, the breeze fluttering the hood over his face, the sunlight piercing the cloth enough to make out light and shade, broad shapes.

'Out the back' was behind a building, under some kind of shade.

'There's a post there,' Gibson said, pushing them against it. 'Sit, both of you, with your backs to it.'

His back against the solid, round wooden post, he touched hands with Jo, before they both eased down to sit on the ground. One of them – probably Checked Shirt – looped cord through the plastic restraints and around the post, pulling his restraints tight against his wrists.

Checked Shirt came back a few moments later, loosening the cord around Nick's neck and dragging the hood over his head. The light hit his eyes, momentarily blinding him. He blinked a few times, the glare easing so he could see the rough machinery shed they were in: earth floor, no walls, only a bent and twisted corrugated-iron roof supported by thick posts and railings. An old hut stood some metres away and dry scrub surrounded them. The Pajero, the Patrol, the bikes and the ute were all there, the ute with a quad bike loaded on the back and the dogs tied to the towbar, sheltering underneath from the sun.

Beside him, Checked Shirt took off Jo's hood, leaning too close in to her, ripping the tape off her mouth in one hard jerk, leaving her mouth bleeding. Leering into her eyes, inches from her face, he wiped the blood off with his finger and licked it suggestively.

Nick tugged at his restraints, tempted to try to rip them apart, and then the man.

Gibson stomped into view with a couple of bottles of water. 'Leave her, Hayes. That's for later. Take his tape off and give him some water.'

Hayes tore the tape off Nick's mouth, jammed his head back and upended the bottle of water into his mouth, almost choking him. He jerked his head down and away, coughing water up while Hayes laughed.

Gibson went more slowly with Jo, giving her a chance to drink, but then drawing the bottle back from her mouth and tipping water down her T-shirt, soaking it over her breasts.

'Oops, bit of an accident there. Sorry, bitch.'

Someone called from the hut, and both men left, leaving the water bottles on the ground, unreachable.

Nick wriggled an inch or two closer to Jo and linked fingers with her despite the restraint cutting into his wrist.

'I know exactly where we are,' she murmured. 'This is Dyson's Hut. It's private property, used as a shooting camp. The National Park boundary is about four hundred metres that way.' She nodded away from the hut, roughly towards the mid-morning sun. 'East-ish. We're on the north-west side of it here.'

'About forty kilometres from where the cadets are searching today?'

'As the crow flies across wild country and two rivers, yes. As roads go, over a hundred.'

'Any roads or properties close by? Anywhere for help?'

'Not much. It's about fifteen k's west to the main Strathnairn–Queensland road. Park is to the east and the south, and most of the north is State Forest. There's not much in the way of phone reception, even if we had one.'

'Shiny took mine. And my weapons.'

He gripped her fingers, leaned his head over to touch hers. 'There will be a search for us underway already, Jo. Even if

Harrison lies his head off, there's no way he could make that scene and our disappearance look innocent. I'm fairly sure I heard sirens in the distance when we turned off the road.'

'I hope so. But we're a long way from there now, and they won't find us easily.' She rubbed her head lightly against his. 'Listen, Nick, if we can't stop them, Ramirez and this lot will keep killing – directly and through drugs. So if it comes to another situation where you can fight, but I've got a gun against my head, then keep fighting. Take every chance you have to beat them or to escape to beat them later. I'd rather have a bullet through my head or whatever, than have more people die.'

The 'whatever' worried him far more than the bullet. Haunted him, but he had to keep a strong front for Jo. 'I made a snap judgement this morning, Jo. Some of them had to be blocking the road further back, as there'd been no traffic through. So, even if I'd been able to deal with the remaining men, there was no escape. Ramirez wants us alive, so I'm banking on us getting another chance, maybe with fewer of them around. This isn't over. And no matter what happens, I'm not leaving you.'

They both fell quiet, listening to the deep rumble of a motorbike engine approaching the house.

TWENTY-TWO

Ramirez kept them waiting at least another hour. The sun shifted high in the sky, close to mid-point, and the temperature continued to rise. Even in the shelter of the shed, with a cross-breeze blowing through it, Jo sweated precious fluid away. But it gave them a rest, breathing space; a chance to build strength for whatever lay ahead and to discuss possible strategies.

Eventually Ramirez emerged from the hut, the others following him, each carrying a rifle or a handgun. Nick straightened, releasing her fingers, shifting away from her and feigning indifference, as they'd agreed.

White T-shirt, jeans, sunglasses – if she hadn't remembered those eyes behind the glasses, Ramirez might have seemed a fit, attractive man. A successful businessman, enjoying the challenge of the great outdoors in comfort. Not a man who incited others to monstrous crimes.

His offsiders – six of them – shifted into a curved line behind him. The kid was there, pale and unsteady on his feet. The other Mexican man wasn't – the one who'd held the gun to her head and belted her.

Feet braced apart, arms folded, Ramirez looked down on them, his eyes obscured by the sunglasses. Determined not to show fear – that would give him too much power over her – she stared back at him, head held high. But Hayes stepped forward and whacked her across the face, the sting making her eyes water.

She got the message. No insolence to the boss. If there'd been any point continuing, she'd have done it, but with both of them disabled, helpless, it made no sense. She lowered her head slightly, and concentrated on the movements and sounds of the men around her.

Ramirez's black leather boots turned away from her towards his louts. 'I gave you a simple extraction task, and you morons totally fucked it up. You lost two men, and left Harrison alive to talk. We'll have police crawling around here before long. I should shoot the useless fucking lot of you now and leave you for the crows and the cops.'

A few of the men shuffled their feet, shifting backwards, maybe ready to run.

'I'll give you one last test to prove yourselves,' Ramirez continued. 'Gibson, Saunders, get them up and uncuff them.'

Under the watchful eye of Ramirez, Gibson didn't grope her as he cut the cord and dragged her upright. But he did twist the restraint tight before he cut it, digging it painfully into her wrists. Bringing her arms forward at last, restoring proper blood flow, she had a moment of light-headedness. Nick stood tall and straight, showing no evidence of weakness.

He stayed half a pace away from her, not touching her and scarcely acknowledging her as he faced Ramirez.

'I've got plenty of information you'd find useful, Ramirez. Business tips. What say we cut a deal?'

No-one stepped forward to hit Nick. Standing with equal confidence and menace as the boss, no-one dared.

Ramirez regarded him coolly. 'I already have my sources, Matheson. I doubt you could provide much additional value. But I assure you, I do intend to have your information, later.'

'What are your plans for us?' Nick asked, as easily as if Ramirez hadn't just alluded to torturing him.

'A test. Since you almost bested these idiots, they need to have another round with you and show me all they've learned. Hayes, handcuff them together.'

Proper handcuffs this time, but they still rubbed on the raw skin where the restraints had chafed her wrists. Her left hand, Nick's right. At least they were side by side, not looped together in a more limiting way.

'I'll give you a five-minute head start,' Ramirez said, 'and then send them after you.' He turned and looked at each of the men as he continued. 'The ones who bring them back – alive – win. The ones who don't, lose. Matheson is mine. The winners can have the woman.'

So, Nick would be tortured for information and she was the prize for the winners. Adrenaline pumping, she had only time for one train of thought: she mentally pictured the water bottle on the ground, and decided which direction to run.

'When does our time start?' Nick asked, his voice cool, unperturbed.

Ramirez glanced at his watch. 'Ten seconds ago,' he answered.

Jo grabbed Nick's hand, swooped up the fullest water bottle and sprinted for the scrub behind the hut, hoots of laughter following them.

Boots thudding, they quickly shifted into a rhythm, keeping pace side-by-side across the paddock. Once among the trees she took the lead, pushing through the scrubby undergrowth, weaving between the taller trees, jogging rather than sprinting because of the obstacles, and trusting that the hard vibrations of their steps would send any snakes slithering in the opposite direction.

'Why this way?' Nick said.

'They can't follow on the bikes, and we'll be hard to see. Plus, this is my territory, not theirs. They mostly stay near roads.'

Branches whipped into her face, scratched her and tugged at her hair, but she kept going, the water bottle in her free hand shielding her from some of it, Nick's hand tight in hers.

Not straight to the park boundary – that might be too obvious, if they knew the area. She turned more south, angled towards it. She had an idea for a hiding place, if they could reach it undetected.

Under the noise of their progress, she heard shouts. Head start? Apparently not.

Another branch struck her face as, among the shouts, dogs barked.

She picked up pace, desperately trying to remember the topographic details beyond the key features. The river carved down into a rugged gorge about four kilometres away. She'd walked part of the length of the gorge, but not every hectare of wild scrub around it.

Rocks. Granite hills or tors made of huge boulders. Boulders that might be both vantage points and hiding places.

She checked the position of the sun, and veered further east. If she remembered the satellite photos correctly, there might be a large tor about halfway to the gorge.

Nick kept pace with her, but he'd received plenty of punches, and the bullet scar on his side was only a few months old. Still healing.

'How's your fitness? Can you run uphill in a while?'

'Yes. Assuming we're not talking Everest.'

Another advantage. Her familiarity with the territory, their physical fitness.

'Are those dogs going to be a problem?' Nick asked, slightly gasping.

'I doubt it,' she replied, her breathing matching his. 'They weren't working the cattle at all – not even an ounce of instinct. All the scents out here will excite them, but I'd be surprised if they stuck to one.'

She ducked under a low-hanging branch, but not quite far enough, her hair catching in it and bringing them both to a sudden stop. She raised their joined hands to deal with it, the handcuff scraping her raw wrist.

Nick saw her wince. 'Hold still. I'll do it.'

Stepping in front of her, close, he reached over her shoulder with his free hand to untangle the snarl, his cuffed hand cupping her face, tender and soothing against the bruises. 'I'll go in front now. Just keep pointing me in the right direction.'

The sharp report of a rifle, loud and reverberating, sent them running again, and she let him take the lead. The tree cover was changing here – less low undergrowth, fewer native cypress pines, more ironbarks, many of them tall and strong. Faster going, but easier to be seen in.

Another rifle shot cracked through air. Close, but not aimed at them. Maybe a roo. Excited yelps sounded a couple of hundred metres away, but headed in the other direction.

She caught glimpses of the granite tor through the trees, rising above the plateau, and they gradually started an uphill run.

'Go around to the east of the tor,' she told Nick, gasping the words. They'd come a couple of hard k's, in stinking heat. They both needed a rest.

She'd not been to this particular section of the vast park, but she'd chosen the east side for two reasons – because she hoped it would give them a view of the direction she planned to take and because she wanted their pursuers to assume they were going past the tor, not up it.

They reached the base of the tor, the huge rocks towering in a pile a good sixty metres high, trees and shrubs growing out at angles among the granite. They continued almost past it, before Jo turned them back.

Halfway up, a large split rock, its entrance shaded by an overhang, offered a possible shelter. She searched for a way to access it, while avoiding the natural paths where sand gathered between the rocks, and tracks would be too visible.

'Up this way. We should be able to manage this.'

Clambering up and over granite boulders while handcuffed required fitness and coordination – fortunately, they had the first and they had developed the second quickly. But she noticed, once or twice, Nick's gritted teeth, slight hesitation, as he used his left leg on large steps up.

'You're hurt. You should have said.'

'It's nothing major. An old injury – exercise will do it good.'

Nothing major. Right. Where she could, she selected a path upwards that put less strain on his left leg.

A small group of wallabies, resting in the shade, leaped up and away from them, and twice lizards scurried off their path. Getting close to the middle of the day, the time most animals and birds hid from the heat. As humans should be doing, too, Jo thought wryly.

The gap in the split rock was just enough to walk between, and opened out to a width inside of a couple of metres. She broke off a branch from a bush before they entered, and brushed away their footprints in the sand near it and as they ventured in.

At the end of the passage in the rock, about five metres long, light spilled into a larger area, and they found a cavern of sorts, made up of vast, tumbled rocks and slabs at all angles, with several gaps leading out to the light. Cool and quiet.

She indicated a flat rock, complete with an almost-even back rest.

'Sit,' she whispered. 'And keep your voice low. Sound carries in these places.'

She unscrewed the cap of the water bottle and offered it to him. Less than a litre between the two of them. Not nearly enough, given the heat.

He glugged a few mouthfuls and then tried to hand it back.

'No. Have some more. Drink half of it. We'll get more at the river.'

Assuming they reached the river. Another shot sounded, close, and a jubilant shout. Voices, laughs and a dog's yelp.

She finished the water in the bottle, listening beyond her gulps, concentrating on where and who and how many. She screwed the cap on the bottle and laid it between them. They held still, silent, hardly daring to breathe, fingers gripped together.

Voices came closer, drifting into the cavern so that she couldn't tell which direction they came from.

And a dog trotted in through the cavern, panting and snuffling, curious rather than particularly following a scent. She held her breath, dead still, while it explored and peed on the wall. But it finally noticed their scent, yelped excitedly and ran over to leap on top of them.

TWENTY-THREE

Four of them pounded in, from two directions: the kid and Gibson through the split, Saunders and the other bloke from the ute through the cavern. Two rifles, two handguns.

Nick hadn't heard Shiny's or Hayes' voices, but that didn't mean they weren't out there.

He and Jo literally had their backs against a wall, and nowhere to run.

He'd finished his scan for his weapon options. The leafy branch Jo had brought in. He passed a short stick broken off it into Jo's cuffed hand. 'Neck or eyes are best,' he'd whispered. 'Or anywhere you can reach.'

The stupid dog, panting and leaning happily against his leg for pats while ripping apart the plastic water bottle, gave Nick two more weapons: sharp shreds of plastic, and a studded leather collar with a metal pin in the clasp, now in his pocket.

He concealed a two-inch piece of plastic in his hand as he and Jo rose to stand, and he purposely unbalanced her so it appeared that they were awkward in the cuffs.

Saunders jeered. 'Look what we have here. The big-shot detective and the interfering ranger. Cute enough bod, I suppose, but a bit old and scrawny. The copper-woman was sexier.'

His mate from the ute laughed, and Gibson grinned, not quite effectively.

Jo tossed her head in disgust. 'Look what *we* have here, Nick. Gutless, low-life scum. They probably even piss where Ramirez tells them to. No wonder he doesn't want to take any of them with him.'

On the slab rock, they had a height advantage, so Saunders had to step up knee-high to belt her across the face with the rifle butt, and he swung it right to left.

Grounded, his strength centred, Nick caught the rifle before impact, using Saunders's own force to twist it out of his hands, topple him sideways and backwards off the rock. Jo's arm, relaxed, flowed with his easily.

The dog yelped and ran out, cowering.

Saunders landed with a thud on his back. He immediately starting swearing and rising, but Nick already had the rifle pointing at him, holding it left-handed so that Jo's wrist carried less strain.

Gibson and the other man had their weapons raised, handgun and rifle.

'Looks to me like you've got a choice, guys,' Nick said. 'You know Ramirez intends to kill most of you, don't you?'

Gibson cast an uneasy glance at the other man, who shifted a little on his feet. Maybe they needed drugs to be brave. Too bad Ramirez hadn't given them any yet today. No reward for this morning's events. Nick worked on the fear, drilling it harder. 'I'm guessing he'll make you draw lots. Or maybe fight it out. I gather he likes to watch, likes to see what the drugs do to you, what kind of animal they turn you into. He likes the power – over you, not just over the poor sods you kill. Oh, and the punishment-fitting-the-crime thing – Mitchell's stealing, Coulter's mistake in being seen – what will he apply to you, do you think?'

'Castration for being wankers and losers,' Jo suggested.

'He's bullshitting,' Saunders said, yanking the handgun from the kid's drooping hand. 'If we take the bitch back, we'll be fine. And she'll pay for her fucking shit.'

Jo moved in close, closed her right hand on the rifle grip, and Nick let her take it, sliding his free hand to his pocket for another weapon. They wouldn't kill her yet, and they didn't want to wound her and have to carry her, although they'd be happy to kill him. But while she had the rifle she had the power to reduce the threats to both of them, and he had his own weapons.

'"Bitch" is such an empowering word,' Jo said. 'No pressure to be "nice". And yes, this bitch can shoot. Feral pests and predators are my speciality.'

The kid collapsed and vomited, and Gibson dropped beside him to lift his head from the dirt, rifle on the ground.

Nick found it easy to feign exasperation. 'Oh, for fuck's sake, Gibson, if that boy means anything to you then get him out of here to a hospital. He's concussed, probably bleeding in his brain. And you know damned well this lot aren't going to let him see sundown. Show some courage and do something decent for once.'

Gibson slid an arm under the lad's shoulders to hoist him up.

'Leave the rifle,' Nick ordered, as he tried to reach for it. 'You'll have your hands full with the boy.'

As Gibson started half-carrying, half-dragging his young mate out of the cave, Saunders charged forward, the other man following suit a moment later, a little to one side.

Aiming to topple them, betting Jo wouldn't shoot.

Not a bet Nick would have made.

She fired as Saunders came close, and he went down with a howl, but the other guy threw himself forward, tackling her legs, toppling her. Nick followed the pull of her arm down, falling on to the man's body, gripping his hair and pounding his head against the stone twice.

Saunders writhed on the ground, a bloodied hand on his knee. He wouldn't be walking far anytime soon.

Nick helped Jo to her feet. Saunders spat foul curses and tried to fight, but Nick kicked him back, held him still with a knee on his neck and a threat to break it while Jo restrained his hands with the dog collar and wrapped a makeshift bandage from the other guy's shirt around his knee.

'If we make it out alive, Saunders,' Nick told him, 'we'll let the authorities know you're here. So you'd better just hope your mates don't find us.'

He searched both of them, found switchblades and brass knuckles. Not well-trained street-fighters, since they hadn't used them, but a welcome addition to his range of weapon options. Weapons he abhorred using, but they were fighting for their lives. For Jo's life. He'd use whatever he could.

Jo tucked a handgun into the back of her jeans, as did he, and they took a rifle each.

'Ready?' Nick asked her.

She nodded, grim and pale. This wasn't her place, her life, but she'd stepped up, held her own when tough men might have failed.

He touched gentle fingers to her scratched and bruised face. 'You've been fantastic, Jo.' He grinned, aiming to bolster her spirits. 'But do remind me never to get on your wrong side.'

He went in front through the split rock, rifle tucked under one arm. Shiny and Hayes were still out there, somewhere. He hoped they weren't waiting, just outside, to steal the prize when the victors emerged.

⁂

Past midday, fast heading to the hottest part of the day. The sun beat down on the rocks of the tor, and there was limited shade – or cover – on the path they ran down.

They'd need water and shade, and more rest, once they'd found them. Dehydration and heat stroke loomed as real possibilities if they weren't careful.

From the tor she'd checked the direction of the river and gorge. Due east. Maybe two kilometres. Half an hour, if they kept moving and the scrub wasn't too rough.

They heard no gunfire, no shouts, no dogs.

The breeze strengthened to wind. Another westerly, but this time she was glad it was at her back, if not actually aiding them, then at least not making it tougher.

Everything ached – head, legs, body, arms – and despite Nick's grip on her hand, reducing pulling on the cuffs, the jostling of the metal rubbed her skin even rawer.

The bush became denser and they had to slow, too much undergrowth, too many rocks and tree branches threatening to trip them on the uneven ground. They both ditched the rifles, needing their hands to push aside branches and climb over fallen tree trunks.

Tiring, her feet heavy and clumsy, she fell once, dragging Nick half-down with her, wrenching her arm and, she feared, his leg.

As she rose to her feet, several crows flew overhead, cawing harshly. She couldn't see far back the way they'd come, but a few wisps of white drifted above the trees. Facing west, she breathed in deeply.

Smoke. Definitely smoke.

'Keep moving. There's a fire. Let's hope we can outrun it.'

Only a kilometre or so. Ten minutes. Ten minutes in which the wind became stronger and the smoke more evident, and burning leaves and embers blew past them.

She veered fractionally to the south-east. Not to the gorge itself but above the falls, where the river flowed more slowly and the land sloped more gently to it. Where they could wade across it at this time of year, and there was a camping area, a cleared parking ground and an access road on the other side.

They were gasping for breath and clear air by the time they made it, the smoke thickening around them.

About to plunge down the slope towards the river, Nick stopped so suddenly she rammed into him.

In the parking area on the other side was an older white Pajero, two men with rifles standing beside it, watching the river.

TWENTY-FOUR

Nick drew her back into the trees, low to the ground, and they crawled behind a stump. Shiny and Hayes. They'd be harder to beat than the others, and they held all the advantages.

'Bastards,' Jo muttered. 'I'm assuming they lit the fire to drive us this way.'

'Likely. What's down this way?' he asked. The river curved over rocky pools, and through low scrub.

'About two hundred metres further down it drops into a steep gorge. Almost cliffs on this side. There are ways down, but they'd be tough in handcuffs, and we'd be visible targets.'

'Not much of an option, then. South?'

'More of this. The river's slow and shallow, but the vegetation is mostly low scrub. Not much good for cover or for a fire break. We'd have to go a fair way along so they couldn't see us.'

'South it is.'

If he wasn't cuffed to her, he'd have tried a decoy, directing their attention elsewhere so that she could get across safely. Not a possibility. They would have to cross over further up, detouring around through the bush to join the access road some distance from the Pajero.

'No. We need water, we need rest and we need to get away from the fire front. The vehicle and the handcuff keys would be bonuses. What are our chances for a bluff?'

Instinct said no, roared to just keep her away from them. 'I want you safe, Jo.'

'That makes two of us. But I can't go much further, Nick. Not another four or five kilometres even before we get back to the access road, and who knows what, then? Hayes wants me. I'm not sure Shiny cares, but he probably would like to thump you a few more times. If this fire is their work, then they had to drive about forty kilometres to get here, so they probably don't know about the others. If they see us crossing, clutching each other, limping, surrendering and begging for our lives, then I bet they'll wait for us to get to them rather than get their feet wet. And they don't know we're armed.'

'It's a risk, Jo.' He ran scenarios through his mind, could see some succeeding, some failing, all dependent on luck.

'Whatever we do is a risk. You could try the I-brought-you-the-woman story again.'

The thought of what they would do to her terrified him so much he doubted he could be convincing, this time.

But he could try to deal with them. Tempt them to quit Ramirez. Offer them information. He could do that convincingly. And they only had to get close enough for him to strike.

'If you're sure you want to risk it, then we'll try it. Can you do a terrified, weeping woman? And if I'm a total bastard to you, will you forgive me?'

She turned on her knees to face him, her scratched and cut hand against his cheek. 'Nick, do whatever it takes. If I'm still alive tomorrow morning, I'll forgive you anything. And if I'm dead before they get their hands on me, I'll forgive you that, too.'

&

It wasn't hard to cry, to cling to Nick, to stumble through the knee-high water and threaten to fall. Harder to actually *not* fall on the slippery stones below the surface, but he only tugged her impatiently when they were on smooth rocks between pools. The water might be refreshingly cool on her legs, but it wouldn't do much for the gun tucked into her jeans, with a wet T-shirt advertising its presence.

She loudly begged him not to do it, to save her, but he just yelled at her to shut up, raising his hand in a threat to hit her so convincing she flinched.

The whole way across the river, the two men stood on the far bank, watching and waiting for them.

'For fuck's sake, will you take this bitch off me?' Nick demanded as they made their way the last few metres. 'Get the bloody key, Hayes. If you get this bitch off me you two can have the deal I was going to give Ramirez.'

'What deal?' Hayes asked.

Jo sobbed more, struck out at Nick. 'You're a bloody traitor. And people *trusted* you.'

He grabbed her flailing hand, twisted it lightly behind her back, held it there with his cuffed hand as though restraining her. Near her gun. She didn't reach for it, yet. Shiny and Hayes were still suspicious, their rifles ready. Interested, but not convinced.

'Information about rivals,' Nick said. 'I know most of the major players, from the inside and the official surveillance. Dates, places, methods for shipments. And I can tell you date and place for a shipment Ramirez has coming in through the north soon. He's not had much luck setting up his network here, doesn't have much decent back-up. He prefers having them murdered to keeping them. You could be next – or you could have the shipment for yourselves.'

His hand, covering the brass knuckles on her fingers, squeezed a warning, and he half-dragged her, stumbling, the last few steps out of the water.

She jerked her head around to Hayes and Shiny, screaming at them. 'You murdering, filthy bastards. You think you're men but you're nothing but cowards.' Hayes came forward, arm rising. Nick released both her hands, and she flicked the safety on the pistol. Her throat flamed but she kept on screaming, holding Hayes' focus, moving her arm around slowly. 'Gutless, no-balls wimps, not even worth spit.'

She pulled the trigger as his blow landed on her, her head jerking one way, her cuffed arm another as Nick rammed a punch into Shiny and another shot exploded.

They all hit the ground. Her head spun and she could hardly see anything before her eyes, nausea bubbling in her throat. But pure panic and adrenaline flooded her system. Something grabbed her ankle and she kicked out, her boot meeting spongy flesh. Another shot echoed in her head as Nick's body rolled into her, and jerked away. The body underneath her pushed up and Shiny's scalp came into focus. She rammed her cuffed hand under his chin. A vice gripped around her upper right arm and she bore down from the elbow with the pistol, squeezing her whole hand and the gun in it as agony tore into her shoulder. The reverberation of the gunshot cracked so loudly near her she dropped her head in shock and pain.

⁓

His left leg burning, Nick eased up on to his right knee, uncaring as his weight pressed on Shiny's chest. Shiny was out, breathing but not conscious. Hayes moaned. Jo lay half over both of them, her face between them, still and silent.

Other than Shiny's bullet in his already-damaged leg, he'd lost track of shots, had no idea who'd shot whom.

Awkward to lift her, with one leg useless and their hands cuffed together, but she groaned and moved herself, yelping as her free arm refused to take any weight. Blood covered half her T-shirt.

'Jo, be all right. Please, be all right.' He moved closer so their joined hands could take her weight.

'I'm okay,' she murmured. 'It's his blood. I think.'

She pushed off Hayes, and he groaned, swore at the bitch, tried to move and swore again. Nick stretched to grip the pistol he'd dropped, raised himself up on his knee again and aimed at Hayes. Blood covered one hip, and his opposite shoulder.

'Hayes, the only move you make without me shooting you is to get the handcuff key. You've got no choices. Shiny won't be any help to you. If you don't have it in your right hand in five seconds I'll starting putting more holes in you. '

He managed it in seven seconds, holding out his hand with the key in his fingers. Nick couldn't quite reach it, without dragging Jo's hand, and with the shoulder of her free arm held immobile, she wasn't able to help.

'Toss it lightly towards me,' he ordered. 'And remember I have the gun.' Hayes's rifle wasn't far from his left hand, but his left arm wouldn't be gripping anything for a while.

Hayes obeyed, and the key dropped within reach. Nick made quick work of unlocking the cuffs, freeing Jo's wrist carefully, yanking his own out of the restraint.

He dragged his shirt off, ripped it into a couple of strips and bandaged his leg as best he could. If an artery had been hit, he'd be dead by now. But he could survive this. He'd done it before.

Now all they had to do was get across the car park and into the Pajero.

'The Pajero keys – who has them?' he demanded of Hayes. 'He does.'

Nick shuffled up a few inches to reach Shiny's jeans pocket, found the keys first try and stuffed them in his own pocket.

With the gun trained on Hayes again, warning him not to move, he snapped the cuffs around his ankles. The handcuff key went into his pocket with the car keys.

'You can't do that! The fire's coming!'

'Too bad. I'll call for help for you. If you're lucky, it will arrive in time. If not, consider who to blame as you choke on the smoke.'

His mouth tasted bitter. He'd have taken them somehow, if he'd had the choice. But with neither Jo nor him in good shape, he couldn't risk another fight.

The smoke was becoming thicker, adding to the effort of breathing.

'My shoulder's dislocated,' Jo said, her voice beginning to betray the pain and shock. 'If you can push it back in, I should be able to help you walk.'

He'd seen dislocated shoulders a number of times, knew the theory. He'd have to do it, now. Her face white with pain, she knelt on the ground, holding still while he gripped his hands around the joint, felt with his fingers for the correct position.

He exhaled a breath. 'Are you ready?'

'Do it.'

With one quick movement, and a smothered cry from Jo, the joint clicked back into place.

'Hope it never heals properly, bitch,' Hayes said.

She ignored him, and rose to unsteady feet, biting her lip, her arm pressed into her stomach. She looked around the area.

'There's a good-sized stick over there. With it and me, you should be able to walk.'

He worried that her voice was flat, her eyes clouded with pain, but she retrieved the stick from near the trees and brought it over. Two inches thick, over a metre long. He wouldn't need to lean on Jo.

Agony as he used the stick to lever his weight up on his good leg, his twice-wounded leg dragging. He breathed in slowly through his nose, out through his mouth. In, out. *Strength. Conviction. Control.* He could do this. Had to do it.

'If you give me the keys,' Jo said, 'I'll bring the vehicle closer.'

He passed the Pajero keys to her. 'Can you drive, with your shoulder?'

She nodded. 'I have to.'

But when she was halfway across to the vehicle, engines roared not far away. Motorcycle engines.

His gut twisted in fear and despair. No, not now. Not when they'd come so close to freedom.

She heard them at the same time he did, and ran for the Pajero.

'Get out of here, Jo!' Nick shouted. 'Get away!'

He could scarcely move, every step a nightmare. Better to have a weapon, ready to aim.

They roared in, two of them, so fast he couldn't get a decent shot, one screeching to a stop beside Jo as she tried to haul herself up into the driver's seat, the other spinning a cloud of sandy dust into Nick's eyes, before knocking him down again with the back wheel.

When the dust subsided, Ramirez held Jo against him, a knife at her throat, and his offsider stood over Nick, a pistol by his side, his boot on Nick's gun.

Nick curled his fingers around the stick. Roughly the size of a staff, he might be able to do something with it. If he could work out a distraction, get that knife away from Jo's throat.

'Get up, Matheson,' Ramirez ordered. 'Or I slice her throat. I want some information from you before I kill you.'

Up. He used the stick to drag himself to his feet. He'd have to master the pain if he was going to do this, make it of no importance. He shifted his feet slightly apart. *Breathe. Balance. Centre.*

The second man took a casual step back, his gun pointing directly at Nick. Good. A better position to strike.

'What do you want to know, Ramirez?'

'What you offered me this morning. Names, people, who's crooked and who can be eliminated. Information is power.'

Jo held still, watching him, the knife resting against her skin. She opened her eyes a little wider – a question.

He gripped the staff tighter, hoping she saw the answer.

'Let's go where I can sit down, Ramirez, and I'll give you all I know.'

Ramirez grinned, and in that same moment Jo gave a small sigh and turned into a dead weight in his arms. Instinctively he gripped her to stop her falling, his offsider turned to see what had happened and Nick struck. The thick stick balanced perfectly in his hand, he hit the gun out of the man's hands in one movement and swept around to land an upward blow under his chin in the next, followed by another crack on the side of his head that sent him toppling.

Four steps, and he would reach Ramirez, bending over Jo, hand in her hair, bringing the knife closer. But Nick saw her hand scrabble in the sand, and she threw the sand in her attacker's eyes.

While Ramirez howled, he made those steps, the pain a hum in the background, not belonging to him.

He struck Ramirez's head, but he still had Jo's hair in his grip, and he slammed her against the car before he turned to circle Nick with the knife.

'I'll kill you, Matheson,' he snarled, keeping just out of reach of the stick, and Nick let him believe that for a few moments.

He turned on the spot as Ramirez circled. *Breathe. Balance. Centre.* Pain did not matter.

'No, you won't,' Nick said. 'You're nothing, Ramirez. You're so twisted you can't function properly. No-one matters to you, and you matter to no-one.'

Ramirez lunged, but Nick was ready. The stick landed with a loud crack against the Mexican's arm, and the knife went flying. Two fast jabs to the knees brought the man down, two quick blows to each side of the head sent him first one way then the other. He finished with an uppercut under the chin, and Ramirez fell backwards on to the sand.

He lay silent, motionless. His companion remained the same.

Nick didn't particularly care if they were alive or dead, as long as they didn't move.

Jo slumped against the tyre where Ramirez had slammed her.

Nick limped across to her, felt for a pulse in her neck, breathing again as she made a small sound, murmured his name.

'I'm here. Everything's all right. We're just going to stand up now.'

She seemed barely conscious. He had to get her into the Pajero, up on to the back seat. And he had to get himself in so he could drive her away from here.

Agony struck his leg again as he pulled her weight up and leaned them both against the vehicle. Agony as he dragged his leg, inch by precious inch, to the door, Jo hanging in his arms. Agony as she jarred her leg against his, trying to find her feet. He stopped, all his weight on his undamaged right leg.

'Can you get into the back, Jo?'

'Think so. Woozy.'

'Lean into me. We'll take it slow.'

Slurring words, dizziness – how many blows had she taken to the face and the head today? He had to get her to a hospital. The Pajero had radio antennas – a functioning radio had to be inside.

He held her to his right, still half-supporting her, but not as a dead weight. He breathed deeply again, made his muscles relax. He would beat this. Pain was only pain. It wouldn't kill him.

She helped him lift her on to the back seat, took some of her own weight and edged across so she could lie down along the seat. There was a towel on the floor, grubby and dusty, but Nick rolled it into a makeshift neck brace and carefully wrapped it in place.

Once in the driver's seat, he started the engine, grateful for the automatic transmission. Unable to reach the police channel from a private radio, he found the emergency channel and sent out a call, requesting urgent medical assistance for a head injury, and ambulances for other injuries, and reporting the fire. He gave directions as best he could.

He turned the vehicle around, stopping a little nearer to Hayes to toss him the handcuff key. Not intentionally, it fell a few metres short. If Hayes needed it badly enough, he'd reach it.

He took the dirt road slowly, juggling the necessity to get to an open, fire-free area for a chopper to land with the need for minimal movement for Jo's head injury. He clarified a few details on the radio, was assured help was coming.

Jo lay silently in the back, unconscious.

There were people and voices and noise and flashing lights in her head and something on her face and she couldn't get any of it straight. Only the throbbing pain was clear and constant, and the nausea.

But there was one voice . . . she listened for it, heard it, lost it . . . heard it again, close. Quiet, near her. Somebody held her hand, very gently. She tried to curl her fingers round it. *Hold on to the hand.*

'Jo, it will be all right. They'll take care of you. You're strong and courageous and you will get through this.' She felt a breath near her cheek, a kiss, feather light. And a whisper, 'Goodbye, Jo. I'll never forget you.'

No, she tried to say. *No. No. No.*

TWENTY-FIVE

'It's okay, Jo. You're in hospital. You're just waking up from an operation.'

Hospital? Operation? She forced her eyes open. Yes. Lights. Faces. Electronic beeps. A bed under her.

'What operation?' She couldn't make her voice work.

'Don't try to talk, Jo. You've got a tube down your throat to help you breathe. You had a bad bang on your head, but the doctors are very happy with you.'

A bang on the head. Yes, she remembered that. Remembered all of them. Remembered running and fighting and being terrified for her life. And she remembered Nick, beside her the whole time, his hand in hers.

She tried to lift her hands, could move but not lift them. They were covered with tubes, and bandages holding them to the bed frame.

'It's okay, Jo.' Someone held her hand, but not the right person. 'We just need to make sure you don't take the breathing tube out. The doctors will come and do that soon, I promise.'

She nodded, understanding. They'd operated on her brain, presumably to relieve some bleeding. But she was okay – she could think and she could understand and she could move both hands and her feet, and when they took the damned tube out of her throat she'd be able to talk.

And the first thing she'd ask would be, 'Where's Nick?'

⌘

They gave him a private room in Strathnairn Hospital. A private room with a police officer on duty outside the door. They also gave him pain meds for his leg, a drip to re-hydrate him, and endless forms to fill out.

What they couldn't give him, for far too many hours, was news on Jo.

Outside his window, Strathnairn's lights shone into the night. He'd heard hospital visitors leaving a while back, and the voices of nursing staff, beginning to ready patients for sleep.

Nick shifted, trying to find a more comfortable position, his leg protesting the movement. His left leg ached, his head ached despite the pain meds, the cannula in his hand for the intravenous fluids ached. Though he strived for any vestige of centred, balanced calm, it eluded him, his mind far too restless.

When Leah poked her head around the door to see if he was awake, he beckoned her in.

'Jo's out of surgery,' she said, in response to his first demand. 'Murdoch spoke with her mother. There was some bleeding in the brain, so the docs have relieved the pressure. "Stable" is the official statement at present, but her mother is pretty optimistic, apparently.'

Bleeding in the brain . . . Hearing the words confirmed the fears he'd endured for hours. Not his worst fears – she was still alive – but 'stable' still covered too broad a range of possibilities. Optimism was good, probably the best he could expect at this stage, but he desperately wanted to hear 'full recovery'.

Leah pulled a chair towards the bed and dropped into it. 'Nick, they do that kind of surgery every day. I had a constable whose head met a brick wall a year or so back. Same kind of op, and he was out of hospital in less than ten days. Jo's young, fit and tough. Trust that she's not going to give up easily.'

No, she didn't give up easily. She'd kept going, kept fighting, all day, facing guns and fists and heat and dehydration and still – even with bleeding in her brain and an injured shoulder – she'd battled Ramirez, struggled to get herself into the Pajero. But now she lay unconscious, far away in Sydney, and all he could do was lie uselessly here and hope she had the strength to keep fighting.

'I guess there won't be any more news until morning.' He spoke the thought aloud.

'No. You know how hospitals are. I'll make sure you're told as soon as I hear anything.'

She didn't ask, didn't tease or comment otherwise on his worry for Jo – just the brisk, practical understanding that characterised their relationship; respect and friendship without emotional closeness.

'Thanks, Leah.' He trusted that she would understand his gratitude. 'So, what's happened? Did you find Ramirez?'

'We've found them all. Most of them are in Tamworth Base Hospital, and some of them are talking, busy blaming each other.'

Nick's chest relaxed, the tight band around it and his spine loosening a little. He'd do the same things again if he had to – he'd been fighting for survival – but leaving injured men out in the wilderness had weighed on his conscience.

He tore a dozen pages off the notebook he'd borrowed from a nurse, and passed them to Leah. 'I've written out my statement, everything that occurred. It should help you piece it all together.'

'Thanks.' She settled back in the chair, skimming down the first page before she glanced up again. 'We've got Harrison. He bullshitted for a few hours until I put him through Haddad Hell.'

Nick had seen it, a few times – the relentless, scathing verbal cyclone that she could keep up for hours if necessary.

Leah grinned. 'Now he's babbling like a baby, trying for reduced charges. Not a bloody chance. He's been in with Ramirez for weeks, probably longer. That coke Jo found at the lookout? It was left for him. The coordinates were in a text message on his phone.'

'Reward for stonewalling the vandalism investigation? It makes sense. If Jo hadn't found Mitchell's body, Harrison might have been the only one to go out there to look into the damage.'

'Yes. Ramirez wasn't happy about the damage. Even less happy about the rifle Mitchell took. I'd say it was the beginning of the end for that group of louts, as far as he was concerned.'

So he'd let them loose, punishing Mitchell and Coulter, silencing Hugh, torturing Shelley for information – keeping his distance, letting them commit the crimes. 'Will we be able to get enough on Ramirez?' Nick asked. He couldn't contemplate the possibility that the man might walk free.

'Even without the rate they're all talking, yes. We have his laptop and his phone, and although his filing system is, shall we say, unique, and half of it's in Spanish, there's plenty there already. Including his file on you, which he gave Harrison to leak. Drugs, money laundering, conspiracy to murder, perverting the course of justice – we'll get him, Nick.'

They had to. He'd be officially off the case now – witness rather than investigator – but if Leah and the team couldn't do it, he'd find a way. 'Where is he now?'

'Royal North Shore Hospital, under armed guard. Don't worry – Jo's at Royal Prince Alfred, not North Shore. If he's conscious in the morning, he'll be charged, and transferred to Long Bay prison as soon as he's out of intensive care.'

She yawned, and checked her watch. 'I've got paperwork to finish, and I should let you get some rest.' Using the armrests of the chair for leverage, she pushed herself to her feet.

She had a long night ahead of her, and although he could – theoretically – rest, probably should, being sidelined by injury sent his frustration levels soaring. With so much to do, cases to build and document, strategies to decide, aftermath to deal with, he doubted his brain would let him rest.

'The two guys on the road yesterday,' he said before she left. 'Can you make sure, when the official autopsy comes back, that Jo is told that their gunshot injuries would not have been fatal?'

'Yes, I saw them. I'll have to wait for the official report of course, but if it confirms that, I'll make sure she knows. She's had enough to deal with, without guilt on top of it.'

Nick could only agree. She was going to need her strength of spirit, her courage and her good sense; all that and more in the weeks and months ahead.

Leah stopped at the door. 'Before I forget, the youngest lad – his name's Jared Gibson – he's here. His brother brought him in early in the afternoon, and at that stage we didn't know the connection. Concussed, and having a reaction to some drugs, but they haven't shipped him elsewhere so I guess he's all right. His brother flagged down the team that went to check Dyson's Hut, and gave himself up. He helped us find the others, and he's given a full statement. He said to tell you that he'd finally had the courage to do the decent thing.'

After Leah left, with little to do and plenty *not* to think about, Nick stared at the ceiling. He was neither glad nor sorry that Ramirez's injuries were serious enough for intensive care. The man had made his choices, manipulated people, tortured and killed – and he'd threatened Jo with the same. Nick had defended her, and Ramirez had reaped what he'd sown.

Now she should be safe from him, wouldn't have to live her life looking over her shoulder, or under police protection.

Unlike him.

He would do what had to be done, but it wasn't a life he wanted to live.

He wanted a life where he could be himself, fully and completely, authentic and *whole*.

He just couldn't see, with the exposure that Ramirez's leak had caused, how it might be made possible.

❦

After a couple of days in intensive care, they moved her upstairs to a ward, and for Jo a distinct advantage of the ward was the large window with a view outside – a view of Sydney, the crowded cityscape not as beautiful as a bush landscape, but she was counting positives, not negatives. Alive, in one piece, with no lasting damage; she'd recover, and be back in the bush before too long. For now, she sat by the window, enjoying the freedom from tubes and monitors, resting, occasionally sleeping, and looking forward to a walk to the cafeteria when her brother arrived later.

A reflection in the window caught her eye, and she turned to the woman hesitating in the doorway, an arrangement of flowers in her hands.

Slim in a simple sundress, dark hair brushing her shoulders, she was distinctly feminine, and yet . . . one look at those familiar eyes, and Jo guessed her name before she introduced herself.

'I hope I'm not intruding. My name's Grace Anderson. I'm—'

'Nick's sister,' Jo finished for her. 'Please, come in, take a seat. I'm so glad to meet you. Have you heard how Nick is? I'm only getting official statements.' And if she didn't get more news soon, now that she was out of intensive care she'd be on the phone herself, hassling Murdoch, Aaron, *anyone* until they gave her a direct number for Nick.

'He's okay.' Grace placed the flowers on the bedside cabinet, and sat on a nearby chair. 'He's out of hospital. He's supposed to be taking it easy, but he's back at work, dealing with the aftermath. The police want detailed statements to support all the charges they'll be making. I'm so sorry that you – that both of you – had to go through such a horrific experience.'

'I survived, thanks to Nick. A detective came to see me yesterday, and I told him all that happened.' She swallowed to moisten a dry mouth, the memories fresh again in her mind after a day or so of post-anaesthetic blurriness. The detective would be back, later today, for a formal statement. She had to make sure she gave it clearly, so there could be no doubts, no loopholes enabling blame to be cast other than where it belonged.

'From the little Nick told me, I gather it was a team effort. He's worried about you, Jo.'

'Everything works fine. I'll be back to normal before long.' Jo pointed to the telephone beside her bed. 'I could tell him that myself if he phoned me. Or if you can give me his number, I'll call him.'

'He's not giving me his direct number.' A small smile didn't quite succeed in disguising her sadness, her pain. 'He said he hasn't replaced his mobile yet, but I can read between the lines. That television report has him worried. So he's protecting me. Protecting you, too.'

I'd give my life to keep you safe . . . He hadn't just meant his physical body. He'd given up his sister, this lovely, compassionate woman, to keep her safe. He would give up . . . she didn't know how to define the bond between them. No promises, no commitments, they'd said, but he'd made that promise to protect her, and he'd meant it.

350

Jo brushed moisture from the corner of her eye. 'I wish . . . God, I wouldn't wish your brother any less than he is, Grace, but I wish his protective streak didn't come at such a cost to him.'

Grace passed her the box of tissues from the bedside cabinet. 'I know. It's what I remember most about him. Where we grew up was an ugly, violent place. When the police smashed some of the organised crime, *dis*organised crime and turf wars filled the vacuum. For many of the kids – even the little ones – bullying and fighting was just the way of life. Nick learned to fight to protect us, not because he ever enjoyed the fighting. And then he joined the police force, and he seemed to have found somewhere he could use his skills for good work. I hoped, when Hugh told me he'd given up the undercover jobs, that he might finally build the life he deserves – that I might get my brother back.'

Tears brimmed in her eyes, and Jo offered her the tissue box.

'I'm sorry,' Grace said, wiping her eyes. 'Some doctor I am. I'm supposed to be cheering you up, but here I am crying into your tissues. I must seem so weak, but I'm just so afraid of losing him again.'

'It's not weakness. I've only known him a few days and I don't know—' She clutched a tissue tight in her hand. 'Grace, I don't know exactly what's between him and me, what we might want. But I'm afraid. Afraid of the threats to him and afraid that if he thinks either of us will be safer without him, then he'll leave. Witness protection, hiding, a new identity – it doesn't matter which, we'd still lose him.'

And she could no longer imagine which might be more

unbearable – losing someone she cared about after only a few short days, or losing someone she loved after five years.

⌀

Two evenings later, with the ward emptied of visitors and the evening hush starting to settle, she took her usual chair by the window, browsing the internet on a laptop she'd begged from her brother to catch up on media reports. Given the lack of contact from Nick, the bare slivers of information she and Grace had gleaned had come from the media.

One headline from the morning caught her eye: *News team sacked.*

She raced through the brief article. A news presenter and a producer sacked. A 'full and unreserved apology' to 'the detective concerned for the misrepresentation of his character and his career'.

They acknowledged multiple errors of fact and judgement, and again, without naming him, stated that the detective had 'no connection to any of the persons named in the original report'.

She rested her head against the back of the chair and watched the lights sparkling across the city.

It had to be some kind of damage-control strategy, not just an apology. But would it be enough?

Goodbye, Jo.

That was the bad dream that woke her from every sleep. Not killers or fires or fighting or running through the bush she loved, scared for her life. Just two gently whispered words.

No. Not goodbye. There had to be a way. They would have to find a way.

☙

Three framed photographs stood on top of the coffin. Hugh in dress uniform, receiving a commendation for bravery. A much younger Hugh, in far less tidy high-school uniform, grinning with Pat and Christie at the camera. And the last, taken just weeks ago, of Hugh and Grace enjoying dinner in a restaurant.

Nick steadied himself on his crutches and faced the small graveside gathering. Very small, the request for a private funeral respected. Three of Hugh's Sydney colleagues stood to one side in dress uniform, with Keith Murdoch and the head of Homicide representing the Police Force officially. A sign of respect. And Grace.

Fresh flowers rested on the graves beside the new plot: Christie, Pat, their parents. It was right that Hugh would lie here with the Matheson family.

Nick drew his inadequate notes from his pocket. He had to start, but he wasn't ready.

A taxi stopped in the lane nearby, and a woman alighted. She wore a simple jade-green dress, classic and unadorned but for a pendant, and flat sandals. A silk scarf was tied around close-cropped hair.

She crossed the lawn towards them.

Beautiful, natural, herself. Discharged from hospital only this morning, and she'd travelled up to Newcastle.

Grace held out her hand in welcome and drew Jo into the small circle.

Nick met her gaze and held it. Everything was right, and he could do this now. Authentic. Whole.

He could honour Hugh as a man who'd risen above a tough childhood, made something of himself through hard work, who'd lived with passion for life and unwavering loyalty to his family and friends. An imperfect man, a complex man who had suffered and feared and loved and made mistakes but also a man who had saved lives and put his life on the line for others, time after time.

Nick looked across the casket at Grace and Jo, and told them, told them all, that he could honour Hugh as his colleague, brother and friend.

☙

She walked with him after the service, a short stroll to a bench under the shade of a tree, peaceful and quiet. The sky huge and blue above them, the sun starting to angle, golden, catching tiny sparkles in granite here and there, birds flitting through trees and graves, chattering contentedly.

He stretched out his injured leg, easing into a comfortable position.

'How is it?' she asked.

'I'll have to take it easy for a while, but it will heal, again, given time. And you?'

Ordinary questions, necessary questions. She looked out over the view, content that they would get to the deeper ones.

'Time and rest, and I'll be fine. The doctors are very happy with me. It's pretty amazing what they can do.'

Time and rest and care, and most things would heal. Bones, muscles, tissue and nerves; hearts and spirits.

But hearts and spirits required different forms of medicine. She reached out a hand, linked her fingers through his, saw his close around hers, still bearing scratches and scars like hers, but strong and sure.

'I read the apology in the news. Will it work to protect your identity? Will you be safe now?'

He nodded. 'Relatively. Nothing's guaranteed. Apparently the original report never streamed out, the file never went online. One of the technical people was on the ball, and pulled it after the first few seconds. HQ ran a risk analysis. A short segment at six-thirty on a Sunday morning that never went online – the initial feeling is that the risk might not be immense.'

It never went online. Relief relaxed muscles she didn't know she'd been holding tense.

'So you're here, not in hiding.'

'Yes. They've put a few other protective strategies in place, as well. Nick Matheson's been doing things, according to official records, when some other people were elsewhere. So, I'm here.' He smiled, and the depth in his dark brown eyes wasn't the dark of fear or despair. 'All of me. Nick Matheson.'

Her smile stretched the tight skin on the side of her scalp, and she didn't care. 'Hello, Nick.'

'Hello, Jo.'

She lifted his scarred hand to her lips, kissed each knuckle, one by one. Hands that fought when needed, to protect, but could be gentle, giving. Strength, for all the right reasons.

'I know I've mentioned it before, but you are a remarkable man.'

He didn't protest, as he'd done before. Dark eyes, peaceful, held hers as he kissed her fingers. 'You're pretty remarkable yourself, Jo.'

She leaned her head against his.

'Do you think we should make time, while we're resting and recovering from our various wounds, to get to know more about each other?'

He folded his arms around her, drew her close. 'Good idea. What do you want to know?'

'The kinds of things we haven't had time to discover yet. Interests, passions, dreams, plans. Although I've already figured out that you probably don't collect stamps.'

'Stamps? As in postage stamps? No, I don't collect them.' He was silent a moment. 'I practise Aikido,' he said quietly. 'It's self-defence, based on a philosophy of minimal harm. That's important to me. I'm thinking seriously about returning to teaching it.'

Protection, minimal harm. The heart, the centre of him. A powerful strength.

'I love the outdoors,' she said. 'Nature awes me – the environment, wildlife, the balances, the way things gradually change yet remain strong. There's so many questions, so much to study and discover. But I also love home and simple things. Friends, family, community ties. It's time I found somewhere to live, not just camp. Maybe a few acres near Strathnairn.'

'You'll stay in the district? I didn't know if . . . whether there'd be too many bad memories, to go back to work there, live there.'

She pulled away just enough to see him properly.

'The land has never scared me. Landscape isn't good or bad or evil or confused, it just *is*. It's beautiful and intricate and incredible. People scare me sometimes, but most astound me with their resilience and hope and their ability to dream and love and to continue on, despite the inevitable challenges. Like you.'

His arm, gentle around her shoulders, drew her close to him again. 'Like you,' he said.

ACKNOWLEDGEMENTS

I wrote this novel while waiting for and recovering from brain surgery, and I am grateful to many people who have supported me throughout the medical and writing journeys. Doctor Rodney Allen and the entire neurosurgery care team at Royal Prince Alfred Hospital have ensured that I am still here to write many more stories, and cared for me throughout with dedication, compassion, and good humour.

My agent, Clare Forster, and publisher Bernadette Foley of Hachette have been patient, understanding, and accommodating, and their encouragement helped me through the rough times. Editors Sara Foster and Claire de Medici took great care in reading the manuscript and their thoughtful suggestions and feedback have improved the book a great deal.

Sergeants Gemma Gallagher and Simon Meehan have again provided very helpful advice on police procedures, and National Park Ranger Emily Ingram generously shared her experiences and answered many questions about the realities of the job.

I am grateful, too, for the ongoing love and encouragement of family and friends, and to the many readers who sent messages and who have been waiting, eagerly but patiently, for a new book from me.

Gordon has been by my side throughout the journey. He endures an untidy house, my distracted writer's brain, and my late night writing timetable, and still believes emphatically that I am a good writer. But, most importantly, he held my hand and talked to me when I was unconscious after the brain surgery, and was there by my side when I woke up. Thank you, joy of my life.

INTRODUCING

DARKENING SKIES

ALSO BY BRONWYN PARRY

Gil Gillespie. Mark Strelitz stopped listening to the constituent expressing his forthright views and glanced across Birraga's main street again. Definitely Morgan 'Gil' Gillespie, sitting at a table outside Rosie's cafe in broad daylight. No longer in witness protection, or wherever he'd been these past few months.

Gil was a man he needed to see, to speak with. Attempting to maintain some level of courtesy, Mark extricated himself from the conversation he'd been caught in with a promise to look into the matter further, and shook hands before he hastened across the street.

Gil rose as he approached, the violent beating he'd endured months ago still evident in the stiffness in his left arm, his eyes narrowed with the same wariness he'd always carried. Growing up they'd never been close, the gulf between their life experiences too great, and Gil's life since then had given him few reasons to trust easily. Three years in prison, then fifteen managing a pub in inner-city Sydney and trying to keep it out of mafia influence. A stark contrast to Mark's experience of university, managing the family pastoral company and grazing properties, and six years serving his outback region as an independent member in federal parliament.

But Gil's stance against the mafia and their unexpected local connections when he'd returned for the first time a few months ago had earned Mark's respect. He'd held the Sydney mafia at bay for years but they'd used bent police and local thugs to get at him, almost beating him to death.

Mark held out his hand. 'Gil! I didn't know you were back.'

'I just arrived.'

'It's good to see you. Everyone was worried, for a while there.' Worried he wouldn't survive the night, after he'd been flown out by air ambulance following a police raid to rescue him. 'You're well?'

Mark could have bitten his tongue. Small talk, awkward and out of place with Gil who rarely practised the social customs that had become natural to Mark.

Nevertheless, Gil answered with only a hint of irony, 'Much better.'

'Great to hear.' Mark paused. Forget polite enquiries. He had to grasp this opportunity, find answers to the questions that had haunted him for a long time. Answers only Gil had. 'Gil, would you have a few minutes? There's a matter I've been wanting to discuss with you.'

Gil hesitated. 'Yeah, I guess so. I've got nowhere to be until six.'

'Thanks. My office is just round the corner – shall we go there?'

His staff had gone home, the electorate office deserted but for the two of them. The afternoon sun through the west-facing windows overpowered the air conditioning, so Mark poured cool drinks and showed Gil into his office.

Mark looked down at his hands, at the glass in them. What happened in this conversation could change everything. Probably *would* change everything.

'Gil, I need to ask you about the accident, with Paula.' The event that tied them together. Eighteen years, half a lifetime ago for them, but not for Paula Barrett, her vibrancy extinguished forever when the car smashed into the tree.

Gil stilled, wary, but Mark ploughed on. 'I've never regained my memory of it,' he explained. 'The medicos think I probably never will. It's just a black hole in my head. But the thing is . . . ever since the other month, when you were here and I had that concussion, I've had dreams, quite often. Always the same – a bloody kangaroo glaring at me in the headlights, a horrendous crunch as we hit the tree.' He paused and took a mouthful of the cold drink, his throat tight. Then he looked Gil straight in the eye, determined to uncover the truth. 'The scene I see – it's always from the driver's seat. I was driving that night, wasn't I?'

Gil stood abruptly, walked to the window and gazed out. 'It's just a dream,' he said.

'I have to know for sure, Gil. I don't know if what I'm dreaming is a fragment of memory or just my imagination. I don't remember anything between my birthday the week before, and waking up in the hospital. But seeing you again, the concussion – one of them's triggered something in my head.

The dream keeps coming again and again and again, and I need to know whether it's real or not.'

'Leave it, Mark.' Gil still didn't look at him, his back rigid, his low voice a rough warning.

A warning Mark ignored. He rose from his seat and pressed harder for answers. 'Can you swear to me that you were driving, Gil? Can you do that?'

Gil finally turned to face him. 'It's ancient history, now. Just let it be.'

No denial. There would never be a denial. The truth was there in Gil's unwavering dark eyes and Mark felt the shift in his life, in what he understood about himself, almost as a physical sensation. 'Why?'

Gil didn't respond.

'Damn it, Gil, why?' Mark demanded. 'Why did you tell them it was you?'

Gil let out a slow breath, and the words came with it, tumbling out after years of silence. 'I didn't. The old sarge – Bill Franklin – was the first one there, and by then I'd got you out of the car and was doing what I could for Paula. I couldn't get to her through her door so I was kneeling in the driver's seat, and Franklin just assumed at first I'd been driving. Then Paula died at the scene, and they didn't know if you'd make it, and everyone was angry, and although Franklin knew by then it was you, not me – well, I guess he figured it was better to blame the feral kid than the town favourite.'

It made sense; more sense than the lies told and maintained for years. 'But why didn't you say something?'

'I was just a kid, outcast, and way out of my depth.' Gil grimaced, and for a moment Mark saw the shadow of the isolated youth in the hardened man. 'It was . . . made clear to me that I was to carry the blame. And then the first night in the remand centre, the threat was delivered – comply, or Jeanie would suffer. I thought I had no choice. The days went by, and you never said anything to contradict the story. No-one would have believed me, without your back-up, and I couldn't risk anything happening to Jeanie.'

Jeanie Menotti – the one adult who'd given Gil a chance, employed him at her Truck Stop Café, demonstrated her belief in him. And whoever was behind the cover-up had threatened her to gain Gil's compliance. Mark clenched his fists tightly, the harshness of Gil's experience worse than he could have guessed. And all his fault.

'Gil, I wish I knew what to say. "Sorry" is nowhere near enough.'

'You don't need to say sorry or any other shit,' Gil said, hard and blunt. 'It's done and gone years ago, and you weren't involved. They stuffed up the rigging of evidence, and the conviction was quashed. I don't have a record. There's nothing to fix. There's no bloody point in bringing it up after all this time.'

No point? Gil had served three years in prison before being able to prove that the damning blood-alcohol report couldn't have been his blood.

'There is if it was my fault,' Mark said firmly, no doubt in his mind. 'Had I been drinking, Gil? Was I drunk?'

Gil ran a hand through his hair. 'You weren't drunk,' he said. 'I was hitching, and you offered me a ride. I was only in the car ten minutes or so before the smash. Paula had a bottle of something, offered it around, but you didn't have any.'

'That doesn't mean I wasn't already over the limit.' It didn't mean that the blood-alcohol report wasn't *his*.

'I saw no sign of it. Look, Mark, the accident was just that, an accident, no-one's fault. Not yours or mine or Paula's or any bloody kangaroo's fault. So don't go being all high-minded and doing anything stupid.'

Stupid? No, he wasn't about to do anything stupid. But justice mattered, truth mattered, and it was his responsibility to clear Gil's name and make the truth known.

The black hole in his memory swirled, a chasm that might yet swallow his life.

ONE

Twenty-four hours on a plane followed by a hot, sleepless night, then early-morning hasty packing and almost nine hours on the road from Sydney to Dungirri, and still Jenn Barrett's brain grappled to make sense of yesterday's out-of-the-blue emails and the phone message that played on a continual loop in her mind on the long drive.

'Jenn, it's Mark Strelitz. I hope you get this before you see it on the news. I need to tell you . . . Gil Gillespie came back to town again last week and I finally had the chance to talk to him about the accident. I still have no memory of it because of the head injury, likely never will. But, Jenn – I was driving, not Gil. I was driving, and Paula died. I have to set the record straight and make sure the investigation is reopened.'

Memories and emotions she'd long ago buried crawled out of their graves and whirled around the stunning fact of Mark's revelation: *he* had been driving when her cousin Paula was killed eighteen years ago. Mark, not Gil Gillespie.

Mark, whose friendship had been the one steady rock in her adolescence, after the violent loss of her parents. Mark, whose affection she'd eventually rejected. Who had been one of the reasons she'd caught the bus out of Dungirri at seventeen, the day after Paula's funeral.

So much for her vow, back then, never to return.

The gravel road wound through the last kilometre of the thick, dry, Dungirri scrub, and the old familiar tension coiled around her spine as she crossed the low wooden bridge over the creek and into the town.

A willy-willy stirred up dust and dead leaves and swirled across the road ahead of her. Dust and death. They still clung to Dungirri, the terminal illness of economic and social decay evident in boarded-up shop windows, long-empty houses and scarcely a soul in evidence, the main street almost as dead as the cemetery she'd just passed.

Why the *hell* had she agreed to come back to this godforsaken hole?

Because of the desperation in her Uncle Jim's voice in his phone message last night, the pleading of her cousin Paul's email. Proud men, both of them, not the kind who could easily ask for help, but out of their depth with this sudden news and worried for Paul's brother, Sean, in prison following his vicious beating of Gillespie.

But Jenn hadn't come back just for their sakes. *She* needed to find out the truth behind Mark's unexpected confession. Unexpected and very public – at a brief lunch stop in a roadhouse somewhere along the way the TV had blared news of his press conference this morning, his shock resignation as an independent member of federal parliament, the reopening of the police investigation at his request.

She gritted her teeth against a wave of nausea. 'Get a grip, Jenn,' she muttered. 'It's only bloody Dungirri. You can sort out this mess and then leave again.'

Approach it like a story. Journalism was what she knew, so she had to stick with that. Be objective, rational. As if Paula hadn't been her cousin, sister, friend. As if Mark were just another politician with a convenient case of amnesia.

At the end of the block, a couple of cars were parked outside the Dungirri Hotel, a 'For Sale' sign attached to the upper veranda, and across the road, a sign advertising ice-cream stood on the path in front of the old general store.

Undecided about what to do or where to go first, she turned into the street beside the shop and parked in the shade of a tree. As she climbed out of the air-conditioned car, the dry December heat hit her, sucking moisture from her skin. Her legs and back stiff from hours of driving after a day in planes yesterday, she walked towards the corner to stretch her muscles.

Apart from slight movement in the leaves on the trees along the street, nothing stirred in the hot afternoon. A bulldozer parked across the road marked the recent demolition of Jeanie Menotti's Truck Stop Café, burned in a fire. A gaping hole in a once-familiar streetscape.

Old habits resurfaced and she refused to allow her gaze to linger on the dilapidated buildings of the Dungirri Showground on the corner where she stood, or the grassed area of the overgrown show ring where she and her parents had once camped while visiting family. Where everything had changed in one terrifying, soul-ripping moment, condemning her to five years in Uncle Mick's guardianship in Dungirri.

Dust, desolation, death – that about summed up her memories of Dungirri.

Steeling herself against the temptation to simply turn around, walk back to her car and drive away, she eyed the hotel from across the street. Time hadn't been kind to it, and she would bet that the accommodation was basic. She could decide later if she would risk staying there, or head into the larger Birraga, sixty kilometres further west.

Right now she needed to re-bury her memories, find her objectivity and focus on making some sense of this mess. Sitting half-in, half-out of the car, she jotted on a notepad the facts as she knew them from her Uncle Jim's emails and the news reports she'd seen. Fact one: Gil Gillespie's return to Dungirri almost three months ago. Fact two: Gillespie's revelations of connections between the Calabrian mafia Russo family from Sydney and the Flanagans, local shady business family and thugs led by wealthy businessman Dan and his sons. Drugs, blackmail, coercion – all the usual organised crime, and she'd seen more than enough of it, the world over. Fact three: Her cousin Sean's involvement with the Flanagans and the Russos, and his assault on Gillespie, believing him responsible for their cousin Paula's long-ago death.

She paused with her pen on the page so long that the ink ran, forming a blot. There lay the crux of Jim's and Paul's concerns

– how Mark's confession would impact Sean, guilt-ridden and in prison, and her Uncle Mick, Paula's father.

She didn't give a fraction of a damn about Mick, but the others – yes, maybe she did. Or maybe this was just personal, about her own needs, her own questions.

Fact four: Gillespie's return to the district from witness protection a week ago, Mark's meeting with him and subsequent public confession and resignation today, after informing the Barretts privately yesterday.

And in that line of her scrawled writing lay the focus of most of her questions and her journalist's scepticism. Just what the *hell* had gone on during that conversation between the two men? Exactly what had prompted Mark to throw away his career so abruptly?

She tossed her pen and notebook on to the passenger seat and yanked the car door shut. The best place to find the truth was at the source. And the source, in this case, lived fifteen minutes beyond Dungirri.

She made herself steady her breathing and started the car. Ask questions, investigate, find the truth. Her teenage friendship with Mark lay firmly in the past, irrelevant now.

The three blocks of the town's main street disappeared into her rear-view mirror and the road ahead ran straight west into the flat, mostly cleared farmland towards Birraga. Only pockets of scrub and the eucalypts lining the road remained, the paddocks brown and withered in the summer sun.

All familiar, this road she'd travelled hundreds – probably thousands – of times. She battled the unsettling sense of being thrust back eighteen years in time by looking for the changes.

The remnants of the old O'Connell wool shed, flattened in a storm when she was a kid, had been replaced by a new steel machinery shed. The Dawsons had installed solar panels on the homestead roof. The property next door to them had new fences.

Small, incremental changes. Nothing that disturbed the shape of the land; the paddocks stretching for miles, the cone of Ghost Hill towering over the plains, the green smudge of trees in the distance marking the Birraga River, snaking its way across the country.

A kilometre or so before Ghost Hill she slowed, shifting down a gear, indicating for the turn-off even though there were no other cars around to notice.

As she made the turn on to the dirt road, a wave of nostalgia caught her unawares. The Kurrajong trees still shaded the short row of mail boxes and the tilting corrugated iron shelter where she'd waited, day after day, with Mark and Paula for the school bus into Birraga High. Despite all the frustrations and unhappiness of her youth and her Uncle Mick's resentful guardianship, the three of them had shared good times and a strong friendship.

'A long time ago,' she murmured, steering her thoughts away from the past. Five kilometres along the track the gates of Marrayin Downs stood open, and she turned into the tree-bordered driveway.

A dusty white ute was parked in the shade of the old red gum in the wide drive-circle across from the century-old homestead, and she pulled up behind it. Mark? His property manager? It was unlikely to be her Uncle Jim over here – he managed another Strelitz property just south of Dungirri. And her Uncle Mick probably hadn't stepped foot at the place since his dismissal had forced them to leave the manager's cottage nineteen years ago.

She spared a single glance towards the old cottage, half-hidden among its grove of trees. No vehicles, no signs of life. Turning her back on the house she'd once lived in – never a home – she straightened her shoulders and walked across the drive circle to the main homestead.

The deep shade of the vine-covered veranda created a refuge from the heat, and her steps sounded on the timber boards with a mellow, half-forgotten resonance.

Long gone were the days when she would have simply called out and walked in through the front door; instead, she pressed the doorbell, heard its chimes echo in the house. Heard, too, footsteps inside. The silhouetted figure she glimpsed through the leadlight window beside the door hurried – but not towards her, away from her, the back door slamming seconds later.

Strange. Definitely strange. The figure was stockier than Mark. Although she hadn't seen him in person for eighteen years, she'd seen him often enough on the TV screen, and he'd maintained his lean fitness. Perhaps it was the manager, or a housekeeper. A ten-thousand-hectare grazing property needed staff to run it. Or perhaps it was a lover or friend – she had no idea of Mark's current domestic arrangements. A few women had been linked to him from time to time, by his side at formal functions.

She pressed the doorbell again, heard it echo through the house. No response. Uncertainty tightened the tension in her spine and she glanced again at her watch – after six o'clock. According to Mark's office manager in Canberra, he'd left straight after this morning's media conference. Unless he'd stopped on the way, he should be home by now.

She'd been preparing herself for this meeting all day, thrusting her fond, youthful memories of the boy she'd been half in love with firmly into the past in order to confront the now former federal politician about Paula's death.

Sighing in frustration, she followed the veranda around to the back of the house. The east wing was new since her day, as were the French doors opening off the eat-in kitchen to a large, multi-level terrace, sloping down the slight hill. She quickened her steps, the low sunlight glinting on the jagged glass in the doorframes. Smashed glass; open doors; a man who'd run away on her arrival.

Nothing moved among the outbuildings beside the house that she could see. In the few minutes she'd waited on the veranda, he'd disappeared.

She hesitated, considering options. Find the manager? She assumed there was one, but he could be anywhere, mustering, fencing, checking dams. Phone the police? She was three steps towards the kitchen phone when she caught the first whiff of smoke, and she whirled around, scanning the view for grass fire in the paddocks, or bush fire in the distance. Either could be deadly in the dry summer heat.

The second whiff of smoke drifted from behind her, from the house, and a fire alarm suddenly beeped to life, high-pitched and loud. Underneath that sound a car engine roared to life somewhere in the distance – possibly down by the old wool shed.

Her sandals crunched on the broken glass on the kitchen floor. She could see the smoke now, thickening in the passageway behind the main rooms of the homestead, the light starting to flicker with a garish glow when she turned into the passage that housed the office.

The door was open, the room a mess, burning papers scattered on the desk and floor, fire already eating the desk chair, the armchairs, and climbing the curtains.

And on the floor behind the desk she could see two feet, clad in dusty leather boots, lying motionless, close to the flames.

◌

Nearing the end of the long drive from Canberra, Mark skirted around the edge of Dungirri, dodging the main street, turning back on to the Birraga Road a kilometre from town. He didn't intend to avoid Dungirri for long, but he planned to go home, shower and change, check his messages for anything he couldn't ignore and then head back to face the Friday-night crowd at the Dungirri pub. There were usually a fair few people there; tonight, with the announcement of his resignation this morning, he expected the pub to be crowded with people talking about it. About him.

Better to face them today, rather than later. His electorate covered a huge area of outback New South Wales, including larger towns like Birraga and Jerran Creek, but in Dungirri they'd known him all his life. And they'd known and mourned Paula. If there was anger, and a sense of betrayal, it would be strongest here.

He passed the rough track that led to the old Gillespie place a few kilometres from town. Somewhere along this section of the Dungirri-to-Birraga road he'd picked up Gil Gillespie one evening eighteen years ago. There was nothing he could recollect to tell him where and why. Nothing but the gaping hole caused by the head injury he sustained in the accident, permanently erasing several days from his short-term memory. Days he would never recover. And while he'd been unconscious in hospital, Gil had been threatened and subsequently confessed to being the driver of the car.

Ghost Hill rose out of the flat plains, still some distance ahead. No matter where he travelled, that first sight of the hill beckoned him home.

Yet today the view of the hill seemed hazy, despite the clear afternoon air. Perhaps his eyes were just tired . . . He blinked a few times to refocus them, and scanned the landscape as he drove. Yes, definitely a grey, smoky haze. Worrying, in this summer heat. But from where?

Coming over a slight rise, he located the faint plume of smoke on the horizon – and he pressed harder on the accelerator. If it wasn't on Marrayin Downs, it was close to it. He turned on the UHF radio, switched it to the emergency channel.

'. . . Seven-four-one-five on Dungirri One Alpha. We're responding. ETA seventeen minutes.'

Seven-four-one-five. As a volunteer with the Rural Fire Service, he knew every one of the local IDs. Even if he hadn't recognised Paul Barrett's voice, he would have known it was the captain of the Dungirri brigade.

Another voice reported in: 'Firecom, Birraga Two Alpha responding. ETA Marrayin thirty minutes.'

Marrayin. His property. And the Dungirri tanker was at least fifteen minutes away.

Mark floored the accelerator.

From the main road he couldn't pinpoint the location of the fire. The trees at the corner of the road obscured the view, but as he sped down the dirt track glimpses across the landscape gradually revealed the worst: not the paddocks, not the wool shed or the shearers' quarters, not the machinery sheds, but the homestead itself. His home.

Smoke spilled from the house, flowing across the driveway and garden. A few metres along the veranda from the main entrance, flames blazed out from the French door of his office, the doorframe, the veranda and the roof above it well ablaze. The old, dry timber in parts of the house would burn quickly and easily – and spread if it was not controlled rapidly.

He drove around the side of the house, straight down to the shed that held the fire trailer, permanently ready with a tank of water and a pump, and swung his vehicle around to reverse in. Focused on his objective, he didn't see the woman running from the house until she was almost at the shed.

Recognition hit hard. Jenn Barrett.

Jenn, *here*, with no warning; no chance to prepare himself for this first meeting in eighteen years, no way to know her thoughts, and no time to find out.

Jenn, with dishevelled hair and dark soot smeared across her face and her light shirt.

He caught her by the arms and she gripped him, her breathing raspy, urgent but not panicked. She never panicked. 'Mark! Jim's inside, hurt. I've moved him out of the office, but I can't—' She caught sight of the fire extinguisher on the shed wall, and left his hold to unhook it from the brace, continuing over her shoulder, 'He collapsed again and I couldn't move him. We have to get him out.'

Jim Barrett. Inside the burning house. All the other questions spinning in his head had to wait. Even Jenn, with smoke-scented hair, a red burn on the hand that had rested briefly on his arm and the thousand tangled emotions between them, would have to wait. He yanked open the back of his vehicle and grabbed his RFS kit bag. 'Where is he?'

'The living room.'

He took the extinguisher from her and set off at a run but she kept pace beside him, explaining in between gasps, 'I closed the doors but that won't last long. The fire's taken hold. The kitchen extinguisher wasn't enough.'

The broken glass of the kitchen door partially answered one question, but smoke had spread in the room beyond it and the enclosed back veranda, leaving no time for details. The light breeze might keep the fire to the front of the house, but there was no guarantee of that.

Adrenaline pumped in his veins and fifteen years of training and experience with the volunteer RFS kicked in. 'Stay outside,' he said, grabbing the fire blanket and his protective jacket and hat out of his bag.

She responded with a 'Harrumph!' – so many years since he'd heard that particular intonation of stubborn disagreement – and he knew she would follow him in. No point wasting precious time trying to argue with her. Yet. He handed her the jacket and hat. 'On. Now.'

The solid doors and mud-brick walls of the original four-room homestead separated the living room from the first addition, providing some protection from the blaze in the office. Some, but not total. As they dodged around the oak table in the dining room, Mark could hear over the din of the alarm an ominous crackling in the roof cavity, and saw the plaster work in the corner of the ceiling start to smoulder.

They had a minute or two, maybe less, to find Jim and get him out.

The knob of the living-room door was still cool to the touch, but nevertheless he opened it warily, holding Jenn back with one arm lest she dash straight in. The smoke was thicker in the room, but he could see Jim sprawled on the rug, motionless, a cream damask cushion underneath his head dark with blood, a large patch of the sleeve of his cotton shirt burned to blistered skin. At least, unconscious, he wouldn't feel the pain.

'I had to move him. We have to move him.' Jenn dropped to her knees beside her uncle, quickly checking his pulse.

Smoke oozed in around the door to the office wing, fire already charring the edges of the door and the cornices above. Mark gave it a blast with the fire extinguisher to slow it down, before checking through the French doors to the veranda, the roof out there already burned. No safe exit that way.

He dropped the extinguisher and knelt next to Jim. 'We'll cover him with the fire blanket. I'll carry him. Can you support his head?'

Jenn nodded and slipped into position, ready to lift. Mark manoeuvred one arm under Jim's back, the other ready to lift his legs, murmuring, 'Sorry, mate, this is going to hurt.'

'Not much choice,' Jenn said, her mouth drawn in a grim line.

He nodded. They had to move him quickly – and hope they did no more damage. He looked at Jenn. 'One, two, now.'

Jim, over six feet and packed with the muscle of sixty years of physical labour, was no lightweight, heavy on Mark's shoulders as he carried him back through the dining room. Jenn used the extinguisher on the flames that licked and danced along the cornice. Both quickened their steps in the rapidly intensifying heat, their focus on the exit.

Smoke smarted his eyes and scratched his throat. Jenn's eyes were red, and she tried to stifle a cough but she didn't stop or slow her pace. In the marginally clearer air in the kitchen they both drew deeper breaths. A dozen more steps and they were outside on the paved terrace, and Jenn coughed again and again.

Beyond the incessant beeping of the smoke alarm, sirens sounded in the distance as Mark exhaled a long breath. He nodded towards the outdoor table on the lower terrace, protected from the sun by shade sails above. 'We can put him there. He'll be safe for the moment till the RFS crew can help him.'

'I told triple-O to send an ambulance, too,' Jenn said, still as level-headed and cool in a crisis as she'd always been.

They gently laid Jim on the wooden table, and Jenn immediately put her fingers to his neck to check his pulse again.

'He's not breathing.'

Hasty fingers tore at the buttons on Jim's shirt and for the first time, her voice caught with a note of panic. 'Damn it, he's *not breathing*.'

AS DARKNESS FALLS

Haunted by her past, Detective Isabelle O'Connell is recalled to duty to investigate the abduction of a child from her home town. She and DCI Alec Goddard have only days to find the girl alive, with few clues, a town filled with suspects and a vast wilderness to search. It quickly becomes a game of cat and mouse, with Isabelle directly in the killer's sights.

For Isabelle, this case is already personal. For Alec, his best intentions to keep it purely professional soon dissolve as his anguish over Isabelle's safety moves beyond concern for a colleague. Their mutual attraction leaves them both vulnerable to their private nightmares – nightmares the killer ruthlessly exploits.

DARK COUNTRY

Most people in the small town of Dungirri have considered Morgan 'Gil' Gillespie a murderer for eighteen years, so he expects no welcome on his return. What he doesn't expect is the discovery of a woman's tortured body in the boot of his car, and new accusations of murder.

Wearied by too many deaths and doubting her own skills, local police sergeant Kris Matthews isn't sure if Gil is a decent man wronged by life, or a brutal criminal she should be locking up. But she does know that he is not guilty of this murder because she is his alibi . . .

Between organised crime, police corruption and the town's hatred, Gil has nowhere to hide. He needs to work out who's behind the murder before his enemies try to harm the few people he cares about. Kris is determined to help him, but will their search for the truth make her the next target?